TIME TAKEN

Out of Time, Book Three

C.B. Lewis

A NineStar Press Publication

Published by NineStar Press
P.O. Box 91792,
Albuquerque, New Mexico, 87199 USA.
www.ninestarpress.com

Time Taken

Copyright © 2018 by C.B. Lewis
Cover Art by Natasha Snow Copyright © 2018
Edited by Elizabetta McKay

Printed in the USA
First Edition
March, 2018

Print ISBN: 978-1-950412-23-5

Also available in eBook, ISBN: 978-1-950412-20-4

Time travel is a precarious business at the best of times, but when Qasim El-Fahkri's mission to the past ends in violence, it has a ripple effect through every level of the Temporal Research Institute.

Rhys Griffiths finds himself caught in the wake of the disastrous jump, his own career uncertain. With the Supervisory Board breathing down his neck, operatives demanding answers to baffling questions, and life outside of work bearing down on him, his only respite comes from Qasim's company. As the professional slowly becomes the personal, they must confront the echoes of their own pasts to try and move forward in the future.

But another past is waiting for Qasim, and there may be no coming back from this one...

For full enjoyment, it is recommended to first read books 1, *Time Waits*, and 2, *Time Lost*.

To the people who travel so far to be safe and free.

Chapter One

THE RAIN HAD finally stopped. The cobbles gleamed in the hazy moonlight, dappled with the warmer glow from the windows of the houses. It was late enough for the streets to be deserted, and the marketplace was silent.

Booted feet tramped by through the streets.

Half a dozen Janissaries. Members of the Sultan's elite guard. All armed with swords and guns. In better days, they would have been a comforting sight. Now, they were the reason people shuttered their windows and closed down their shops at night. With tensions rising across the city, it was better to stay out of their way.

In the shadows between the stalls, a dark figure crouched out of sight.

It wasn't the best idea.

Less than three feet away, there was a broad gutter cutting through the road, ankle-deep with the waste of the day. Even with the breeze from the Bosphorus, it stank.

A donkey turd bobbed by.

Qasim El-Fahkri made a face, leaning further back into the shadows and away from the gutter.

It was going to be a relief to get back to the twenty-first century, a time with better hygiene and less danger.

Something brushed against his shoulder.

Only a few years earlier, Qasim would have screamed like a kid, fallen over, or added a sample of his own to the gutter. Thankfully, he'd been on enough missions to know how to control himself, even if his heart was slamming against his ribs and he'd snapped his mouth shut so hard he'd gashed his lip.

There were no shouts and, whatever it was, it didn't have fingers or a grip on him or a knife at his throat.

He twisted around.

A cat was standing on the cobbles, within arm's reach, glowering at him as if he had mortally offended it for getting in its way. *Standard cat, then.*

Relieved, he turned his attention to the soldiers. They were at the edge of the market now. He just had to stay out of sight a little...

The cat yowled.

Qasim whipped around. "Shh!" he hissed. "Please, shh!"

The cat either didn't speak panicked human or didn't care and yowled again. The soldiers weren't leaving. Their footfalls had turned, coming back, approaching.

Qasim glanced around wildly. There were only two exits from the marketplace, and one of them was definitely not available, on account of the swords and the men attached to them.

The cat wasn't shutting up either.

Some part of his brain must have been operating because he grabbed the sodden creature and shoved it down the front of his robe. It squirmed but, mercifully, didn't remember it had claws. Qasim wrapped his arms over his chest and held his breath.

The footsteps came closer, paused, then moved away again.

Qasim exhaled, closing his eyes.

Too close. Far too close.

Cautiously, he slid closer to the edge of the market stall and peered around it. Between the other stalls, he could see the soldiers heading for the gate. All five of them were marching briskly, and he waited until they were out of sight, then slipped out from behind the stall and straightened up.

Maths. Bollocks! Always a weakness, but he'd never failed to count to six before.

The lingering Janissary—sneaky bastard—grabbed at him.

Everyone thought Qasim was cool in a crisis, which was frankly hilarious. He was the proverbial swan: majestic on the surface, paddling like mad underneath.

Still, there was always a bit of him that seemed to know what it was doing, and it dinged the man hard across the head, hard enough to send him reeling and crashing into the nearest stall.

The cover on the stall gave way, taking one of the support beams with it. The silence shattered as wood and canvas and a full-grown, fully armed man crashed down on the cobbles.

Qasim turned and ran. Behind him, the fallen soldier was yelling. There was some very vulgar Turkish in there, nearly beyond Qasim's vocabulary, but enough for him to feel offended on behalf of his mother and goats.

The streets were a labyrinth—one he'd memorised as much as possible in the weeks leading up to the mission. *Just in case*, Dieter and Gulshan had both insisted, and as Qasim ducked down a passage and skidded around a corner into a broader alleyway, he wanted to kiss them both.

There was a wail from inside his robe, and the cat wriggled against his chest, but there was no time to stop or release it. "Shh," he panted as he vaulted over a staircase wall and dropped into the alley below. He ducked under the stairs to catch his breath.

From the street above, the shouts of the men chasing him rang out.

For once, he appreciated the curfew. The drama at the Hippodrome had people on edge. It wasn't official, but with Janissaries raising arms, people preferred to take refuge indoors. A political storm was about to break. No one wanted to be caught in it. It also meant no one would flag the guards down and let them know where he was. Problem was he was out in the dark with roaming bands of Janissaries and had a rendezvous point at least a half a mile away.

"Where are you?" Tahmila's voice was a breath in his ear. "I'm here already."

He sighed with relief. She'd made the rendezvous point. One less thing to worry about. He leaned out cautiously from beneath the stairs. It sounded like the soldiers were spreading out, but none of them had come near his hideout yet. "Half a mile. Long story."

"Fifteen minutes."

No pressure at all. Qasim eased out of his hiding place and glanced around to get his bearings. The trouble with moving away from the main square was so many of the smaller alleys were practically identical. If he went down the wrong one and hit a dead end, he might well end up hitting a very literal dead end a short time later.

The cat shifted under his robes. It felt like it was curling up and making itself comfortable. Of course, it bloody was.

He slunk forward, darting from one patch of shadow to another. The clouds were thinning, and the moonlight was growing brighter. He slipped between two rows of buildings, clinging as close as he could to the walls. People were still awake inside the houses. Lamps were lit. Voices carried. The scents of woodsmoke, spices, and cooking meat made his stomach gurgle.

No one noticed him. The soldiers seemed to have fallen away behind him. Still, there was no reason to be reckless. He yanked his boots off, balancing precariously on one foot then the other. Dirty feet could be washed, but the rap of a boot's heel in the silence could be as deadly as yelling and waving his arms.

He turned into another alleyway and continued north. Under his robe, the cat started kneading at him. He hissed between his teeth as claws dug through his shirt.

"Why haven't I dropped you yet?" he whispered, peering down through the collar of his robe. In the darkness, the cat was damned near invisible.

"Me?" Tahmila. Again.

He made a face as he stepped into another narrow passage and then swore as a rope strung across it caught him right across the forehead. Always with the unexpected clotheslines. He ducked and hurried onwards, hoping to hell it was just rain and not blood or cat doings soaking through his clothes.

Ahead of him, the passage widened into a broader avenue, and he approached the corner of the building with caution, his heart pounding. Two blocks to go and he would be home free.

Boots clattered on cobbles nearby. Qasim slammed against the nearest wall, sinking into the shadows. A low wail rose from his robe, definitely with claws in the skin underneath it, but he held his breath, biting his lips, and tried to work out how screwed he was.

Voices raised. Not close enough to make out their words. Shouted, but not loudly. At least half a block from one another. The thump of running footsteps. Calls for support. He strained his ears, trying to work out how screwed he was. Something about movement.

The cat started squirming and struggling inside his robe.

He grinned down at it.

Movement, eh?

He pressed his shoulders against the wall, counting down from ten to slow his heartbeat, and listened as they drew closer and closer. Two of the voices were clearer now.

Qasim yanked down the collar of his robe and squeezed. The cat erupted, yowling. It shot out into the light. One of the soldiers yelled in surprise, and there was the crack of a rifle being fired. The other snorted in disgust and berated him for a false alarm and for not even being able to hit a target three paces in front of him.

Good. Qasim released a trembling breath. *Just turn around and—*

"You!"

Qasim whipped around. Another soldier at the other end of the alley. One of the men from the marketplace. Well, not quite so clean an escape as he'd hoped. He sprinted out of the alleyway as fast as he could and sent the two cat-startled soldiers spinning.

Adrenaline and a three-second head start were good enough. He pegged it as fast as he could, grabbing at corners of buildings to whip himself into the winding maze of buildings without breaking his pace. They were chasing him now, and, well, who didn't like some added spice in their reports?

"Coming in hot," he panted, running full tilt towards a mound of stacked timbers, praying like hell it would hold as he scrambled up it and onto the wall it was braced against. He glanced back. Still coming, but in armour, they would have no chance. Especially, if some absolute bastard shoved his foot against the pile of timbers and sent them cascading down.

A shot whistling by his ear ensured he wouldn't stay to see the ensuing chaos. He launched himself off the other side of the wall. It was farther than he expected, and he grunted and stumbled when he hit the ground. Pain shot up one ankle, but it was better than being shot. Something brushed his leg, and he flinched, half expecting arrows. No. Small, furry, and glaring at him.

Qasim laughed breathlessly. "Same to you," he rasped, stumbling to his feet. Since it had made itself useful before, he scooped the cat up again and broke into a hobbling run. The familiar warehouse doorway—their assigned rendezvous point—was up ahead.

Without warning, shouts and pounding feet came at him from all directions. His heart plummeted to his stomach. He was close, but so were the soldiers. The white fire of pain in his leg was nothing compared to the thought of the Grand Vizier being ripped into confetti by an angry mob led by the very men he was fleeing.

"Qasim?" Tahmila was starting to sound worried. "There are soldiers coming this way."

"Yeah. About that long story..."

"Qasim! What do we do?"

He braced one hand against the wall, wincing. He couldn't run, not when his leg was hurting so much. If he missed this jump, there was no way he'd make it out of the area and to the second rendezvous point. "I can see the door. Get through. I'll follow."

"You're lying."

He laughed, hobbling on as fast as he could. "Bluffing. It's called bluffing."

The door was only yards away, but the shadows of the Janissaries, cast by flickering torches at the far end of the street, also loomed closer. They were coming in fast.

"Go," he repeated, sinking into an alcove packed with baskets and straw. He closed his eyes and took an unsteady breath. There was only one option if he wanted to get out alive. "Tell them I'll try for a jumping flash in two minutes."

"You're insane!"

"Start the count the second before you get through. Two minutes. Go!"

He didn't listen to her protests, glancing out into the street. There was no way to the door without being seen. He squinted around the alley. Straw and baskets. Not exactly useful. He glanced up and grinned. Bloody clotheslines everywhere.

"Qas. Two minutes."

He raised his eyes to the sky, casting up a prayer, and pushed off from the wall. Either he was about to make the most spectacular exit in TRI history, or he was about to die horribly trying.

Chapter Two

"ALL RIGHT," RHYS Griffiths braced his hand on the edge of the workstation. "Connection in one minute."

He didn't have to say anything, given the countdown clock glowing on the screen, but it was his first time in charge of a temporal mission. It felt better to do everything by the book.

Rhys had joined the Temporal Research Institute nearly four years earlier, and it had taken a hell of a lot of work to get to this point in his career. He was on the verge of being promoted to Team Supervisor, a big step up from being one of the support team. No more running about for a supervisor. Now, he would have people running about for him.

On paper, Team Supervisor sounded like a tedious job, but no. Not when there was time travel involved, and he was responsible for sending members of his team into the past. He'd seen them through prep, he'd made sure his tech team were all coordinated, and now...

Right now, the two agents under his supervision were in Istanbul, doing on-site recon into the fall of Sultan Ibrahim in 1648. They had an assigned pickup point. Rhys always hated the wait. Most agents made the first pickup, but if worst came to worst, there were always two later ones, just in case.

Knowing didn't make it any easier.

The countdown clock was getting lower.

Rhys risked a glance over his shoulder.

Jacob Ofori, his supervisor, was sitting in to monitor him. He'd been doing spot checks through the whole mission, from the start of prep right up until the temporal jump. Protocol, but it made Rhys nervous in case he cocked anything up.

He glanced at where the empty frame of the temporal gate was visible in the gate room. The gates were all closed up in secure bunkers deep beneath the TRI compound. It wasn't anything special, just a metal doorway rigged with cables.

"Connection in ten, nine..."

Rhys's heart was pounding as he counted down.

On zero, the gateway filled with a charge of brilliant light as the connection was formed.

"Close on fi—"

A figure leapt out of the shimmering door of light, trailing robes and veils.

"Jumping flash!" she screamed. "Two minutes."

Rhys heart thundered, but everything else seemed to be freezing around him.

Jumping flash. Right. Yes. He'd learned about them, and…Christ, what did you do when they happened?

The gate winked out.

"Ben—" Jacob called out. "Find me a surplus. Malia, keep the live count." He appeared by Rhys's side, and Rhys knew he'd fucked up. He should have known what to do. "Istvan, we need a med team on standby."

Rhys glanced up at him. "Jacob…"

"Not now." Ofori's dark eyes were on the screen. "Flash first. Ben, talk to me."

Ben Sanders was staring frantically at a mess of codes on his screens. He was, by all accounts, as brilliant as his father, Tom Sanders—developer of the temporal gates and creator of the TRI. If anyone could find a way to fix things, he was the one to do it. "Early closure on twelve yesterday and leftover from ours now. Should give us a three-second window."

"It'll have to do. Istvan?"

"Med team on standby."

"Count?"

"On-screen now."

Jacob leaned forward, bracing both hands on the desk. Rhys pressed his fist into his twisting stomach, praying he wouldn't be sick, as the numbers winked down. Flashes didn't happen. They'd told him they didn't happen. Urban legends. When an agent ended up in such a dangerous situation, they had to risk an immediate pickup, or they might not make it out alive. Temporal gates were a balancing act anyway, with massive power surges anytime a body passed through them. Opening up a second link within the same twenty-hour window made them even more unstable. Four years in the TRI and he'd never heard of someone being desperate enough to do one.

"Reconnection in ten!"

Jacob's eyes were fixed on the screen. "Ben, ready on my mark."

Rhys's nails were biting into his palms and his teeth into his lip.

"Three, two, one—now!"

The gate flared to life, three heart-stopping seconds of blinding light, then darkness as the gate blinked out.

"*Alhamdulillah!*" A male voice. Qasim El-Fahkri. "Made it!"

A second figure was visible in the gate room now. Qasim was leaning against the wall as if he had just fallen in, barefoot and filthy. Rhys sagged; he could breathe again. Both agents safely home.

"Thank Christ," Jacob said to murmurs of agreement from the tech team. "Good to have you both—"

"Qasim," Tahmila Samuels, the other agent, interrupted, her voice shaking. "Your side."

Rhys couldn't make out what she was seeing until Qasim pressed his hand to his side. When he turned it palm up, visible to all the cameras, it was dark and wet.

"Um." He blinked owlishly at the camera.

"Get the med team in, Istvan," Jacob ordered. "Rhys, with me."

Rhys fell into step behind him as they headed out of the monitoring hub. Jesus, if Jacob hadn't been there, he wouldn't have gotten the gate open in time or had the med team in place or any of it.

"Don't beat yourself up," Jacob said as if he could read his mind. "You know how rare a jumping flash is."

Rhys wished it made him feel better, but it didn't. "I still froze."

"No one will blame you." Jacob led him into the glass-walled lift. The doors slid closed, and the lift headed up to the more secure communication chambers on the fifteenth floor. "This is an exception, not a rule."

Rhys leaned against the handrail. "Yeah."

"Rhys," Jacob said quietly. "I'm serious. He's home. He's upright and talking. It's going to be fine."

Rhys managed a quick, if unconvincing, smile. "I know." He pressed his hands to the handrail. "We were trained what to do if it happened, but it—I just—" He shook his head, frowning. "I knew what to do. I remember the training, but..." He shook his head again. "Sorry. I should have done better."

"Your team would have helped if I hadn't been there."

Rhys nodded.

They would have. Some of them had been working at the TRI from the beginning, seventeen years earlier. Even Ben Sanders, who wasn't quite nineteen, had been involved for longer than Rhys, stepping into his late father's shoes when he was fourteen. Of all the people to have on a jump tech team, Ben was the best he could have hoped for.

"What happens now?" he asked, though he could already guess the answer. "I mean, you said yourself this is an exceptional situation. I know the protocol for someone being hurt, but not this."

Jacob ran a hand over his face. "I'll have to run point with you." Rhys's heart sank. This had been his chance to show what he was capable of, and now he'd blown it. "Being wounded is a special kind of shitstorm, but the fact he did a flash? It's not going to be a fun ride. You'll still be handling the standard elements—the data sifts and the external assessors. But the rest of it..." Jacob shook his head with a sigh. "The last time a flash happened, I didn't get home for a fortnight. Kit is going to wring my neck for being here for another one."

Rhys winced. If Jacob's laid-back boyfriend didn't like it, Marc was going to have a field day. "That bad?"

Jacob nodded with a grimace. "Count yourself lucky. You'll get to witness all the fun and games without having to deal with the paperwork." He glanced around as the lift came to a halt and the doors slid open. "Better see how bad it is before upstairs start chasing us."

"Would someone in the team tell them about it?"

Jacob led him down a broad corridor. "We don't have to. The Supers keep tabs on exactly how many gates are open. They'll know there was an extra connection already."

"There's a surprise." Rhys disliked the Supervisory Board as much as Jacob did.

When the TRI had been forced to go public with time travel, half of the United Nations had insisted on an international oversight committee to ensure neutrality and prevent any agent from tampering with someone's past. It led to the formation of the Supervisory Board, which oversaw all the decisions about destinations, targets, jump duration, and so many bureaucratic details which made life much more difficult for anyone working within the TRI.

Jacob headed into one of the communication rooms. The screen projections illuminated with a touch as soon as the door was shut, and Jacob typed in a code before pressing his palm to the console. The video link to one of the medical quarantine bays lit up on the screens, showing a pile of cut-away clothes and, now, so much more blood. It was vividly and sharply real.

The transfer from the gate room had been impressively fast, even with the internal pod system adding a boost. Their med team—always prepped during a jump—had rarely been needed. Still, they knew exactly what to do and had done it, and now, Qasim was in the best possible hands.

The team was visible in decon suits and masks, fully covered for protection from any historical infection. They were working around one of the beds. Their patient didn't sound happy about it given how much he was complaining. He didn't stop until his partner stepped closer to the bed.

"Qasim, if you don't stop talking, I might finish you off myself."

"But I'm fine!" Qasim El-Fahkri exclaimed from the middle of the huddle.

"Is he?" Jacob asked over the comm.

The team must have been expecting him, because not one of them flinched.

"Knife wound," one of the doctors said. "Looks worse than it is, but it's still pretty bad. We're patching it now. Some minor flesh wounds, a cracked rib, a twisted ankle, blister burns on his palms."

Rhys sank onto one of the chairs, relieved. He wrapped his shaking hands over his knees.

"I'm fine," Qasim repeated.

"Tahmila," Jacob said. "If he causes any trouble, you have my permission to knock him on the head with a bedpan."

There was a silence, and then Qasim's voice piped up hopefully, "I'm mortally wounded and should not be smacked by my partner?"

Despite the sick feeling burning in his throat, Rhys couldn't help snorting. Qasim's sense of humour had picked a funny time to show up.

"There's something else," Tahmila added. "He brought something back with him."

"Not my fault!" Qasim exclaimed.

Rhys glanced at Jacob, who was rubbing his forehead with his fingertips. "Explain."

Tahmila stepped out of shot for a moment and returned, holding up her bag gingerly by the strap. "This."

Something popped out of the top of the bag, a tiny head peering around.

"A cat?" Rhys leaned closer to the screen. In the middle of all the panic and mess and blood, it felt surreal. "You brought back a cat?"

Qasim shoved one of the medical crew aside. "Who is it? Doesn't sound like Ofori."

"It's Rhys, Qas." Jacob nodded reassuringly at Rhys and then at the screen. "I'll be sharing point with him for the remainder of this particular mission."

Qasim went very still and quiet on the bed. "On a scale of one to dead, how much trouble am I in with those on high?"

"Gaping knife wound and miscellaneous other injuries should give you a clue," Jacob replied. "Don't you worry about the Board for now. I'll deal with them." He frowned as the door chimed. "Speak of the devils…" He rose from the chair. "Right. Qasim, I need you to shut up and let the med team work. Mila, get the cat into some kind of box, and it'll be moved to a separate quarantine to be checked when we can get a vet approved. I'll buzz back in as soon as possible."

He disconnected the video link. "Here we go."

"Upstairs?" Rhys guessed from the expression on Jacob's face.

"A minion from on high, I have no doubt," Jacob confirmed. "You should stay put. I'll be back as soon as they'll let me." He opened the door. Rhys got a glimpse of a lean figure with long, dark hair before the door shut.

Rhys glanced back at the blank spot where the projections had been. To think he'd been worrying about his promotion and his prospects while Qasim El-Fahkri had been getting stabbed. He took off his glasses and pressed his finger and thumb to his eyelids. *You selfish bastard.* He shook his head. *It's just a job.*

It was, technically, but things were never simple.

He propped his elbows on the desk and rested his head in his hands. Later. He could worry about it later. Now, he had to keep his supervisor hat on and be ready when Jacob got back.

Chapter Three

QASIM FIDGETED.

Debriefing was always his least favourite part of a mission anyway, but now he was doing it from a bed, in the scud. To add insult to injury, he wasn't even allowed to have an hour-long hot shower. *Hammams* were all fine during the mission, but he'd been excited about a shower for days!

Still, not like he could argue with a great big cut in his side. He squinted down at his bare chest and the steri-panel that the team had put in place. They'd put a needle in him too and lots of nice medicine. His side didn't hurt now, so it couldn't be as bad as everyone said, even if he could to see some of his ribs through the blood. He poked the bandage to be sure. *Squish.*

"Qas. Mila."

Qasim peered up at the link to the briefing room on the wall. Two people were in the room, and Qasim beamed as he recognised them. "Hey! Mila, look!" He gestured to the screen. "Jacob's back."

Tahmila gave him a look. "He only went away because you ran into a sword."

Qasim frowned at her. "Dodged. I dodged a sword."

"Not very well." She pulled her chair up alongside the bed. "They let you escape faster than usual, Jacob."

"They need details before they can give me a good yelling-at," Jacob Ofori said. He'd been with the TRI a long time. Qasim remembered, once upon a time, time travel was a big secret, and Jacob was the one who found out about it, and because of him, everyone knew. He'd been a policeman then. Now, he was...

Qasim frowned. Now, he was bossy. Yeah. He was the bossiest of bosses, who made sure everything they found out when they time travelled was sorted out and made into sensible bits. Lots of bits.

Tahmila nudged him, and he glowered at her, affronted. "Jacob asked you a question."

Qasim cocked his head, returning his attention to the screen. "Question?"

Jacob raised his eyebrows. "Your digi-lens. Will you be able to take it out?"

Qasim touched the skin under his right eye. It was puffy too. Ah. Yes. The man with the sword came *after* the man with the fist. He tugged the lid down with his fingertip. "If Mila helps, yeah."

"Great," Tahmila said wryly.

"It can wait until the swelling goes down," Jacob said.

Qasim nodded. Clever man, Jacob. Very clever. And he'd brought a friend. Another man, all short and pink and blond where Jacob was all big and tall and dark. Qasim peered at him. Ah! Him! Yeah. He had a name. "Mila?" he whispered. "Who's'a little fat ceiling baby again?"

Tahmila's head whipped around so fast he leaned away to stop her knocking heads. "What?"

Qasim nodded towards the screen. "Little fat ceiling baby. Only, no wings. And clothes. And not a baby? 'S his name again?"

Tahmila was staring at him like he was nuts. "What are—" She stared at the screen and then at him. "You mean— It's Rhys Griffiths. You remember? He's the supervisor for this jump?"

Qasim peered up at the screen. The briefings were a long, long time ago. Four-hundred-and-something years and some days. Long time. Couldn't be expected to remember everything. With all the words and maps and history and everything else, he hadn't had room to fit in a ceiling baby in his head too. Which was a shame because he was sure he would have remembered lovely big blue eyes.

He tilted his head. Sometimes, pretty things showed up in the strangest places, and he clasped a hand to his chest. "*Subhan'Allah.*"

Rhys Griffiths—Rhys, Rhys, Rhys...sounded like cheese— peeked at Jacob, then down at his screen. It was glowing, turning his pink face blue.

"Qasim."

It brought his brain to a standstill as if he'd run into a wall. Only Ummi and Abi and Tette ever used his name like a big smack on the nose. Wasn't good when Jacob said it. Nope. Not good at all, so he smiled hopefully, because it sometimes worked.

"Yeah?"

"You want to explain to me how you ended up resorting to a jumping flash?"

Qasim nodded gravely. "Men. With swords."

"I heard."

Qasim pointed to his chest. It was all scratched. "And a cat."

Jacob's eyes moved towards Tahmila. "Can you enlighten me?"

"But she didn't do a flash!" Qasim protested indignantly. "I did! And I can do an actual flash if I lift the blanket!"

Tahmila caught his wrist. Her eyebrows were down in one big line, and that only happened when she was cross or worried or really tired with no coffee. "Can you maybe be quiet for a minute? I'll talk to Jacob, okay?"

"But I—"

She squeezed his wrist. "You need to count the scratches on your chest. We need an exact record of your injuries."

It sounded like a serious job. He peered down at his chest and started to count, but he tried to listen too because he was a very good agent and he was very good at doing lots of important things at the same time.

She was talking fast: separated at the mosque; couldn't find each other after; planned to rendezvous over comms; the city on curfew; soldiers in the streets.

"Cat!" Qasim exclaimed. "Cat in a marketplace!"

"We gathered," Jacob said.

"It's gone now." Qasim peered around the room. "Where did it go? Doesn't it know we're not allowed to go out?"

"They're bringing in a vet to check it," Tahmila said, patting his wrist. "In case it has anything."

"Like us?"

She nodded. "Like us. Usual quarantine stuff."

Smart. Careful. Qasim nodded. "It's mine now, yeah?"

Jacob scratched at his chin. "I don't think we can open the gate to lob a cat through it, but upstairs might want to put it down as a precaution."

"No!" Qasim sat up indignantly. No killing the cat! Not when it helped! "No! S'my cat! Saved me from nasty men with swords!" Jacob fixed him with a stare, and he sank against the pillows, pulling the blanket up to his nose. "S'mine."

Jacob rubbed the middle of his nose. "Right. Okay. Elwin's going to love this."

Qasim nodded happily. Always wanted a cat.

"I know there are the rules for humans and samples," the ceiling baby said. "I've never heard of anyone bringing a live animal through the gate with them."

"No. Apart from some DNA and plant samples, this would be the first time for anything bigger than lice or fleas." Jacob was doing a frowny face. "I don't know if the Board'll be happy to let a historical artefact run wild, but since it can't be sent back—"

"A cat," Qasim interrupted, "isn't a butterfly."

Jacob's attention was on him again, like a big-boss teacher. Qasim pulled the blanket back up to his nose and peered over it at Jacob, who was studying him. "Tahmila, did they mention how many painkillers they gave him?"

Tahmila reached up to tuck the blanket over Qasim. She smiled at him, and it felt better than peeking at Mr. Grumpy Face. "Does your side hurt?"

He shook his head and poked it. "It's squishy."

Tahmila caught his hand. "Don't poke it. You'll make it worse." She turned to Jacob. "I'm guessing a lot."

Jacob rubbed his hand over his face. "Right. Qas. Put the blanket down."

Qasim reluctantly obeyed. "Am I in trouble?"

"Not just now." Jacob was doing his dad voice. "You need to get some rest, okay?"

Qasim frowned. "Will I be in trouble later?" he hazarded. "If I'm not in trouble now?"

Jacob snorted and glanced at the angel man. "Even when he's drugged to the eyeballs, he's always thinking in a thousand directions at once." He returned his stare to Qasim. "We'll talk about it when you've rested. Your debrief can wait."

Qasim nudged Tahmila. "The doctor in the spacesuit already debriefed me. Cut 'em off and took 'em away."

She laughed and pushed him down on the bed. "You're still daft." She glanced at Jacob. "I'll make sure he doesn't do himself an injury while we're stuck in here."

"Full debrief in twelve hours, then," Jacob said.

Qasim waved at him and the pretty little angel man. "Night."

The projection went out.

"You should rest." Tahmila smoothed his hair. "You need to heal."

Qasim lifted the blanket to peek at the bandage. "I have a hole."

"They've sealed it up. You'll be fine as long as you don't poke it." She perched on the edge of his bed. "You didn't need to let me go first. I could have helped."

He smiled up at her. "No, silly." He groped for her hand. "Because then you would have a hole too, and it would be bad." He lifted her hand up and kissed her knuckles "It's only a little hole, and we're all fine. *Masha'Allah.*"

She smiled at him, but it wasn't a full happy smile. "Yeah." She squeezed his hand. "You get some sleep, and once they decide whether you can keep it, we can pick out a name for your new furball."

Qasim let her tuck the blankets over him, all soft and clean. "Pisi."

Tahmila made a funny squeaky sound. "Pisi? Really?"

Qasim nodded. "He's a Turkish cat, so I have to speak to him in Turkish because he won't understand me if I speak Arabic at him."

"So, it's not because it's a stroppy little bastard?"

He blinked at her, indignant. "He's my Pisi."

She shook her head, smiling. "You're ridiculous."

He gazed solemnly at her. "So I won't forget." He turned onto his not-holey side, rubbing his cheek against the pillow, and yawned. "*Tisbah 'ala-khair.*"

Cool fingers brushed his brow again as he closed his eyes. "Good night to you too, sleepyhead."

Chapter Four

"HE'LL BE ALL right, thank Christ."

Rhys shared the sentiment. Even with all the bullshit that was going to rain down on them, Qasim was back and alive, which was the important thing. "He's going to need some extra recovery time after this."

"And then some." Jacob turned in his chair. "Let's hope tomorrow he remembers more of the mission than he did your name."

Rhys smiled wryly.

Qasim hadn't paid much attention to him during prep, too caught up in his research. Even when he was standing still, he always seemed ready to jump into action like a tightly wound spring. He was one of their best agents, and everyone agreed he was a charmer.

The fact he was nice-looking was a bonus of working with him. Dark laughing eyes, black hair, and the rare but brilliant smile over the historically accurate beard he was contractually obligated to keep. He suited period costumes, but Rhys had to admit he suited his bright-coloured, much-more-fitted, modern clothing more.

"Introducing yourself to someone who's trying to cram geopolitical history into their head in record time is never going to be memorable," Rhys said.

"You're not wrong." Jacob chuckled. He was massaging the back of his neck, his head tilted back and eyes closed. "When he's in mission mode, the kid is all research and nothing else." He opened one dark eye and shot Rhys a wry smile. "Ceiling baby, eh?"

Rhys couldn't help laughing. It was partly relief, but he thought it was daft. Sweet but daft. "I've been called worse. We'll say it's the drugs talking." He switched off his folio, the screen winking out. "About the mission…"

"I don't know." Jacob sat up in his chair, and even though he was knackered, there was a glint in his eyes. "I think we should pay attention to this ceiling baby thing. Until we get the debrief, it's not like we can do much else, yeah?"

Rhys raised his eyebrows. "Jealous, are we?"

Jacob's laugh echoed off the walls. "'Course," he said, grinning. "Everyone knows I'd look amazing stuck on a ceiling with wings and a tiny strip of silk hiding my unmentionables." He glanced towards the door when it chimed. "Hold on…" He tapped a button on the console in front of him, unlocking the door. It slid open.

Rhys frowned in confusion. "Ben?"

Ben Sanders nodded in greeting, but his attention was on Jacob. "Is he okay?"

Jacob smiled. "He's going to be fine." He propped one arm on the back of his chair. "What's up? You know I'll be down in five minutes to tell everyone what's going on."

Ben pushed his fingers through his hair. "Right. Yeah." He cleared his throat. "I need a word about the flash." He jerked his head slightly in Rhys's direction. Teenage subtlety at its best. "Privately."

Rhys had to turn away. Simple as that, he was put on the sidelines of his own mission. He didn't blame Ben for it, not when it was blatantly obvious to everyone involved he had no idea what he was doing.

"Rhys is supervisor on this mission. You can tell us both," Jacob said. "Is there a problem?"

Ben hesitated. He appeared to be picking his words carefully. "Not a problem exactly, but…" He fell silent. Rhys glanced up to see the young man's face twisted in indecision. "There's something. I—it's—I'd prefer to discuss it with you."

"It's all right," Rhys said quickly. "I don't think I'd be much use anyway. I've never seen a flash before."

Jacob glanced at him, and Rhys tried to make his smile convincing. "All right. We're done for the night anyway. Qasim's going to be out for the count for a few hours, so we'll debrief in the morning."

"You want me to go upstairs and give them an update?" Rhys inquired as he got up. Sitting on the sidelines was bad enough without something to keep him busy.

Jacob rubbed at the hollow of his cheek with his thumb. "It's not like there's much to tell them. You can nip down to update the team about Qas's condition, then write up what we got from Tahmila so far and send it on to me once you're done. Tomorrow won't be an easy day."

Rhys paused at the door as Ben dropped into the seat he'd vacated. "I'll find one of the rooms in H-block in case anything comes up overnight."

"You could go home," Jacob pointed out. "It's not like much can happen while Qas is drugged to the gills."

While his own bed was tempting, there was a message from Marc sitting in his inbox saying he wouldn't be home until late because he had a work night out. Another one. Rhys had experienced the afterglow before. With an agent in the med bay and his work snatched from under him, he knew he wouldn't be in any mood to deal with it.

"With a mission still technically active?" He forced a quick smile. "I don't think so. You'd do the same, and you know it."

Jacob chuckled wryly. "Don't act like it's a good thing, Rhys. I'm a cautionary tale."

"And you love it." He nodded respectfully. "I'll see you back here in a few hours."

"Eleven hours, forty-five minutes, not a minute sooner."

Rhys couldn't help himself. "Careful. You might be losing your workaholic edge."

Both Ben and Jacob laughed. "Oh, sod off." Jacob waved him away. "Go and enjoy your night of self-inflicted captivity."

Rhys offered Ben a quick nod and withdrew from the room. Before the door closed, he heard Ben say, "I saw something interesting in the log—"

Whatever it was, it would mean nothing to Rhys. He'd sat through the standard training about how the temporal gates worked and knew there was some...computery rubbish behind it, but it could have been written in Chinese for all he knew. Thank God it wasn't a part of his job.

After popping back into the tech team and letting them know all was well, he headed to the lift, contemplating whether to find an office or make sure he had somewhere to sleep first. The report could be done anywhere, so H-block was the first priority.

Once, the TRI had been a small, secret operation, working out of an office building, using three gates, and managing one mission every few months. Now, there were daily missions all over the place from a dozen gates concealed in a network of bunkers below the compound.

The main building was their communication hub and where most of the administration, briefings, and research work was done. Their compound had four other buildings, all of them closed up inside secure perimeter fences and walls to keep out prying eyes.

He walked into the main courtyard and glanced around. The warehouse off to his right housed the prop facility, where the tools and clothing the agents used were designed and made to appear as accurate as possible. The smallest block next to the main building was the transporter hub, where staff would be shuttled out of the secured base to their transport links.

On the far left, there was the quarantine block. From the outside, it seemed like any other glass-walled office structure. Inside, it had the strictest security links and internal pod connections of anywhere in the compound. Anyone or anything that had travelled to the past would end up there on return. El-Fahkri and Samuels were in one of the medical bays somewhere on the fifth floor.

The final one was the H-shaped staff accommodation block directly opposite the main building. The west wing of the H was restricted to agents in prep lockdown, where they were quarantined for a month before their jump in order to do their mission prep and make sure they didn't take modern illnesses back with them. The east wing was for the staff who were either involved in missions or who had worked too late to go home for the night.

The vast open courtyard between the buildings was lit by the evening sunlight. It was a pleasant place to sit. There was a round pond in the middle, circled by a flagstone path, benches and a wide ring of grass. Agents had a warped sense of humour. They called it the Last Glance.

Rhys made his way around the pond and down the path to H-block. Sam Phelps was behind the desk watching a film projected above it but brushed it away when Rhys reached him.

"Room for a small one?"

Sam brought up a screen. "Just the one night?"

"Yeah. Bed and access to the canteen, and I'm good."

Sam studied the screen and then made a flicking gesture. Rhys's folio chirped as the digital key was picked up.

"Room fourteen, floor three," Sam said. "Canteen is open another two hours."

Rhys nodded, heading for the east wing doors.

The building could have been any hotel in any part of the country. The halls were plain, and his room had a bed, a wardrobe, and a table and chair. There was also a small bathroom attached. Not exactly homey, but enough to be comfortable while working on the first draft of Tahmila's comments.

First things first, though.

He opened his folio and tapped to connect to Marc's. He wasn't sure if he was relieved or disappointed when it went straight to inbox. It wasn't late, so Marc and his colleagues were probably still in the office.

He hesitated and then smiled. "All right, *bach*? I won't be able to get home tonight. Work's gone a bit...shit. They need all hands." He touched two fingers to his lips and blew a kiss towards the camera. "Take care and have fun. I'll see you tomorrow night."

It was a lie, but it felt kinder than the truth. He sighed as he disconnected the link and turned his attention to Tahmila's report.

The summary was finished in less than an hour. There were a lot of details needing clarification, and they still needed to collect the data from their digi-lenses. The TRI had started using them a couple of years earlier, and their data collection rate had shot up.

Still, what Tahmila had provided so far didn't explain how Qasim had almost ended up skewered. It was one thing to get separated from your partner. It was another thing to end up with a sword in your ribs.

Qasim El-Fahkri was an agent with a reputation. He'd been chosen for the mission *because* he was known for his caution and attention to detail. Yes, the report confirmed tensions had been much higher than expected in the city, and there were Janissaries on the streets, but something must have happened for them to attack him.

He'd been desperate enough to try a jumping flash, knowing they were as risky as staying put. He'd been put in a situation that had forced him to risk his life. It meant the soldiers hadn't been about to listen to persuasion or excuses.

It could just have been the climate, Rhys thought, running his thumb along his lower lip pensively. After all, there'd been protests and Janissaries rising against the Sultan. Everyone would have been on edge about it all. It could have been as simple as some frustrated men jumping the first person they came across.

He closed down his folio screen and pushed up his glasses to rub his eyes.

There was no point in making wild guesses. In a few hours, he would know for certain anyway.

The halls were quiet as he made his way down the stairs. A few people lodged in the building, but the shifts at the TRI could vary depending on team, mission, access, and a thousand other factors. He saw a few familiar faces and nodded in greeting as he headed to the canteen.

Over the muted conversation in the room, one voice rang out loudly.

"What the fuck's happening, Rhys?"

Rhys stopped short, barely across the threshold, and searched for the speaker. Two people were hurrying towards him: a thin, pale, brown-haired man and a tall, shapely, dark-skinned woman, who was also munching her way through a bowl of creamed rice. She waved a spoon at him.

Ah. No one liked to be accosted by the in-house historians, especially not the historians they were meant to be working with.

"Dieter," Rhys said with a quick smile. "Gulshan."

Dieter Schmidt, the TRI's longest-serving historian and linguist, stopped in front of him and canted his head. "Come on, Rhys. Jacob buzzed us. Said the debrief's on hold. Something about El-Fahkri getting himself fucked up."

Rhys winced. "You know what I know."

Dieter and Gulshan exchanged looks. There was close to a twenty-year age gap, but sarcastic eye-rolling was one of the gifts they shared.

Rhys sighed. "Fine. We know El-Fahkri and Samuels got separated. We know there was something like a curfew in place. She made it to the rendezvous, but he was late. The guards got between him and the gate. He made it out, but not before they got a few licks in."

Gulshan took her spoon out of her mouth. "He's going to be okay?"

"As far as they can tell." Rhys gazed longingly in the direction of the serving windows. "Look, I'm hungry, I am. I'll come over once I've got something to eat, all right?"

Dieter waved towards a busy table. "We'll keep a seat for you."

Two minutes later, Rhys set down a plate of steaming stew and dumplings and took a seat to find all eyes on him. "What?"

Gulshan wagged her spoon at him. "You didn't say he did a flash."

Rhys scanned the faces around the table. None of them were on his technical team. "Who told you that?"

Dieter tapped the side of his nose. "Got our sources. So it's true?"

Of course, the news would get out. Rhys sighed and picked up his cutlery. "Yeah. It's true." He tucked into his food, ignoring the babble of questions until he'd downed several mouthfuls of steak before it got cold. "Look"—he reached for his glass—"you know the rules. I can't talk about an active mission."

"It's practically over," Gulshan pointed out. "Debrief and it's done, right? Report write-up aside."

Rhys met her eyes as he ate another mouthful.

"Christ on a cracker, he's doing an Ofori," Dieter said with a snort.

Rhys tilted his glass towards Dieter. "Thank you."

"That," Dieter said, "wasn't meant to be a compliment."

Rhys just smiled and continued to eat.

Chapter Five

SLEEPING BECAUSE OF lots of painkillers was good. Those same painkillers wearing off was bad. It was even worse when they wore off as you were lying on your side with the lovely great big sword wound in it.

Qasim gave a strangled squeak, rolling onto his good side.

It didn't help much, the pain spreading over his ribs like wildfire.

"Ohhhh...," he groaned, "oh...s'not good."

"Qasim?"

He forced his eyes open. Everything was hazy. There was someone coming closer, and he squinted. If he was still confined, then there was only one other person who should be there. "Mila?"

Tahmila leaned over his bed, concern all over her round face. "Who else would it be?" She brushed her cool hand across his brow. "Do you want some more painkillers or something?"

He nodded, wondering if she would take offence if he threw up all over her.

Tahmila straightened up and moved away from the bed. He took deep breaths and tried to ignore the dull ache that felt like it was pulsing through every inch of his body.

The room was coming into focus around him. It had been a long time since he'd ended up in the med bay. It was the smell. He hated the smell of the place. All sterile and clean and clinical.

The monitor by his bed chirped, and a chill touched at the line in his hand. Fresh batch of painkillers: cool and straight into the bloodstream. He breathed out slowly, waiting for them to kick in.

"They won't be as powerful as the ones they gave you last night," Tahmila warned as she sat next to him. "We've got a debrief to do, and I don't think you being out of your tree again would be any use to anyone."

He tilted his head to peer at her. "Again?" He frowned, trying to recall anything beyond his clothes being hacked off and being as surprised as everyone when a cat catapulted into the face of the attending physician. "I thought they knocked me out."

Tahmila's face was a picture. Her lips pressed together and her shoulders shook. Never a good sign.

"What did I do?" he asked. "I didn't try and get naked or something?"

She pressed her fingertips to her lips, struggling against a smile. "You...might have called Rhys Griffiths an angel."

Qasim stared at her. "Rhys Griffiths?"

"You know? Our supervisor?"

An image came to mind of a short plump man with glasses, a warm smile, and a mop of curly blond hair. Qasim had met him, but he'd been so caught up in prep, he couldn't remember much of what they'd said to each other. Still, he seemed nice enough. Complimenting him wasn't a crime.

"An angel?" he echoed. "Doesn't sound so bad."

Tahmila patted his hand. "It's more...*how* you said it."

"...how?"

"Fat ceiling baby. Direct quote." She was trying to hide her grin. "And then, you went all moon-eyed and sighed."

Qasim stared at her. "No."

"Mm."

"Please tell me you're the only one who heard it."

She shook her head, her hair tumbling around her shoulders. "Griffiths, and Ofori as well."

Qasim turned his face back into the pillow, wondering if it was possible to suffocate himself before she could stop him. "Nooooooo."

"As metaphors go, I was impressed," Tahmila said consolingly. "You were pretty far gone."

He peered at her out of the corner of his eye. "Did he seem annoyed? Griffiths?"

"To be honest, I was too busy trying to stop you from popping your wound open to notice." She ruffled his hair. "Don't worry. Ofori is discreet, and I won't breathe a word of it."

"Promise?" he muttered around a mouthful of pillow.

"Would I lie?"

She made a good point. Of all the people in the TRI, she was the one he trusted most and who knew him best. They'd worked together on both sides of the gate, and she'd seen the good and the bad sides. It was also why he was lying in the med bay with a sword wound across his ribs.

He groped for her hand and squeezed it. The blisters on his palms throbbed, but it was nothing compared to his side. "Thank you."

She smiled. "Don't mention it." She squeezed his fingers too. "How about we get you something to eat, and then we can see about getting your lens out?"

He nodded gratefully.

Fifteen minutes later, when the projected screen lit up on the wall for the debrief, Qasim was still working his way through a bowl of scrambled eggs. His whole body ached from the exertion of the past few days, and even lifting the spoon felt like a challenge.

Tahmila had dragged over her chair to sit by Qasim's bed again and waved in greeting.

"Morning, you two." Jacob was seated at the middle of the table in the communication room with Dieter on his right and Gulshan and Rhys Griffiths on his left. "How are you feeling, Qasim?"

Qasim swallowed down a mouthful of egg. "Sore, but all right." He risked a glance at Rhys, who was tapping at his folio. Qasim couldn't help staring. Suddenly, his comment made sense. The man was like one of those chubby little cherubs painted on a church ceiling, only all grown up and wearing a suit. Qasim hastily dragged his eyes to Jacob. "D'you mind if I finish breakfast? It's taking a bit longer than usual."

"Take your time. Tahmila can do the initial debrief. You can supplement anything she misses."

Qasim nodded gratefully, digging his spoon into the bowl of lukewarm eggs.

Tahmila took a sip of coffee and then launched into a thorough breakdown of their mission.

All things considered, it had been straightforward: expand on known details of the coup that dethroned the Ottoman Sultan Ibrahim with perspectives of the residents of Istanbul. There'd been an additional request—if possible—for information pertaining to Kösem Sultan, the Sultan's mother, and her role.

Qasim and Tahmila had arrived several days before the coup, when the city was already on edge, but before the Janissary uprising and the death of the Grand Vizier at the hands of the mob. They'd gone as close to the Hippodrome as they dared. No one in their right mind wanted to rile up the Janissaries, especially when they were already up in arms. It was a brave— and stupid—man who crossed the elite soldiers.

Still, Qasim and Tahmila had gotten close enough to see the numbers involved and mingled in the marketplaces and mosques in the guise of a merchant and his wife from the provinces visiting her family. Despite the tensions in the city, there were always people who would talk over food and drink. They hadn't lacked sources.

The ongoing war against Venice was a sore point. Most people spoke angrily about how the Venetian blockades had whittled down supplies to the city for months. In addition, the Grand Vizier had levied exorbitant taxes on a population already struggling. The Sultan was blamed for it. It was his war, after all. Given the level of anger, the people's revolt and subsequent bloodshed came as no surprise. Qasim and Tahmila's extraction had been on the night before the coup happened.

By the time she was done, Qasim's bowl was empty.

"Anything to add, Qasim?" Jacob prompted.

Qasim shook his head. "She's covered everything I would have said." He hesitated and, unable to help himself, added, "Except the inn by the marketplace. I would cut off my right foot for another portion of their lamb."

Dieter snorted in amusement, and Gulshan shook her head, smiling. Rhys Griffiths even laughed, and there was a glint of humour in those clear blue eyes.

Qasim hid a relieved grin. No grudges being held, then.

"You said people talked freely about the gathering at the Hippodrome?" Gulshan inquired.

Qasim nodded. "People in the market didn't expect it to go anywhere. They were frustrated, but they'd seen one coup fail, so they didn't really expect another so soon to be so successful. When the Janissaries got involved, people sat up and paid attention. No one messes around when the Janissaries stick their oar in."

"Plus, people who are trying to make a living don't want to get involved in the big issues," Tahmila put in. "It's like any rebellion—until it starts affecting them, they're willing to sit by and let the rebels get on with it or get squashed, whichever comes first."

"People are people," Dieter said. "Say what you like, but at least we're consistent buggers."

Jacob chuckled. "I'm going to bask in the glow of your heart-warming cynicism for a moment."

"Eh." Dieter shrugged. "Cynicism. Realism. One and the same."

"What about the *Valide*?" Griffiths asked. Now he was aware of it, Qasim recognised the deep, lilting voice from the prep meetings. It was a nice voice, warm and rich, and with a bit of a Welsh accent. "Did you hear anything about her?"

Qasim glanced at Tahmila in inquiry. There had always been speculation about the role of the Sultan's mother in the coup, but it was difficult to get accurate information that wasn't biased or hearsay. The first days of the mission had been fruitless, and they hadn't had time to exchange information about what they'd learned before the last visit to the mosque.

"I didn't get anything," he admitted. "I think the circles we were moving in were too low down the social ladder. Met a few men with opinions about women trying to grab power and such but nothing solid."

Tahmila nodded. "The best we could manage were the rumours and speculation about how she was trying to take the throne for herself. It was practically impossible to get near any of the royal women. I tried speaking to some of the Jewish women who did business in the seraglio, but you'd have more luck getting blood out of a stone."

"Discretion is a currency of its own," Gulshan agreed. "The ladies of the palace would need it, and if you have their trust and their business, you don't risk it for petty gossip."

"There's plenty of information on the lenses," Qasim added. "Hopefully, you'll be able to get a better read on the numbers than we could. There was too much going on for us to hang around and count heads."

"And you didn't want to draw more attention, did you?" Griffiths said.

"Well..." Qasim offered a sheepish smile. "I fluffed it."

Griffiths actually chuckled. "You got back mostly intact. That's what matters, isn't it?" He rubbed thoughtfully at his chin with the ball of his thumb. "Can you tell us how you got separated? Tahmila said you found each other when you left the mosque, but she turned around, and you were gone."

Qasim spun the spoon in circles in the empty bowl with his fingertip. The metal handle hummed along the china rim. There were some things Tahmila didn't need to know.

"The streets were clearing in a hurry after prayers," he said. "I got caught in a crowd, and by the time I managed to get free, Tahmila had turned a corner, and I couldn't see her." He stilled the spoon and glanced up at the quartet. "I didn't want the guards to get suspicious about the random guy running about like a madman. Meeting up at the rendezvous seemed like the safest bet."

"I'm assuming from the gaping knife wound," Jacob said, "keeping a low profile didn't work."

"Sword," Qasim corrected, recalling the gleam of metal in torchlight. He hadn't felt it strike. Running on adrenaline and terror by then, he supposed. It still didn't seem like it had really happened. If not for the pain and bandages, he might not have believed it. "More like a narrow scimitar, if you want to be precise." He gingerly put one hand to his side. It was still aching. "I was taking the long route through the marketplace to avoid them. It didn't work. There was some running involved. And climbing."

"They must have blocked both ends of the street the house was on," Tahmila put in. "By the time I jumped, they were almost on top of me."

Qasim nodded in confirmation. "I had to get in through the roof. Thought they might not notice, but they heard me. Came bashing in through the door." He waved vaguely to his swollen face. "One got too close, so I kicked him in the bollocks. The next one was smarter and used his sword."

"And then you did the flash?" Dieter asked, leaning forward intently.

Qasim's focus drifted as it all came crashing back: beyond the panic and the mad beat of his heart in his ears, he'd stumbled, barely dodging the blade. The Janissary raised his sword again, and there was a flash of light. The doorway. The way out. He'd dived for it, the soldier's curses of shock and fright still ringing in his ears.

The blade and the torchlight. Silver metal and shining gold. It was moving down. It would have hit him. A second later, half a second, and he'd have been dead. Dead and left behind and pieces in the gutter.

His chest was too tight, like his ribs were closing in, and he tried to take deeper breaths. They were rasping in his throat, panting.

Fingers wrapped around his. Warm fingers. His hands were cold. Shaking. He blinked at the hand on his, then at its owner. Tahmila. She was saying his name, but he could hardly hear it. He folded over the edge of the bed and was sick all over the floor.

"Cold," he whispered. She moved, and blankets bundled around him. She climbed up onto the bed, hugging him in his blanket nest. Safe. Warm. She was stroking his hair, and he closed his eyes tight, shaking. All the fear and panic and everything else bubbled up, and it was all he could do to keep breathing.

"It's all right," she murmured, rocking him as if he were a baby. "You're all right. You're home."

Chapter Six

"SEEMS LIKE DELAYED shock." Jacob finally returned to the communication room. He'd slipped out to speak more privately with the doctors. "He didn't have a chance to process it all last night."

"And thinking about it triggered the memories," Rhys murmured, glancing at the screen which still showed the medical bay. "Poor bastard."

Jacob glanced over to the opposite side of the room where their colleagues were at work. "They're already on the footage?"

Rhys turned to Dieter and Gulshan. Both of them were in the half-reclined viewing docks. The wraparound screen projection gave each of them the full perspective of the two agents in high-resolution detail, and the headphones meant they could completely immerse themselves in the world Qasim and Tahmila had returned from. Gulshan had already scaled the footage up and was adding markers on things worth noting.

"I don't think they'd want to watch the cleanup." Rhys turned back to Jacob. "I know technically we need to do a full debrief of the last leg of the trip, but is there any way we can skip it this time? I mean, we have the footage. We don't want to make things worse for Qasim."

Jacob's eyes flicked to the screen showing the med bay. "I was thinking the same thing. If the digi-lens data shows enough, he won't need to talk about it."

Rhys sighed with relief. It was rubbish, sitting out here, not being able to do anything for Qasim. He disconnected the feed. At least he could deal with the report. "Do you want me to write up the summary of the debrief? It'll give me something to do while these two are working."

Jacob raised his eyebrows. "You sure?"

Rhys shrugged, glancing again at the blank space where the med bay projection had been. "I need a distraction. Didn't expect to have an agent almost die on me on my first mission as supervisor."

Jacob nodded in sympathy. "It shouldn't have happened, but sometimes, you can't help history. You know the standard format?"

"Yeah." Rhys opened up his folio. The summary was the easy part. The full report, written with historical analysis provided by Dieter and Gulshan and their experts, would come later. It was what the client would pay through the nose for. The summary was an outline of what they could expect. "I'll send it up to you for a check when I'm done."

Jacob rubbed at his eyes. "Maybe take your time with it, yeah? I'm going to need a lot more coffee where I'm going."

"Hell?" Rhys suggested wryly.

"Close enough," Jacob said with a grimace. "H-Elwin. I swear to God, it's like bashing your head against a brick wall with him. 'How could an agent end up getting so badly injured in the field?' he asks. Jesus, I don't know— When you send him into a violent political coup by the bloody army? It's a mystery!"

Rhys couldn't help smiling. Elwin was the head of the Supervisory Board and, based on Jacob's frequent tirades about him, you'd think Elwin was personally trying to make Jacob's life as difficult as possible. "You should say that. Exactly that."

"And find out how much I like being unemployed?" Jacob snorted, shaking his head. "I'm too old to find a new job." He nodded towards the two historians. "Let me know if they come up with anything interesting."

"Will do."

It took more than an hour to write up the information. Rhys played back Tahmila's words, but there wasn't much to add. She had been clear, and he'd taken plenty of notes. He glanced over at the two historians, still listening intently to their footage, and brushed his hand over the sensor. The link to the med bay opened up again.

The bay was deserted, except for Qasim tucked up in his blankets in his bed. The mess beside the bed had been cleaned up, and according to the engaged beacon, Tahmila was in the bathroom. No doubt washing her partner's vomit off her.

Qasim had a folio illuminated in front of him and was playing chess against a computer. Even across the feed, Rhys could see how much Qasim's hand was still shaking as he moved the pieces around. He needed a distraction more than anyone.

Rhys hesitated, checking to make sure Dieter and Gulshan were oblivious, and carefully touched the control panel. As the supervisor of the mission, he'd been authorised to use access codes. No one had cancelled them when Jacob took over.

A small beacon flashed on Qasim's screen. He frowned at it, and then touched it. Immediately, the widescreen view of the med bay shrank into a close-up of Qasim's face. Rhys knew his own would be projected in the same way to the other man.

Qasim blinked foolishly at him. Up close, he was even paler, which could be the blood loss or shock or both. Still, Rhys couldn't help but notice the sudden flush of colour across his cheekbones.

"Um."

Rhys smiled. Tahmila had probably mentioned what he'd said the night before. Better to humour him rather than let him get all worked up about what had happened. "That's all I'm getting today? Hardly any effort at all, is it?"

"What?" Qasim's dark eyes widened in surprise.

Rhys leaned forward, bringing himself closer to the microreceptors, so Dieter and Gulshan wouldn't overhear. "Well, when you started going on about my secret identity last night, I was thinking I'd finally get the recognition I deserve for it." He winked.

Qasim gaped at him. For a grown man, he was as wide-eyed as a cartoon character. "Your secret identity?"

Rhys nodded solemnly. "Fluffy wings. Bit of silk. On good days, a Frisbee on my head."

Qasim was shaking again, but from the confused smile on his bruised face, it was from mirth. He shook his head in disbelief. "No—no offence." His breathing was laboured. "That's what you called me for?" He hesitated. "Do—is—do you need more information?"

There was a hitch in his voice. Of course, he wouldn't want to talk about what had happened with anyone, especially someone he barely knew. Trauma was a bastard that way.

"Nah," Rhys said. "I finished my report and thought I'd see what you were doing. See if you fancied a chat, eh?"

"A chat." Qasim tilted his head, his black hair flopping over his forehead. Something in his expression said there was a lot going on behind the eyes. Calculating, working out what was happening. "Thanks for your concern, but you didn't need to check in on me because I've been left unsupervised."

It was no surprise he'd figured it out. He was a smart man. Rhys propped his elbow on the table and rested his chin on his knuckles. "You got me, but I wanted to interrupt your game as well."

For a moment, Qasim seemed confused, and then stuck out his chin mutinously. "Why? Going to tell me to get some rest?"

Rhys shook his head. "I was going to challenge you since you're obviously getting your arse kicked by a machine."

Not for the first time, the other man seemed wrong-footed. "You...want to play me?"

Rhys smiled at the wary interest in Qasim's face. Good. If he didn't want to be treated like an invalid, Rhys could help. "No, I'm going to beat you." He touched several keys, and the frame with Qasim's face shrank into the top of the screen. A new chessboard appeared in front of him. "White or black?"

There was an eager glint in Qasim's eye. "Age before beauty."

So he was going to give sass, was he? Well, Rhys had plenty of experience giving and receiving. "So, not just a fat ceiling baby, but an old, ugly, fat ceiling baby?" He widened his eyes and let his bottom lip wobble.

Qasim squinted at him. "Is this psychological warfare? Are you messing with me, or did I actually offend you?"

Rhys moved a pawn and hid a smile. "Let's see if you can figure it out."

It didn't take long to realise Qasim was the better player. They'd barely made a dozen moves by the time Tahmila returned, because Rhys kept second-checking every move before he made it. Qasim knew it as well.

"Who's playing?" Tahmila's face appeared beside Qasim's, a towel wrapped around her head. She blinked, surprised. "Oh! Hi, Rhys."

Rhys waved in greeting, but Qasim put a hand into Tahmila's face and shoved her gently but firmly out of shot.

"Don't distract him," he said with—what Rhys felt was—unnecessary glee. "It's his move, and he needs to concentrate."

"Qasim." Her voice drifted in, reproachful. "Didn't you warn him?"

"Warn me?" Rhys inquired suspiciously.

Qasim's expression was innocent, and he shrugged, blankets rucking up to his ears. "He said he was going to beat me. I smelled a challenge."

The top of Tahmila's head appeared in the frame. "He used to play competitively when he was fifteen."

Qasim shoved her head out of shot again. "Lies. All lies."

Rhys couldn't help chuckling. "Really?"

Qasim nodded. "I was fourteen."

It made too much sense, especially given the way he assessed the board and moved his pieces less than a blink after Rhys made his own moves. He knew the game much better than he'd let on and was thinking ahead.

"Cheating?" Rhys feigned indignation. "It's not exactly fair play, is it?"

Qasim's face split in a contagious grin. "Ah, the sound of surrender I hear?"

It was a playful side of him Rhys hadn't seen before. Every other time they'd spoken, Qasim had been caught up in training and research. There hadn't been any time for a gleeful chess cheat. It was a pleasant—very surprising—change.

"Do you think I'd give you the satisfaction?" He made his move.

It was embarrassing how deftly Qasim got them to checkmate. He didn't even need to say it. He just leaned back against the pillows and let Rhys hum and haw and stare at the board until he realised how soundly he'd been beaten.

"Damn."

Qasim snickered. "Good game."

Rhys snorted in amusement. "You don't need to patronise me."

Qasim flashed a grin again. "That was polite. I can do patronising, if you want."

"Don't encourage him!" Tahmila called from off-screen. "I'm stuck in here with him."

Rhys closed down the board, returning Qasim's frame to full screen. "Would you believe me if I said I let you win, since you're wounded?"

Qasim's eyes danced. There was some colour in his face, and Rhys felt more than a little smug he'd helped put it there. "Not a chance, but if it'd soothe your bruised ego, we can have a rematch when I get out of here. Let me see you really try."

In the background, Tahmila was hooting with laughter.

"I'd offer to bet against you." Rhys tried to keep his face straight but couldn't help saying, "But I get the feeling if I did, you'd end up seeing the secret identity in person."

This time, it was Qasim who started laughing, then yelped and clutched at his side. "Ow!"

Rhys winced in sympathy. "You should get some rest."

Qasim made a face. "I'd be fine if you didn't make me laugh." He shifted on the bed. "Thanks, by the way."

"For what?"

"Letting me kick your bum." Qasim smiled a smaller, more sincere smile. Even though they'd only been playing for half an hour, he was much more relaxed. It was something to keep a note of in the future.

"I don't think 'letting' came into it," Rhys said with a laugh. He raised his voice: "Tahmila?"

Her head poked into the shot again, her hair hanging in damp ringlets around her face. "Yup?"

"Make sure he gets some rest." Rhys remembered how Jacob had spoken to them the night before. "Sit on him if you have to."

"Hey! That's not—" Qasim's words were muffled by Tahmila's hand over his mouth.

"As you say, Mr. Supervisor, sir," she said with an evil grin at her partner.

Rhys terminated the connection and sat back in his chair.

In less than half an hour, he'd learned more about Qasim than he had from El-Fahkri's HR record and their previous encounters. The HR version was interesting from a management perspective: efficient, quick on his feet, adept at taking in new information. The kind of person you'd want as an agent. The human version, the person who had beaten him at chess and poked fun at him, was something else.

He smiled. It would be interesting to get to know the man better.

Chapter Seven

"HOT! HOT! TOO hot!"

Tahmila leaned into the shower and swept her hand down the control. The temperature of the water dropped to a bearable level, and Qasim sighed in relief, leaning forward into the stream. Some kind soul had thought ahead and set up a waterproof chair so he didn't have to try to stand on his wonky ankle, which was double its normal size.

It had been a bit of a crap morning, all things considered. Pain and vomiting and...

He shuddered, recalling the vivid moments of the flash and the wall of panic dropping on him. It had been a good few years since he'd had a panic attack. His hands shook as he worked the soap into a lather and tried to remember all the little techniques which had become second nature back then.

Chess had always been one of his favourite ways to divert his attention from a trigger.

He didn't know how Rhys had guessed it would help when he offered to play. Maybe Rhys didn't even realise. It could have been a coincidence. Either way, it had distracted him enough so he could get a grip on what remained of the anxiety.

Salat would help too. It always did. There was something comforting about the routine of the prayers five times a day. It felt like a stable anchor when the world went awry.

"Mila!"

"Yeah?" She was on the other side of the misted screen.

"Can you get me something clean to wear?"

She pattered away through to the other room.

Qasim concentrated on scrubbing and rinsing himself and turned down the pressure of the water to carry out his ablutions. It took longer than usual, his wound pulling sharply as he lifted his arms to wash each part of his face and his head in turn. Leaning down to wash his feet was worse, but he wanted to do it. He'd missed several prayers already, and if his hands were shaking and he was aching in places he didn't even know he had, he could manage this one.

When he was done, Tahmila returned to help him out of the shower, one shoulder tucked under his arm. He gave her a stern glare. "This is the first and last time you get your grubby, lascivious hands on my poor, helpless totty."

She made a face at him as she helped him sit on the towel-covered toilet lid and started towelling him down. "Babe, I'd rather swallow a cactus."

Qasim couldn't help laughing as she firmly towelled his hair. "Lies. I've seen you checking me out."

She lifted the edge of the towel to peer at him. "Yeah. What the hell is that and why is it pretending to be human?" She handed him another towel. "Don't push yourself, all right? I'll dry as much of you as you need me to dry."

He nodded gratefully, risking a glance down at himself as he gingerly dried himself. His chest was a mass of bruises and the steri-panel was still in place over the...

His hands were shaking again, and he closed his eyes, taking slow breaths.

Tahmila covered his hands with hers. "What do you need?"

He forced his eyes open again. "Salat. I need salat."

She nodded and retrieved one of the towels, working her way up from his feet as he worked his way down from his shoulders as much as his throbbing ribs would allow. It took effort to get into the standard quarantine threads, and he didn't bother with socks as she helped him to his feet.

A prayer mat was laid out on the floor.

"I checked the position for you," Tahmila said, helping him hobble over. "It should be in the right place."

He managed a smile. Trust Mila to think ahead and get everything set up for him. "Thanks."

"What are partners for?" She helped him down to the mat. "I'll go and clear up the bathroom for now. Give us a shout when you're done, and I'll help you back up."

It was one thing to answer the call to prayer on a mission and sit with other Muslims in the great mosque of Istanbul. The med bay wasn't a holy place. It didn't have the same tranquillity, but it offered the quiet he needed here and now. With a wound in his side and the memory of his near-death, there was plenty to be grateful for.

Qasim sat with his bad leg stretched out before him. It wasn't as if he could manage to stand, let alone kneel, but at least he could complete salat. He took slow breaths, clearing his mind of all concerns and distractions.

In the quiet of the medical bay, he prayed.

It was amazing the difference it made. In spite of the pain in his side and the ache in his leg, there was a calm settling over him for the first time since his return. Even when he was done, he sat, eyes closed and hands loosely clasped in his lap, basking in the peace of it.

He was still sitting there when his folio chirped.

After three vain attempts to get upright, he resorted to yelling for Tahmila, who saw him sprawled on his face and started sniggering before she hauled him to his foot.

"Did you want to prove you're a strong independent man?" she said in a tone of mock consolation.

Every step was making it difficult to catch his breath, so Qasim responded the only way he could by sticking his tongue out. Spikes of heat were jabbing down his side, and every heartbeat throbbed in his ankle. He sat gingerly on the edge of the bed, groped for his folio, and flicked the screen out. There was a message flagged in the corner from Rhys Griffiths: *Got someone here who wants to talk to you.*

The pain was momentarily an afterthought, and Qasim stared at the screen with trepidation. Normally, until the initial draft of the report was done, no one except the supervisor and historians were meant to have contact. "Um. Someone wants a chat."

"Apart from the super? Weird."

"Yeah." Qasim's heart thumped hard. Maybe he was in enough trouble to bring down the higher-ups. Still, it wasn't as if he could say no. He typed a quick acceptance.

A moment later, a video link connected.

Rhys nodded in greeting. "Qasim. Sorry to disturb you again."

Qasim tried to smile. "You said there was someone to speak to me?"

"Someone who wanted to make sure you were all right." Rhys turned the camera and a younger, more worried face appeared in the shot: Ben Sanders, one of the operations team. They'd worked together before.

"Ben!" He raised his hand in greeting. "Hey! Good to see you!"

Ben ducked his head and grinned. "*Salaam alaikum.*"

Qasim smiled. "*Wa'alaikum al-salaam.*"

Ben made sure to always greet Qasim the same way every time their paths crossed. He was a sweet kid and still ended up pink-cheeked every time he talked to Qasim. An agent-thing, Qasim figured. It carried a certain mystique.

The boy stared at him through the screen. "Are you okay? I saw you come back. They said you were stabbed."

"Only a little bit." Qasim winced and gestured vaguely around him. "Stuck in here, a bit sore, but I'm going to be fine, *Insha'Allah*."

"*Insha'Allah*," Ben echoed, sounding relieved.

Tahmila leaned into the frame and waved. "Hi, Ben!"

Ben waved at her too. "I wanted to ask you about the flash, if it's okay?"

Qasim hesitated. "What about it?"

Ben leaned forward intently, arms folded on a table. "Technical stuff. You know we don't normally reopen a gate in the same twenty-four-hour window?" Qasim nodded. "Did you notice anything weird when it connected?"

"Er..." Qasim glanced at Tahmila, who shrugged.

Ben must have sensed his bewilderment. "Um. Like, was anything different? The colour? The light? The sound? Did it seem stable? There were some anomalies in the log, so I was wondering if it messed up the connection or something."

Qasim stared blankly at the screen, remembering the blaze of light and the familiar chilly feeling of passing through it. "I didn't really notice," he said apologetically. "I only really had time to see it open and jump through it."

Ben's face fell. "Right. Yeah." He shook his head. "Sorry. It's just..." He sighed. "There was something familiar, and I wondered if it affected the gate. It was...there were notes about it, but..."

He trailed off, but he didn't need to explain.

More than ten years earlier, Tom Sanders—Ben's father, and the pioneer of time travel technology—was killed by a thief sent from the future to steal his work from his home. Tom had tried to escape through a temporal gate and was killed when the thief short-circuited it. Most of his old records and data were stolen and had never been recovered. The few remaining documents were far from complete.

Qasim couldn't imagine how it must feel to try to piece together the fragments of his father's shattered legacy. On top of everything else, the poor kid had lost his mother to time travel when he was a baby. The TRI were all the family he had left.

Still, it wasn't as if Qasim had had the time to stop and examine the gate when he had to make as fast an exit as possible. "It didn't feel any different. I mean, it felt and sounded and smelled the same when I went through." He paused, frowning. "Should it have been different?"

Ben chewed on his lower lip. "I don't think so. I'll have to check the readings again." He managed a quick smile. "Thanks. I know you need to rest."

Qasim waved his hand dismissively. "I don't mind having someone calling in. It's going to get dull in here, and, well, I'm stuck with Mila." He managed to duck before she swatted him across the back of his head. Ben laughed, but it sounded forced. "I tell you what—if I think of anything, I'll get Rhys to call you in, okay?"

Ben nodded. "That would be brilliant. I just..." He rubbed his forehead with the heel of his hand. "You know when something's right in front of you and it's...just out of reach, and you know if you can just get to it, it'll make things make sense?"

Qasim remembered days of staring at walls and sitting and chewing his nails to ribbons while his mind ran in circles. A long time ago now, but the memories were still there, gnawed into the scars on his fingers. "More than you know, kiddo. At least you have a brain on you. You'll figure it out."

Ben's expression brightened. "Thank you," he said again, and the video disconnected.

"Poor kid," Tahmila murmured. "It must be so frustrating for him."

Qasim nodded, switching his screen off.

Sometimes, he wondered if it wouldn't be better for Ben to step away from the TRI altogether. The boy was a legal adult now. He didn't need to tie himself to the organisation that had been the albatross around his father's neck. He didn't need to, but oh, he wanted to. The TRI was the last connection he had to his parents.

There could be no denying Ben knew what he was doing better than anyone. His father had taught him when he was tiny, and he had turned out as smart as his old man. It was a tragedy neither parent was there to see the incredible leaps their son had made with their technology.

"If anyone can figure it out, it'll be him," Qasim said, setting the folio on the cabinet beside the bed. He leaned against the pillows, exhaling as pain spread across his side. "D'you think they could get me some more of those nice painkillers?"

She reached for the comm connection. "I think they may even give you the strong ones."

Qasim touched his hand gingerly to his side. "Good."

Chapter Eight

THE SCREEN WINKED off.

"Was it any use?" Rhys asked.

Whatever Ben had been asking about, it was definitely beyond Rhys. Most techs had never asked questions when he'd been the support on other missions, but Ben was different. Ben knew the code well enough to see when something was wrong. It was probably why he'd been given a higher-level clearance than the other techs.

Ben frowned at the place where the screen had been. "Maybe. I don't know." He pushed his fingers through his short, sandy hair, leaving it standing in all directions. "I'll need—"

Both of them turned in their seats when the door opened. Rhys's heart dropped like a rock at the sight of Mariam Ashraf. The director of the TRI didn't just show up without warning.

"Has something hap—" Rhys began.

She ignored him, her eyes fixed on Ben. For someone even smaller than him, she still managed to be terrifying. "Explain."

Rhys glanced sidelong at Ben, confused. The boy had gone a sickly shade of grey. "Playing at?" Rhys asked and then groaned inwardly. Oh, the mission was getting better and better. "He didn't have authorisation to speak to Qasim, did he?"

"*He* didn't have authorisation." Mariam folded her arms, her expression grim. "He managed to get hold of the clearance codes of someone who did. Funnily enough, the system flags me when someone else uses my codes."

Rhys stared at Ben. "What? Why?"

"I needed to know!" Ben said, rising from his chair. "What harm is it doing if I talk to him about it?"

"About what?" Rhys frowned up at him. "Is this about the code-thing you talked about last—"

"Yes." Mariam cut across him, her eyes still fixed on Ben. "This is about the 'code-thing.' And this is about the fact Jacob told you not to ask him, because the last mention of the flash during the debrief triggered a panic attack." Ben opened his mouth to argue, but she held up one plump hand. "Don't even try and make any excuses. You know Jacob's word is law in this situation."

"Aunt M, he wasn't liste—"

"Something," she snapped sharply, "you're demonstrating well enough yourself." She strode towards him, dark eyes flashing. "Qasim is injured and clearly traumatised by what happened to him. Of all people, you know what it's like. You don't get to override his well-being to slake your curiosity. He needs to recover, not relapse."

Ben's pallor vanished as colour flooded his face. "I—it—if I didn't find out now, he might not remember! And he was okay!"

"You couldn't know he would be okay," Mariam said angrily. "I understand this is important to you, but I'm not having you risking the health and well-being of *any* of our agents because of a hypothetical theory."

"I didn't even ask about—"

"No." Mariam held up a hand. "Like I said, you don't get to make excuses. You were given an order. You not only disobeyed it, but you lied to your supervisor *and* violated security protocols to do so."

Ben rose, opening his mouth as if he was about to start shouting back, so Rhys scrambled up. "It was my fault. I didn't think it was normal for a tech to have access. I should have checked with you before I let him call. It's on me."

Both of them turned to stare at him as if he'd grown a second head. He held up both hands.

"I'm only saying," he said, hoping his hands weren't shaking too much, "it's done now. He's got his answer, and Qasim's fine."

A muscle was twitching in Mariam's cheek, her lips pressed together in a tight line, but she nodded. "I'll speak to you later." She jerked her head towards the door. Ben, seeing the sense of it, grabbed his folio and fled. Mariam sighed as the door closed behind him and lifted a hand to rub her brow.

Rhys sank back into his chair, rubbing his hands together. Christ, he hated arguments, and he hated the knots twisting up his stomach when they happened.

Mariam sat down in the other seat a moment later. "Sorry you had to see that," she murmured.

Rhys shook his head and darted out his tongue to wet his suddenly dry lips. "A boss has to do what a boss has to do."

"Boss and mum," Mariam sighed. "Not a great pair of roles to roll into one."

He frowned in confusion, then remembered what Jacob had told him years earlier: When Ben was orphaned, Mariam was the one who'd taken him in. His dad's oldest friend and the closest thing to family Ben had left, Jacob said. And now, Ben was a stubborn teenager who had both a mother and a boss to rebel against and the brains to get away with it.

He risked a glance at Mariam, who was drawn. "I'm sorry. I didn't think to ask anyone. I—he said he was authorised. The code checked through."

"Mm." She exhaled slowly. "He knows you don't know all the protocols yet. That's why he waited until you were in here on your own."

Rhys flushed, squeezing one hand around the other. "Sorry."

She offered him a tired smile. "Don't be. It's Ben Sanders. People still see him as the wunderkind. Most of the time, they're right." She got back to her feet and tapped the ID button pinned to her hijab. "Next time, check whether the user ID he's using matches this before you give him any access, okay?" She sighed again. "I'm going to have to change the passwords on everything again."

"Again?" Rhys echoed. "He's done this before?"

She laughed quietly. "You don't raise a baby computer genius without being hacked at least once." She glanced at the door as it slid open again. "Jacob."

Jacob frowned as he came into the room. "What happened?"

"Ben."

Jacob groaned. "Shit."

"It's dealt with for now." She walked by him towards the door. "I'll speak to him later."

Jacob nodded, then turned his attention to Rhys as the door closed behind her. "He wanted to talk to Qasim?"

Rhys nodded. "I let him." He shifted self-consciously on the chair. "Sorry."

Jacob rubbed his hand over his eyes. "My fault. I should have guessed he wouldn't take no for an answer. He's a stubborn little shit when he wants to know anything." He lowered his hand and glanced around the room. "At least our historians weren't in the audience."

Rhys nodded. Dieter and Gulshan had barely been gone for five minutes on their lunch break when Ben showed up. But maybe it had been Ben's plan all along. They'd know the protocol better than a wet-behind-the-ears supervisor.

"What's going on with the code?" he asked tentatively. "It must be important if Ben had to speak to Qasim."

Jacob sighed, shaking his head. "It's nothing to do with the mission or the jump. He's fixated on a recurring piece of code, and he got it into his head Qasim might be able to give him some useful information about it." He raised his eyebrows. "Did he?"

Rhys thought back on their conversation. "No. Not really. He only said the gate felt exactly the same as it usually does."

If it meant anything to Jacob, he didn't show it.

"Right." He sat up a little straighter in the chair. "Well, it's out of his system now. He asked the question and didn't get much of an answer. I hope it's enough to satisfy him."

Rhys nodded. "I think it helped Qasim as well—the distraction, I mean."

"Yeah." Jacob had a knowing gleam in his eye. "Not just him either."

Rhys knew he'd overreached his authority by calling in to chat with Qasim, but it had been for a good cause. "It happens." He said it without breaking eye contact. "And it wouldn't hurt to give him some more, even if it is bending the rules a bit."

Jacob chuckled. "Not a criticism, Rhys. Just an observation. At least you have the authorisation to make the connection." He pushed off from the chair. "The med team let me know he's been dosed for the afternoon. You don't need to worry about him anymore today."

It was easy to say, but Rhys knew he'd be worried until Qasim was on his feet. He already had a few ideas about making things easier for Qasim's remaining time in quarantine. They'd have to wait for another day, though, when he could risk bending the rules a bit further.

"Is there anything else I can do now?" He hoped he sounded casual.

Jacob glanced over at the two vacant stations where the historians normally worked and shook his head. "Afraid not." He studied Rhys. "You've been here every day since the mission prep, haven't you?"

Rhys hesitated, treading the fine line between keen and obsessive. "It was my first time supervising. I wanted to see it all through."

"Understandable. But since it's been delegated up to me, I think you've earned a break." He nodded towards the door. "It's almost finishing time, and you've been doing more than your share of hours. Take an early one. Boss's orders."

"But what if something—"

"Something comes up?" Jacob sounded amused. "Our agents are safely home, and we know what happened. Our historians have the footage to work through. You'd just be sitting on your hands."

It would be nice to see home by daylight for a change. Even if the mission follow-up would be at the back of his mind, he could enjoy the break for a night. If he got home early enough, he could even throw together a meal to surprise Marc.

"You're sure I won't be needed?" he asked, getting up.

Jacob's answer was a finger pointed towards the door.

Less than half an hour later, Rhys was on the monorail to the transport hub. He considered sending a message to Marc, but surprising him sounded better. He smiled as he thought about it. A good meal, maybe a bottle of wine, and see where the evening led.

He picked up his pod from the dock at the transport hub and headed in the direction of the city, stopping off to pick up shopping on the way. He and Marc lived in a modest flat in a large block in the northern suburbs. Once in a while, he'd thought about moving, but budgets being what they were...

Still, it was home, and Rhys smiled as he stepped into the hall. Home was always a welcome relief. The lights came on at his call, and he carried the shopping through to the kitchen, but his heart sank at the sight of it. The counters were a mess of half-made food. There were fragments of a broken plate in the bin. He didn't want to guess what was clogging the sink. There was also a note stuck to the fridge: *I'll clean up when I get home tonight.* It was too familiar: the after-effects of one of Marc's nights out.

By the time he'd cleaned up enough to make a start on dinner, it was already getting late. By the time dinner was ready, Marc should have already been home. By the time the food was stone cold and Marc's folio had gone unanswered, Rhys was worried sick.

He called Marc's colleagues to see if any of them knew where he was, but no one did. A meeting, one suggested. Or maybe the gym. Or, or, or. So many suggestions and no real answers. He paced the floor, tried to chime Marc again and again—food, hunger, appetite all forgotten.

When his own folio chirped nearly an hour later, Rhys flicked open the screen at once. There was a text message, just a line from Marc: *Client in town. Will be late.*

Rhys stared at it and closed the screen down. The dread and panic faded, but they left something dull and aching in their place. He set the folio aside carefully. He had no right to feel angry. After all, he'd done the same thing the night before. They both had to work. He knew how important Marc's consultancy was, just as Marc knew how important Rhys's promotion to supervisor could be.

Still, when Rhys'd stayed at work to deal with the mission, at least he'd bothered to send a message in advance. At least he'd tried to make his excuses.

"Enough," he muttered to himself. The food was cold, but it would keep, and he wasn't hungry anymore. He packed it into the fridge, showered, tried to watch some telly, tried to read, tried to occupy himself. The flat felt too quiet and too empty.

In the end, he gave up and went to bed.

It was pitch dark when someone sprawled on top of him and a wet mouth pressed against his ear. He jerked awake and snapped his fingers for the bedside lamp.

Marc grinned at him. Even without the smell of alcohol, Rhys would have spotted the telltale gleam in his partner's eye at twenty paces.

"All right?" Marc was enthusiastically working a hand under the covers, fumbling for Rhys's shorts.

Rhys caught his wrist. "Marc, what the fuck?"

Marc propped himself over Rhys on his other arm, rubbing his hips against Rhys's legs through the blankets. "Been a while. Fancy it?"

Rhys stared at him. It was never good when Marc was in that kind of mood. Rhys shoved the blankets aside and pressed a hand to Marc's shoulder to keep him at arm's length before he could take it as an invitation.

"Just a minute, *bach*." He swung his legs over the side of the bed and got up.

"But where are you going?" Marc demanded, grabbing at his shorts.

Rhys managed a convincing smile. "You know we keep all the stuff in the bathroom." He unhooked Marc's hand from his shorts. "You get undressed and under the covers. I'll be back in a bit."

Marc nodded blearily, frowning as he tugged at the buttons of his shirt.

Rhys retreated into the bathroom, closing the door behind him. He didn't lock it. He'd never needed to lock it yet. The *yet* was getting to him, though. 'Yet' felt like it might still happen.

It wasn't that Marc was an arsehole. When he was sober, he was great, but the social drinking was the reason Rhys had resorted to stashing all their sex gear in the bathroom. It gave him an out if Marc ever came home in that state, which was happening more and more often. Clumsy, messy, and sometimes painful shagging wasn't how Rhys enjoyed spending his nights.

He padded across the cool tiles of the floor and sat on the toilet lid.

Five minutes was usually enough. Ten at a push.

It was easier than getting into an argument Marc wouldn't remember, and Rhys wouldn't forget.

By the time he slipped out of the bathroom and back into the darkened bedroom, Marc was already snoring. He hadn't finished undressing, sprawled facedown on the bed, one shoe on, shirt hanging off his arm.

Rhys managed to arrange the covers over him without waking him and then made his way through to the living room and sank onto the couch.

At some point soon, they'd need to talk about it, but the thought made Rhys feel sick down to his stomach. It felt like such a petty thing when Marc was such a good partner so much of the time. They never fell out. It felt safer. It was all right: no anger and disappointment or those taut, tense silences.

Rhys ran a hand over his eyes.

It'd be all right. They'd be all right.

He reached up and pulled the blanket down off the back of the couch. It wasn't the first time he'd slept there, and it wouldn't be the last. Still, he had a home. He had security. Maybe he hadn't gotten the promotion, but he also hadn't been stabbed, and he still had a roof over his head.

It would be all right.

It had to be.

Chapter Nine

"GIVE ME YOUR first four priorities."

On the other end of the video feed, the pair of trainee agents exchanged looks. As usual, they had one male and one female agent to cover both sides of the gender divide in missions. "Um…"

Qasim raised his eyebrows. "You should know this."

"Make sure the environment is safe?" Nilufer guessed.

"Make sure your partner is with you," Ibrahim added.

Qasim nodded, leaning back against the pillows as the two conferred. He and Tahmila had been training the pair before their prep for Istanbul started, and it seemed like a fortnight without their teachers had had an impact.

He'd been surprised when they'd chimed in.

In normal circumstances, only the mission supervisor and their two historians would be given access. The only reason he could think of was because he was injured. Maybe the Board wanted another pair of agents who could pass in Islamic cultures ready to go in case he needed extra time off.

"Blend in!" Nilufer exclaimed. "Get blended in as soon as you can."

Qasim disguised a wince of frustration with a wince of pain and made a show of pressing his hand to his ribs.

It wasn't that they wouldn't be able to do the job ahead of them. They would. Ibe and Nilufer were good and given the time needed, they'd be great agents, but time was a luxury the Board didn't always allow, which struck Qasim as ironic in an agency built for time travel.

Tahmila was a sterner teacher. "Are you kidding? Four basic rules and you've forgotten them already?" She was sitting next to Qasim's bed, one arm propped by his hip. "Do you remember the acronym?"

Ibrahim nodded. "BEEP. But I can't remember the other *E*."

Tahmila held up her hand, folding down four fingers. "*Blend* in, check your *Environment*, remember your local *Etiquette*, and keep your *Partner* close. BEEP."

Qasim sniggered and got a finger poked in his ribs. "What? It's a rubbish acronym."

Tahmila glowered at him. "I made it up."

"I know," he replied, widening his eyes. "Why d'you think it's rubbish?" He turned back to the screen. "She's not wrong, though. Looking the part and blending in isn't going to be enough if you don't remember how to behave."

Sometimes, he thought as Tahmila took over the lecture, *even that's not enough*. Istanbul had proved it. He'd done so much prep. He'd accounted for every possibility. It should have been fine, but it wasn't, and now, he was stuck in a med bay pretending he was a good example for new agents.

Tahmila had no clue, either.

As far as she knew, it was just bad luck.

His hands were shaking again. He clasped them together in his lap and tried to pay attention to what Tahmila was saying. Something for Nilufer about remembering modesty and humility even when men were being men. He should laugh. It was a gentle jab at him, and he could sense Tahmila's eyes on him, but his hands were shaking, and it was harder to breathe.

She was sitting on the bed in a heartbeat, and her hands were on his. "What do you need?"

She could always tell, even if there weren't any outward signs.

"Beads."

She ran around the bed to the cabinet on the other side and pulled out the string of prayer beads. There was something comforting in the repetitive rhythm as they clicked between his fingers. Neither of them spoke until he laid them in his lap and released a shaky breath.

"Sorry."

Tahmila gave his knee a pat through the blankets. "You took care of me the time I got the squirts. I think I've got the easier job." She tilted her head. "Was it something I said?"

Qasim shook his head. "Me, this time." He laughed ruefully. "Set myself off. How smart is that?"

She took one of his hands careful to avoid his blistered palms. "Well, you never were the brightest candle on the cake, were you?" She tugged a finger against his. "You didn't throw up on me this time. I consider it progress."

He rubbed her fingertip with his thumb, offering a small smile. "But that's how my people show affection."

She leaned closer and pulled him into a hug. "Because you are a disgusting peasant." She kissed him firmly on the cheek as he wrapped his arms around her plump body. "And why I think you secretly enjoyed my encounter with Delhi belly."

He made a face at her. "We were in Alexandria."

"Eh. Different continent, same burning bum." She glanced over her shoulder. "Want me to ring the new starts back in? I disconnected them."

Qasim considered it. As long as he focussed on the agents and their training and didn't let himself think about his own cock-ups, it would be all right. "Go on, then. Someone needs to get them ready."

It wasn't so simple, but it was easier with Tahmila beside him. By the time they were done, Nilufer and Ibrahim looked as if they were the ones who had just come back from a mission, wrung dry of everything they knew.

"I think we scared them," Tahmila said with satisfaction.

"You enjoyed tormenting them a bit too much," Qasim observed.

She grinned. "I have to take my pleasure where I can." She nodded towards the door at the far end of the window-lined bay where there was a small gym. "Mind if I leave you for a bit?"

Qasim smiled crookedly. "You must be bored if you want to exercise."

She flexed dramatically. "Need to stay in shape for Boris. He'll never forgive me if I can't walk him properly."

Qasim couldn't help laughing. "Not for the husband, but for the dog? Your priorities are wonky." He waved a hand towards the gym. "Go and get sweaty. I'll be fine for a bit."

As soon as she was gone, he picked up the beads again. If he focussed on them and didn't let his mind go wandering, he would be fine. Trouble was the blister burns on his hands still hurt, and the more he moved the beads, the more acute the pain became.

He was half tempted to call Tahmila back, but it wouldn't be fair. She already had to deal with him at night. After the first nightmares, she'd ended up cradling him until morning.

He chewed his lip. There was chess on the computer, but it wasn't the same, not when he needed a good distraction.

He couldn't say why he did it, but he flicked open a folio screen, found a tiny icon of a pair of flapping wings, and sent it to Rhys Griffiths. It seemed like a good idea at the time, but as soon as it was gone, he groaned. Mistake. Stupid mistake. It wasn't as if they were friends, and no agent lobbed cartoons at their supervisor.

He pressed the heels of his hands against his eyes.

Tired.

That's what he was. Tired and mind running in circles and not thinking straight. And drugs. Yeah. The painkillers were making him all wobbly.

His folio chirped.

Qasim lowered one hand, squinting at it, and then lowered the other.

A message from Rhys was waiting on the screen.

Bored?

Qasim hesitated and then sent: *Sorry.*

To his astonishment, Rhys didn't respond with words but with a tiny dancing angel animation. It had a hula hoop. No. It had a halo it was using as a hula hoop. Qasim snorted.

Sexy, he responded and then winced at how inappropriate it sounded.

Another icon appeared—a wink. *What I do on a weekend.*

Qasim couldn't help laughing, relieved.

A video connection blinked at the corner of the screen, and he brushed his finger over it, opening the connection.

Rhys was on the other end, as haggard as Qasim was feeling. "All right?"

Qasim managed a nod, though he knew his face betrayed him. Always did right after a panic attack. "Bit of a morning."

"Yeah?"

Qasim shrugged a shoulder. His stupid erratic brain was nothing for his supervisor to worry about. After all, he was paying his therapist for something. "Nothing a dancing angel didn't help."

Rhys smiled and deep dimples appeared in his cheeks. "Did its job then, didn't it?" He leaned forward, closer to the camera on his end. "Want to have a game?"

Relief spread through Qasim, pushing down the lingering tension. "You've got time?"

Rhys scratched his fingers through his blond curls. "Weeeeell, technically, Jacob's handling a lot of the business because of the flash, so I have time to kill." He raised his eyebrows. "Trying to avoid playing?"

Qasim huffed in mock indignation. "No. I just don't want to get in more trouble for distracting you." He tried to grin as he said it, but he had a feeling it wasn't very convincing. "I'm enough trouble as it is."

Rhys gazed at him from behind his neat rectangular glasses. "You know, if you're going to give me lip, I'm going to make this harder for you."

He glanced sideways, and from the way he was moving, he had another screen open. "Right. Pawn to D5."

"What?"

The dimples appeared again. "You've forgotten how to play already?"

Qasim peered at his screen. "I can't see the board."

Rhys cupped his chin in both hands and widened his eyes, even more cherubic than ever. "Oh, did I forget to say you'd be playing blind?"

Qasim blinked. He'd played blind before, but it was ages ago. Remembering the board and the moves was one of the biggest challenges he'd given himself. It took all his concentration and a lot more work than a normal game.

Well, if that wasn't a distraction and a half...

"Go on then," he said, pushing himself up in the bed.

By the time he'd taken three pieces, he had his eyes closed and was tracing out the moves on the covers over his lap. When he managed to check Rhys the first time, Qasim was smiling. It took longer than their first game, but he still won in the end. He opened his eyes.

"Not as hard as I thought."

Rhys wrinkled his nose. "I don't know. It took you a while, didn't it? I think you could do better."

"Yeah?" Qasim tugged at the edge of his covers and cautiously suggested, "Same time tomorrow?"

Rhys flashed his dimples again. "I'll see if I can squeeze you into my busy schedule of sitting and writing notes." He waved cheerfully. "Get some rest. I want you fighting fit for our next round."

"Your next beating, you mean?" Qasim grinned at him.

"I might just be testing you for weakness," Rhys said with a sniff.

"Uh-huh." Qasim laughed and pressed a hand to his side as his ribs pulled against the wound. "And there's a sign I need to be a good patient." He smiled. "Thanks."

Rhys shrugged with a smile and disconnected the video.

"Aw. I missed all the fun," Tahmila said, so close by Qasim almost jumped off the bed. She was sitting on her own bed, several feet away, reading. She grinned at him. "You didn't even realise I'd come back in, did you?"

Qasim glanced at the space where his screen had been. "I was distracted."

Tahmila chuckled. "I saw." She climbed off her bed. "But enough excitement, I think. I'll get some food in, and then you're having a nap."

"Yes, Ummi."

Tahmila, mature as ever, stuck her tongue out at him.

Chapter Ten

THE WALLS OF the briefing room were covered in projections. Rhys brushed some aside to see the ones below. Every hour, he was taking the fresh notes and images Dieter and Gulshan had put together, sorting through them, and putting them in order on the digital boards. It took a lot of attention, sifting out any duplications, but he was glad for the distraction.

Things were...not great at home.

They hadn't talked, him and Marc. Not the way they needed to. It was all his stupid fault. If he'd slept better, if he hadn't already been on edge about the mission and his job and everything else, he might not have snapped at Marc for the first time in the five years of their relationship. And because he snapped, he panicked and tried to explain, and when he explained, he made things so much worse.

The bathroom. He'd told Marc about the bathroom. About how he wondered if, one day, he'd have to lock the door to keep Marc at bay. Marc got upset and no wonder. Then Rhys was a coward and hid at work for three days.

When he went home after, things had changed. Not in big ways, but in ways that made their flat feel wrong and tense. It was depressing, and what made it worse was all the little ways he wasn't even trying to stop it. He could. He wished he wanted to, but he was so tired.

By comparison, a mission going wrong felt simple. When he wasn't entertaining Qasim—who was bored to death in quarantine—with badly played chess, the mission data was keeping him busy.

A three-day mission took at least ten days for the basic sift. The more complicated and in-depth the mission, the more time it would take. They'd already been working on it for twelve days and finally reached the last few hours of the third day.

It was because of Qasim and Tahmila. The amount of data they'd collected was more than anyone expected. Both of them had mixed with the locals in the mosque and at the baths. Several times, Qasim had managed to join conversations with men over thick, dark coffee. Gulshan wouldn't stop going on about how well he'd nailed the accent.

Rhys scaled up some of the images of the Hippodrome. There were a lot of soldiers—Janissaries, he recalled—and the mood seemed tense. There were close-up images of people surrounded by notes about their clothing, rank, and age. It could have been any military protest in any part of the world. The only real differences were the clothes and the lack of hand-painted banners.

"Die..." Gulshan's voice caught Rhys's attention. He turned to both of the historians. Gulshan had frozen her footage and was beckoning Dieter over. "Come and have a listen to this. I'm not sure if I'm hearing it right?"

Dieter dragged her screen wider as Rhys went to join them. "What am I listening for?"

"You'll know," Gulshan said, shifting the projection in his direction.

Rhys leaned in over their shoulders as the footage played. It was evening, before sunset, and they were seeing through Qasim's lens as he made his way towards the mosque. Gulshan turned up the volume on the footage. There were a lot of voices overlapping, and she darted her fingers along the controls, shifting the balance. One voice became clearer, though still muffled.

Abruptly, Qasim looked back over his left shoulder. He glimpsed a couple men and then faced ahead again. The small panels registering his vital signs showed a brief spike in heart rate.

Dieter frowned and replayed the few seconds again.

"What is it?" Rhys asked quietly.

Dieter and Gulshan exchanged looks.

"I did hear it right, didn't I?" she said.

"Unless we're both hearing things," he agreed.

"And for those of us who don't speak Turkish?" Rhys inquired.

"Is he the one?" Gulshan quoted. "He... I'm not sure how this would be phrased. I think they think he's asking too many questions about things he shouldn't? Something like that? They've gone a bit...dialectic."

Rhys stared at the screen, then reached down over Dieter's shoulder and replayed it. "They said it here?" Gulshan nodded. It was just before Qasim turned and his heartbeat picked up. "Is it possible they made him?"

"As an outsider?" Dieter nodded. "Sounds like it."

Rhys had a horrible premonition of how the rest of the footage would play out. "Skip to the final half hour."

"But we only have a couple of hours left," Gulshan protested. "Wouldn't it be better to do it in order?"

Rhys shook his head. "Now."

They skimmed forward through the final visit to the mosque and a blur of images of men in conversation with Qasim. From the way his eyes were darting around, Qasim was on his guard. When he left the mosque, he scanned around again. For a split second, his eyes settled on two men. The men who had spoken. They turned away when he met their eyes.

Qasim searched out Tahmila. She uncurled her finger in the direction of a side street, and he nodded, but as soon as she was out of sight, he turned into the crowd heading in the other direction. He mixed in among them and then broke off into a side alley. He muttered to Tahmila that he would meet her at the rendezvous point, before glancing out into the street. The two men were speaking with some Janissaries.

What followed was enough to settle Rhys's heart in his throat. The Janissaries were hunting Qasim. He was hiding, running, making his way through the tangle of streets. Gulshan couldn't be sure whether they thought he was a spy or a traitor, but they were after him.

"Fucking hell," Dieter murmured as the flash of light gave Qasim his escape route. "Why didn't he say something?"

Rhys reached down and stopped the footage. There was only one reason he'd kept it from them. "Tahmila. He didn't want to upset her."

"It'll be in the report," Gulshan said. "They have to sign off on it. She's going to find out."

"Yeah," Dieter agreed, "but they'll be out of quarantine by then, so he can run the fuck away before she can smack the shit out of him."

Rhys rubbed his forehead with his fingertips. "Jacob's going to be thrilled with this development."

"And then some," Gulshan agreed. "You want us to finish the sweep before you tell him in case there's anything else in the interim?"

Rhys considered it. "I'll let him know what we think happened, but you're finishing the sweep to make sure." He stepped away from their chairs. "We'll need to work out what to do with El-Fahkri."

Once they were back at work, he sent a line to Jacob about what they'd found. Jacob replied several minutes later saying he wasn't surprised, and he would come down shortly.

Rhys sent up an acknowledgement and tapped his fingers on the table, frowning. Qasim must have known they would find out. He'd probably been waiting for it. He'd sat through the lectures about putting himself in danger without complaint, even though everything he'd done was to save his partner.

A touch connected Rhys's folio to the med bay camera.

Tahmila was lying on a blanket in a patch of winter sunlight by the window, her head propped on a pillow, her attention on whatever she was reading. Qasim was halfway up the room, lounging in an armchair. He was playing some kind of game on his folio, his fingers dancing across the screen. Always finding some way to occupy himself.

Rhys hesitated and then sent a note to Qasim: *We know what you did.*

On his screen, Qasim flicked his game aside and opened the message. He tensed, darting a wary glance up in the direction of the camera, then back at his screen and typed rapidly. *Did I just wake up in a horror film?*

Rhys smiled crookedly. Of course, he would try to dismiss it. *You know what I'm talking about. After the mosque.*

He wasn't surprised when Qasim scrambled to his feet and limped towards the bathroom, taking his folio with him. As soon as the bathroom door closed, Rhys's folio chimed to let him know a video link was incoming.

Qasim was sitting against the edge of the sinks. "You haven't told Mila?"

Rhys shook his head. "We just reached the end of the footage."

Qasim grimaced. He'd regained some of his colour, but he was still haggard and pale. "She's not going to be pleased when she finds out."

Rhys propped his chin on one hand. "And when she finds out you lied?"

"Not lied!" Qasim held up a finger. "Omitted. Two totally different things."

"As near as makes no difference," Rhys countered.

Qasim ran a hand over his head, rumpling his hair. He raised his eyes to the ceiling. "I don't want her to think it's her fault." He sounded tired and much younger. "She hates it when I get hurt."

Rhys wasn't surprised. Qasim and Tahmila had been friends for years before they were headhunted for the TRI. Everyone knew they were as close as siblings. "I'm not going to tell you what you should do, but I thought you should know Jacob'll want to speak to you when you're out of quarantine."

Qasim leaned back against the mirror and closed his eyes. "Yeah. Figured." He opened one eye. "Will you sit in and stop him from tearing me a new one?"

Rhys chuckled. "You think you're in my good books, Mr. El-Fahkri?"

Qasim lifted his head, wary. "Are *you* going to tear me a new one?"

"Me?" Rhys inclined his head. "I think I'll omit that information just now."

Qasim stared at him, then made a face. "I see what you did there. Not subtle."

It was tempting to laugh at the indignation on his face. "I never said I was." Rhys glanced at the corner of the screen. A message incoming. "I need to go. You...do what you need to do. Or not. It's your call."

"If you bribe Jacob to be nice to me, I'll let you win a game," Qasim blurted out. "And you can tell people."

Rhys laughed. "But where's the fun there? I'll beat you one of these days *and* get to see Jacob go through you like a dose of salts."

Qasim snorted. "You're not as sweet and innocent as everyone thinks."

Rhys smirked at him. "I never said I was sweet or innocent. Didn't anyone ever tell you not to judge a book by its cover?"

"Not when the book played chess with me every day to stop me getting bored while I'm stuck in here." Qasim leaned closer to the camera as if scrutinising Rhys carefully. "So, not sweet and innocent. Little bit evil. Likes chess. About right?"

Rhys chuckled. "I'll let you work it out." He disconnected the link. It made him smile to think how Qasim had decided to tease him. Once he got past wary formality, it seemed like Qasim would poke fun at anyone, including his superiors.

On the far side of the room, the door slid open.

Rhys turned in his seat to see Jacob enter. "Good timing."

"Yeah?" Jacob touched the panel to close the door behind him.

"I was just done warning Qasim that you're coming for his hide."

Jacob raised his eyebrows. "How scared was he?"

"He asked me to come and hold you back," Rhys replied, smiling, "so I'd say eleven on a scale of one to ten."

Jacob looked pleased. "Can't have them getting complacent." He swung around to the two historians. "Right, kids. What do you have for me?"

Chapter Eleven

"COME ON. COME on, come on, come on, come on!" Tahmila was bobbing on her toes at the door of the medical bay.

Qasim grinned as he headed towards her. "I'm not that bad, am I?"

She rolled her eyes at him. "No offence, but I really miss fresh air."

Their two full weeks of quarantine were about to end and, as usual, Tahmila's reserve had shattered in the last ten minutes. She was good at waiting until the last moment when she became as impatient as a toddler at a birthday party.

"Count yourself lucky," Qasim said, running his fingers through his hair. "I'm about to go and get a bollocking from Jacob. *Insha'Allah*, I won't get fired."

Tahmila leaned closer to him, slipping her arm through his. "They wouldn't fire one of their best agents, and you know it." She rested her head on his shoulder. "You got me out of there intact, and you didn't die. Those are two good things."

He'd confessed everything to Tahmila after his chat with Rhys two days earlier, despite his misgivings. She'd swatted him around the head, then cried and hugged him and told him what an idiot he was. All things considered, it could have gone worse.

Trouble was, he *had* still ballsed up some of the mission.

"I brought back a cat and a gaping sword wound," he pointed out. "Don't think he's going to be throwing me a party. And I breached protocol. And I was obvious enough to get made by a couple of blokes at the mosque, so everyone'll know I didn't do enough prep. And I—"

Tahmila covered his mouth with her hand. "If it was so bad, they'd've let you know already." She tapped the end of his nose. "Try and focus on the bright side."

Qasim wished it was so easy.

It was the lack of sleep.

The lack of sleep and the pain.

And the medication.

And the fact he'd cocked up.

Normally, he could keep his mind in check, but not this time. The thoughts were already whirling around in his head, and catching them was like trying to catch dust motes in a stream of sunlight. She must have seen it in his expression because she rose up on her toes and hugged him tightly.

"You have my line," she murmured close to his ear. "Any time."

He tried to laugh, his arms around her. "What if there's a sock on the door handle?"

She leaned back far enough to smile at him. "Then I'll take five minutes to reply." She brought her hands around to cup his face and drew his head down to kiss him on the end of the nose. "Mitchell knows what we're like after a mission."

"What I'm like," Qasim corrected, releasing her and stepping away.

"What *we're* like." She caught one of his hands, squeezing it. "Like always."

Winding down was always tricky. It was different every time, but regardless of how the mission went, it was easier to do it with someone who'd been by your side and seen what you'd seen. Thankfully, Tahmila's husband understood. Mitchell always had a spare bed ready for Qasim, just in case.

"I'll hold you to it," Qasim warned. "And I'm not taking Boris for a walk again."

"You will," she said smugly. "He owns you too."

The light beside the door illuminated, and they stepped apart as it slid open. Even though it only opened into one of the internal pods, the air felt fresher. Qasim took a deep breath and shot a smile at Tahmila, who was beaming from ear to ear.

"Here we go."

The ride from the quarantine unit across to the main building took a couple of minutes, and they emerged into the sterile pod station. Cool air rippled down from outside, and Qasim shivered as they made their way towards the service lift.

"You go on," he said as the lift shot up. "I'll meet you there after Jacob tears me limb from limb."

She leaned in and kissed him noisily on the cheek, earning a groan of mock disgust and a flap of his hands. "You'll be fine." She skipped out when the door opened on her floor.

A few floors up, the lift opened again into a brightly illuminated hallway. Qasim glanced at himself in the polished surface of the floor-to-ceiling windows and hastily straightened his shirt. It never hurt to be respectable when you were speaking to a man who could decide your future. He hurried along the hall, passing several doors before he reached Jacob's office.

Despite the fact the door was shut, he could hear voices inside, though not the words. Jacob was definitely in there, and one of the other speakers sounded like Mariam Ashraf, the current director of the TRI. The third voice wasn't quite so clear.

Qasim sighed with relief. If Jacob didn't think their meeting was top priority, then maybe Qasim wouldn't be in as much trouble as he feared. He glanced about and then went over to sit on one of the chairs standing against the opposite wall.

He'd been sitting awkwardly for what felt like ages when the door slid open and a young man stormed out.

Qasim sat up, surprised. "Ben?"

Ben Sanders paused, his eyes lighting up. "Qasim! You're out of quarantine?"

"A few minutes ago." Qasim got up, smiling. He recalled something Rhys had mentioned about the flash, when they were playing chess one day. "I heard I have you to thank for getting me a doorway."

Ben shrugged, ducking his head, colour blooming on his cheeks. "Just moved around some power. Didn't want to leave you there."

"Which worked out for me, didn't it?" Qasim knocked him on the shoulder playfully. "What about you? Did you have any luck with those mysterious anomalies?"

Ben's smile faded. "No. They've shown up before, but I'm still trying to find the connection." He glanced over his shoulder at the half-open door and offered Qasim a wan smile. "I need to go. I'll see you later, maybe." He started off down the hall, and then paused. "I'm glad you're all right."

"Me too," Qasim called after him.

He approached the door. Through the gap, he could see Mariam Ashraf and Jacob Ofori. Jacob sat behind his desk, rubbing his brow with one hand. Mariam stood, examining a shimmering projection.

"Surely, he understands what happened," Jacob was saying. He sounded tired. "We've explained as many times as we can, and he knows his father's theory as well."

Mariam shut down the projection. "He wants to believe it."

"But it's impossible."

"And he knows," Mariam murmured. "Logically, he knows. But returning to the house, getting all of his dad's things, it was bound to dredge things up. Telling him I'd be retiring didn't help, and then this...mess happened. It's been too much all at once." She sighed. "Give him time. Let him process it. Grieve."

Jacob nodded, now rubbing at his eyes with both hands. "This place never makes things simple, does it?" He lowered his hands and tilted his head, spotting Qasim.

Qasim reared back, mortified to be caught eavesdropping.

"It's all right, Qas." Jacob's chair creaked as he got up. "I was expecting you."

Qasim sheepishly pushed the door wider. "Sorry. I saw Ben leave and thought you might be free."

Mariam smiled as he entered. She was as drawn as Jacob. "Don't worry. I was just going." She patted him on the shoulder. "It's good to have you home, Qasim. Try not to scare us like that again, all right?"

He nodded, mouth dry, and stepped aside to let her out. The door slid closed behind her, and he turned his full attention to Jacob, who was still standing behind his desk. He was a good man, but sometimes he could seem terrifying.

Jacob motioned to the vacant chair opposite him. "Sorry, we were running late."

Qasim managed a crooked smile. It didn't sound like the start of a severe dressing down. He approached the seat and sat down. "Rhys said you need a word with me."

"I think you know what it's about."

"Apart from my exciting new scar?" Qasim knotted his fingers together in his lap.

Jacob reminded him of a reproachful schoolteacher. "Apart from that, yes. You know the protocol for maintaining contact with your partner, Qas. Running off without informing her what was happening was reckless."

Qasim nodded tightly. "I know. I didn't—" He exhaled. "I didn't think it would go the way it did."

"No one ever does," Jacob pointed out. "There's a reason we work in pairs—so if anything does go wrong and only one person gets through the gate, at least the other can confirm what happened."

Qasim couldn't meet his eye. "I didn't want Mila to panic."

"Let's be honest. Of the two of you, which one is more likely to panic?"

Qasim managed a sheepish smile. "Not Mila." He combed his fingers through his hair again. It was still damp from the shower. "Am I going to get a bollocking from upstairs?"

Jacob frowned. "We're hoping not. They've got the summary of the mission, and we provided some of the footage. Hopefully, the fact you completed the mission and both got home with no permanent damage should be enough."

"Hopefully," Qasim echoed.

"There might be some wrist slapping, but you and Mila are both safe."

Qasim couldn't help smiling in relief. "I knew working my arse off would serve me well."

"Yeah." Jacob snorted. "Who knew making yourself indispensable would make you indispensable?" He nodded to the door. "You should head down to check on Dieter and Gulshan's work. I've buzzed your family to let them know you'll be out of here by four."

Qasim got up. "You didn't have to."

"And you know your mother would be bugging us if we didn't."

"Well, you're not wrong," Qasim agreed with a laugh. "Ummi does like to have a timetable. She has cooking to do after all." He paused. "What's going to happen to the cat?"

"Ah. Your stowaway." Jacob leaned back in his seat. "We got a vet in to run some checks. Turns out you just stole someone's pet."

Qasim winced. "Really?"

"Mm. Well fed, healthy, used to being handled." Jacob seemed to be struggling to contain his mirth. "You don't do things by halves, do you? All those guards and the chase, and you had time to steal a family pet as well? Time traveller gone rogue..."

Qasim shifted his feet self-consciously. "Well. Kind of. So...what happens to him?"

"If the vet's checks are clean and upstairs approve, you *might* be allowed to keep it." Jacob held up a hand when Qasim opened his mouth. "Might. There's no guarantee here. They might have to put it down. It's staying in quarantine until a decision is made."

"Can I see him, at least?"

Jacob raised his eyebrows. "It's not your sick father."

"He saved my life," Qasim said. "If he's going to get put down, I want to at least give him a cuddle before he goes."

Jacob considered him. "I'll see what I can do." He waved towards the door. "Now go and get on with your work."

Qasim nodded but stopped at the door. "By the way, I wanted to thank you."

Jacob raised his eyes. "For what? Not ripping you a new one?"

"That too." Qasim rubbed his neck. "I don't know whose arm you twisted to get access for Ibe and Nilufer, but I appreciated the distraction."

Jacob shook his head. "It wasn't me."

Qasim blinked at him. "It wasn't?"

"You have your supervisor to thank."

"Rhys?"

"Unless you have a different supervisor I don't know about." Jacob smiled. "He managed to make a good case, and upstairs listened. He thought you might want to be kept busy."

"Yeah." Qasim couldn't help frowning. "That—he didn't need to."

"No," Jacob agreed, "but he did it anyway." He motioned towards the door again. "You've got work to be doing and a supervisor to thank."

Qasim nodded and hurried out into the hall.

He didn't know what to think. It was one thing for Rhys to take the time out of his day to play chess once in a while, but if he'd noticed Qasim needed a distraction and had even managed to persuade upstairs to provide one...

No one went upstairs unless they had to, but Rhys had done it to keep Qasim entertained.

Qasim shook his head with a crooked smile as he stepped into the lift. Rhys was going out of his way to surprise him. There weren't many supervisors who'd make so much effort for their agents.

Tahmila was already sitting with Gulshan and Dieter when he reached the report room. Every inch of the wall was scattered with projections, and he turned in a slow circle, taking it all in. He was always surprised by how much information they gathered.

"All it needs is your approval."

Qasim spun around to face the speaker: Rhys.

They'd met in person before. Okay, it was just one time, and planning for prep had distracted Qasim, but he'd forgotten how short Rhys was. He was half a head smaller than Qasim and was holding out a soft, pink hand.

"Welcome back," Rhys said, and Qasim blankly reached out and shook his hand, wondering how he'd managed to forget Rhys's smiling blue eyes. The video links didn't do them justice. They really were brilliantly blue. Like the sea on a bright summer day.

Aaaaaaaaaaaaand he was still shaking Rhys's hand and staring at him like an idiot.

"Sorry!" He pulled his hand back. "I had something—oh! Right! I was going to thank you."

"You were?"

Qasim nodded. He had a horrible feeling he was as red as a tomato. "For getting Ibe and Nilufer to chime in. It—they were a good distraction."

Rhys's smile popped dimples in his cheeks. "I like a successful plan, I do."

"And the chess," Qasim added quickly. "I liked the chess."

Rhys ducked his head with a laugh. "You mean you liked kicking my arse six ways from Sunday?"

Despite himself, Qasim grinned. "Well, it didn't hurt." He rocked onto the balls of his feet. "Now I'm better, I might see if you're as bad in person as you were online."

"Hey!" Rhys protested indignantly, but his eyes were dancing. "I played bloody well."

Qasim diplomatically nodded, pressing his lips together to keep from laughing. "Mm." A flash of colour over Rhys's shoulder caught his attention. All humour was snuffed out as he recognised what he was seeing: two of the Janissary soldiers outside the mosque. Qasim's breathing hitched, and one hand moved instinctively to the *misbaha* at his waist.

Rhys must have noticed his line of sight. He glanced over his shoulder, then hurried across the room and scaled down the images. Qasim ran the string of beads through his fingers. It was just a picture. Nothing to get worked up about.

"Sorry," he said hoarsely as Rhys returned to him.

"Nothing to be sorry for," Rhys said with a comforting smile. "Of course, you wouldn't want to see those arseholes again." He nudged Qasim's elbow with his hand. "Come on. The sooner we get these checks done, the sooner you can get out of here and back to your mam and dad."

Qasim nodded gratefully. "Please."

Chapter Twelve

FOR THE FIRST time since the mission started, Rhys could relax.

The internal historians had done their part, and now, all they needed was for the agents to go over everything before they brought in the external experts.

The data had been divided up into blocks. It had all been annotated with translations attached. Daily updates had been sent through to the pair in quarantine at the end of each day for their amendments. This was their first time seeing the whole and their last chance to add anything they thought was missing.

Tahmila and Qasim weren't doing things by halves. Tahmila had pulled a chair in front of the wall of projections and was going over each block. Qasim stood behind her, his arms folded, his eyes darting across the wall. Once in a while, he pointed to a section of the wall, and they would both study it. Tahmila was taking notes on a folio in her lap.

"I feel like I'm back at school," Gulshan confided in a mutter. She sat with Rhys and Dieter at the table in the centre of the room. "Please, miss, is my history report all right?"

Rhys was watching the two agents. "Better they do it now than when we bring the externals in. We need it to be as good as possible before they lay hands on it."

The last thing they needed were irate academics throwing a fit. It was bad enough they had to deal with protesting scholars daily, but if the academic community heard rumours the in-house research teams were cutting corners, it would give them a reason to demand unrestricted access to everything.

"Those two know what they're doing as well," Dieter added. "Of all the agents you want checking your work, you want Mr. Anal-Retentive and Little Miss Thorough Notations."

"I heard that, you prick," Tahmila said without turning around, the sweetness of her tone belying the words.

Rhys chuckled. "I'm fairly sure it was a compliment, Tahmila."

"From Dieter? Really?" She tilted her head. "I think I just passed into a parallel dimension."

Dieter winked at her. "No one'll believe you if you tell them."

She shook her head, smiling, and turned back to the projections. "Arsehole." She nudged Qasim's hip. "Qasim? Still with me?"

Qasim was still rocking on the balls of his feet. Rhys watched him carefully. It was the fight-or-flight reaction again, too much nervous energy pent up. Qasim was breathing shallowly as well. Rhys could see the tension boiling off him.

They were coming up on the final hours. Bad enough to have to review a mission that hadn't gone as planned, but to relive the moment when you'd almost died wasn't what anyone needed. Especially not with an audience.

"I think this could take some time," Rhys said to Dieter. He nodded towards the door. "How about you and Gulshan go and get something to eat? See if they can package up something decent for these two as well. It'll need to be *halal* for Mr. El-Fahkri."

Gulshan started to say they were nearly finished, but Dieter could be a sharp one. Maybe he'd noticed what Rhys saw as well, or maybe he was smart enough to take a hint when it was given.

"We're due a tea break anyway," he said, stretching as he got to his feet. "Come on, Gul. Don't look a gift break in the mouth."

The second the door was closed, Rhys got up. "Qasim."

Qasim didn't turn. He was still rocking back and forward, his eyes fixed on the projections. "Yeah?"

"I don't think we need validation of the last twenty minutes of the footage."

If he hadn't been watching for it, he might not have noticed the shudder that ran through Qasim's body. "It's standard protocol," Qasim said, his voice clipped.

Rhys made his way around the table. Tahmila had twisted in her chair and reached up to touch Qasim's arm, but Qasim didn't notice it. He was paler, his lips pressed to a tight line.

"Standard protocol under normal circumstances," Rhys murmured. "But to be honest, you were showing off—running around, climbing on walls, rescuing kittens. Nothing useful at all, really."

Qasim's shoulders sagged, and he laughed hoarsely. "What can I say? I live to be an action hero." He shifted an arm and unfolded his fingers to squeeze Tahmila's. "You'll miss my exciting chase sequence."

She pulled his hand down and pressed her cheek to it. "I've seen you climbing over the back of my sofa. I think I can imagine how it went. Arse over tit?"

Qasim nodded and then managed a frail smile for Rhys. "You're sure you don't need to see it again?"

Rhys shook his head and met the other man's eyes. "Believe me, once was more than enough."

The relief and gratitude in Qasim's expression said more than words. He sniffed hard and cleared his throat. "We should probably finish with when we leave the mosque, then, yeah? Some dialogue and gossip, before I went all stuntman."

"That would do," Rhys agreed. "Dieter and Gulshan should be back with food by the time you're done with it."

Qasim turned his attention to the screen, unfolding his arms for the first time since he'd joined Tahmila. He braced his hands on the back of Tahmila's chair. "Where were we up to?"

She swivelled around and pointed at an excerpt of the video. "Our last visit to the bazaar before we ate."

Rhys returned to the table and sat, watching them from across the room. The difference in Qasim's stance was dramatic. He was casually leaning on Tahmila's chair, gesturing to different frames as Tahmila skimmed through the footage. He even sounded brighter, which was definitely a good thing.

They were done with the footage by the time Dieter and Gulshan returned, carrying boxes of food. Tahmila lifted her folio in one palm and, with great deliberation, tilted it in the direction of Dieter's workstation and flicked the file.

"Great," Dieter grumbled cheerfully as his station chimed, registering the pickup.

"Got to keep you busy," Qasim said, stretching his arms over his head. "Can't call myself Mr. Anal-Retentive if I don't keep your on your toes."

Dieter snorted as he set down the boxes of food. "So you heard me, eh?"

Qasim nodded and tapped his ears. "Fully operational." He glanced at Tahmila. "You can tuck in. I need to nip upstairs for salat."

Gulshan watched Qasim leave. "He's perked up a bit, hasn't he?"

Tahmila's smile was convincing, but now that he was paying attention, Rhys could see how forced it was. "Pleased the mission's done with," she said as she pried open a box of noodles and vegetables. "If you can do your thing, we'll do one last check and be off. I'm dying to get outside."

Rhys took a few minutes to sort out the amendments, dividing them up between Dieter and Gulshan, and returned to the table, where Tahmila was finishing her box of noodles.

"You not eating?" she inquired around a mouthful.

Rhys shook his head. "I can wait."

She studied him, glanced at the two historians to make sure they were busy, and said softly, "Thank you. I mean, for not making him go through it all again."

He shook his head again. "It was nothing."

She scraped together the remains in her box, peering in at them. "No. It's not nothing." She raised her eyes to his. "That. The chess. Even just sending him messages while we were quarantined. It helped more than you can know."

"You're my team," Rhys said. "I mind my own."

"I like it. I think we'll keep you."

He chuckled. "That sounds ominous."

Her eyes glinted. "You have no idea."

"It wasn't a big deal." Rhys smiled. "I'm his supervisor. It's the least I could do. What kind of super would I be if I didn't make things as comfortable as possible for my agents?"

She smiled as if she knew something he didn't. "You noticed, and you did something. A lot of people don't." She twisted the last of the noodles around her fork and shot an impish smile at him. "Especially not after he calls them what he called you."

He couldn't help chuckling. "I've been called a lot worse. I hope he doesn't feel too embarrassed about it."

She shrugged. "As long as you don't spread it around, he'll be okay." She dragged another box closer, opened it up, and peered in. "He's not one who enjoys being laughed at, is our Qasim."

It didn't come as a surprise to Rhys. Not many people did like it. "I don't see why anyone else needs to know. After all, it's a private nickname."

Tahmila's lips twitched. "I'll be sure to let him know you said so."

"Said what?" Qasim inquired.

The door had opened so silently neither of them noticed.

Tahmila beamed up at him. "About name-calling being a private matter."

Qasim stared at her, and his face burned as bright as a beacon. "Oh." He glanced cautiously at Rhys as if he expected a lecture. "Right. Yeah." For want of anything better to do, he threw himself onto a chair and snatched one of the boxes of food marked with an *H*.

Rhys could see the tension return to Qasim's shoulders and sighed inwardly. For all their conversations and all those silly icons he'd found of angels, he'd hoped Qasim realised he wasn't upset about the description. It seemed not.

Well then. Desperate times called for desperate measures.

"I can't have everyone else knowing about it, can I?" he said as haughtily as he could. "Got to protect my aggressive, dangerous reputation."

Tahmila choked so hard she ended up coughing up cake, and to Rhys's relief, Qasim's face broke into a smile.

"I think what Mila is trying to say is 'yeah right,'" he translated. "Possibly with more swearing."

Tahmila nodded fervently, mopping crumbs and cream off her face and shirt, her cheeks still round with the food she hadn't sprayed all over herself.

Rhys winked at them, then got up to check on the historians and leave them to eat in peace. Still, he was close enough to hear Tahmila cheerfully complaining about what a snarky git Rhys was. When he heard Qasim laugh, he knew things could be all right.

There was plenty for them to work through, but once Dieter and Gulshan read Tahmila's notes, they could see what they'd missed. The footage and data passed back and forth between them several more times before both sides said they were done.

"Home time?" Qasim was the first one to say it. He sounded a lot happier now the worst of the work was out of the way.

Rhys was flicking through the screeds of data. Even though Jacob would be doing the report, he liked to make sure everything was in order. "I'd say we're good to go. I'll pass this up to Ofori, and you're done for the week."

Tahmila gave a happy whoop, flinging her arms in the air, and Qasim did a little jig on the spot. After the chaos of the mission and the blood and pain and exhaustion, Rhys smiled at how carefree it was.

Dieter seemed to agree, snorting with amusement, "Agents. Always so fucking adorable." He got up. "If you'll excuse me, I have a fine piece of Hungarian man flesh downstairs waiting to get me home and fuck me silly."

"Too much information, Die," Gulshan said, laughing as she got up and walked to the door with him. She waved back at them. "Have a good break."

Tahmila glanced at Qasim. "What about us? You ready to head out?"

Qasim didn't immediately reply, but when he did, he said, "Rhys?"

Rhys sent the file on to Jacob before glancing up, confused. "Yes?"

Qasim was fiddling with the buttons of his coat. "You heading back to the transport hub?"

Rhys stared at him for a moment too long and then smiled. "I will be, yes."

"Want to join us?"

It wasn't a long journey, about fifteen minutes, but Rhys had to admit it was nice to be asked. He hadn't even thought about going home, but with company to the hub, it would be easier. After a fortnight of tension and worry, seeing Qasim recovered and on his way home would be a good way to end the mission.

"I think I can cope with it," Rhys said. "As long as we all get where we need to be."

"Be warned," Tahmila said as she pulled on her coat and scarf. "This one'll spend the whole journey mooning out the window."

Qasim made a sound of indignation, but he was smiling. "Only a little."

In the end, it wasn't as bad as Tahmila suggested. Qasim did spend much of the journey standing by the window and gazing out at the frosty landscape whizzing by as the monorail sped towards the transport hub, but he still joined in the conversation.

"At least it'll be a break, eh?" Rhys suggested as they chatted about their plans for their forthcoming week off. "I mean, a week away from this place has to be good. Some rest and relaxation and everything."

"Ha!" Qasim snorted. "I think I'd do another week in Istanbul."

Rhys frowned at Tahmila, wondering if he'd touched on a sore spot.

"He's exaggerating," Tahmila said, grinning. She was sprawled across two seats, hands behind her head, eyes closed. She cracked one eye open to squint up at Rhys. "Three sisters, their eight kids, Mum, Dad, and Nan and aunts and uncles all waiting to celebrate his homecoming as if he'd been away for a year."

Rhys couldn't help laughing. "A welcoming committee?"

"Mm. Every single time." Qasim rubbed at the end of his nose with his fist. "If I'm lucky, Ummi'll leave her brothers and sisters out of it this time." He shuddered. "Ai, *habibi*, you are so thin! You have not eaten well! You must eat! Here! Eat this! And this! You must not be so thin! And your hair! It is too long. Do you want the neighbours to think our son is homeless? A starving homeless man?"

Rhys covered his mouth to stifle a chuckle. "Bit of a caretaker, is she?"

Qasim's expression softened. "She just remembers what it was like when she first got here and how hard it was for her and my sisters. Forty years, and yet..." He sighed, turning from the window. "She worries. That's all."

"God knows how she's going to react when she finds out about the..." Tahmila waved towards his side. To Rhys's astonishment, Qasim actually swore. His eyes widened in horror, and he clapped a hand to his mouth. "You hadn't thought about it, had you?" Tahmila said with a crooked grin.

"No." Qasim stared from one to the other in panic. "Is it too late to go back? She's going to kill me!"

Tahmila sat up, peering out of the window. "We'll find out in about two minutes."

Qasim sank into one of the seats. "I could tell her it was a paper cut?"

Rhys raised his eyebrows. "Really? An eight-inch paper cut?"

Qasim pushed his fingers through his hair. "Quick." He got up again. "Quick. Shave my head. It'll distract her."

"Tell her at the end of the week," Rhys suggested. "Bask in the celebration and tell her later."

Qasim stared at him, wide-eyed. "She'll know. She has creepy mother-knowledge powers." The carriage passed under the arch of the station roof. He batted down at his shirt and jacket, trying to smooth any creases, then dragged his fingers through his hair. He squinted at his distorted reflection in the windows. "If I die, I'm coming back to haunt you."

He was almost hyperventilating. Out of sympathy, Rhys took him by the shoulders, drawing him around from the window, and waited until Qasim met his eyes. "In the name of my secret identity, I swear to God if you try to haunt me, I'll exorcise you into a teapot."

Qasim dissolved into laughter, only a little hysterical. "It better be a nice teapot."

Rhys shook his head. "Ugly. Floral. With a face on it. Maybe even one of those ones where the tea comes out the nose." He patted Qasim on the arm, admiring the horrified awe on his face. "You'd better not die, then, eh?"

"You really are evil, aren't you?" Qasim breathed, shaking his head. "No one would believe it."

Rhys smiled as the monorail pulled into the platform. "All part of my evil charm." He stepped aside and raised his hand to his temple in a mock salute. "Good luck."

Qasim straightened up and stepped out onto the platform. Even though the security doors were at least thirty metres away, a chorus of voices reached them, calling out Qasim's name. Rhys shot a wry smile at Tahmila, who was leaning against the doorway.

"Should we stay here until the tide ebbs?"

Tahmila stepped out onto the platform with a smile. "He loves it. Complains every single time, but wouldn't change it for the world." She raised a hand in greeting, and Rhys leaned out the door to see a group of half a dozen people welcoming Qasim. A small girl was waving enthusiastically at Tahmila. "You did it again."

"Did what?"

"Were kind." Tahmila smiled. "He might not realise it, but you were."

Rhys shrugged, watching as a tiny sturdy lady with a colourful headscarf embraced a beaming Qasim. *It must be nice to receive such a warm welcome.* "He seemed like he needed it."

"And you noticed." She straightened up from the door. "Again. I appreciate it." She offered her hand, which Rhys shook. "We'll see you in a week or so."

He nodded. "Try not to get in too much trouble."

She flashed a grin at him. "Not too much. Just enough."

Chapter Thirteen

AUNT YASMIN AND her brood had left. Uncle Abdullah, Aunt Mirmah, and Qasim's oldest sister, Aisha, were still there. Various children were snoring on the couches and in the spare beds. Tette was in the kitchen again, brewing up another pot of tea.

"Shame it's a school night."

Qasim glanced up with a smile as his father approached and sat beside him on the couch. "It's the only reason Yasmin left," he admitted. "You know she loves a good dinner."

His father twisted his face in an exaggerated wince. "I remember. Not a fan of my cooking, though."

"To be fair," Abdullah said, raising his small cup of coffee, "who is?"

Mirmah swatted her husband reproachfully on his knee. "At least he tries."

Qasim sat back, laughing as his father launched into his familiar defence of macaroni and cheese as a good meal for growing children. His father would never admit it was the only thing he'd ever been able to cook, which was why they'd lived on it and takeaway anytime Qasim's mother was away.

Aisha leaned over from the chair next to Qasim's. "We should set up a cookery competition between them. Something Ummi could do standing on her head."

Qasim hid a grin behind his knuckles and replied as quietly, "Abi's would still turn into mac and cheese. He possesses some kind of dark and cheesy magic."

To his delight, Aisha snorted out loud. They exchanged looks, and he had to duck his head to keep from laughing again. It wasn't quite enough to stifle another yawn, though. It was almost midnight, and it had been a very long and very busy day.

It was the trouble with gatherings like this after every successful mission: what started out as a small family meal would expand into several hours of food and talk. It was always difficult to excuse himself, especially when he was more than happy to see them all. All the same, falling asleep under a pile of children when he had a healing wound was a bad idea.

He managed to negotiate himself out from under Rocky, Uncle Abdullah's youngest. "I think I need to head to bed." He passed his nephew down to his father and smiled apologetically. "The painkillers they gave me are pretty strong."

"Ai, you should have said something!" his mother exclaimed, getting up. She hurried over to him, checking him over. Her plump hands were warm and soft, and she frowned sternly at him. "You will rest and get well. Plenty of rest. Stay in bed tomorrow."

"Ummi, I'm fine," he protested, smiling. "I'm only tired."

"Hm." She motioned him towards the door. "Bed."

A chorus of farewells rose from the couch as he headed to the door. He wasn't surprised to find his nephews Youssef and Hassan in his bedroom, playing with his video games. Ever since childhood, his sisters had always known how to break through his security measures, and they'd obviously taught their sons.

"Out," he ordered, jerking a thumb towards the door.

"We're in the middle of a mission," Hassan protested. "You can't make us stop in the middle of a mission."

Qasim raised his eyebrows. "I could pull the plug."

Youssef snorted. "Scared we'll beat your hit scores?" he asked, grinning with more confidence than any spotty thirteen-year-old deserved to have.

Qasim looked down at him, then at the screen. So that was how it was going to be? He sat on the end of his bed and reached down to log himself into the game. He pulled on one of the sensor gloves and smirked at both boys. "If you last five minutes, you can play for half an hour, all right?"

Hassan glanced at his cousin warily. "Sef..."

"There's two of us," Youssef said. "We can win this time."

Four minutes later, they were bundled out the room, protesting he'd cheated. Qasim shut the door behind them and sighed with relief. It was great to spend time with family, but after weeks of having someone in the same space as him, there was nothing like a bit of solitude.

As usual, his room was much neater than he'd left it. His mother couldn't help herself. There were fresh linens on the bed, the shelves and units had been dusted until they gleamed, and she had even topped up his supposedly secret stash of sweets in the bedside cabinet. He popped one in his mouth and sprawled out on the bed. It was good to be home.

He propped his folio on his chest, dragging the screen to hover over him. It was no surprise there was a message from Tahmila: *Since I haven't heard about anyone bursting from eating too much, I'm assuming you're okay. Chime if you need anything.*

He sent a thumbs-up icon, then swept the message away. There was another beneath it. This one didn't have any text, just two knight chess pieces side by side. He could guess who it was from before he even read the name and, snorting, sent his response.

Knight knight? Really?

To his surprise, Rhys responded less than a minute later: *I thought you'd like the pun.*

Qasim grinned. *Don't you mean the pawn?*

Ouch.

Qasim sniggered into his hand. *What? It was a good one.* He sat up against the wall, studying the screen. He knew what he wanted to ask, but trying to find a polite way to phrase it was the trick. *Don't you have something more fun to do than check in on me?*

Just me and a book. And it's not a very good book.

Qasim pulled an image from one of the collection taken by his sister a few hours earlier, when they were still all piling in from the mosque. He was barely visible in the middle of it, sat on by at least three children of various sizes. He flicked it Rhys's way. *Next time, feel free to join us and distract the halflings.*

Good God. That's your whole family?

Qasim laughed out loud. *Whole? Nah. That's only Ummi's—Mum's—side. Dad's lot are in Leeds and London.*

Is it fun or chaos? It sounds like it could be either.

Both. It was always noisy and messy and loud, but it was family. Anything else would seem strange. He stifled another yawn and glanced at the clock. *I'm going to have to send you back to your book. Been a long day.*

I'll cope. The text was accompanied by an image of a chubby little cherub.

Qasim smiled, shutting down his screen. There were a lot of decent people at the TRI, but not many of them socialised outside. It was something about the place. Fascinating to work there, but intense and so secretive and closed in. Tahmila was the only one who he regularly stayed in touch with.

And now, Rhys Griffiths.

It was a surprise. He hadn't expected Rhys to have such a dry sense of humour. He seemed like he should be a stuffy, boring man, but he wasn't. The suits and ties were as much a façade as the innocent pink face and curly hair. No one looking at the man would expect the glint in his eye and the smirks.

Qasim glanced across the room to his shelves. Somewhere in the stacks of boxes, he had a chess set. It was fun playing at a distance, but nothing could match sitting across a board. There was something about working out another player's tells, seeing their face tense in thought, watching their eyes as they considered their next move.

Rhys would probably be an expressive player.

Qasim grinned. Come morning, he could find the pieces and offer a game somewhere outside the restrictive walls of the TRI. Part of it was curiosity, to see whether Rhys dressed like a librarian away from work as well.

Someone tapped at his door.

"Yes?"

His mother poked her head in. "Do you have enough water? Blankets? Are you warm?"

He smiled. "I'm fine, Ummi. I just need to change and get under the covers."

She hummed, watching him with concern. "You can change on your own? There isn't too much pain?"

In demonstration, he raised and lowered his arms, then poked his side. "All good."

"*Alhamdulillah.* That's good." She fussed with the end of the shawl draped around her shoulders, a gesture he knew as well as he knew himself. He slid off the edge of the bed, knowing why she was really there: the afternoon had been an overwhelming blur, and they hadn't had a moment alone. She had fussed and fretted as much as she could with company, but she'd put on a brave face.

When he held out his arms, he wasn't at all surprised when she bustled across the room and hugged him. He pressed his cheek to her bowed head, revelling in the familiar scent of her perfume.

"I'm happy you are home safe, *habibi*," she whispered, her voice cracking. "This job you do, it is too dangerous."

"Uncle Patrick is a fireman, Ummi," he reminded her gently. "At least I don't run into burning buildings for a living."

She drew back with a sniff and reached up to lightly cuff the side of his head. "He does not get stabbed with swords."

He ducked with a laugh. "One sword, Ummi! And not even stabbed!" He had glossed over the second swing of the blade and how close it had been. She didn't need to live with the extra fear. He caught the end of her scarf and dabbed at her cheeks. "You'll need to go and put your face back on if everyone else is still downstairs. You don't want them thinking you're sad to have me home."

She caught his hand in both of hers. "They'll understand why." She pressed his knuckles to her brow.

He drew his hand from hers to hug her again. The last thing he wanted to do was cause her any distress, but his job was his job. No matter what he said, she would worry. "I'm home and I'm safe and they won't send me on any dangerous missions for a long time now."

"*Insha'Allah!*" She glowered up at him sternly, her dark eyes gleaming and wet. "If they do, you tell this boss of yours he will answer to me."

Qasim laughed, wiping her cheek again with the end of her shawl. "I'll let them know." He then leaned down and kissed her silver-threaded black hair. "You shouldn't hang around up here. You know Tette sees an unsupervised kitchen as an excuse to cook all the things you don't like."

His mother spun around so fast he had to step back. Despite their closeness, the battle for the kitchen between his mother and grandmother bordered on legendary. It wasn't that either of them particularly wanted to have control of it, they just didn't want the other to. It was a matter of principle.

"Good night, Ummi!" he called after her before closing the door.

Chapter Fourteen

THERE WERE VOICES raised in Jacob's office.

Rhys hesitated in the hall. He was meant to be meeting Jacob to go upstairs for a meeting, but he really didn't want to open the door. There had been enough tension at home, and the last thing he wanted was to walk into another argument.

When there was a lull, he touched the sensor to notify Jacob he was there. The door slid open a moment later, and three faces turned to him. Jacob was on one side of the desk, which was covered in a mess of papers, with Ben Sanders and one of the engineers—Kit Rafferty—on the other side.

Ben was flushed, his mouth a thin line, and Rafferty was grim-faced.

"We have the meeting," Rhys said carefully.

Jacob subsided in his seat with a sigh. "Oh. Right. Yeah." He rubbed his forehead, then turned back to Ben. "Can we talk about this later?"

"What's the point?" Ben snapped, snatching up the pages from the desk. They seemed to be centuries-old documents in plastic sheaths. He slid them into a file and shot a dark look at Rafferty. "It's not like anyone is even listening to a word I'm saying."

"Ben—" Rafferty began.

"What? You're infallible? You know everything about the gates because my dad gave you a job?" Ben snarled, shoving the folder into his bag. "I'm telling you the coding was the same during the flash. It proves there was a connection!"

"Ben," Jacob said, rising. His voice was quiet but firm. "You know your dad said—"

The boy's shoulders slumped. "I know. When a gate short-circuits, it..." He took an unsteady breath. "Someone in transit would...it would...it would be terminal." He lifted his chin defiantly. "That doesn't mean he was right." He glowered at Rafferty. "Or you."

Rafferty opened his mouth to argue, his pale, freckled cheeks turning red, but Jacob raised a hand.

"Ben, come back this afternoon, okay? We'll talk about it then."

Ben stared at him, nodded, and spun on his heel to stalk out of the room, shoving by Rhys as he went. Rhys was tempted to run out into the hall too. Anything to get away from the ugly tension in the room.

Rafferty breathed out noisily. "You didn't need to stop me."

"Yeah, I did." Jacob massaged his temples with his fingertips as he sat down again. "The kid's having a hard time of it, Kit. You going off at him wasn't going to help anything right now."

Rafferty shook his head. "He needs to face the facts. If he keeps on grasping at any straw, any bit of rogue code, it's going to drive him nuts. When Mariam leaves—"

"Kit..."

"When Mariam leaves, who's going to handle him? You know she's the only one who can talk him down when he gets worked up like this. This isn't a hypothetical. We've only got her for a few more months."

"It's his dad. If my boy had been lost, I'd be the same." Jacob met his boyfriend's eyes. "Once she's gone, he loses the keys to the kingdom. Can you blame him for going after it so hard?" He exhaled. Rhys shifted awkwardly, standing like a pudding by the door. "Sorry you had to get dragged into the argument, Rhys."

Rhys could only nod. It put his own problems in perspective. "I should have waited outside, but the meeting... I thought you'd started early."

Jacob winced. "God help us if it goes down like this." He got up from behind the desk and glanced back at Rafferty. "I'll talk to Ben alone, okay? If he's got any notes worth passing on to you, I'll get them to you."

Rafferty nodded and headed for the door.

Rhys waited as Jacob gathered up his folio and his cup of coffee. "Not the best start to the day?"

"It's always a bloody Monday." Jacob sounded knackered as they headed across the hall. "Is it too much to ask for them to start yelling at me on a Friday afternoon?"

"When you can walk away? I doubt it." Rhys touched the control by the lift door. "Do we know what this meeting is about yet?"

Jacob nodded. He didn't seem thrilled. "The Supervisory Board have assessed our reports on Qasim's...incident. They want to talk about how we can 'ensure the safety of our operatives without diminishing the efficacy of their roles.' Also known as how not to get our people dead and cause extra paperwork."

"Jesus wept," Rhys groaned at the irony.

Ever since he joined the TRI four years earlier, the paper trails had grown by the year. Every single action had an equal and opposite amount of paperwork. Even requesting a different piece of wardrobe or prop had to be formally submitted, which was daft because they were working *with* the costume and prop producers while they researched. It added more hoops to jump through all in the name of having paperwork for every damned thing.

Of course, it meant when anything happened which didn't match the exact details of their mission outline there were a new array of hoops set out for them. Human fallibility was a variable that didn't work so well in neatly organised timetables.

"It's going to be a complete waste of our time," Jacob said, looking as unhappy about it as Rhys felt. "But if it means they can check the boxes and Elwin can feel important by signing another scrap of nothing, we have to sit through it."

Rhys made a face. "I should have brought my tinted lenses. I could have caught up on my sleep." Even as he said it, he knew he should have kept his mouth shut. Jacob might have laid down his police badge more than a decade earlier, but it didn't mean he'd kicked the detective habits.

"Something up?"

Rhys shook his head. "The usual." He could feel Jacob studying him and wondered how much he would notice: the creased shirt, the not-quite-styled hair, the bags under his eyes from a night of tossing and turning and trying to work out how to speak to Marc. Old habits died hard, and he'd smiled as if everything was all right over breakfast. Stupid, stupid, stupid.

"Right." Jacob focussed on the doors as they opened. "It's that bad?"

Rhys grimaced as they emerged into the light-filled hallway. "Well, it's not good." He nudged his glasses up his nose. "It'll work itself out."

Jacob nodded sympathetically. They stopped outside one of the larger conference rooms. "Word of warning"—he glanced at Rhys—"if it's O'Donohue, be careful what you say."

"What? Why?"

"He's a watchful bastard, is all," Jacob replied, straightening his tie. "Elwin's first minion. I get the feeling he has his finger in more pies than we know about. Acts like butter wouldn't melt, but he's too sharp for his own good."

Rhys slanted a glance at him. "Bit like you, then?"

From Jacob's expression, he wasn't taking it as a compliment. "Also, when you see him, try not to stare. He does it on purpose to throw you off."

"Does what?" Rhys asked, frowning.

"You'll know when you see him." Jacob swept his hand over the control panel by the door.

There was one man sitting at the end of the table, his hands folded on the surface. Rhys couldn't help feeling like he'd wandered into a business-wear catalogue shoot, which only worsened when the man turned towards them and inclined his head.

"O'Donohue," Jacob said coolly. "Good to see you."

O'Donohue rose from the chair and held out one of his hands. "Jacob, please. I've told you to call me Lysander." He turned a perfect smile framed by a perfectly trimmed beard in an almost perfectly symmetrical face to Rhys. "And Rhys Griffiths, isn't it?"

Rhys nodded, staring at him as he shook O'Donohue's hand. Tailored suit, blue-black hair in a long ponytail, and ink-dark eyes. It wasn't that the man was good-looking. He was *too* good-looking. It was weird, like seeing someone step off a film poster, all pristine and polished.

Jacob cleared his throat.

Rhys blinked at him, startled, and realised, yes, O'Donohue was doing 'it,' whatever it was, on purpose. He turned his attention back to O'Donohue who was gazing placidly at him. Ha! If he thought Rhys could be so easily distracted, he had another thing coming. "Are we getting started then?"

O'Donohue motioned for them to sit. "Mr. Elwin asked me to come on his behalf."

"Is there anything to be added to the report?" Jacob was rigid and straight-backed in his chair, his hands folded on the table.

O'Donohue gazed at him and then tapped the tabletop, which illuminated. He flicked a file towards each of them. Rhys opened his file, skimming through a statement that sounded like a politician had written it. It was all carefully phrased and neatly packaged, a very sterile view of the business.

"You know the lives of our agents have to be our number one priority," O'Donohue said. Rhys tried to pick out his accent. It sounded like American, but not quite. "The Supervisory Board always aims for minimal risk to our staff."

Rhys wanted to point out they were the ones who made the decisions about which missions they took. Not a one of them had ever come to briefings and prep weeks. He opened his mouth to speak, but Jacob pressed down hard on his foot before he could say anything.

"You want to say something, Rhys?" The perfect, placid smile was still in place. Rhys would take any money the man would smile exactly the same way if he was told his house had burned down and he'd lost everything.

He shook his head. "I'm good, I am."

O'Donohue raised a dark eyebrow. "No need to be shy, Rhys. I'm here to help you help your team."

Rhys glanced at Jacob, who was frowning.

"Mr. Griffiths." Under the softness of O'Donohue's voice, there was a core of steel. "If you don't mind."

Jacob nodded curtly, and Rhys turned back to the other man.

"Here's the thing—" Rhys began. O'Donohue was watching him, his head tilted slightly to one side. It was unsettling. "Look, you lot choose the jobs, yeah? Mr. Elwin has the final say and everything?"

"Correct."

"Then—" All he had to do was stick his neck out and ask the big questions. Ask why they took jobs in politically unstable zones. Ask why an agent would be directed to go near someone or something dangerous. Ask why the money seemed to take priority over the lives they insisted were so important. It was all he had to do, but O'Donohue was Elwin's second, and he was watching with the cool expression that gave nothing away. It was enough to put Rhys's back up.

"Then?" O'Donohue prompted.

Rhys pressed the balls of his thumbs together. "Do you do the research before you take the job?" It was *nearly* the big question, but Christ, he wanted O'Donohue to stop focussing on him.

O'Donohue laced his fingers together on the table in front of him. "Mr. Griffiths appears to have a very low opinion of the Supervisory Board, doesn't he, Jacob?"

Rhys felt sick. No wonder Jacob had tried to warn him about keeping his mouth shut.

"Mr. Griffiths has dealt with the serious injury to a member of his team and spent the past fortnight providing emotional support for him," Jacob said. "He asked a question. You haven't replied."

To Rhys's relief, O'Donohue glanced at Jacob. For a moment, the mask dropped, and there was a hint of warmth and amusement in his expression. "Ah. You got me." He returned his attention to Rhys, and it was as if someone else was looking at him. "Yes. We do research. Not as extensively as your teams, but enough to assess the risk." The mask slid back in place, and a dark brow arched. "Answer enough?"

Rhys could only nod and bite his tongue to keep from saying anything.

The meeting continued exactly as Jacob had predicted; all the standards lines about improved safety and well-being were trotted out. Support teams of psychologists and doctors would be available. It was all the same old cack spouted again. Rhys wished he were somewhere else.

It was the start of a pretty crap day.

Three hours of meetings, two more of report writing, and bits and pieces filled up the day and left Rhys with a thumping headache. For once, he switched his pod to autopilot and sank back to doze as he headed for home.

To his surprise, Marc was there before him for a change. From the smell of it, dinner was in the oven, but the kitchen was empty, and the bathroom door was closed. The shower was on in the bathroom, and Marc was singing tunelessly, muffled by the door. A nice normal night at home for a change.

He hung his bag on the hooks by the front door, kicked off his shoes, and sprawled on the couch with his folio. The screen hovered in front of his face as he leafed through the messages he'd missed during the day.

One of them was a blinking note from Qasim.

Rhys opened it then laughed. It was an image of Qasim holding a chess set in a wooden box and gesturing dramatically to it, his eyes widened in feigned wonder. There was a single line scrawled over the picture: *Your move.*

He considered before sending a reply: *On your week off? You must be bored.*

To his surprise, an incoming video chimed only a minute later.

Qasim waved on the screen. "Family stuff is on hold until the weekend." He didn't bother with a greeting. "Everyone else is working, so it's me and Ummi and Tette for now. There's only so much caretaking I can handle."

Rhys couldn't help smiling. "Is there lots of feeding?"

Qasim glanced around as if someone might be listening and leaned closer. "An attempted meal every hour. I swear Ummi's trying to get me so fat I won't be able to move or go back to work next week."

It must be nice. "So I'm your escape?"

Qasim beamed at him. "If there's one thing she likes more than making sure I'm fit, it's knowing I've got friends. She'll be delighted for me to go out and play with someone." He shook his head, grinning. "It's like I'm still twelve."

Rhys sat up and scratched at his head thoughtfully. He was due a day anyway, especially now the mission was close to finished. "I'll see what I can do, but it depends if I can get the day off."

Qasim leaned off-screen, and when he returned, he bounced a knight in front of the camera and tilted its head to peer quizzically at Rhys. It was daft, and Qasim was smiling and relaxed, and it made up Rhys's mind for him.

"I'll arrange something," he promised.

"Yay!" Qasim leaned sideways and waved. "Hi!"

Rhys, startled, glanced over his shoulder. Marc was standing there, towelling his hair. "All right, *bach*?"

"Don't let me interrupt." Marc raised a hand in greeting to Qasim and headed towards the kitchen. Rhys watched him go and must have been frowning when he turned back to the screen.

"Sorry," Qasim said with a sheepish smile. "I didn't realise you had company." He wiggled the knight at the camera. "Let me know if you have time."

"I will," Rhys agreed and cut the connection. He remained where he was for a moment and ran a hand over his face before getting up. Marc hadn't seemed too pleased, which wasn't good. Rhys made his way to the kitchen. "You're home early."

Marc nodded, stirring a simmering pot on the hob. "Thought I should make an effort." He glanced at Rhys, and when he smiled, it was almost convincing. "One of your friends from work, then?"

"Qasim?" Rhys nodded, leaning against the door frame. "One of my team."

Marc lifted the pot off the heat. "Ah."

Rhys felt the familiar prickle of unease. The unsaid words. The tension. Normally, he'd have let it go, made his excuses and gone to freshen up for dinner. He didn't know who was more surprised when he demanded, "What do you mean 'ah'?"

"Nothing." Marc glanced at him, his dark brows pulled down. He sighed. "It's just—you never talk to colleagues outside of work."

Rhys straightened up from the door frame. "So?" The impulse to turn and walk away was strong. To find somewhere to wait it out. "You talk to colleagues outside of work all the time."

Marc frowned at the pot, prodding the contents with the ladle. "You were smiling." He didn't sound angry. That was something.

"It's not a crime," Rhys said quietly. "I'm allowed to have friends. I'm allowed to smile at them."

When Marc met his eyes, it was worse than anger. It was disappointment, and it was like a punch in the chest. "Do you know how long it's been since you've smiled at me like that?"

Rhys wanted to retreat, to go and sit quietly somewhere until he could pretend everything was all right, but all right had been months ago before the drinking and money troubles and the problems which had built and built.

"He's just a friend."

"You said." Marc smiled unhappily. "We should eat before this gets cold."

"Marc..."

Marc shook his head. "You said. Just a friend. I—" He shook his head again. "Let's just have dinner, all right?"

They sat in silence on opposite sides of the table. Rhys's appetite was shot. He picked at the warm stew and tried to work out something to make things better. Easier. Not this unbearable quiet tension that made him feel sick to his stomach.

"I supervised my first mission," he finally said, prodding a piece of meat. "Qasim was on the team. He got hurt. Almost fatal." He chased a piece of carrot around the plate with the fork-skewered meat. "He—it was hard for him. I've been trying to help. The last fortnight. I was trying to help."

Marc swore softly. "You didn't say anything."

Rhys forced himself to raise his eyes from his plate. "How could I? I've no idea what I can tell you anymore." He took a shaking breath. "I don't know what you might say on your nights out. Nor do you."

Marc's fork clattered on his plate. "I'm not that bad!"

Rhys's hands were shaking, but, here and now, there were words he needed to say. He'd ignored them for too long already. "You are, *bach*. You never asked me why I sleep on the couch so much."

"You said I'd fallen asleep across the bed!" Marc was flushed across the cheeks. "If this is about you locking yourself in the bathroom again..."

Rhys swallowed hard. "You scare me when you're like that. You're not *you*. I don't know what you'll even do. What you'd remember if you did it."

Marc looked stricken. "Rhys..."

Rhys carefully put his cutlery down on the plate and lined it up straight. It was his fault it had gotten to this point. "Should have said something before. Sorry." He pushed the chair back. "I'm— I don't think I can eat just now."

Mercifully, Marc didn't try to stop him as he pulled on his coat and headed for the door. He managed to get half a block before he had to sit on the nearest flight of steps and take gulping breaths, trying to gather himself.

It was good. He'd said what needed to be said. It was good, even if he felt like he was about to throw up what little he'd managed to eat. Maybe it would make things better. Maybe. Or maybe not. Either way, the truth was out now, and Marc knew.

He sat for ages. Long enough for his arse to start aching and his hands to get cold. He picked himself up and headed back in the direction of home.

Marc was waiting, sitting on the couch with his coat on and a bag at his feet, and he rose when Rhys walked in.

Rhys hesitated at the door. "What's going on?"

Marc smiled uncertainly. "Apparently, I've been a massive arsehole." He picked up his bag and crossed the floor. "I thought I'd give you a bit of space. Some time on your own, so you don't need to worry about me bothering you. I've called my parents. They've got the spare room ready for me."

Rhys's eyes stung. "You don't need—"

Marc lifted one hand to brush Rhys's cheek. "Yes, I do." He leaned down and kissed Rhys. "Next time, don't keep secrets from me, all right?" His eyes were as bright as Rhys's. "So a week? Or do you want some more?"

Rhys could only nod, lost.

Marc studied him and then pulled him into a hug. "You can chime me when you're ready, eh?" He pressed his lips to Rhys's cheek again. "Take care, yeah?"

And, as if it was easy, he walked out, and Rhys did nothing to stop him.

Chapter Fifteen

QASIM PROPPED HIS cheek against his fist, his eyes half-closed.

The first weekend hadn't been as relaxing as he'd hoped. Restful would have been too ambitious, but family time usually helped him wind down from a mission. It would have been fine if the mission had been like any other, but not when it had sent him home with nightmares.

More than once, he'd ended up sitting on the floor by the bed, staring at his folio and wondering if he should contact Tahmila. The first two nights, he'd restrained himself. She deserved a break after all. Instead, he'd spent hours playing video games before retreating back to bed. The third night, he'd given in and chimed.

Thankfully, he'd seen his therapist by noon on the following Monday.

Eleanor Bailey had been treating him since he was twelve, when everything had gone tits up. His parents had moved house for the first time in his life, after his sisters started marrying and moving out. They relocated to a new town, a new neighbourhood, a new school with new people. With puberty on top of it all, the whole world had been changing too fast and had become impossibly terrifying.

Dr. Bailey was the one who helped him find a way to get a handle on it. His visits to her were rarer now, but once in a while, they became necessary. Missions could get to you unexpectedly.

She knew loosely about the TRI, and it always amused her that missions didn't usually faze him. Surely, she would say, going back in time and being in a totally different society and culture was as extreme as you could get? He remembered the first time she asked him and how much it had puzzled him. Why didn't it get to him? It should have. By rights, he should be climbing the walls every time.

In the end, he realised what it had to be; it was because it was a mission.

If he had a job to do, exact parameters to follow, and a specific assignment, then it was simple. He did his research; he did the job, exactly as instructed. Cause and effect. Go on the mission, don't change the timeline, return from mission intact. Simple.

The nightmares were new, though. So was the scar.

Dr. Bailey listened as he explained what had happened. Like Tahmila, she'd seen him fall apart too many times for him to be embarrassed by it. When she talked him through the emotions, it helped. She laid out options and alternatives, and, for once, he agreed that something to help him to sleep—and hopefully stay that way—would help. A fortnight of broken sleep had left him exhausted.

A follow-up appointment was already on the books, so he took her advice and her medicines, and managed to get through a few more days. The nightmares still came but with less frequency. Knocking himself out for a few nights helped.

Thankfully, he still had his family to distract him. Ummi hauled him with her when she went out, and even when he was alone, Tahmila and Rhys both made sure to stay in contact. It was comforting to know they were there, even if his brain's stupidity was his own problem to deal with.

No, not stupidity. Trauma. Trauma was a cause. Nightmare was an effect. There was always cause and effect. It made sense, even if he wanted to stifle his screams in the pillow every time he woke up, soaked with sweat and shaking.

The wound was all but healed. The scar was going to be impressive, but it didn't hurt anymore. He still found himself running his fingers along the length of it, remembering the hot stickiness of his blood and seeing his ribs between his fingers. It was healed. It should have been the end of it, but, of course, his brain was having none of it.

It was best to keep busy and occupied. He spent hours at the mosque, went on daytrips with whichever family members were available, and now, he was waiting at his favourite café with a box of chess pieces and a battered chessboard.

Somehow, Rhys had managed to wrangle some time off. Probably because Jacob was dealing with a lot of the paperwork. Qasim had no idea why his supervisor would want to use his free time to hang out with him, but if it meant distraction chess with someone he liked, Qasim was happy to take it.

The board hadn't seen daylight for nearly a year. The set was the only one he'd ever owned. It was a bit the worse for wear, but all the pieces were still there, neatly tucked into their rightful places, even if they were a bit battered and chipped.

Once he'd ordered himself a hot chocolate with enough sugar to blow the mind of an unsuspecting toddler, he set out the board. And since he was—as always—stupidly early, he started a game to keep himself occupied until Rhys arrived.

He'd already taken six pieces when a shadow stretched over the table.

"Having fun?" Rhys inquired.

Qasim grinned up at him. "Warming up." He gave his fingers a wiggle. "Need to make sure I'm in top shape."

Rhys smiled, but he seemed more tired than the last time Qasim had seen him. "Taking the advantage." He undid his jacket. It was a brown leather number with a fuzzy collar, vintage fighter-pilot chic. It was mismatched with the shirt and wool vest beneath it, but somehow, it suited him.

"You want something to drink? Or eat?" Qasim offered. When he was knackered, sometimes a warm drink or snacks helped.

Rhys's smile brightened. "I see your mother is a powerful influence on you." He sat on the opposite side of the table and touched the panel to hail a waitress.

Qasim pulled a face at him and reset the board as Rhys ordered a coffee and some biscuits. He couldn't help glancing across the table, studying the other man. It was a force of habit—too many missions where spotting the little details was critical.

As always, Rhys was clean-shaven, but there were a couple of tiny nicks. His hair was a mass of golden curls, a little messier than usual. His shirt was creased, but it didn't mean anything. Some people didn't like pressing their clothes. The cufflinks caught Qasim's eyes. They didn't match. Qasim squinted at the nearest one.

"Army brat?" he guessed once the waitress hurried away.

Rhys looked startled. "Excuse me?"

Qasim tapped his own cuff, and Rhys lifted his arm. It was impossible to miss the way his expression clouded and his whole body tensed, as if he'd just realised he was wearing them.

"Oh. Yeah. I didn't realise I'd picked them up." He tugged his cuff around, moving it out of his line of sight. "They were my dad's. He—well, he doesn't need them anymore."

Qasim felt like an idiot. "Oh. I'm sorry."

"Eh?"

"Your dad. I didn't realise he... he was...y'know...gone."

To his astonishment, Rhys laughed, and the tension evaporated.

"No!" Rhys shook his head. "God, no. He's not dead or anything. Just living somewhere warm with short sleeves."

Qasim buried his face in his hand, part mortified, part relieved. "Well, this is embarrassing." He jolted in surprise when Rhys's foot knocked against his, and he peeked between his fingers.

"My fault." Rhys was smiling. "I'm a bit shit at explaining, I am. Don't worry about it."

Qasim rubbed at his forehead. "That was a spectacular bit of misinterpretation, there."

"Good call on the history, though," Rhys said. Qasim could see—not for the first time—Rhys was trying to reassure him. "I don't know many people who would've spotted it."

Qasim wrinkled his nose. "Just doing my job." He smiled as the waitress returned. She set down a mug of rich, creamy coffee and a bowl of tiny chocolate biscuits. Qasim eyed them doubtfully. "Why not get a couple of big ones?"

"Stakes," Rhys said, pulling the mug towards him. "I didn't think you'd want to play for money."

Qasim raised his eyebrows. "We're playing for biscuits?"

"Unless you want to play for dignity." Rhys made a shocked face. "Do you want to end up nuddy in a public place?"

Qasim tried to suppress his grin. "You're...very confident. Deluded, but confident." He rotated the board. "I tell you what—I'll let you start."

Rhys cracked his knuckles. "Prepare to diet."

Qasim snorted into his hot chocolate. "Not your most intimidating threat."

"What about 'Eat shortbread!'?" Rhys smirked when Qasim spluttered again. "What? Did you think I was going to make this easy for you?"

"Do you think I'm so easily distracted?"

Rhys propped one elbow on the table and cupped his chin in his hand. "I don't know, but I'm going to have fun finding out."

Qasim ducked his head, grinning. He slanted a glance up at Rhys. "It's on."

To Qasim's satisfaction, Rhys was an expressive player. It was true he kept trying to distract Qasim with dry commentary and suggestions for moves, but Qasim had many years of experience playing with people who were trying to beat him by whatever means they could. He also had plenty of experience turning distractions back on his opponent.

"Can I ask you something?" He moved another pawn.

Rhys took the pawn and pushed the plate of snacks towards Qasim. "With your mouth full."

Qasim picked up his first biscuit, nibbling it as he surveyed the board. "Your dad. You said he was living somewhere warm."

"Mm."

"Retired or on a holiday or what?"

Rhys glanced over the top of his glasses. "Retired." His voice was curt.

"That's all I get?" Qasim cocked his head. "So, not dead but retired and living in a land without cufflinks?"

Rhys took a sip of his coffee. "Croatia. He's living in Croatia with my mam."

Qasim tapped his thumbnail against his lower lip, watching the other man. Rhys didn't seem happy. Yeah, he didn't seem unhappy either, but there wasn't the usual glint in his eye. Something about his parents—or maybe Croatia—bothered him. "And you on your lonesome over here?"

One side of Rhys's mouth turned up. "What can I say? I love a damp, cold climate." He took another one of Qasim's pawns and waved it at him with mock-pity. "Ha! You're losing your edge."

Qasim didn't need to check the pieces to know his next move. He was still chewing his second biscuit as he swiped one of Rhys's bishops clean off the board. He didn't even say anything as he nudged the plate towards Rhys.

"I asked for it, didn't I?" Rhys said ruefully.

Qasim couldn't help feeling a little guilty. "Distracted by interrogation. Sorry."

Rhys's tense expression eased. "It's all right. I just—it's like—most people don't ask." He considered the board before peering up at Qasim. "A bit random is all."

Qasim chewed on his bottom lip. "How about you get to ask about mine then? Only fair."

Rhys chuckled as he moved his queen. "I know more about your family than you do about mine."

"Oh, yeah? Prove it."

"Three sisters. Eight kids. Aunts and uncles in Luton, Leeds, and Manchester. A short mum who wears colourful hijabs." Rhys popped a biscuit into his mouth. "How am I doing?"

Qasim stared at him. "Okay, you weren't meant to remember it all."

Rhys smiled. "I pay attention too."

Qasim knocked off one of Rhys's pawns with a knight. "Well, not enough."

Rhys grumbled but was smiling as he picked up another biscuit and wedged it into his other cheek. He noticed Qasim trying not to grin and widened his eyes and wiggled his nose.

Qasim stifled a snigger. "Great manners, there."

Rhys took a bow from where he was sitting. He swallowed the biscuits and delicately dabbed at his mouth with a napkin. "What can I say? I'm classy, I am."

They managed to both hold a straight face for a few seconds and then dissolved into laughter.

Chapter Sixteen

THE LATEST BATCH of missions were being assigned, according to the gossip Rhys heard in the canteen.

Elwin and his fleet of winged monkeys always picked the jobs. Rumours and whispers suggested if private clients offered a gift here or took someone out for a pleasant meal there, their application would be pushed up the queue, but no one wanted to be the one to find out if it was true. However the missions were picked, they were passed down to Mariam who would liaise with the agents' handlers, who made the decisions about which agents were assigned to which job and the supervisor who would be allocated to oversee it from beginning to end.

In Rhys's case, there was no new job waiting.

He was being benched, and it was frustrating as hell. Even though Jacob had taken over as supervisor the moment it had all gone tits up, Rhys's name was still beside the Istanbul mission. Until the report was completed and approved, he was stuck with it. All he wanted was a good distraction, and this wasn't it.

The agents were free to move onto the next mission. They never crossed paths with the external historical examiners. All digi-lens footage was edited to blur their faces and keep them anonymous. The last thing they needed was someone on the outside knowing what they did for a living. There were always people who would try to use and abuse their position.

Rhys was curious about where Qasim and Tahmila would go next. Hopefully, something straightforward—a basic recon with no chance of any sweet, good-natured agents getting stabbed.

"You're not being subtle," Jacob said one afternoon.

Rhys glanced over at him. "What do you mean?"

Jacob was smiling. "Your 'I wonder where my agents will be going this time' spiel. I know you're fishing for hints, but until it's confirmed they can tell you, I'm afraid you're in the dark." His dark eyes were glinting. "Since when have they been 'your agents'?"

Rhys rubbed the back of his neck self-consciously. "Mutual decision. Or so Tahmila said."

"Yeah?" Jacob was openly grinning now. "Should I set up a Supervisor Adoption Kennel?"

Rhys rolled his eyes at him. "We're meant to be working here, *boss*." He nodded towards the table of experts, who were poring over the footage. "Babysitting the historians."

Jacob nodded, slouching in his chair. "Yeah. Can't exactly leave them to run wild. No one likes free-range historians. They nibble the wiring and shit in your shoes if you leave them alone."

Rhys forced himself to keep a straight face. "Mice. You're thinking of mice."

"I know what I'm about," Jacob said haughtily. "Have you ever left a historian unsupervised?"

"Only Dieter...and I get your point."

Jacob snickered and glanced at his watch. "I've got a meeting pencilled in with Ben and a couple of the techs. D'you think you'll manage to control this band of savages until I get back?"

Rhys considered the table of historians, all of who were concentrating ferociously. "I think I'll survive." He checked his own watch. "I'll get them downstairs for lunch as well, in case your meeting runs over."

Jacob rose, bracing one hand on Rhys's shoulder, and leaned down to confide, "It's like herding cats. Don't trust them. They'll walk all over you."

Unsurprisingly, the group of historians were well behaved. One or two of them occasionally asked a question, but Rhys spent most of his time tweaking the draft of the report. It was a matter of pride to make it as perfect as possible. His name was going to be attached to it alongside Jacob's, and he wanted people to remember it.

By lunchtime, the visitors were happy to be escorted down to one of the assigned dining rooms. Pre-ordered meals were waiting for them, so Rhys felt no guilt as he retreated out of the room and left them chattering excitedly among themselves.

Technically, he was meant to stay with them in case any of them wandered off, but since there was only one door and he was loitering outside it, it wasn't as if they could escape.

There were nooks in the opposite wall with chairs, so he slouched into one, closing his eyes for a moment. It wasn't hard work, supervising the externals, but it wasn't exactly the most interesting job in the world.

His folio chirped and he sat up reluctantly, opening his eyes. There was an incoming message, so he opened the screen. His heart sank.

All right, Rhys? I just wanted to see how you were. It's been a few days, and I hadn't heard anything from you. Please let me know you're all right. M xx

Rhys stared at it blankly. Marc. He'd said he would stay away until Rhys chimed him. It was six days ago now. Marc said he'd give him a week. He'd *said*. The last day was gone because Marc didn't want to wait. There was no way to avoid it again. No way to ignore it.

The worst part was that Rhys didn't know if he wanted to reply at all. It was the coward's way of getting out of it; Marc said he'd only come back when he was chimed, and if he wasn't chimed...

Rhys closed the message, took off his glasses, and rubbed at his eyes with both hands.

"Shit..." he whispered.

"Something up?"

Rhys grabbed for his glasses and shoved them back on to see Jacob walking down the hall from the lift. He hadn't even heard the doors open. "No. Nothing. Just things at home. Forgot to get the shopping in."

Jacob's expression suggested he didn't believe a word of it, but thankfully, he didn't press for details. "You got everyone down okay?"

Rhys nodded, forcing a smile. "Had to break out the cattle prod with a couple, but as soon as they saw the food, they were happy enough." He started to rise. "I know I should probably have stayed in there with them but—"

"I think they can manage to feed themselves." Jacob studied Rhys a bit too intently and then jerked his head in the direction of the lift. "How about you get something at the canteen? I'll take the next hour to give you a break."

"I'm fine."

Jacob raised an eyebrow. "A TRI supervisor turning down a break? Come on, Rhys. You and your crazy talk." He motioned towards the lift. "You'll be working late on the report again, so you need to get a break and a decent meal. That's an order."

Jacob always spotted his bad days, and Rhys hated himself for hating it. Jacob never said as much aloud, but he had a way of taking some of the pressure off. In some ways, it was good, because Rhys never took all the breaks he was entitled to. In other ways, it made him feel like he wasn't nearly as capable as he wanted to be. It was bollocks, of course. They'd never have trialled him as a supervisor if he weren't capable. But it still nagged at him.

"I'll be back over at one thirty," he said stubbornly.

Jacob stepped aside. "Not a minute sooner."

As soon as Rhys got outside, he knew Jacob had the right idea. The fresh air cleared his head, and for a moment, he basked in it. He walked across the courtyard towards H-block and made his way through to the staff canteen, which was already filling up. He hurried to the counters, piled a tray with an assortment of sweet and savoury things, and turned to hunt down a free chair.

"Rhys!" Tahmila rose, waving. "Over here!"

It took some careful weaving and ducking to get through the bustling crowd to the table where Tahmila sat opposite Qasim. Qasim beamed around a mouthful of food and waved a fork at him while Tahmila dragged her tray out of the way to make room for Rhys.

"I didn't expect to see you two around," Rhys admitted as he sat down. "Don't you have your briefing today?"

Qasim nodded, swallowing his food. "Had. We finished fifteen minutes ago."

The urge to ask where they were going was overwhelming, but Rhys focussed on his food. He was on a break. You didn't talk business on a break. "Any plans for the rest of the day, now it's out of the way?"

"I'm going to see Pisi," Qasim said happily. "They've finally agreed to let me keep her."

"Pisi?" Rhys inquired, puzzled.

Tahmila rolled her eyes. "The cat."

Rhys pressed his knuckles to his mouth, trying to keep from laughing. "You...you called the cat Pisi?"

"It's Turkish!" Qasim said, offended. "What's wrong with it?"

"As someone who doesn't speak Turkish, it sounds like a description of her personality."

"Hey!"

Tahmila nudged Rhys, grinning. "You know what's even better? It means 'kitty.'"

"I think it's a good Turkish name for a Turkish cat!" Qasim exclaimed. "You can't judge me. You called your dog Boris Yelpsin!"

Rhys burst out laughing. "Really?"

Tahmila didn't seem at all embarrassed. "Latest in a long line after Alexander Muttskoy and Vladimir Shih Tzutin." She picked up a cupcake off her tray and broke it in half. "My family, we don't forget those who wronged us."

"Be careful," Qasim warned ominously. "If you piss her off, she'll name her dog after you."

Tahmila snorted and pinged a chocolate chip at him. "If you're going to be cheeky, I'm off to sit outside." She pushed her chair out from the table. "I'll be in one of the research rooms when you're done. I want to get started as soon as we can."

Rhys couldn't help but notice the way Qasim's smile tightened.

"I'll see you there."

Rhys waited until Tahmila was out of earshot and said as casually as he could, "I don't blame you," he said as casually as he could. "I wouldn't want to get back into prep mode already either. I mean, you're just back as well."

To his relief, Qasim smiled and exhaled. "Yeah. It's...well, it's a mission. We have a job to do. Can't sit about, doing nothing." He was picking at his food, and his plate was still half-full. *No wonder his mother was trying to feed him up.* Qasim put his fork down. "Do you want to come down and meet Pisi?"

"Mm?" Rhys raised his eyebrows, his mouth filled with rice and meat.

"Well, Mila can't. Cats make her sneeze." Qasim shrugged self-consciously. "She's still in the quarantine block, and I—" He hesitated and drew himself up. "I'm not keen on going back in there on my own. I know it's ridiculous, but there it is."

Rhys wasn't surprised. "Of course. Let me finish this, and we can go over."

Fifteen minutes later, they were in the internal pod on the way to the quarantine basement. The cat was housed in one of the storerooms. It was generally used as a collection point for any accidentally acquired antiquities. Some had been destroyed, but occasionally, a weapon or a tool or a piece of clothing that made it back would be distributed to historians. It was better to stay on their good side, and bribery always worked.

There was a floor-to-ceiling cage constructed in one of the corners of the room, large enough to give the cat space to climb and entertain herself. As they approached, he could see a pair of suspicious yellow eyes peering down from one of the upper shelves.

Qasim reached for the lock and pressed his thumb to the identification panel. It clicked open.

"Are you allowed to go in?" Rhys asked.

"They said she's all clear," Qasim replied, closing the door behind him. "No bugs or fleas or anything nasty." He smiled, all the tightness in his features softening as the cat leapt down from shelf to shelf and wound herself around his ankles, purring frantically. Qasim crouched down, running his hand the length of her back. "They just want to keep her here for a bit longer, and since I'm off on a mission soon, it's easier for everyone."

Rhys sat outside the cage, watching as the cat all but pushed Qasim onto his bum. The mass of purring grey fur settled in his lap, tilting her head into his hand as he petted her.

"I was going to ask," Rhys said carefully. "I thought you were getting extended leave because of..." He motioned to his own side.

Qasim frowned down at the cat. "They need someone to hit one of the Islamic empires. Timurid or something." He shrugged. "I don't mind going back in." He smiled, but it wasn't his usual confident smile. "Better to get back on the horse, or whatever it is they say."

Rhys stared at him, the meeting with O'Donohue and all the corporate bullshit about what was best for the agents coming back to him. Apparently, what was best didn't matter if there was a mission to be done. "But you're not the only agent who can take the Islamic cases."

"Omar and Cyra are already in pre-prep for their next one," Qasim murmured, stroking between the cat's ears, "The SB wants this one out of the way to a deadline."

"What about Ibrahim and Nilufer? They've been in training for months now."

Qasim actually laughed. "Those two aren't even close to ready. Ibe's still relearning his spoken Arabic. He'd stick out like a sore thumb." He shrugged again, as if he wasn't worried sick about it. "It's an easy one this time. A bit of recon, celeb spotting, sightseeing. Nothing to worry about."

Rhys wanted to shake him and tell him it was all right to say no; he needed time to rest and recover from his injury. But it wouldn't do any good. At least it was an easy mission. It was something to hold on to.

"How's the report going, anyway?" Qasim asked.

Rhys leaned his shoulder against the cage. "You'd think they were watching porn, the noises some of them made when they saw the footage." It wasn't much of an exaggeration. "They're getting through it pretty quick. Quicker than I expected. The first run was pretty good."

Qasim smiled a little smugly. "Tahmila and I know what we're doing."

"I thought you lot were meant to be all humble and modest," Rhys said, lips twitching.

Qasim snorted. "I can be sober and upright and pious, but occasionally, once in a while, I can be proud of the fact I'm bloody good at my job." He lifted his hand so Pisi could wriggle around. "So..." He glanced at Rhys. "Any chance you'll be done before we officially start the next brief?"

Rhys hesitated. As much as he wanted to work with Qasim and Tahmila, it wasn't likely. Once the second check was completed, the report still had to be tightened up into a coherent whole, and even if Jacob was helping, it would take time. He shook his head. "I'm stuck with this one a bit longer. I don't even know if I'm allowed to know where you're going."

"It's not a top secret one this time," Qasim said, scooping his cat into a more comfortable position. "Sunny Otrar, early fifteenth century."

Rhys frowned. "Never heard of it."

"Same." Qasim was still watching the cat, a distant expression in his eyes. "It's one of the lost cities of the Silk Road. Pretty big back in the day." He laughed, but it sounded brittle. "No coups or anything going on when we're there. Just some old war lord called Timur on his last stop before he snuffs it."

"Nice and simple, then," Rhys said, hoping he sounded reassuring. "No invasions or wars or anything to worry about."

"Nope." Qasim was staring down at the cat, his hand shaking on her back.

Christ, anyone with eyes could tell the man wasn't ready to go back on another mission, and here he was, stuck with it and trembling, and Rhys had the door open and was in the cage with his arm around Qasim's shoulders before he could even think about it.

Qasim leaned into him mutely.

"You don't need to go," Rhys said. "They have to give you recovery time. They can't force it."

Qasim shook his head. "If I don't go on this one, I—" He shook his head again and took a shivering breath. "I need to get back to it as soon as I can. If I don't, if I sit and wait and stew, I don't think I could— I don't think I'd be able to."

"Has anyone ever told you you're stupidly brave?"

Qasim laughed weakly. "Only when they're giving me a lecture." He turned to Rhys. "I'm sorry I screwed up the mission for you. I know it was your first time supervising."

Rhys stared at him blankly. Of all the people to be apologising, it wasn't the man who had been wounded saving his partner's life. "You're an idiot." Qasim's eyes widened in surprise. "I mean, you didn't screw up the mission. You completed it. It's not your fault there were soldiers who were a bit stabby."

Qasim broke into a crooked smile. "A bit stabby?"

Rhys had never been more relieved to see a smile and nodded. "Historical term, you know. I did a lot of research, I did." The tension in Qasim's shoulders relaxed, and the other man started laughing in earnest. As Qasim leaned against him, Rhys couldn't help smiling.

Chapter Seventeen

PERSIAN WAS A nightmare.

Qasim hated it, but he'd feel awful if the sweet woman who was trying to teach him realised. The only good thing was that he and Tahmila were given more pre-prep time for lessons. It was easier for Tahmila. She'd always enjoyed languages, so most of her time was spent helping him understand the new conjugations between their assigned blocks with their tutor.

"No." He pushed his screen aside. "No more."

She gave him a patient look. "You were doing fine."

He rubbed his face and groaned into his palms. "Can't we just say I'm mute?" He peered between his fingers at her. "It would be easier. A poor mute idiot who wanders around and stares at everything."

She didn't even dignify him with a response.

"I don't see why I have to learn another one! Three is enough for anybody, and it's not like I can't just use Arabic! The place was part of a Muslim occupation *and* a crossing point for travellers from all over the place."

"You know why," she replied. "We don't know how common Arabic was with the locals. It's better to be on the safe side."

"Flah!" He flopped forward and knocked his forehead on the table. "My head is full."

She reached over and ruffled his hair. "It's time for prayers anyway. Do what you need to do; clear your head, get some food in you, and I'll meet you back here in an hour."

He lifted his head enough to peek at her. "Really?"

"Well, if the alternative is watching you smack your head on a table..." She drummed her fingertips on her chin. "Hm. Tough decision."

He scrambled up, bent to kiss her on top of her head. "You are a queen among women."

She waved him away. "I know, I know."

There were a couple of former meeting rooms in the research department of the main building. They weren't designed for prayer, but they weren't used much otherwise. Though no one had actually said anything, the one on the eighth floor ended up being used by the women and the one on the sixth floor was for the men.

It was nice to share the space and the time with people within the TRI. It felt different compared to praying alone or praying with family. There was something about being among colleagues who knew exactly what their jobs entailed and the risks they took.

"We need to get somewhere bigger," Ibrahim complained as they emerged afterwards. The group scattered in different directions, but three of them headed for the lift. "I'm sure you're not meant to be sitting on each other."

"We could try for the training suite?" Qasim suggested as the lift started moving. "Unless they have visiting groups in, they leave the floor clear."

Omar snorted. "Yeah. Good luck getting access authorised."

"Outside?" Ibrahim inquired. "There's the Last Glance."

"Maybe in summer," Qasim said, smiling. "I'm not risking hypothermia because it's a bit of a squash." He glanced at his watch as the lift slid to a halt. "I'll see you later, yeah?"

Ibrahim waved and Omar nodded as they stepped out into the hall.

Qasim continued down to the bottom floor and headed across to the H-block canteen. There was a small canteen in the main building, but it didn't have such a varied menu. He gravely considered all the options. Ummi was already gearing up for Ramadan, which meant a lot more traditional food was sneaking in and a lot less chips.

Spicy chicken and chips with peas won out. He added a side of toffee pudding and a couple of rolls before searching around the hall for someone to bother while he was eating.

One table was surprisingly empty, given how busy the canteen was, but since the tabletop was covered in folders and files and their owner glowered up when anyone approached, Qasim couldn't blame people for backing off.

"You're really not in the mood for company?" he asked as he approached.

Ben blinked at him, and his scowl faded. "What?"

Qasim mimicked Ben's glare. "That. You were scaring people off." He peered down at the table, puzzled. The papers were old, some only fragments, and really should have been in an archive instead of a canteen. "What's this?"

Ben hastily pulled the papers into a stack. "Something I'm working on." He motioned to one of the empty chairs. "Sit down, if you want. I don't mind."

Qasim grinned at him. "I feel special."

To his amusement, Ben flushed. "It's not a big deal."

Qasim set his tray down and tucked into his lunch. "A bit old school for you," he observed as Ben started sliding the sheaves of paper into plastic files. "I don't think I've ever seen you work in analogue before."

Ben had stuffed one of the sheets halfway into a folder, but he hesitated, pulled it out, and tentatively offered it to Qasim. "Maybe you can help."

Qasim nodded. "Okay..." He took the page carefully. It had a small piece of parchment attached to it, rumpled and tattered as if it had been folded many times. The text was in brown ink, parts faded beyond legibility. It appeared to be some kind of letter, but part of it had been torn in the past, also ripping the text in half. Qasim squinted at the words. "My dearest Thomas and Benjamin..." He paused, frowning. "What is this?"

Ben stared down at the table. "Read it and tell me."

It took some effort, but the general gist said the writer was safe and well and anticipated seeing them again soon.

"I don't understand," he finally said, laying the paper on the table and sliding it towards Ben. "It's an old letter. What's so special about it?"

"My dad had it and some others like it."

Qasim shook his head, confused. "Why?"

Ben was silent for a moment and finally met Qasim's eyes. "I think it was from my mother."

There were some stories no one in the TRI was meant to know, so, of course, everyone did. It was an internal urban legend: when Tom Sanders invented the first temporal gate, his wife volunteered to go through it, but something went wrong, and she was never seen again. Tom Sanders spent the rest of his life trying to find her.

"Oh," was all Qasim could say.

Ben tucked the sheet back into the folder.

"So the stories were true?"

Ben shrugged. "Mariam always said she died in an accident." He closed the folder up. "He had a gate in the basement. Mariam said it was his prototype. I mean, she said it was for research but if—" He huffed out a shaky breath. "This— I couldn't think of any other reason he'd have things like this."

Qasim looked at the folder, then back at Ben. "But why is it so important now?"

Ben laughed, bright and brittle. "Because I got the worst birthday present ever when I turned eighteen—all my dad's stuff. The house. The safes. The storage units." He pressed his knuckles to his mouth, and when Qasim reached across the table to touch his arm, he threw up his hands angrily. "It's stupid! It's nearly eleven years ago, and it's stupid and—"

"And they're your parents," Qasim said softly. "Of course, you're going to get upset."

Ben shook his head again. "No. No. There's more." He fumbled with his folio, opening up a batch of projections of other old letters. He shoved them across the table to Qasim and sat back, pressing both fists to his mouth again.

Qasim pulled the projections closer, spreading them all out.

These documents were different. Some were in better condition, but the ink was still faded. The handwriting was different. They were only addressed to a 'Benjamin,' and the signed ones showed 'Thomas S' at the bottom. Most of them were about travelling and being away too long.

"I went searching," Ben whispered. "After I found the ones from—the ones that might have been from my mum. It— I know it's stupid, but I thought if he searched for letters from her, maybe I could find some from him." He motioned to the scattered images. "I found so many, but these…"

Qasim wished there was a gentler way to put it when he said, "Ben, you have no idea how many letters in the past were about travelling and not getting back in time. I've seen hundreds of the things. I mean, it would be great if it was possible, but your dad—"

"I know." Ben's voice was sharp as a pistol crack. "I know. The gate short-circuited. He's dead. Everyone keeps on reminding me. I *know*." He shut down the images. "But isn't it possible, just maybe, they could have been wrong?"

Qasim chewed his lip. "If it short-circuited—" He shook his head. "I'm not the best person to ask. I just go through the gates. I don't know how they work."

Ben's eyes were wet, but he blinked hard. "I know they think I'm going nuts, but what if it's him? What if the gate didn't do what everyone thinks it did? What if it threw him back in time instead?"

"Can that happen?"

Ben shook his head. "I don't know." He buried his head in his hands, his elbows propped on the table, and took a gulping breath. "I don't know, and I know more about this technology than anyone. If I don't know, how can we be sure it didn't happen?" He pressed the heels of his hands against his eyes. "Dad's gate…" He lowered his hands, shaking his head. "They don't know how much Dad's gate could do. All the information was stolen. Maybe… I don't know." He stared back across the table at Qasim. "No one even tried to find him. No one thought—"

"No one thought to search for a dead man," Qasim murmured. He rubbed at his jaw. It was a hell of a lot to pin all your hopes on—a handful of old letters that might or might not have been written for you. "Where did you find them?"

A guilty flush flooded Ben's face. "I-I did some online searches."

And somehow got hold of the original copies? Very few collections were willing to lend out their archives to the public, unless…

"Oh no," Qasim groaned. "Ben, don't tell me you used our clearance!"

The flush went from pink to scarlet. Ben scanned the room frantically, before whispering urgently. "No one cares! I didn't take anything important! They were just…found in the old offices and ended up in archives and no one else was going to do anything with them!"

"Mariam won't be happy about this."

Ben winced. "Yeah. No. She wasn't." He propped his elbows on the edge of the table and wrapped his fingers around his forearms, squeezing until the knuckles were white. "She doesn't believe it."

Qasim couldn't blame her. Even if someone did want to send a letter to the future, there were so many problems to be taken into account: where to address it, when it could be found, something to confirm who you were. Mariam had been one of Tom Sanders's closest friends. If she didn't see a message, if she didn't believe any of the documents were from Tom, then they probably weren't.

"It could just be a coincidence," he said carefully.

Ben stared at him. "No."

"Ben—"

"No! I can't believe that. There's—it's not just the letters! There's— Why does everyone think I'm imagining this? Do I seem crazy?"

Qasim shifted uncomfortably as Ben's raised voice was drawing attention. He held up a hand, placating. "Okay. Okay. Tell me what you think happened."

Ben subsided in the chair, shaking his head. "I don't know." His face was creased with distress. "They— I think Dad used to use his gate. I think... I don't know...I think he went back to find her."

Qasim stared at him. "Into history? Without any prep or anything?"

Ben shrugged helplessly. "I know they haven't told me everything. I know they didn't want to upset me. I remember the gate. I remember the light. I just..." He knuckled at his forehead. "The gate had to connect to somewhere for him to use it. It had to. He couldn't have gotten out of the basement if there wasn't some kind of connection. You can't go through a closed door."

"Okay. So, the gate could open?"

Ben leaned across the table. "I think he went somewhere he'd been before."

"What? How could you know?"

Ben hesitated and then pulled out his folio. He opened up four images and laid them out side by side in front of Qasim. They appeared to be identical logs, and Qasim raised his eyes to Ben in confusion.

"The anomaly in the code," Ben explained in a whisper. "This is what I saw on the screen when you did the flash."

Qasim's heart was bashing against his ribs. "All of these?"

Ben shook his head, a fevered gleam in his eyes. He touched each of the images. "This is your flash. This one is the Farraday flash six years ago. Her gates were opened three minutes apart. This one is Singh's flash eight years ago. His gates were six minutes apart." His finger was shaking as he pointed to the last image. "And this is the output they salvaged from Dad's computer. It's the *same*. That means the gate *must* have connected with somewhere he'd visited before."

Output that only appeared when a gate connected to the same place and time within the same twenty-four-hour window. Qasim studied each one, trying to find some difference, but Ben was right. They were identical. "But what about the short circuit? I thought those shut down the gates?"

Ben held up both his hands, palms facing each other, about a foot apart. "The open gate—" He clapped, and the sound carried over all the noise of the canteen. He was staring at his hands, still pressed together. "The short circuit. That's—everyone believes it's what happened."

Qasim was very glad he hadn't eaten much. No wonder Ben wanted to believe any other possibility. "Did you speak to Mariam about it?"

"Yeah. 'It's impossible. Even if you're right about this anomaly, we don't know when or where the letter came from. We don't have anywhere to start.' She doesn't believe me." Ben pulled the folders together into a pile. "Like Jacob." He glowered accusingly at Qasim. "Like you."

"Hey, don't put words in my mouth." Qasim leaned over the table and caught Ben's wrist. "I'm just saying…" He squeezed Ben's wrist. "Don't pin all your hopes on it, all right?" He tried to smile, but Ben's stricken face made it difficult. "I know you want to believe it's possible, but you *know* there's a fifty fifty chance that it isn't."

Ben shifted his shaking hand to cling to Qasim's wrist and whispered, "I know." Qasim didn't know what else he could say, and Ben withdrew his hand. "Thanks." He gathered up his folders. "For not calling me crazy."

"I time travel for a living. Who am I to judge?" Qasim tried to smile again. "How about this? If I ever get lost in the past, I'll definitely send you a letter, so you'll know if it's possible."

"Okay." Ben smiled weakly, stood, and walked away.

Qasim watched him go, sighing quietly. Grief got to people in different ways. He could only hope Ben would figure things out.

Chapter Eighteen

THREE WEEKS OF external examiners and the report still wasn't done.

Rhys was starting to wonder if they were doing it on purpose. Interesting architectural features, they said. Unexpected details on the uniforms, they said. A colour of dye that wasn't meant to be in Istanbul for another seventy years, they said.

Bullshit, Rhys said. Only very quietly. Under his breath. When they definitely weren't paying attention.

He hadn't managed to keep his frustrations hidden from Jacob, who sympathised but reminded him, no matter how frustrating it was, the historians couldn't be kicked out. Even if the clients didn't care whether the Janissaries' uniforms had buttons, there would be some history nerd who would get very excited about it. The clients didn't care about how many layers there were to the turbans. For fuck's sake, they didn't need to know all the spices being sold at one stand in the market.

Unfortunately, one of the historians had found some important graffiti in the background, and another was doing an analysis of the banners and flags in the Hippodrome. As long as there was any chance of any useful information being found, Rhys was stuck. Meanwhile, more missions were happening.

Marc put the icing on the cake of frustration.

He'd grown tired of waiting. He showed up one evening—sober, thankfully—and demanded to know when he could come home. He went on about how hard it was to be apart, about how much he missed Rhys, how much he missed their home. It shouldn't have been a surprise. Marc loved his big gestures, and, once upon a time, his keenness to be back might have been sweet.

It was Rhys's fault too. He'd been avoiding it all, hoping if he didn't reply, Marc might actually realise Rhys wanted more time. Lots of it. All of it, even. He'd ignored Marc's messages and quietly hoped it would be enough.

And then Marc was there, in front of him, expecting to be welcomed back with open arms, as if Rhys's fears and concerns could be put aside. As if hours spent sitting in a cold bathroom, dreading what might happen, were nothing. As if it could be forgotten and not rest like a rock in Rhys's belly every time Marc came home late.

The straw finally broke the camel's back, and for the first time, Rhys couldn't keep the frustration—the anger—in anymore.

People didn't think he got angry. Marc definitely didn't. It was the appearance, Rhys knew. Look small and chubby and harmless and everyone assumes you're a mild-mannered doormat. Especially when he did his best to avoid any conflicts and kept all his problems to himself, to keep them from burdening anyone else.

The trouble was…

The trouble was the little things piled up, and when he did lose his temper, it was like a firework. He had a long fuse, but it could only burn so long, and when he finally exploded, it was never good. The only mercy was that it was brief—a flare of fury burning out as abruptly as it began. Anger was exhausting. Anger didn't help. It never had.

Marc got the full force of it.

"You never listen, do you?"

Marc seemed puzzled as if he couldn't understand what he'd done wrong. "I did! I gave you space, and you—"

"Space. I ask for *one* week. *One*! And you can't even give me that!" Rhys's heart was thundering in his ears, so loudly he could barely hear himself speak. "But it's always the way with you, isn't it? I tell you what I want, but no, you know better than me, and you just bulldoze in as if what I want doesn't matter!"

Marc recoiled like he'd been slapped. "I neve—"

"Bullshit!" Rhys exclaimed furiously. "Fucking bullshit! You *always* decide everything for us! Holidays! Restaurants! Pods! Christ, I left you alone for a week, and you replaced half my fucking wardrobe!"

"You *needed* new clothes!" Marc protested. "I thought you liked them!"

Rhys stared at him in disbelief. "You never even *asked* me! You picked out things *you* liked and assumed I would like them! You chucked out all *my* things *you* didn't like and expected me to be happy about it!"

"You never said anything!"

"Of course, I fucking didn't!" Rhys shoved his fingers through his hair, trying to gather himself. "Jesus, Marc, you're hot and young and smart and you were with *me*. D'you think I wanted to risk doing anything to chase you away?" He threw his hands up. "Don't you remember how many times I suggested places for a trip, but you just laughed and said it would be shit? D'you really think I wanted to go on those clubbing holidays? Or on the skydive? But you wanted it, so I made myself do it because I wanted to keep you fucking happy! And now, I ask for one thing, and I don't even get that!"

Marc stared at him. "I thought—you never—" His face crumpled. "You could've said something!"

Rhys sagged to sit at the table and propped his elbow on it. Christ, he was tired, and the rage was draining away, leaving a gaping, aching hole instead. "I tried. In the start. You didn't listen."

"I did!"

Rhys shook his head. "Heard. Not listened." He took an unsteady breath. "I—I'm not one to make a fuss. I...don't do confrontation. I had a nice, handsome man who wanted to be with me." He shook his head again. "It—it was safer."

Marc sat at the other end of the table. He was pale and shaken. "So, you just...what? Put up with me?" The pain and confusion in his face made Rhys turn away ashamed of himself. "D'you even *like* me?"

Rhys recoiled. "Yes! Christ, yes! Of course I like you! And loved you and all!"

There was a long silence as they both realised what he'd said.

"Loved." Marc's voice was dull. "Not anymore, then?"

"Marc..." Rhys's heart was in his mouth. "Shit, Marc..."

Marc didn't look at him. He pushed the chair back and straightened up as if he was a hundred years old. "Thank you for finally telling me. I—it's something I needed to know." His voice was brittle with the edge of tears. "I'm sorry I made you so miserable. I didn't mean to."

"Marc!" Rhys rose so fast he knocked his own chair over.

Marc held up a hand. It was shaking. "Don't. You've said enough." He swallowed hard, licking his lips. "I—it's better if I go, I think."

Rhys could only watch as Marc walked back into the bedroom. It was as if he'd turned to stone and was still standing there, shaking, when Marc came back out with two of their cases in his hands. They stared at each other across the room, and Christ, Rhys wished he could find something— anything—useful or kind or *anything* to say, but he was wrung out, and there was nothing left to help or fix the mess he'd made.

If there'd ever been a chance for them to salvage what was left between them, Rhys knew he was the one who'd smashed it to pieces in those few minutes.

Marc's eyes were wet, and he took an unsteady breath before he spoke. "I'll come back for the rest of my stuff another day."

It was the last time Rhys had seen him.

Babysitting historians wasn't enough of a distraction to keep him from going over everything he could have done to try to make things work. It was as much his fault as it was Marc's. Maybe more his. If he'd said something sooner; if he'd spoken to Marc instead of hiding from it all. Maybe they would have argued about it, but maybe it would have been better. Maybe not.

He tried to call Marc. To explain. To apologise. To...to something. Marc wouldn't take his calls. He wasn't surprised. If Marc had unconsciously put a wedge between them, he was the one who had hammered it home and split them apart. The relief didn't matter, even if it was the right thing for both of them. It didn't stop the guilt from bearing down on him for hurting Marc.

Then there were the little realities to deal with: sole responsibility for the mortgage again, a single income instead of joint, the cost of running and maintaining a pod for his commute, replacing any of Marc's share of their possessions. Rhys had budgeted so carefully. Everything was...just enough. Just enough for him. Just enough for his parents. Only just enough, but not anymore.

It was all too much to think about, and it was so hard to keep his temper when people were giving him funny looks, when he was being abrupt and snappish. Easier to go and sit outside, away from everyone. March was still colder than it had any right to be, but he had his coat and hat, and it was enough.

He was sitting on the bench at the Last Glance when someone approached, footsteps crunching on the gravel. His historians were having their lunch, and most of the staff were in the canteen. He glanced back, relieved to see it was only Qasim walking towards him.

He was bundled up in a coat, his hands shoved in his pockets. "Mind some company?"

Rhys slid sideways to make room on the bench. "Avoiding the canteen?"

Qasim nodded, taking a seat a foot from him. Rhys nodded down at the space by him, and Qasim grimaced. "Trust me, you don't want to be within breathing distance of me at this time of year."

"Oh?"

"You try going without a drink all day," Qasim replied ruefully. "Your mouth won't thank you."

"Ah." Rhys could begin to imagine. He leaned back. "How's it all going? The fasting?"

Qasim shrugged, the shoulders of his coat riding up to his ears. "Same as ever. Sugar crashes. A lot of grumpy people trying to fit in a prayer room." He smiled quickly. "You know you're into the second week when you start talking about a giant plate of chips instead of Persian greetings. Mila's about ready to throttle me."

Rhys almost smiled. "Not an issue I've thought about before."

Qasim grinned. "Count yourself lucky. Persian is a pain in the backside. Still, I've got until Eid to practise, before they start all the historical training."

Rhys was surprised. Normally, agents would head into prep within a fortnight of being briefed. "They've delayed the prep?"

"'Til the end of Ramadan," Qasim confirmed. "I pulled the big holy day celebration card on them, and they agreed I could delay the mission."

Rhys's eyebrows shot up. "Really? The Board delayed an urgent mission? Out of the goodness of their hearts? So you could go to your big religious do?" He shook his head. "I smell bullshit."

Qasim took a hand out his pocket to scratch at his ear. "I...might have taken your advice and applied a well-placed guilt trip over my near-death experience. Recovery time and how much my family would hate it if I missed Eid, especially when I came so close to missing it." He gazed up at the sky. "I mean, it's not exactly untrue or anything. If I let them shut me in, Ummi would bring down her wrath, and there would be no survivors."

Any other day, the image would have made Rhys laugh, but not today, and it was his mistake. He should have forced it and pretended everything was fine.

Qasim turned to him, studying Rhys too closely for his liking. "You all right?"

Rhys nodded, tried for one of those smiles everyone knew, but it was too much effort, and he was so damn tired. "No. No, I'm not." His hands were curled in fists in his jacket pockets. "Marc—my partner—left me."

"Oh." Qasim sounded genuinely shocked and sympathetic. "He's the man I saw when I called you?" Rhys nodded. Qasim scooted closer and knocked his elbow against Rhys's. "I'm sorry."

Rhys kept his eyes on the fountain in front of them. There was still water flowing, despite the cold. "We both cocked up." He inhaled and exhaled slowly. "Can't point fingers." Qasim was studying him closer now, and he couldn't bring himself to meet Qasim's sympathetic gaze. He didn't want the concern. He didn't deserve it. "It'll be all right."

"Mm." Qasim settled back against the bench. "That's why you're out here?"

Rhys shrugged.

Qasim knocked elbows with him again. He didn't say anything else, just sat there, and Rhys was grateful. It felt rubbish being on his own, but there were too many people in the TRI who would ask all the questions he didn't know how to answer yet.

They were still sitting there when Qasim's folio chimed, muffled in the depths of his pocket.

"I need to get in," he said, unfolding from the bench. "Mila'll be waiting." He hesitated and then blurted out in a rush, "I know it's probably the last thing you want right now, but if you'd like some company tonight, my family is getting together for *futoor*. S'when we break our fast for the night and there's more food than you can shake a stick at. You'd be more than welcome."

Rhys blinked at him, startled. "I can't invade your family do..."

Qasim waved a hand. "It's not invading. It's practically tradition. We like to be hospitable, especially during Ramadan." He shrugged. "You don't have to, but there's always room for one more."

God, it sounded better than going back to an empty flat and searching for somewhere new to live. Company and people who weren't colleagues, and good food and anything that wasn't wallowing in misery for a few hours.

"If I won't be in the way," he said, getting up.

Qasim laughed. "You've seen the numbers we're working with. You'll be the easiest of the lot. Anyway, my dad's away on business as well, so you'd be filling a gap."

Despite everything, Rhys smiled at Qasim's enthusiasm. "Drop me a line of where and when." He paused, frowning. "Do I need to bring anything?"

"Maybe some flowers for Ummi, and you'll be fine." Qasim groaned dramatically when his folio chimed again. "Mila's getting grumpy." His eyes danced. "She's not even got a sugar crash as an excuse. Natural grump, her."

Rhys watched as Qasim hurried towards the main building.

No one had warned him how kind Qasim could be. Intelligent, focussed, and protective, he'd been warned about. Not the gentle smiles, the concern, the honest-to-goodness kindness. He hadn't expected it, and it stole his breath away.

It would be better not to think about it. Friendship was a precious thing. There was no reason to get stupid and attached and make a mistake and ruin everything. Especially after the train wreck he was still picking his way out of.

He pushed his hands into his pockets and followed in Qasim's wake. There were historians to collect and babysitting to be done.

It was amazing the difference anticipation made to a rubbish day.

In the afternoon, Rhys had plenty of time to research the fast-breaking and check if there was anything he should do. Qasim dropped a line less than an hour after they'd left each other, with an address and a time to arrive "so you don't need to worry about the praying part."

Once the historians had returned to their accommodation for the night, Rhys headed towards the city. While he lived on the north side, Qasim and his family lived closer to the centre. It wasn't until his pod pulled up outside the house that he had a sudden twinge of panic. It was a beautiful detached house with a lovely front garden and a row of high-end pods parked vertically in the drive. Suddenly, his shirt and wool vest felt too casual for a house.

Before he could change his mind and rush away for a change of clothes, the front door opened, and Qasim was there, framed by the warm light. *So much for a quick getaway*, he thought ruefully as Qasim—and the small child sitting on his back—waved. He climbed out of the pod and pressed the grav-thruster control on the rear panel to tilt it up to park beside the rest. No escape now. He pulled on his best smile and walked to the front door, flowers in one hand, chocolates in the other.

"Right on time," Qasim said, smiling. He was dressed down in a loose, collarless shirt, the sleeves rolled up to his elbows.

"You brought sweets!" The girl at his shoulder beamed at Rhys. "Are they for me?"

Qasim gave Rhys an apologetic eye-roll. "No, Leila. You already have sweets." He crouched down and set her on her feet. "Can you fetch Sitto for me?" The girl scampered into the house as Qasim straightened up. "You don't have to stay long, if you don't want to. If they get a bit much and you need out, let me know."

Rhys eyed him suspiciously. "Are you trying to scare me?"

Qasim laughed, stepping aside to let him enter the broad, brightly lit hall. "I'd consider it a caution, so you don't try to sue the pants off me for trauma."

Rhys stepped into the hall. There was a giant pile of shoes by the door. He toed his own off to add to the pile. Beyond the closed door to the left, the noise of at least dozen voices, talking and laughing, floated out along with rich, sweet and spiced scents, all mixing together and washing over him. It smelled amazing, and his stomach growled, making him wince in embarrassment.

"Good call," Qasim muttered as one of the doors opened, and his mother bustled out, adjusting her veil over hair. "Ummi'll be delighted you came with an empty tank." He put a hand on Rhys's shoulder, nudging him forward. "Ummi, this is Rhys. Rhys, this is my mother."

Rhys could immediately see Qasim in the bright, laughing eyes and warm smile.

"You are welcome in our home," she said carefully, and her smile brightened even more when Rhys held out the flowers and chocolates to her.

"Thank you for your hospitality," he said, relieved when she took the flowers and sniffed them. She handed them off to one of the children loitering behind her and hurried to the living room door, beckoning him.

"Please, come."

The minute Rhys stepped into the room, it was like being hit by a wall of sound. Greetings were called from all sides, and he remembered enough to recall the right responses. There were at least twenty people of all ages, and Qasim's mother took him by the arm, guiding him around the room, giving his name to each of them.

Rhys couldn't help noticing Qasim didn't join them. Instead, he hung around at the door and laughed as Rhys was passed around like a newborn to every one of Qasim's relatives. Welcomed and introduced for at least fifteen minutes, his cheeks had been left grazed raw by warm, stubbled, and bearded kisses.

He was standing, dazed, in the middle of the room when Qasim finally reappeared by his side and pressed a plate into his hands.

"You look like you could use a seat," he said, grinning.

"Mm." Rhys nodded gratefully. Qasim took charge of it, yelling in Arabic to a couple of the teenagers to clear a space on one of the three couches lining the walls of the huge living room. Around them, conversations started up again, and the attention seemed to have moved away from him.

Qasim slouched beside him and picked up a date from his own plate. "Coping?"

Rhys stared around the room, feeling out of his depth. The most family he'd ever had in one place didn't even come close to this, and it had been at his nan's funeral. More often than not, it had just been him, his parents, and, sometimes, his mam's sister. "Is it always like this?"

"More or less," Qasim said, smiling. He pulled a couple of forks from his breast pocket and held one out. "You've earned a nibble."

Rhys had no idea what he was eating: some kind of rice and meat dish. It was hot, spiced, and delicious. As he ate, he let his eyes wander, taking in everything. The far end of the room had several tables covered in a sprawling buffet. People were going back and forth between them and the other half of the room where pouffes, beanbags, and the couches took up all the space.

Two identical girls were playing a board game with a younger boy on the floor. A toddler slept in the lap of a wrinkled old lady, who was chain-drinking glasses of some kind of tea. There was a heavy-set, red-faced man with ginger hair who was both out of place and perfectly at home in the middle of all the dark-haired, dark-skinned family. Some of them were wearing what Rhys considered to be traditional Muslim clothing. Others were dressed informally. They all seemed to be having a great time.

"They're really all relatives?" He couldn't help asking.

"Direct and in-laws only," Qasim confirmed.

Rhys shook his head, dazed, trying to wrap his head around living with so many people in his life.

He'd only just finished the mountainous plate of food Qasim had filled for him, when Qasim's mother brought over another stacked with small pastries. She smiled encouragingly, balancing it on the arm of the couch beside Rhys, and then hurried off without saying a word.

Qasim must have noticed the bemused expression on Rhys's face. "She worries about her English around new people. Some idiots were...less than polite when she first arrived and was still learning. Kind of shook her confidence." He gazed in his mother's direction with a brief smile. "She'll be fine once she knows you." He leaned over Rhys and took one of the pastries. "The flowers were nice."

"Did she like them?" Rhys asked, picking up a pastry. It seemed to be packed with chopped nuts and was layered and sticky. When he bit into it, it was crunchy and soft and flaky at the same time.

Qasim seemed surprised. "Of course." Rhys couldn't help remembering his gran fussing over any flowers she was given, making a show of them being put in a vase and displayed. "Is this because she gave them to Kamila?" Qasim didn't sound annoyed, just curious.

"I'm being daft, I am." Rhys laughed self-consciously. It was always the way, not wanting to disappoint anyone and always second-guessing himself. "Don't worry about it."

Qasim gently nudged him. "The only reason she passed them on to someone else was so she could give you her full attention. A guest is much more important than a gift." He smiled and nudged Rhys again. "She loved them."

Rhys smiled in return, more relieved than he'd expected. "I wanted to make a good impression. Especially when it's such a special time of year for your family."

Qasim laughed and patted him on the knee. "You're doing all right." He got up and took Rhys's empty plate. "Want some more?"

Rhys held up the deeply stacked plate of sweet pastries. "I think I've got enough to work on here."

Qasim nodded, then headed off across the room to the tables of food. His space beside Rhys was immediately occupied by one of the identical girls, who looked about six. She pushed her braid over her shoulder, straightened her dress, and gave him a good, hard stare.

"Are you Uncle Qasim's friend?"

Rhys offered her a pastry from the plate. It seemed like the safest thing to do. "I think so."

She chewed on the pastry, staring at him, unblinking. "Why do you have glasses? Are you blind?"

"Only a little," he said, pushing said glasses up his nose.

"My daddy shoots lasers in peoples' eyes to fix them," she informed him solemnly. "Why don't you shoot lasers in your eyes?"

Rhys had to smile. "Because my eyes are funny, and doctors don't like them." He leaned down close. "People think I'm smart because I wear glasses. Because only smart people can wear glasses. But I'm not smart." He put one finger to his lips. "Don't tell anyone."

She giggled and then widened her eyes innocently when a shadow fell over them.

"Causing trouble, Ranim?" Qasim was standing there, holding two glasses of tea.

"He wears glasses because he's really, really smart," Ranim declared and then scrambled along the couch to make space for Qasim.

"Is that right?" Qasim sat, handing Rhys one of the glasses.

Rhys kept his face straight. "Absolutely." He took a sip of the tea, which was sweet and strong enough to make him catch his breath. "Please tell me you don't eat and drink like this all year around."

Qasim burst out laughing, drawing every eye in the room. "If we did, we'd have trouble getting out the front door." Ranim scrambled to sit in his lap, nestling against him, her head on his shoulder. She caught his wrist and pulled his glass closer to take a sip of his tea. Qasim gazed down at her fondly. "This month is special."

Rhys glanced at Qasim and said quietly, "Thank you. For inviting me. For sharing it."

"I thought it might help."

Rhys nodded. It was a hell of an understatement. He offered the plate to Qasim, who juggled his tea and niece to free a hand to take another pastry. Rhys set the plate down in his lap and picked up another one too. "If I get fat." He paused. "If I get *fatter*, I'm blaming you."

Qasim snickered. "More of you to love?" He widened his eyes in mock-innocence.

Rhys snorted and elbowed him. Qasim's snickers grew louder as he nudged Rhys in return.

For a house packed to overflowing with so much noise and so many people, Rhys was surprised he didn't feel as uncomfortable as he normally would. A fish out of water, yes, but a fish with good company and good food and nothing to worry about.

He ended up with the second of the twins—Zeinah—on his lap when Qasim declared it was story time. The children rushed together to sit eagerly at Qasim's feet, and Rhys listened as he started telling an exciting adventure of Murad, the noble bandit of Baghdad.

From the sound of it, it was a character they all knew well. They all shouted out his secret weapons: his magic flute of sleepiness, his spiky stick with sharp bits, his accursed ice-cream maker. They all oohed and aahed in the right places. They jumped when he roared like the Hydra. They cheered when Murad got away, rescuing a princess from the evil vizier.

Rhys noticed the conversations around the room had trailed off. The rest of the family was listening with amused indulgence. Qasim was a natural storyteller, and it wasn't just the kids who enjoyed his stories.

By the time Qasim reached the end of the tale, Rhys was starting to understand why story time was so popular with the parents too. The smallest of the kids who'd been running around excitedly all evening were sleepy and much easier to bundle into their coats.

Qasim passed Ranim up to her father and glanced at Rhys. "It'll take them about fifteen minutes to get ready, so if you want to slip away first, before the drama kicks off..."

"Drama?" Rhys inquired.

"At least one of the kids will realise they're about to be taken home and be unhappy about it." Qasim scrambled up and lifted Zeinah up from Rhys's lap. "Go and grab your shoes and coat, and I'll try and keep the peace."

Rhys glanced around at the children gathering up their toys and the parents sorting through a giant pile of coats, which had appeared from some other room. It was organised chaos, and he was beginning to see what Qasim meant, so he bolted for the hall.

Qasim's mother was there and smiled knowingly, holding out his coat.

"Thank you," he said, wishing he could express how much he'd enjoyed the evening. "It was wonderful."

She smiled, deep lines creasing around her eyes and mouth, and reached out to take his hands between her plump warm ones. She smelled of cloves and sweet, floral perfume. "You are welcome," Her dark eyes were warm. "Thank you for coming."

She slipped back into the living room, and he pulled on his coat, frowning when he noticed a bulge in one pocket. He put his hand in and found a small plastic box. Lifting one corner of the lid and grinned. Someone must have noticed how much he'd enjoyed the pastries—baklava, Qasim said—and gave him enough to last a few days. He tucked it in his pocket and turned his attention to finding his shoes.

The living room door swung open again. Rhys glanced up to see Qasim step out into the hall and pull the door shut behind him, cutting off a child's squalling. "It begins," he said ominously.

Rhys snorted, fishing through the pile of shoes. "You love it."

Qasim laughed, leaning against the wall. "A little." He was more at ease than Rhys had ever seen him at work, loose-limbed and relaxed. It suited him. "I'm glad you came."

"Me too." Rhys stepped into one shoe, then the other, and pulled the laces over. He glanced towards the living room. "They won't mind if I leave without saying goodbye?"

Qasim laughed again. "They'll be jealous. You saw what your welcome was like. Usually, leaving is exactly the same. You get special dispensation since I told them they scared the seven hells out of you."

"You didn't!" Rhys exclaimed in indignation.

Qasim's grin was radiant. "No." He slid his hand over the console by the front door. "But you should have seen your face."

Rhys gave him a reproving glare. "Sometimes, you're a little bit evil."

"Coming from you? I'll take it as a compliment." Qasim stepped out onto the porch with him. The night had turned cooler, and Rhys was close enough to see goosebumps rise along Qasim's bare forearms. His breath misted on the air. "Should be a nice night for you driving home."

"Yeah." Rhys fiddled with the fastening of his coat, not quite sure how to say goodbye. He glanced up at Qasim. "Let's say I didn't run away from your family. What kind of farewell are we talking? I mean, I'd hate to ruin a tradition or anything."

Qasim shrugged. "Pretty much the same as before." He took Rhys's shoulders and leaned down and kissed him on each cheek, right, then left, and...

And Rhys totally forgot that, inside, they had kissed him three times. He started to nod and Qasim was already moving for the third kiss on the right cheek and halfway there, their lips met.

Chapter Nineteen

QASIM'S MIND WENT blank.

It didn't happen often.

But then, he didn't end up kissing his supervisor often.

He recoiled, eyes wide. He could still taste the sweetness of baklava from Rhys's lips. Rhys was staring at him, and his tongue darted out along his lower lip. Qasim's attention was immediately drawn to his mouth again, soft and pink and inviting. He forced his gaze to Rhys's eyes.

They're darker. His eyes are darker.

"Qasim—" Rhys began. His face was red and his voice caught.

Qasim's hands were still on Rhys's shoulders. *Should have lifted them away. Should have broken the connection. Kept at a distance. Not touching. Definitely not being completely stupid and drawing him closer.*

"Try again," he said, and his voice hitched. "Have—have to do it properly."

One kiss to the right. One to the left. Another to the right, and Rhys's breath was warm against his ear and his heart was drumming and he didn't know which one of them tilted their head first, which one of them moved slightly, enough...

It was sweeter, pastry and honey and rose water still dusting their lips. Rhys's tongue darted against his, and Qasim couldn't stop himself from burying his hands in Rhys's curls. They were so soft, like heavy silk, and Rhys's hands were at his waist.

He was drowning in it, a warm body against his for the first time in so long, hands on him, lips on his, breath against breath, hearts pounding.

But...

But, but, but...

He jerked back again, forcing his hands from Rhys's hair, forcing himself back, back, back. Bad idea. Such a bad idea.

"Sorry!" He retreated a step. "Sorry." He half waved, then darted into the house, slapping his hand on the console to close the door because—hey! How better to totally ruin a lovely night than by kissing your semi-boss—

who had just split up with his boyfriend—and then slamming a door in his face?

He sank to sit against the bottom of the door, propping his elbows on his upraised knees, and pressed his face into his palms.

"Idiot," he whispered under his breath.

So what if Rhys was funny and sarcastic and had the loveliest eyes and the wickedest smile? It was stupid because he was practically Qasim's boss, which was a multitude of levels of messed up. And then there was his break-up.

Qasim knocked his head against the door once, twice, three times.

Too many thoughts were swarming and none of them good.

Oh, of course, great start, Qasim, great start. Not just snogging your boss but snogging your boss who is probably rebounding from a long-term relationship, and wow, it would be so healthy. And just throw yourself at him, on your parents' doorstep no less. Class act, there. Couldn't just go and find some stranger in a pub. Had to go and get attached to someone you shouldn't, you moron.

Stranger in a pub would have been so much easier, but no. No, no, no. It never worked. Tried it and all bad. Needed those little connections, those smiles, someone who would play chess and be funny and everything else Qasim liked in a person and never realising he was falling little by little, until he—like a complete muppet—snogged them on his doorstep.

And at Ramadan as well!

He knocked his head against the door again.

"Mum!"

His eyes flew open at Youssef's voice.

He hadn't noticed the living room door open or the kids piling into the hall. He scrambled to his feet, trying to force on a smile. "There you are. I was beginning to think you'd forgotten me." He opened his arms and received a cascade of hugs but didn't miss Youssef watching him or the way the boy sidled up to his mother.

Qasim turned his attention to the kids, because it was easier to distract himself with little hands tugging at his and hugs and making promises and keeping secrets.

As shoes were donned and farewells were made, Qasim glanced out of the door. Rhys's pod was gone. Of course it was. What kind of man would hang around after he'd had the door slammed in his face? And how was he going to explain it? *Oh, I'm sorry I'm a little bit stupid and did something idiotic, and then reacted like I'm brain-dead.*

As excuses went, it was rubbish. Rhys probably wouldn't want to work with him again, and things would be awkward if they were assigned the same mission, and it would mess everything up and they'd been getting along so well, and he'd gone and made a cock-up of it because Rhys had pretty eyes and was...was...

He jolted when someone touched his shoulder and turned to find Aisha, his eldest sister and Youssef's mother, beside him. She slipped her arm through his, her bracelets clacking against his forearm.

"Ismail's taking the kids home," she said, "but I'm helping Ummi clear up, and then we could have a game."

He knocked his shoulder against hers gratefully. Of all of his sisters, she was the one who knew him best. She was the one who had pushed his parents to find Dr. Bailey.

By the time everyone had left, it was already well past ten o'clock. Qasim and Aisha bid their mother and grandmother goodnight, then retreated into the deserted living room. It felt so much bigger now it was empty. Qasim sank onto the couch.

Aisha sat cross-legged, facing him, and opened out her folio. Of all the family, she was the only one who could match him. They'd learned to play together all those years ago. Even on the morning of her wedding, when he was hyperventilating in his bedroom, terrified she would be gone and never come back, she found the time to sit with him in all her wedding finery and play a game.

"Which side?"

He touched the whites, and she smiled. He couldn't remember when they had started the tradition, but they often played when things were filling his head, overwhelming him. White meant he would—could—talk. Black...black was less good.

They were seven moves in before he spoke.

"I messed things up with Rhys."

"Oh?"

He took one of her pawns. "I...we...I kissed him. At the door."

Aisha took a sharp breath. Enough for him to know he had surprised her. "A man again?"

Qasim nodded. The last time, it had been Erika, an exchange student at his university. She was Danish. Brilliant. Not afraid to tease him mercilessly. Three months of friendship and then attraction hit him like a steamroller. Then she went home to Denmark and it wasn't the same.

The time before that had been Murad. The...difficult time. It was when Qasim stumbled out of the closet to his family. There were a few who tried to push him back in. Mercifully, most of his family stood by him. Murad hadn't been so lucky.

His sister moved her bishop. "He seems like a good man."

Qasim hesitated before moving a rook. "I shouldn't have. He's my...well, he's sort of one of my bosses." He shook his head. "Shouldn't have done it."

Aisha claimed one of his knights. "One question, did he kiss you back?"

Qasim blinked at the board. He'd had moves in mind, but they were all gone, and her question was ringing in his head like a gong. Hadn't even thought of it before. Too busy expecting the worst.

He lifted his hand, tracing his fingertips along his lower lip.

Rhys...

Rhys had kissed him back. They had both kissed each other.

"Oh," he said softly.

"Mm." Aisha's eyes crinkled when she smiled. "You should take it into consideration. It's kind of relevant."

It definitely pushed away some of the thoughts. Still, it couldn't squash the loudest ones: *he's your boss, it'll make things weird at work, he's rebounding from his boyfriend, he only did it because you started it, he was lonely, and you took advantage.*

He forced himself to focus on the board. The pieces had to move. He had to work out where to go next.

Aisha reached over the board and smoothed his rumpled hair as he stared at the squares. "You're adorable, you know." He raised his eyes to her. "Don't need to act so shocked. I can give you a compliment once in a while."

He made a face at her. "Some warning might be nice."

She laughed. "I'm serious. I think he must have noticed too."

Qasim snorted. "Yeah, right."

"Kiddo." She cupped his cheek in her hand. "I saw you two talking and the way you were laughing together. He was looking at you exactly the same way you were looking at him." She patted his cheek. "I just didn't realise why."

He poked at the board, moving his knight. "It's not a good idea."

She smiled fondly. "When is it ever?"

They subsided into silence as the game continued. There were still thoughts crowding in on him, but he put all his focus on the game. They had a running tally of the number of times they'd beaten each other over a dozen years. She was ahead of him, and the last thing he wanted was to give her another victory.

"Oh no..."

Qasim raised his eyes from the board. There were three possible moves she could make and inevitably, all of them would lead to checkmate. "Your move."

She made a face and then batted over the projection of the king. "Not bad, kiddo."

He sprawled against the arm of the couch. "Thanks, Aisha."

She tapped the beacon to call for a taxi-pod, and then snapped her screen away and smiled at him. "What are big sisters for?" She unfolded from the couch and extended her arms. "Now come here, give me a hug, then get your bum to bed. You have work in the morning."

He hugged her. "Yes, Ummi."

She cuffed him fondly across the head. "And try to think of our next game, okay? I'll be playing white and my first move will be 2.d4."

He wrinkled his nose as they walked through to the hall. "Not exactly original."

"It was good enough to beat you before. It'll be good enough to beat you again." She leaned in and kissed him on each cheek. "And it won't be a Queen's Gambit or a Dutch Defence."

"Right..." He frowned, thinking about the other opening moves she had used. "Right." He scratched the end of his nose. "You've got until Eid to set a rematch. After Eid, I'm off the grid for a few weeks."

She pulled on her coat and smiled. "I'll check my work schedule and see when Ummi and Abi want me to bring the kids around again."

"All the time," Qasim said at once. "Honestly."

"I'll check." She laughed and gave his shoulder a warm squeeze. "Now go and get some sleep, all right? And remember our game."

She knew how much it helped as a distraction, and he was grateful.

He switched the lights off and made his way up the stairs. Ummi had left his light on for him, so he made it without injury, and he sat on his bed. His folio, lying on the bedside table, was blinking. Messages received. He hesitated and then picked it up.

Despite knowing it would probably undo all Aisha's work, he opened out the screen. Two senders: Tahmila and Rhys. He chewed his lip and touched Tahmila's. It was the safer option.

How'd it go? Did they scare him?

He picked at his nails, staring at the message, and sent a reply before he could change his mind: *Went well up until we kissed and I freaked out and slammed the door in his face.* He didn't know what he expected her to say, but she replied in seconds.

About time. Not the door slamming. The rest of it.

Qasim blinked at it in confusion. *What do you mean?*

She sent a tiny icon of a cackling face. *Really? You were mooning over him when you were high as a kite. I was wondering how long it would take your conscious brain to catch up.*

I was?

Don't tell me you hadn't noticed the flirting either?

Qasim stared at the screen.

A moment later, Tahmila added: *How many times has he implied getting naked with you? I mean, come on. Really.*

Qasim started to protest, but his brain helpfully reminded him about Rhys's jokes about his secret identity and the allusions to strip chess.

Did I flirt back?

Tahmila sent a laughing emoticon. *Slightly. Go and have...fun dreams, lover boy.*

He rolled his eyes and tapped to the next sender.

There were a dozen messages from Rhys. They were halting, awkward, mostly filled with apologies and attempted explanations.

The final, most recent one was a video.

Qasim hesitated and then opened it.

Rhys was sitting in front of a couch in a dimly lit room. He was a mess. His curls were sticking in all directions as if he'd been running his fingers through them. His vest was gone. The top buttons of his shirt were undone. He didn't even seem to realise the video was on.

"Right," he finally said, frowning into the camera. He held up a half-full glass. "Liquid courage. Gets the words out." He examined the glass. "Not good with the words." He took another drink then removed his glasses and rubbed at his eyes. "I like you." He gave his drink a reproachful look, then leaned out of shot and returned with a bottle of Scotch. "The thing is..." He poured himself another measure of whisky and sighed. "The thing..."

He rolled his head and stared at the ceiling for a moment, then peered into the camera. "You're so kind, Qasim. I mean, you have no idea. You didn't need to be kind to me. Didn't ask you to."

His eyes were bright, and Qasim was shocked to hear a tremor in his voice. Rhys always seemed so contained even when he was unhappy.

Rhys knocked back the finger of whisky, and then rubbed at his brow with his knuckle. "I didn't...it wasn't about Marc...or any of my bullshit." He wasn't looking at the camera now, and he seemed older, tired, and a little sad.

"You were kind," he said again, so softly it was barely audible, "and sweet and...and you invited me into your home. All because I wasn't happy." He shook his head as if he couldn't understand, and Qasim pressed his fingers to his mouth, his own eyes stinging. "I'm sorry if I ruined everything but when I—when we—" He rubbed at his eyes again. "You—I like you. A lot. I know it's bad timing. I know." He laughed, brittle and sharp. "Don't even know if you— whether you're—"

He set aside his glass and gazed at the camera. "You make me feel all right, you know. Even if we're just friends. You make things feel...better." He smiled faintly. "So. Yeah. If—if you don't mind me being a silly arse, I'd still like to play chess with you. Got more biscuits and everything." He rubbed the end of his nose with his fist and exhaled noisily. "Yeah."

He leaned forward and switched off the video link.

Qasim stared at the blank screen, then shut down his folio.

It was a complication. Not just a little one either.

He propped his elbows on his thighs, pressing his fists against his mouth. He'd kissed Rhys. He had done it. He hadn't been pushed or forced or coerced. He'd started it, even though it had ended badly last time with Murad.

It was different this time round. This time, he wasn't a frightened, confused teenager. Ha. No. This time he wasn't a frightened teenager. Confused, yes. So confused. He rocked back and forth, staring at nothing.

It was the worst time of year for it as well; the holiest of months wasn't the time to realise your bisexuality might actually still be unexpectedly alive and kicking.

Ramadan had to be his priority. Stupid brain and body chemistry could wait.

He tipped onto his side on his bed, uncurling one fist to chew on his thumbnail. It was better not to think about it. Not even the sweetness of the syrup, so sticky on Rhys's lips. No. Better not to think about it at all.

Chapter Twenty

LIFE WAS A bit of a mixed bag for Rhys.

Three days short of a month, the report was finally finished. Jacob was running the last checks, which meant Rhys had completed the last day of historian-sitting. He was already assigned a new mission—Europe, sixteenth century—with confirmation he was to be supervisor.

Those were all good things.

It didn't balance out the epic cock-up he'd made at Qasim's house. It had been a lovely night. The whole family was so welcoming, and then he'd gone and put his mouth where he shouldn't have. More than once as well. Okay, Qasim had kissed him back, but then, he'd also run away.

Rhys knew Qasim was a practising Muslim. Yes, there were going to be queer Muslims, but it didn't mean they were going to kiss a Welshman on their doorstep. Or kiss a man at all, if the expression on Qasim's face was anything to go by.

Written apologies felt stilted and awkward, so he'd only added to the cock-up—no, bad choice of words—the...confusion by getting hammered and apparently sending a drunk video to Qasim. He'd been far too embarrassed to watch it and had no idea what he'd said. Whatever it was, it wasn't enough to bridge the divide between them.

It wasn't as if they weren't getting along. They were. They would talk and even laugh sometimes, but Rhys could see the careful, self-conscious edge to it now, as if they were both watching what they were saying and doing. He knew *he* was, in case he tripped and fell and landed on Qasim's mouth again.

The trouble was...well, the trouble was he really wanted to trip and fall and land on Qasim's mouth again. Qasim was good. He was kind and generous and sweet and funny and tidy as well.

Friendship would be enough, but attraction was impossible to switch off.

At least, he thought wryly, he had plenty to distract him: the break-up with Marc and the division of their possessions, putting his flat on the market, balancing his budget all over again. It was almost enough to stop him noticing how often Qasim tended to lick his lower lip or glance at him through his lashes.

It was the best kind of torture when they met, giving him the eye while very carefully keeping him at arm's length. It had become a routine as well. When it was raining, they would entertain Pisi for an hour; if it was dry out, they'd meet at the Last Glance after Qasim's noon prayers.

On that particular day, Qasim was already at the bench when Rhys arrived. He was occupied with braiding thin strands of colourful thread into ornate bands. He'd been doing it for the past few days since the weather had started to warm up and he could take his hands out his pockets. He said they were for his nieces, but Rhys guessed they helped distract him from the hunger of the fast.

"Any details about the target yet?"

Rhys shook his head. "This one is a bit of a mysterious one."

Qasim glanced at him. "Could be going for royals. They like to keep those ones quiet."

"Mm." Rhys nodded. He glanced up at the sky. It was grey and overcast, but the rain wasn't due for a couple of hours. "They've told me I need to be in lockdown with my team as well."

"Seriously?"

It was unusual by all jump standards. Agents were in prep lockdown for quarantine reasons, but supervisors were generally allowed to come and go. However, their communication was always monitored, and they worked under the unspoken warning that since they were the only people who left the base, any leaks to the public or press would be attributed to them.

"They don't want to take any chances." He tilted his head towards Qasim. "We might end up stuck on the same floor in H-block."

Qasim's tongue darted out, pale pink against his lips. "Oh. Okay."

Rhys looked back at the sky. Going into prep lockdown for a month or more was bad enough but being in an enclosed space with the man he had a crush on and nowhere to go sounded like a recipe for disaster. Spending an hour with Qasim here and there was bearable, but to be around him all the time?

"I can ask Jacob to make sure we don't get in the way of each other," he offered.

"What?" Qasim sounded genuinely bewildered. "You—would you prefer to stay away from me in there?"

Rhys folded his hands together in his lap, watching the shadows stretching between his fingers. "It might be easier for both of us. I mean, you'll have prep to do, and I've got my agents."

"Oh." Qasim had stopped braiding. "Right. Yeah." He gave a barely audible sigh, then asked, "All the time?"

"Qas—" Rhys began.

Qasim shook his head. "I mean, I'm not saying we'd need to spend all the time together or anything, but..." He hesitated and eyed Rhys, uncertain. "I like to spend time with you. It's— You make things fun." His smile was careful. "Some fun in lockdown might help."

Rhys wanted to insist it was a bad idea—that the more time he spent around Qasim, the more time he wanted to spend with him. He should insist, but Qasim seemed half-hopeful, half-worried.

"Some fun wouldn't hurt," he agreed and, without thinking, squeezed Qasim's knee. Both of them froze, staring at Rhys's hand, and Rhys withdrew it as if he had been burned. "Shit. Sorry. Sorry."

Qasim licked his lower lip again and fixed his eyes on the braided band he was working on. "It's okay."

"Is it?" Rhys couldn't be sure. Before, they would casually knock elbows and prod each other, but now, he was treating Qasim as if he were a fragile piece of glass which might shatter on contact.

Qasim was silent for a few seconds, frowning at the braid in his lap. He tied off the loose threads and then slid a little closer on the bench. "Give me your arm."

"What?"

Qasim beckoned with his free hand. "Your arm." Rhys held out his arm. Qasim looped the braided bracelet around his wrist and knotted it. Qasim met his eyes as his fingertips brushed the inside of Rhys's wrist, sending his pulse racing. "You can touch me, Rhys. I won't break."

It was a pleasant thought, but Rhys lifted his hand free, making a show of examining the bracelet. Anything to keep Qasim's fingers from running against his wrist. He touched the band, smoothing it against his skin. "What's this for?"

Qasim smiled. "Because we're friends. At least, the girls say they're friendship bracelets. Or something." He ducked his head, shrugging. "It's ridiculous."

Rhys suspected he was smiling like a moron. "I like it, I do." He turned his wrist as the sun played on the rainbow band. He met Qasim's eyes.

"Thanks." He laughed ruefully. "I've lost a lot of stuff this month. Getting something new is nice."

"The break-up?" Qasim winced. "I bet it's all rubbish."

Rhys fingered the braid as he gazed at the man who'd made it. A little bright spot making all the crap easier to deal with. "It's not great. I'm going to ask about using an H-block room as a layover now the flat's on the market."

Qasim nodded. "Until you go into lockdown?"

Rhys nodded.

Putting the flat up for sale hurt, but not as much as he had expected. It had been home since he joined the TRI. It was safe and comfortable, but it also came with all of the memories of Marc, both good and bad. It was their first place together. Rhys had bought it, but Marc's salary had supported him. There was relief and grief in seeing the paperwork, a definite line drawn under everything they'd had.

"D'you have somewhere to put your things?"

Rhys blinked. "What?"

Qasim nodded towards H-block. "I don't think the rooms in there are made to store furniture."

"Oh. Right." Rhys rubbed his brow. "Shit. I didn't even think."

"Well, you *have* been working so hard for the past few weeks," Qasim said innocently, but was fighting down a smirk. "I mean, it's not like you were sitting on your backside, doing nothing but watch boring historians."

Rhys stifled a chuckle. Moments like this reminded him why he was willing to hang around like a love-struck idiot: Qasim could make him smile so easily. "You're going the right way to get a kick."

Qasim wrinkled his nose and grinned at him. "I tell you what—I'll give you Uncle Abdullah's details. He does storage for international companies. I'm sure he could find a decently-priced storage unit for you."

"You don't have to—"

"I know." Qasim reached over and patted his hand. "Friends. It's what we do."

It was such a simple statement, but, Christ, it had been so long since anyone had been so kind without wanting anything in return. Rhys turned his hand to—appropriately—squeeze Qasim's fingers. He then released them. "Thank you."

Qasim brushed his thumb along his fingers where Rhys had touched him. He chewed on his lip as he gathered up his box of threads and scrambled to his feet. "I should get back. Tahmila's determined to make me understand sentence structure."

"A fool's errand," Rhys called after him, twisting on the bench to watch as Qasim started towards the building.

Qasim spun around. "I'll tell her you said so!"

Rhys remained where he was for a few minutes more. He ran his finger along the braided bracelet again.

Was he reading too much into it? It was a personal thing, a bracelet like this. And Qasim had touched him without flinching and told him they could touch. It was a good thing, wasn't it? Maybe there was still some chance? But if there wasn't, his friendship with Qasim had shaken things up anyway. It had been a while since he'd fancied anyone, and now this.

It was only a matter of time before it started affecting his work.

He got up from the bench and headed towards the main building. There was one person he could always go to about his problems, who could be trusted to be discreet about them.

For once, Jacob was alone in his office when Rhys entered. The projections on his screen and dotted around the walls were all too familiar.

"Just finishing the final checks," Jacob said, rubbing at his brow with the knuckle of his thumb. "Give me two minutes."

Rhys nodded and sat on the opposite side of the desk.

A few minutes later, Jacob finished whatever he'd been reading and shut the report down. "Something bothering you?"

"Ha." Rhys folded his fingers and pressed his thumbs together. "Where to start."

"Shit." Jacob shifted in his seat. "That sounds ominous."

Rhys glanced up at him. "I'm selling my flat. It's on the market now, and the estate agent seems to think it'll go pretty quick."

Jacob raised his eyebrows. "I didn't know you and Marc had any plans to move."

Rhys smiled tightly. "Marc's out of the picture. Just me. I need something new." He took a quick breath before Jacob could try to offer sympathies. "If it sells, I might be in this...lockdown mess with my new mission. I need somewhere to stay to get it cleared out so if it goes while I'm in lockdown, I don't have to worry about it."

Jacob was watching him with a little too much concern. "You want off the mission? You barely take enough of your holidays as it is. A break-up and moving house is a pretty good reason for taking a week or two."

Rhys shook his head. "I need to be doing something. I already started packing things up. I just..." He rubbed at the end of his nose with his fist. "I don't want to be there anymore. Can I take a room in H-block until it's done with? Until I find somewhere new?"

"Of course," Jacob murmured. "Whatever's easiest for you. We can get one of the suites assigned instead of just a basic room, if it's going to be for a few weeks."

"Basic'll be fine," Rhys demurred. "I'll be switching into lockdown in ten days anyway." He hesitated, then asked, "Do you know why the lockdown?"

Jacob shook his head. He didn't seem too pleased about it. "This one is coming in sealed from on high. I asked O'Donohue why. He looked like he'd sucked a lemon and said it was a special request." He shrugged. "Given the period, it could be anything."

"Qasim guessed royal encounters or something."

"Could be," Jacob agreed. "Something significant anyway. Or something we're being paid a lot for with extra secrecy." He half smiled. "You said you wanted something to distract you. I think this'll be the perfect thing."

Rhys cleared his throat. "There's something else."

"Jesus." Jacob laughed in disbelief. "Years you've been here, and nothing comes up, and now, everything at once?"

"Like buses," Rhys agreed. He rubbed at his left palm with his right thumb. "You know I've been keeping Qasim company."

Jacob nodded. "It definitely helped when he was in quarantine."

Rhys pressed his thumbnail into his palm. He'd always hated talking about personal stuff, especially at work, but this was where his personal and professional lives were colliding. Jacob was the best person to talk to about it. After all, his partner worked in the TRI as well.

"It's...there have been...developments."

Jacob's chair squeaked. Rhys reluctantly raised his eyes from his hand. Jacob was in full boss stance, one elbow on one arm of the chair, chin propped on his knuckles. The other hand was tapping on the other arm of the chair. "Developments?"

Rhys cleared his throat again. "I—there—" God, he hated talking about it. "I like him."

"Ah."

Jacob was like that. No intonation at all to give away what he was thinking.

Rhys folded his hands together again. "I thought you should know, since we'll be going into lockdown at the same time."

"And is this a mutual thing?"

Rhys hesitated and then shook his head. "I don't think so, but he's a friend. That's all."

Jacob ran a hand over his beard, watching him. "You don't think you're going to do something stupid?"

"No." Rhys toyed with the bracelet with his thumb. "But it doesn't mean you can stop yourself from getting distracted by someone you fancy."

One side of Jacob's mouth turned up. "You have no idea how right you are." He straightened up in his chair. "Is it going to be a problem?"

Rhys drew the bracelet round again, the knot catching on his nail. "I don't know." He shrugged. "I'm a bit out of practise with this fancying-people thing. Thought you should know, in case it gets awkward in there. In case..."

"In case you need a work-related intervention?"

Rhys shook his head. "I don't even know. I don't know if it's just that or if it's everything else and all. It's been a weird couple of months."

Jacob nodded. "I'll keep an eye on things." He studied Rhys. "You sure you're okay? It's a hell of a lot to be happening all at once."

Rhys pushed his curls from his forehead. "It's strange, but it feels normal." He shrugged. "I got used to handling a lot of shit when I was small. Keeps me from turning into a broody mess, doesn't it?"

"It's one way of looking at it." Jacob touched a control on his desk, opening the door. "I'll see you in the pre-brief tomorrow when we pick the tech team. All the techs are fighting to get out of this one. There aren't many who want to be stuck in lockdown as well."

"And they say temporal agents get worked up over nothing." Rhys snorted. "See you tomorrow."

By the time he got to the lift, he was feeling better. It made a difference to have someone watching his back and making sure he wouldn't make things worse.

Chapter Twenty-One

QASIM WASN'T USED to having an audience.

Aisha hadn't been able to find time between their last game and Eid for their rematch. She'd apologised, but he realised too late it was a ruse. She was smiling far too widely when she presented him with his Eid gift after she and her family arrived at the house after the morning prayers.

The gorgeous midnight-blue shirt wasn't a surprise. The brand-new traditional chess set sculpted in cream and black marble was.

Once everyone had eaten their fill, the dining tables cleared away, and the children occupied with their toys and games, Aisha dragged one of the coffee tables over in front of Qasim. "Rise and shine."

He cracked open one eye, wanting nothing more than to lapse completely into his food coma. "It's post-food nap time."

She grinned at him. "Nice try. You owe me a game." She tapped the tabletop. "Bring it."

"Ummi!" Qasim turned imploringly to his parents. His father was talking to Nasreen, Qasim's second sister, while his mother appeared to be drowsing, her head on her husband's shoulder. "Ummi, Aisha's bullying me."

His mother smiled sleepily. "Play nicely with your sister, Qasim. It is not a day for fighting."

Aisha smirked at him as he pulled out the new board. He made a face at her and turned his attention to his new possession. The board was hinged to create a beautifully lined box for his new pieces. It was varnished and polished to a lustre. Each piece clicked as he set it on the board. He turned one of them over.

"They aren't anything like the usual ones."

"Historic pieces for the history boy," she replied. "Elephants and viziers and soldiers, oh my."

The pieces were different shapes, but the game was played the same. Within half a dozen moves, several of their nieces and nephews had gathered to watch. By the time eight pieces were taken, Youssef was running a commentary for the people on the far side of the room.

"No pressure." Aisha grinned across the board at him.

Qasim rubbed at his forehead, examining the pieces again. There was something familiar about the gambit she was playing, but he couldn't put his finger on it. Aisha was smiling like a cat. She'd always been good at bluffing, and he could never read her, which he considered unfair.

"You should throw the horse-thing at the king," Rocky declared. "It would knock him down."

"That's not how chess works, stupid." Ranim snorted. "You can't just throw, can you, Qasim?"

"No," Qasim agreed, scanning her pieces. "No throwing." He moved his fortress forward, into the line of Aisha's elephant. It was an obvious trap, but he hoped she wouldn't notice the second and third traps beneath it.

She raised her eyebrows, laughing. "Really?"

She deftly dodged trap one and trap two, but he had to fight down a grin when she walked straight into trap three. Or so he thought, because it turned out she'd set her own traps, and all at once, he was an elephant short. "Wait—"

Aisha leaned back smugly on her stool, spreading her hands, as her children hooted triumphantly and hugged her.

"She hasn't won yet!" Hassan said. "It's only check. It's not checkmate!"

Qasim's heart was racing but in the good way. He loved a challenge, and Aisha wasn't one to pull her punches. They both knew whoever lost here, in front of the whole family, would hear about it every time they crossed paths until the next year.

He leaned forward, staring at the board, his elbows propped on his knees.

Distantly, he heard the doorbell ring. It was probably some of the second or third cousins from across town. It always took them a while to make the journey after prayers. He didn't even bother to glance up as he considered his options.

"This is an unexpected surprise," he heard his father say. "Come in, please. You're welcome."

"I don't need to come in." The voice was so familiar Qasim's head snapped around in response. "I just wanted to drop by a present for your family."

Rhys.

His heart leapt. Every day since that night—and the kiss—they'd seen each other at the same time. Every one of those days, Qasim had kept his hands occupied, tucked in his pockets or braiding strands of coloured thread or petting the cat. He'd been so good, so restrained for the whole month.

Day in, day out, he'd tried to keep his focus on the holy month. He prayed, he fasted, and he absolutely and definitely didn't kiss the smiling blond with the sugar-stained lips. Sometimes a thought slipped in, but it was just a thought, and he had been so strict with himself.

And now, Rhys was here, as if he could tell Qasim wanted to see him.

Before Qasim could even get off the couch, his father had not only talked Rhys out of his shoes, but into the living room. Rhys smiled sheepishly around the room, wielding a brightly wrapped parcel like a shield. "Um...*Eid Mubarak.*"

Qasim started to get up as a cascade of family members descended on Rhys to welcome him.

"Our game's been rained off, eh?" Aisha murmured, shooting Qasim a smile. "Did you know he would be coming?"

Qasim shook his head. He had a feeling he was grinning like an idiot as he wove around the cluster of nieces and nephews to reach the other man. He leaned down and kissed Rhys warmly on his cheeks, trying not to think about the last time he'd done it, trying to resist the impulse to do the same again. "You should have said you'd be coming."

Rhys smiled crookedly at him. "I didn't plan on coming in." He held out the parcel. "I wanted to thank you and your family for your hospitality the other day, and today was the one day I knew you'd all be here."

Qasim started laughing. "And now, you're trapped." He gave the box a careful shake. "Is it safe for the kids to open?"

"If you don't mind them getting even more sugar?"

Qasim shot daggers at his sister, then handed the box down to little Qasim, her youngest, who squealed in excitement, pulling at the paper. Ranim and Zeinah immediately joined him.

Rhys smiled at Qasim. "I should head off for now. I just wanted to wish you a happy holiday."

"Aw, that's cute," Malika, Qasim's third sister, sighed. "He thinks he gets to walk out without having tea."

"Really, I don't need anything," Rhys said. "I—"

"Would be very rude if you didn't stay for at least one glass," Qasim muttered out of the corner of his mouth. "You're going to have to throw yourself on the sword, unless you want them to think you're an uncivilised heathen." He was desperately fighting a grin. "I thought you English people knew the importance of tea."

Rhys sniffed haughtily. "I'm Welsh, I am."

Qasim grinned at him. "Then we'll have to teach you proper Englishlamic tea etiquette."

Rhys gave him a warning look. "One glass, right?"

"Mm. Yeah. Of course." He steered Rhys over to the couch. "That's how it works. Just one."

Rhys subsided onto the couch. "I'm not going to be leaving in less than an hour, am I?"

Qasim couldn't resist squeezing his knee as he sat beside him. "Now you're getting it." He smiled as his mother bustled through from the kitchen with fresh glasses of tea for them. "Thanks, Ummi."

To his surprise and pleasure, Rhys thanked her in Arabic. Oddly accented Arabic, but it made Ummi's face light up. She beamed at Rhys and gently pinched his cheek.

"He is a good one, this one," she said in Arabic to Qasim. "I like him."

Rhys kept nodding politely until she bustled away again, and then leaned towards Qasim. "I said it right, then?"

"You did." He knocked Rhys's elbow with his. "I'm glad you came."

Rhys shrugged, as if he wasn't smiling as widely as Qasim. His gift was wide open, and handfuls of sweets were being passed around the room. "I wanted to thank you again for the other night."

"Did I hear you right?" Aisha approached, carrying a plate of *ka'ak*. "You wanted to thank us for throwing you in the deep end?"

"Best way to learn to swim." He sounded confident, but Qasim could see the nerves. He was being polite, but he was minding himself as well. "You're...Aisha, aren't you?"

She offered the plate like a reward. "Well remembered."

Rhys snagged one of the cookies. "I might need to ask you for some chess tips. It's embarrassing how easily this one keeps wiping the floor with me."

Aisha smirked at Qasim, and he made a face at her. "Oh, it would be my pleasure. You should reset the board, Qasim. I'll be back, and we can give him a lesson."

Qasim shook his head as she walked away. "This isn't fair." He started resetting the pieces on the board.

"I didn't realise those were chess pieces." Rhys leaned forward.

"Old-fashioned Persian one, yeah." Qasim offered him one of the elephants. "Viziers instead of queens, elephants and horses instead of knights and bishops. They all do the same thing, though." He couldn't stop himself elbowing Rhys. "Like you getting checkmated."

Rhys laughed. "I think I'll be able to take you one of these days, *cariad*." He blinked as soon as he'd said it, as if it was a slip of the tongue.

Qasim frowned in confusion. "Car-what?"

Rhys self-consciously ran his fingers through his hair. "It's Welsh. Don't worry about it."

"No fair," Qasim said in mock-indignation. "Can't call me a name, then not tell me what you said."

Rhys turned over the elephant in his hand. Qasim fought back a smile when he noticed his bracelet still tied around Rhys's wrist.

"Sweetheart," Rhys finally said, his voice barely above a whisper.

"What?"

Rhys glanced nervously at him. "*Cariad*. It means sweetheart."

Qasim's heart skipped a beat, and for a moment, he forgot how to breathe. He stared at Rhys. He'd told himself he would make a decision once Ramadan was over, and now it was, and now Rhys was sitting beside him, being nice to his family and calling him pet names and...

"Abee!" Qasim froze at the sound of his mother's voice from the hall. She sounded startled, and if it was indeed her father at the door, he wasn't surprised. He scanned the room urgently for Aisha, who'd gone pale. She must have heard it too.

Of all the timing...

"What is it?" Rhys asked quietly. "What's wrong?"

Qasim felt sick to his stomach. "My grandfather just arrived."

Rhys must have seen something in Qasim's expression, felt the sudden tension in the room. "Do you want me to get out of the way? If this is a family thing, I can make myself scarce."

Qasim wanted to say no. He wanted to grab Rhys's hand, keep him there as a reassuring presence, but he nodded. It wasn't fair to drag Rhys into their family problems.

"Please," he whispered. "Please. It would... It's better you're not here."

Rhys nodded at once, and Qasim couldn't have been more grateful he didn't ask what was happening. He drained his cup of tea and rose. "I should probably get to work." He declared it loudly, even though Qasim—and every one of the adults in the room—knew it wasn't the reason. "I'm sorry I can't stay."

"Maybe another day." Qasim rose too, and he felt a sudden swoop of nausea. They would cross paths in the hall, Rhys and his grandfather.

Rhys reached up to pat his shoulder and met his eyes. "Definitely."

Good manners would mean seeing him out, but Qasim felt rooted to the spot. He could only stand and watch as Rhys left and twitched when someone touched his shoulder. Aisha. She'd moved to his side without him even noticing.

"You okay?"

He shook his head. Every year it was the same. It was Eid. It was the time when you had those awkward encounters with family members you avoided all the rest of the year. He glanced towards the patio doors behind the dining table and back at Aisha.

She squeezed his shoulder. "I'll make your excuses."

He couldn't have been more grateful when the kids cleared a path for him. The same old story every year, and they knew enough not to ask him why he always made himself scarce. Zeinah trotted after him.

"I can come with you," she said, reaching up to take his hand.

He shook his head, crouching down to face her. "I'm just going to get some fresh air. You should go and give Jedu a hug when he comes in." He forced a smile. "He'll be happy to see how big you are now." He drew his hand from hers and gave her a gentle nudge. "Go on."

As soon as she stepped away, he slid the patio door open and slipped out. It was a cool morning, still crisp and bright, and he sank onto the steps that led down to the lawn.

If he were lucky, his grandfather wouldn't stay long. He rarely did, not since he'd left the family home ten years ago in a storm of rage and blood. Somehow, he had found out about Murad. Qasim rubbed his thumb along his lower lip. There was no mark now, but it didn't mean he didn't remember the pain when his grandfather had struck him.

Qasim had never seen his mother get angry before that day, and from everyones' reactions, neither had his grandfather. Qasim had knelt, numb and bloody and blank, as they raged at each other. In the end, his grandfather ordered her to make a choice: her father or her son. She didn't even say it. She just sat beside Qasim and took his hand. And then, his grandmother sat on his other side glaring at her husband in quiet defiance, and Qasim had knelt there, tears rolling down his face, as he fractured his family.

It was the day Jedu had left the house, but Eid...Eid was when families were meant to gather, and his grandfather was nothing if not a pious Muslim.

Qasim folded his arms on his knees. The muffled voices carried through the glass-paned door. His sisters would try to persuade his grandfather to see him, and he knew how it would go. It was easier to take himself out of the equation and wait quietly until he was gone. Ummi would never ask it of him, not when she was the one who had cleaned the blood from his face.

Minutes ticked by, and eventually, he heard the door slide open behind him.

"Thought you might need this." His father sat next to him and offered him a mug of tea.

Qasim took it gratefully, wrapping his hands around it. "Thanks, Abi."

"They're seeing him off now."

Qasim nodded, sipping the tea. It was sweeter than usual. Ummi's touch, there. Extra honey.

His father was silent for a few minutes, then quietly said, "This is your home. Not his. You don't need to leave when he comes."

Qasim gave his father a crooked smile. "We both know it's easier. He'd make a fuss if I was in there too." He blew the steam on his cup and took another careful sip. "Ummi has enough to worry about without everything kicking off again."

His father patted his shoulder. "You're a good son, but sometimes, you need to be selfish too." He used Qasim's shoulder to push himself to his feet. He'd always seemed so invulnerable, but now Qasim could see the signs of age starting to creep in. "Come back in."

Qasim nodded. "I'll finish my tea first, Abi. Tell Aisha to get the board ready."

His father ruffled his hair. "Of course."

Qasim gazed out over the garden, the mug warm between his hands, his father's words echoing in his ears: sometimes, you need to be selfish too.

Chapter Twenty-Two

THERE WAS SOMETHING comforting about petting a cat.

Rhys didn't know how long he'd been sitting in Pisi's enclosure, but it was long enough to drive away the worst thoughts. The cat was a purring puddle in his lap as he combed his fingers through her fur over and over.

What had happened at Qasim's house had been far too familiar. He'd recognised the change in the air the second it happened. He wished he hadn't, but it was instinct. That kind of tension got under your skin. Once you knew it, you never forgot it. All it took was one person, one word, one action.

As much as he hated to admit it, he'd run away. Yeah, Qasim had agreed it would be better for him to leave, but he couldn't deny every hair on his body was on end, and he'd needed to get the fuck out.

He'd crossed paths with Qasim's grandfather in the hall. The man didn't seem like someone who could turn the mood of a house, but you could never tell. He must have been in his eighties, not much taller than Rhys, bony and gaunt.

Qasim's mother was there, trembling with suppressed emotion, so Rhys had made sure to set himself between her and the old man when he said goodbye and thanked her for her hospitality. She had clasped his hands and nodded and walked him to the door herself.

It felt wrong, such an oppressive, anxious mood in a family so warm and welcoming, but then, every family had one: the one person who could be guaranteed to ruin any occasion simply by showing up. He remembered being in Qasim's place, sitting on a couch, rigid and dreading what was coming. A different time. A different place. Different circumstances.

He gently rubbed between Pisi's ears. "Why are people arses?" The cat apparently didn't like having her ears rubbed and turned her head to nip at him. "Right, right!" He lifted his hand away. "Message received."

Pisi settled down and nuzzled her chin along his knee.

Rhys leaned against the wall of the enclosure and sighed. He felt sick. The hot, unpleasant nausea in the middle of his gut. He had no reason for it. It was so frustrating. It wasn't his issue. It wasn't his family showing up and bringing him grief. Not this time. The memories it stirred were enough.

He was still sitting there half an hour later when a notification rang through the speakers: the lower levels were about to be locked down.

"Sounds like date night is over, Pisi," he said, scooping the cat up in his arms and setting her down in her basket on the shelves. As he made his way to the gate, she sat like an Egyptian statue, her tail curled around her paws. "I'll wander by tomorrow."

In ten minutes, he was out of the lower levels and headed across the courtyard to H-block. The room Jacob had arranged for him was one of the bigger ones with a living room and its own small kitchenette. Before tonight, he hadn't expected to cook. The canteen was good enough for food and a chat with anyone else who was around. Now...now, he wanted to sit quietly in his room with no one bothering him.

By the time he'd warmed up a pan of soup, it was dark out. He sat at the table by the window, opening his screen to return to the miserable task of house hunting. He had a second screen glowing beside the first, a reminder of his budget.

It was depressing.

It wasn't as if the TRI paid poorly. For the calibre of people they hired and the jobs they did, they needed to pay well to guarantee quality. The trouble was he had too many financial commitments already. Too much money going out without ever passing through his hands.

Rhys propped his elbow on the table, resting his forehead against his fingertips as he skimmed through all the decent-sized flats he couldn't afford and the shoeboxes he could.

His bowl was still half-full and stone-cold when there was a buzz from the door.

Rhys turned in his seat, surprised. H-block didn't tend to be very social. It was usually only the haunt of workaholics and people stranded by transport links.

He shut down the screens of his folio, then went over and touched the monitor by the door. His heartbeat picked up at the sight of Qasim, wrapped up in a coat. The door slid aside, and Rhys knew he should have done the normal, human thing and said hello, but instead, he said, "What are you doing here?"

Qasim held up a couple of bags. "Since you missed out on food."

Rhys stared at him for a second too long, then remembered his manners and motioned Qasim in. His heart was racing again. The last thing he'd said before Qasim's grandfather showed up flashed into his mind: sweetheart. And Qasim hadn't replied. But if he was showing up at his place, it had to be a good sign, didn't it?

"I didn't think I'd see you tonight."

Qasim ducked his head, a small smile on his lips. "I guessed as much." He kicked his shoes off, carried the bags over to the kitchenette, and started to unpack them. There were at least half a dozen boxes, including a transparent one stuffed with baklava and cakes.

Rhys shut the door and walked towards him, pleased but puzzled. "I thought you'd still... Isn't this..." He frowned, shaking his head. "I thought this was a time for you to be celebrating with your loved ones."

Qasim glanced at him. "Who says I'm not?"

Some of the tension knotting up Rhys's insides melted away. "Yeah?"

Qasim's ears were going pink, and he smiled down at the box he was holding. "Mm." He raised his eyes to Rhys. There were shadows under his eyes, but he seemed more relaxed than he'd been the last time Rhys saw him. "Have you eaten already?"

Rhys glanced at his half-full bowl of cold soup. "Not very well."

"Good, good." Qasim beamed. "I brought enough for both of us." He searched around the tiny kitchenette for somewhere to set things down and shook his head. "This is rubbish." He sifted through the boxes, reading what was scribbled on the lids in Arabic. "Right..." He held out two large boxes to Rhys. "Take these over to the table and open them up. Should be the salad, bread, and falafels."

"Are you trying to make me explode?"

Qasim grinned. "I'm just getting warmed up." He undid his jacket and shucked it off his shoulders. He was wearing a gorgeous collarless dark blue shirt underneath it. Rhys's mouth went dry. Showing up, saying what he was saying, looking so bloody tidy. Please God, he wasn't misinterpreting the signals. Qasim noticed him staring and waved a hand. "Go on. Table. I'll sort the rest out."

Rhys hastily moved everything off the table and started opening the boxes. Each of them was filled to the brim, and Qasim was wedging more boxes into the microwave.

"You know there's only two of us, don't you?"

Qasim glanced back over his shoulder, eyes dancing. "This is how it's done."

Rhys shook his head with a rueful smile. "I'm starting to wonder why there isn't an obesity epidemic in your family."

Qasim snorted. "You lot do the same at Christmas."

"Point." Rhys returned to the kitchenette, gathering cutlery and plates from the shelves. Qasim was humming to himself as he sorted through the other boxes. "You seem happier." He wanted to kick himself for blurting it out. "Than when I left, I mean."

Qasim nodded, though he did frown. "Yeah. I'm sorry you had to see...well...it." He shook his head. "Long story. Lots of drama. Not a lot of fun." He smiled crookedly, but Rhys could hear the brittleness in his voice. "He... Eid is when he visits. It's a bit awkward."

"Felt like mine at Christmas," Rhys confessed.

Qasim winced in sympathy. "Yeah?"

Rhys hesitated. It was always difficult talking about his family, but Qasim deserved to know. "It's why I left." He shifted the plates and cutlery in his hands, watching the metal slide against the china. "I—it was—it felt a bit too close to home." He tried to smile. "Daft, eh?"

Qasim was looking at him as if he was seeing someone new. "You have homophobic arseholes too?"

Rhys carried the plates over to the table and set them down. "No," he finally said. "Funny. He got on at me for everything else, but never that." He didn't have to turn to know Qasim was watching him, and he forced a quick smile. "Family, eh? Can't live with them, can't throw them off a cliff."

"So the police say." Qasim agreed. "But Ummi and Tette—my nan—still kicked him out."

Rhys was surprised. "The tiny raisin-shaped lady?"

Qasim burst out laughing, and Rhys immediately felt better. "Yeah. That's Tette."

Rhys returned to the kitchenette to fetch the glasses. "It's easier to keep them long-distance if you can."

Qasim met his eyes. "Croatia?"

Rhys examined the glasses in his hand and nodded. "For the good of his health," he said, as if he wasn't the one who had suggested it and been such a good son, getting them somewhere warmer to help with his poor old dad's lung.

"Well, tonight, we forget all about those tits and stuff our faces."

"That sounds great," Rhys said fervently.

Qasim pulled open the microwave door and a waft of fragrant steam made Rhys's stomach gurgle. Qasim burst out laughing. "I don't think you're going to have any trouble with the meal, do you?"

Rhys rolled his eyes, but already, he was feeling a hundred times better than he had half an hour before.

It wasn't so much a meal as a proper feast. There were two kinds of meat. There were spicy and nutty grains and rice with noodles scattered through it. Rice rolled up in leaves. Dips. Flatbreads as big as his head. At one point, boxes were stacked on the spare chair because there was no space on the table.

Over it, they talked, and the time flew by. Qasim told him about the more enjoyable parts of his day. Rhys told him about the new trick he was trying to teach Pisi. They both speculated about the nature of Rhys's next mission and whether they would be allowed to chat with each other while they were in lockdown.

"I don't see how they can stop us," Qasim said, refilling his glass with water. "We're going to be closed in. It's not as if any of us can leak information."

"This mission is one of those top-secret ones. Sealed envelopes and everything. Jacob's in a huff because they won't tell him." Rhys examined the dessert box. "Even if they keep us on separate floors, we'll still have access to the closed-circuit server, won't we?"

Qasim's expression brightened. "True. You can tell me where your agents are going."

Rhys raised his eyebrows. "Do I seem like the kind of person to leak top-secret information?"

Qasim clutched a hand to his chest, shocked. "Not even to me?"

Rhys fought back a grin and picked up a sweet, sticky cake. "What do I get in return?"

Qasim studied him speculatively, and Rhys could take a wild guess about his train of thought based on the colour flooding his cheeks. Well, if that was the way of things, he knew how to make it worse.

He met Qasim's eyes and deliberately licked the syrup from the cake off his fingertips.

There was definitely no mistaking the flash of heat in Qasim's eyes or the way he caught his breath. He pushed his chair back and circled around the table. Rhys gazed up at him, heart thumping. Seemed he might have been reading the signals right after all.

"Looking for something?"

Qasim darted his tongue along his lower lip, then leaned down and brushed his lips against Rhys's. There was such caution there, and all Rhys could think was: *slowly, slowly, slowly.* He tilted his head back a little, parting his lips in encouragement, and smiled against Qasim's lips as long, strong fingers cupped his cheek, and Qasim kissed him again.

When Qasim drew away, he searched Rhys's face, his cheeks flushed. Rhys had never seen anyone so hopeful and nervous at the same time.

He rose from the chair and sank his fingers into Qasim's hair, drawing him down to kiss him again. The tension holding Qasim rigid evaporated, and, in a heartbeat, there were arms around him.

Qasim was the one who broke the kiss again, breathing hard. Not enough practise, Rhys thought, amused, brushing his thumb along the younger man's cheek. Enthusiasm in spades, but apparently, he'd forgotten how to breathe in the middle.

"Relax," Rhys murmured, leaning up to kiss him lightly. Qasim tried to claim his mouth again, but Rhys drew away, shaking his head. "I'm not going to have you pass out on me because you ran out of air."

Qasim wrinkled his nose and stuck out his tongue. "I want to kiss you."

Rhys drank in his flushed face, his shining eyes, and his lovely finger-tangled black hair. "And I want to do a hell of a lot more than that." He slid his hand down from the nape of Qasim's neck, curling a fingertip under Qasim's collar, brushing his skin. A full-body tremor ran through the other man. "How about you?"

"I—" Qasim nodded, his breath escaping in a gust. Through the fine fabric of his shirt, Rhys could feel how fast his heart was beating. He laughed suddenly. "I—it's—I haven't. Before, I mean. There was...I had a-a friend. Murad. But..." He shook his head.

That was enough to give Rhys pause. And then something Qasim had said hit him: homophobic arseholes. Christ, Qasim had already come out to him, and he hadn't noticed. No wonder he'd frozen when his grandad showed up, and Rhys was still there. "Ah."

Qasim licked his lips nervously. "Yeah. Wasn't the best family dinner I ever had when they found out."

"I bet," Rhys said softly. "Jesus. I can only imagine how hard it was."

Qasim tried to smile. "It's in my *fitra*. I didn't make myself this way. Told them as much."

"But they didn't see it that way?"

"*He* didn't." Qasim shrugged. "My faith and my sins are between me and Allah." He curled his fingers against Rhys's back. "I'm trying to be a good man and a good Muslim. If it's wrong to act out of love—" He hesitated, catching himself.

It was as if Qasim had yanked the rug out from under him. "Act out of love?"

Qasim delicately pushed a curl of Rhys's hair from his brow. "Why do you think I came?" He smiled self-consciously. "Sorry. Got all serious on you there."

Rhys's world had been given a shake. "There's nothing to be sorry for." He stepped back far enough to give them both a little breathing space and took Qasim's hands in his. "It's...we..." He stumbled on his words, not sure what he could or wanted to say. It had only been a couple of months. It was far too fast. But...

But whenever he saw Qasim, his heart lifted. The man could make him smile without even trying. He was kind and good, and every time Rhys thought about him, it made him happier than he'd been in months. When Qasim had arrived at his door, after the day of bad memories and misery, his presence and company washed everything else away.

He stared up at Qasim.

"Oh," he said faintly.

Qasim's brow creased in worry. "What's wrong?"

Rhys took a deeper breath and laughed faintly. "I'm an idiot, I am." He looked back up at Qasim, feeling peeled naked. It was too soon to say anything, too soon to be sure, especially so soon after Marc. "How about we give it a try? Us, I mean. See how we go?"

Qasim smiled, and for a moment, it took Rhys's breath away. "Officially?"

Rhys couldn't help smiling in return. "Yeah." He lifted Qasim's hands up between their bodies. "Will you, Qasim El-Fahkri, walk out with me?"

Qasim burst out laughing. "Bit old-fashioned, isn't it?"

Rhys tried to keep a straight face. "I'm a traditionalist."

"Go on, then." Qasim's smile faltered a little. "About the...other stuff, though... I—it's—I know it's also old-fashioned, but I was kind of saving myself."

Rhys squeezed his hands. "No hurry. We take our time. See how you feel as we go."

Relief lit Qasim's face. "Yeah. Yeah, sounds good to me." He curled his fingers against Rhys's, and the heat was still in his eyes. "But the kissing...can we do some more?"

Rhys swallowed hard. It was going to be the mother of all exercises in restraint, especially after almost two months without a proper shag. It didn't help when Qasim was all flustered and rumpled and eager and then saying he was waiting. "If you want."

Qasim's mouth was on his in a heartbeat, and Rhys's breath caught when Qasim nibbled on his lower lip and then sucked on it. He pulled back, raising his eyebrows.

"Said I wasn't experienced." Qasim met Rhys's eyes, his own glinting. "Didn't say I was completely useless."

"I'm not convinced you're not trying to kill me." Rhys caught him by the hip. "First the food, now the most kissable virgin?" He shook his head. "If I survive the night, I think I should get a medal."

To Rhys's delight, Qasim started laughing. "You could kick me out."

Rhys pointedly stared him up and down in the very nice and fitted shirt and the trousers which left just enough to the imagination and those mussed waves of hair falling forward over his dark eyes.

"I could," he agreed, "but it'd be rude, especially when you came all this way." He rubbed his thumb along his chin. "What could we do, d'you think? Don't want to get you too excited. Want to play a game?"

Qasim's eyes shone. "You know I wouldn't say no."

Rhys couldn't help the slow grin. "We never did have our high-stakes game, did we?"

He wasn't surprised when Qasim blushed to the roots of his hair. "Are you trying to get me naked?"

Rhys let his gaze drift again. "I have no clue where you get these ideas."

"The fact you're a dirty great pervert?" Qasim was grinning too. "Your folio?"

Minutes later, they were sitting on either side of the coffee table, the board projected on the surface. It started like any other game, but Qasim was quicker than usual. When he took the first of Rhys's pawns, he also took a sharp, excited breath.

Rhys slowly and deliberately removed his watch.

"Cheating." Qasim snorted.

"I could do worse."

"Ha! Don't think flirting will distract me."

Rhys smiled. "What if I told you what I would do with you, if I had you in my bed?" Qasim looked up from the board warily, and Rhys propped his elbows on the table and cupped his chin in his hands. "Distracting?"

"Uh. No. Not something anyone tried."

Rhys knew how people saw him. He'd learned to use it years ago. Big eyes and an innocent face but a mind seven levels below the gutter and falling. Combining the two was enough to throw anyone off their game. And in strip-chess? Well, it was practically the rules.

He pulled his glasses down his nose, gazing over the top of them. "I'd want to put my mouth on you." Qasim was trying his best to keep his attention on the game. "All over. Anywhere I liked. Anywhere you wanted."

"Th-that's nice."

Rhys leaned forward to move another pawn. "Or fingers. Either. Both." He sighed and kept his voice a low murmur. "Find all the ways to make you squirm and shiver and..."

"And...?" Qasim sounded a little breathless.

Rhys smiled up at him and knocked one of his castles aside. "Pay and display."

Qasim frowned, blinking in surprise. "One time," he said, fumbling with the buttons of his shirt. "You managed it once. You won't again."

Rhys pressed his tongue to the back of his teeth to keep from saying anything as Qasim opened the front of his shirt and slid it off his shoulders. Jesus Christ, he was just as beautiful as Rhys had expected, lean and lithe with a scattering of dark hair across his chest and forearms. And there was the scar, curving down across his ribs. Qasim self-consciously moved an arm to cover it.

"Don't worry about it," Rhys said, lifting his eyes to Qasim's. "I know how you got it. It's nothing to be ashamed of." He nodded at the board. "I think it's your move."

Qasim rested one arm on the edge of the table. Closer now, Rhys admired the light and shadows playing across the lines and hollows of Qasim's chest.

"You were saying," Qasim said, shaking him from his sightseeing.

"About how I would make you squirm, wasn't it?" Rhys rubbed the nail of his thumb against his lower lip, and when he caught Qasim looking, he flicked his tongue out over the ball of his thumb. "Mm. I get the feeling you would try and keep it quiet, wouldn't you? Biting your lip to messes, especially if I sucked you off, eh?" Qasim's breath hitched. "I would as well.

And you'd watch me, and you'd have your fingers in my hair and I wouldn't let up until you said my name so we'd both know who was making you come."

Qasim's eyes were wide as saucers. "I—uh—"

Rhys ducked his head in mock shyness and sucked on the tip of his thumb. Qasim swallowed hard, and Rhys tilted his head, blatantly peeking down at the front of Qasim's trousers. His misbehaviour was definitely having the desired effect. Gaze now locked on Qasim's, he slid his whole thumb into his mouth.

Qasim's left hand curled against the edge of the table. "That's cheating," he said hoarsely.

Rhys withdrew his thumb and stared at it in feigned shock. "Really?" He bit his lip and widened his eyes innocently. "Having trouble concentrating?"

Qasim cleared his throat and forced his attention to the game. His fingers were still white-tipped on the table as he reached out with his right hand and nudged a bishop across three squares.

Rhys clicked his tongue and took an undefended pawn. "Oh dear."

Qasim shook his head, staring at the pieces as if they had betrayed him. "But—I didn't—you—"

Rhys tugged at the front of his shirt. "You know the rules. Socks off."

A blush had been lingering around Qasim's ears since the game started and now spread, flushing across his face and chest. "I don't— I'm not wearing any socks."

Rhys smiled like a cat. "Well, this is turning out to be a short game, isn't it?" Qasim was so flustered Rhys had to smile. "Let's make this fair, eh?" He undid the top couple of buttons of his shirt, then pulled the whole lot over his head and threw it aside. He'd never be as tidy as Qasim, but he didn't mind. The world was made up of all shapes and sizes, and in his case, he was short with a comfortable layer of fat to soften all his edges and a downy blond coat. "How's that?"

Qasim ducked his head, his smile returning. "I think you're making these rules up as you go."

"Maybe, but you've still got your trousers on." Rhys motioned to the spot in front of him. "Let me help."

Qasim only hesitated for a second and then walked around the table to stand in front of Rhys. His hands were shaking, Rhys noticed. Instead of reaching for the buttons, he reached for Qasim's hands, lifting them to his lips.

"If I'm being too much, let me know," he said. "I know I can...get a bit carried away."

Qasim drew one of his hands free and sank his fingers into Rhys's curls, leaned down, and kissed him. It was still cautious, but the fire was definitely there. "It's different," he murmured against Rhys's lips. "I like it."

Rhys darted out his tongue to lap Qasim's lower lip. "Yeah?"

Qasim swallowed and nodded. He brought Rhys's hand to the front of his trousers. "Bit of help?"

The familiar heady rush of desire surged through him as he hooked his fingers over the waistband of Qasim's trousers, pulling him another step closer. Qasim stumbled in surprise, his hand dropping from Rhys's hair to his bare shoulder instead. It was scorchingly hot, and Rhys had to force himself to keep his eyes on Qasim's as he ran his finger inside the waistband of his trousers.

Qasim caught his breath, his fingers digging into the meat of Rhys's shoulder. "Still evil..."

Rhys chuckled, leaning forward to press a kiss to Qasim's belly. "You have no idea." He unfastened the top button of Qasim's trousers with a flick of his fingers, then the second, and raised his eyes to Qasim's face as he moved both hands to Qasim's hips and started dragging his trousers down.

Qasim braced both hands on Rhys's shoulders as he kicked his trousers off, leaving him in nothing but a pair of very snug shorts. "Um."

Rhys stared at the barely hidden eyeful right in front of him. The test in restraint had suddenly become a lot more immediate. His voice was hoarser than he intended as he asked, "You sure you want to go on?"

"Think you'll win by default?" Qasim's voice was unsteady.

Rhys could only nod, distracted by how warm and firm Qasim's hips were against his hands. If he'd thought his words could be distracting, it was nothing compared to a gorgeous, mostly naked man standing right in front of him, blowing every thought out of his head.

"Right." Qasim stepped away. He was still flushed but smiling. "My move?"

Rhys couldn't help admiring how widespread the blush was. Jesus Christ, he was definitely going to need a cold shower. "You've not much left to lose."

Qasim burst out laughing. "It's your turn now."

Rhys moistened his lips as Qasim sat on his side of the table. "Yeah. Mine."

Qasim gazed at him through his lashes. "I think I have an unfair advantage now."

"Yeah?" Rhys hoped he sounded casual. He had a horrible feeling he didn't. He also had a horrible feeling his glasses were going to steam up and give away exactly what he was thinking.

Qasim was smiling like a cat as he leaned down on one forearm. "Yeah." He nodded at Rhys. "You've stopped using your words."

Well, yes, Rhys wanted to say. *The man I fancy is practically naked in front of me, and my head is full things I really, really want to do and words have kind of gone out the window, thanks for asking.*

"I'm concentrating." It wasn't completely a lie.

Qasim covered his mouth with his hand, his body shaking with stifled laughter. "Right." He studied the board, then moved another piece. "Your turn."

Rhys stared at his pieces. It should have been simple, but for some reason, he had completely forgotten how every single piece could move.

'Some reason' propped his chin on his hand. "Problem?"

Rhys glared at the board for a moment longer, then knocked over the King. "Can we just go back to the kissing?"

Qasim laughed, pushing the folio out of the way. "Yes, please."

Chapter Twenty-Three

QASIM ALWAYS TRIED to be a good houseguest.

He'd woken with a start at the muffled beep from his folio in the other room, and it had taken him a moment to get his bearings. A strange bed in a strange room was enough to make his heartbeat pick up, until he remembered where he was and recognised the warm weight of a hand resting on his belly.

He made sure not to disturb Rhys when he slipped out of the bed to go and shower and purify himself for the morning prayers. When he was finished, he tried to tidy up some of the mess left from the night before. It didn't take long.

It was the downside of being an early riser, he thought as he padded through to the bedroom. He'd never been able to get back to sleep after Fajr, but it felt rude to poke his host awake so early.

Rhys was sprawled out on his side just as Qasim had left him. Without his glasses on and relaxed in sleep, he seemed much younger. He had one hand tucked under his head, the other arm flung over the space where Qasim had slept.

Qasim smiled as he shed his fresh set of clothes—brought in case he stayed and put on for salat—and sat on the edge of the bed. Things had changed the night before. There was a side of Rhys he'd only seen hints of, someone who seemed much more vulnerable in spite of all his confidence.

It was why he was willing to stay, no matter how tempting it might be.

Now, even though he wasn't tired, the idea of crawling back into a warm bed was more inviting than it had been in years. He slipped under the sheets and eased his way across the bed, trying not to disturb Rhys.

He was unsuccessful, but only in the best way. Rhys rolled towards him and flung an arm and a leg possessively over him, burying his face in Qasim's neck. His breath was warm against Qasim's skin, and Qasim shivered pleasantly.

"'Lo," Rhys murmured, nuzzling Qasim's jaw.

"You're awake, then?"

Rhys hummed drowsily, draping a thigh across Qasim's hips.

Last night had been fun, but kissing was as far as they'd gone. Rhys had been so careful when he touched him, even though Qasim could tell how readily he would have done more. Once, Rhys's hand strayed a little too low, and Qasim froze like a startled deer.

The evening could have gone one of two ways.

Thankfully, Rhys was as good as his word. He kissed Qasim once more, then yawned and drew back, declaring he was getting tired. It was the food's fault, they'd both agreed. They were too full and drowsy, and it was probably wise to get some sleep. Rhys was the one who'd said it out loud. Qasim hoped Rhys couldn't tell how relieved he was.

It wasn't as if he was scared of sex.

It was...

There was still so much to consider. A man wasn't meant to sleep with anyone but the one he married, for one thing. The fact Qasim was head over heels for another man was an added complication. No. Not a complication. A...different perspective, depending on who was asked.

One thing he was sure of—if he was going to marry anyone, it would be the person he loved, regardless of gender. Whether he had sex with them beforehand, whether he could be sure, whether he could restrain himself...

It didn't help Rhys was half-asleep and rubbing his soft, warm thigh against Qasim's groin with only his shorts as a barrier between them.

Qasim closed his eyes, trying to ignore the heat rushing through him. He should have expected it, crawling back into the bed. Curling up close to someone he wanted was a stupid, stupid idea, but here he was, and he took a sharp breath as Rhys's privates rubbed against his hip.

It was one thing for him not to sleep with Rhys. It was another to expect Rhys to be as celibate as a monk.

Maybe he couldn't take anything more from it all, but he could at least offer a little relief. He could feel the blush spreading across his face as he tentatively eased his hand down between the two of them, his knuckles skimming Rhys's belly. It drew a muffled sound, not quite a giggle, from Rhys, who was still nuzzling at his neck.

Qasim slipped his hand a little lower and hesitated. It had been years since he dared to touch another man. Not since he was a teenager, before everything went wrong, and Murad was sent away to Pakistan. New, but not new. Familiar, but not. His heart was thumping in his ears, and he swallowed hard.

Rhys brushed the tip of his nose against the corner of Qasim's jaw. "Don't have to."

"I know," Qasim whispered back, then curled his fingers around Rhys's shaft. It was something else new—Rhys wasn't circumcised. Curiosity always got the better of Qasim, and what was meant to be sensual, turned exploratory. "Huh."

Rhys rubbed his chin along Qasim's shoulder, pushing his hips against Qasim's hand. "I like turtlenecks, I do."

Qasim snorted. "You're so weird," he murmured as he tightened and shifted his grip when Rhys hardened against his palm. Part of him thrilled at it, but the other part was still there too, thinking of what else they might do, whether it would be wrong, if it might hurt, that he might regret it all...

Rhys's lips brushed the corner of his. "Y'smell nice."

Qasim tilted his head enough to claim a brief kiss. "Showered. For prayers."

"Mm." Rhys smiled at him. He looked mussed and innocent, which was quite a task since he was grinding himself lazily into Qasim's palm. He moved his hand in a circle on Qasim's chest, his eyes still half-closed. "Hand's good for me."

Qasim blinked. "What?"

Rhys slid his hand down to cover Qasim's. "S'good for me. Don't need more." He kissed the corner of Qasim's mouth again. "Got time."

Qasim uncurled two of his fingers to loop around Rhys's. "Yeah?"

"Got totty in my bed." Rhys yawned. He moved his thigh to a less compromising position over Qasim's thigh, which helped a lot. "Got a stiffy and a hand on it. Not a bad way to wake up." He nuzzled his way to Qasim's ear. "I can wait."

Qasim couldn't help laughing weakly. "Hand it is."

It didn't help as much as he'd hoped. Rhys had rubbed against him long enough to rouse him anyway, and Rhys's rapid breaths against his throat, the thrusts against his hand, the slickness, hot and wet against his fingers, was a reminder of it. He bit on his lips, his other hand clenching in the sheet beneath him to keep him from reaching for his throbbing member.

Rhys wrapped his hand around Qasim's briefly, encouraging him to squeeze more firmly, and then slid his hand to spread on Qasim's belly. "Good...yes, *cariad*..." He groaned when his hips stuttered. He pressed his mouth to Qasim's throat, drawing on the skin, and Qasim choked on a gasp—an electric charge shot through him. He must have tightened his hand, because Rhys hissed against his throat and bucked against his fist. Qasim felt the hot spatter on his skin.

His hand was slick too, still moving, and he felt hot and tight and breathless down to his toes. All he had to do was offer—ask—and Rhys could...

With a gasp, he released Rhys and rolled away. "'Scuse me!" He scrambled out of the bed and stumbled to his feet.

Rhys peered up at him short-sightedly. "*Cariad*?"

"I—" Qasim leaned against the wall, trying to steady his breathing. He was hard, and it wasn't just going to go away, not with Rhys right there. "Shower—" He stared around the room to find the door. "I-I'll be back in a minute."

He made his way through to the bathroom as fast as he could and turned on the water. Cold. He winced as he stepped under the spray, and after scrubbing his hands leaned against the tiles as the water sluiced over him. He thought of salat, tried to concentrate on anything but the demanding ache low in his body and the chill seeping into his bones.

Under his breath, he started unsteadily singing a *nasheed* he'd learned at his mother's knee, the words lost in the rushing water. If he concentrated on it, he could push his desire away. The tiles were hard and cold, and he sang.

Little by little, the ache abated, but his teeth were chattering, and he was freezing. He turned up the heat of the water until he stopped shivering, then scrubbed at himself all over, washing away any traces of what they—he—had done.

He stared down at his hand as the bubbles flowed off his skin. Some part of him should have been ashamed for allowing even those touches, but he wasn't. Had he put his own hand to himself, then yes, but not for Rhys, not for giving pleasure to the one he might love.

By the time he was done, a towel wrapped around his waist and another draped around his shoulders like a cloak, he was warm again, and his skin was as wrinkled as an old date.

As soon as he opened the door, he was hit by the scent of fresh coffee. Rhys was in the kitchenette, humming along with music on the radio. He wore a patched dressing gown and was flipping slices of French toast.

Qasim cleared his throat self-consciously.

Rhys smiled over his shoulder, and all Qasim's dread melted away. "Finally. I thought you were trying to dissolve yourself in there." He waved the spatula towards the pan. "Do you like French toast? I was going to do bacon, then I remembered you don't eat anything pig-based, do you?"

"No," Qasim said, relieved. "No, to the bacon, I mean. Yes, to the toast."

"Good, good." He jerked his head towards the table. "There's a pot of coffee and one of tea as well. Help yourself, and I'll bring this over when it's ready."

Qasim nipped into the bedroom to get dressed before heading to the table. Rhys had been busy. It had been wiped down and laid, with mats and cutlery and plates already in place. The condiments were arranged in the middle and were flanked by the pots of tea and coffee.

"I feel like I'm in a restaurant," he said as Rhys carried the pan over.

Rhys smiled at him. "Feel free to tip the waiter." He served up the toast onto their plates and set the pan on the stove. "So"—he sat opposite Qasim—"what do you plan to do with your last day of freedom?"

Qasim picked up his fork. He'd been trying to avoid thinking about it. "Family dinner." He smiled crookedly. "If you think last night was filling, you won't believe how big things get on my last night before a mission. You'd think I was going away for a decade, instead of a few weeks."

Rhys blinked, surprised. "And you still came over to spend time with me? I'm flattered."

Qasim stretched out one leg beneath the table, brushing his ankle against Rhys's. "It might be the last time I see you for a while as well. I wanted to spend some time with you before I go."

Rhys stared at him, colour blooming on his cheeks. "Oh." He examined his plate, cutting into his toast, and Qasim snickered.

"You're blushing."

Rhys gave him a look. "Am not."

"Are." Qasim couldn't help feeling delighted. Rhys was always so calm and cool, but when he got flustered, he forgot about using his quick tongue and even pouted. It was adorable. Qasim leaned forward over the table. "I think you like me."

This time, Rhys snorted. "What gave it away?"

Qasim just laughed, slicing into his toast with the side of his fork. "What about you? When's your lockdown scheduled?"

"Tomorrow as well," Rhys replied, drizzling some tomato sauce onto his toast.

"Any plans?"

Rhys shook his head. "Flat-hunting. Again."

Qasim wrinkled his nose. "No luck so far?"

"Nothing I can afford."

That caught Qasim by surprise. Agents were well paid because of the risks of the job, but he'd assumed the TRI wouldn't be frugal when it came to the rest of the staff. "I didn't think flats were so expensive. If you're selling your old one as well..."

For the first time in ages, Rhys's expression closed down. "Nothing in my budget." There was the same abruptness when Rhys's family was mentioned. It was as if there was a huge gaping hole in front of Qasim, a topic he could risk falling into or one he could safely skirt around.

Better to part on good terms than to push for information Rhys didn't want to give.

He smiled, a little forced. "Something'll come up."

Rhys relaxed at once. "I hope so."

They talked as they ate, about the mission and about what they could do when they were both out of lockdown and quarantine. In the time it took them to get through their breakfast, they had two future dates lined up, one at a fancy Syrian restaurant Qasim's family frequented.

Once they'd cleaned up, Qasim packed up his empty boxes from the previous night and reluctantly glanced towards the door. "I should go. Ummi will want me to be at home to help her prepare for tonight."

Rhys made it easier. "Then you'd better go." He came closer and rose on his toes to kiss him, and Qasim leaned into him, sinking a hand into Rhys's hair. When Rhys had him breathless, he stepped back without warning. Qasim yelped in indignation, and Rhys blinked innocently at him. "Call it a promise of things to come when you get home."

Qasim laughed a little hoarsely. "Evil."

"Of course."

Qasim was still smiling as he set out from H-block to head for home.

It didn't come as a surprise to see an extra pod already at the house when he arrived. Even though there were boxes of leftovers from the day before—a potluck provided by eight families was extensive—his mother and one of his sisters were in the kitchen again.

"Ummi, you know we could just go out for dinner," he called through as he toed off his shoes.

"Ha!" His mother leaned out of the door, indignation all over her face. "You know they don't make your favourites the way I do."

"Of course not," he agreed, wandering in, and kissed the top of her head. "Morning, Aisha."

Aisha was stuffing some vine leaves. "Good night?"

Qasim wished he didn't blush so easily, but it wasn't something he could help. "It was all right."

Her lips twitched, and she motioned to the side of her neck. "My, they have big mosquitos in your work."

Qasim clamped his hand over the ruddy bruise Rhys had left on the side of his throat. "Shut up."

Aisha sniggered. She shuffled sideways to give him some room. "So, are you going to stand there looking pretty, or are you going to help?"

Qasim squeezed her waist in passing as he headed for the sink. This was what he always missed when he went on his missions. "I'll show you how it's done," he said, as he scrubbed his hands. "You might be a bloody good doctor, but your *yalangi* are crap."

Behind him, his mother chuckled at Aisha's indignant exclamation, and he smiled.

Chapter Twenty-Four

BEING IN LOCKDOWN was strange.

Rhys didn't mind it, but some his team weren't thrilled. They didn't think it was necessary, since they wouldn't be going to the past anyway, but the bosses had made their decision.

Some of them were at least showing a bit more sympathy for the agents and the compulsory quarantine now. Once in a blue moon, someone came back with a stomach bug or minor injury—or in Qasim's case, a gaping sword wound. But in Rhys's four years with the TRI, it was the worst he'd seen. It all seemed overkill based on a worst-case scenario.

Still, it wasn't so different from supervising from the outside. He was sitting through the briefings in person instead of by video link. He talked things through with the rest of the team. He reported any problems to Jacob on the secure internal lines.

He could also socialise with Qasim and Tahmila, who were considered discreet enough to be allowed near them. It kind of knocked his farewell to Qasim on its arse, but if it meant time with Qasim, he didn't mind. He could only begin to imagine how stifling quarantine would be for an agent after a mission.

The most surprising thing was the difference between the lockdown wing and the standard sections of H-block.

The rooms were larger and less like a hotel suite and more like a private flat. They could request groceries and cook for themselves if they wanted, or they could eat in a dining room, which was more like a high-class restaurant. There was a quiet room lined with couches and bookshelves like an old-fashioned library. All right, yes, they had to wear the clothes provided for them, and they were assigned blocks in the day when they were confined to either their workroom or quarters, but for a temporary prison, it was the best kind.

"I knew it had to be comfortable," he told Qasim and Tahmila over breakfast in the dining room on the second morning, "but this is ridiculous."

Tahmila grinned at him. "If you're going to put people in confinement for a month and you want them to keep working for you, you have to make it pretty bloody good for them."

Qasim nodded as he buttered toast. "Have you seen the cinema yet?"

Rhys stared at him. "You have a cinema?"

"We." Qasim nodded, smearing jam on the toast. "Cinema. Michelin-star restaurant. Swimming pool. Strip club." It was only when his lips twitched, his eyes dancing, that Rhys realised he was being teased. Qasim's face broke into a grin. "Sucker."

Rhys propped an elbow on the table and cupped his chin in his hand. "You know I would be, given the chance."

Tahmila snorted into her coffee as Qasim blushed scarlet.

"Shut up," Qasim mumbled into his breakfast.

Tahmila held a hand up to his cheek. "Quick! Get me some bread. I could toast it nicely."

Qasim swatted her hand away, but he was fighting down a smile. "You're lucky there's no one else around to hear you being all filthy."

Rhys laughed. "I've had many, many years of protecting my image. I don't slip up so easily." He stirred up his bowl of porridge. "Is there really a cinema?"

"Only a small one," Tahmila said. "A dozen seats and a popcorn machine and the film archive."

"We could go," Qasim suggested, knocking his ankle against Rhys's under the table. "If you want."

It felt like such a normal thing to do in such an unusual situation. "As long as we can sit in the back row."

Qasim rolled his eyes, but he was grinning. "You're such a pervert."

Tahmila sniggered, nudging him in the ribs. "You love it."

Qasim's grin softened to a smile. "It's all right." He shoved his chair out. "D'you want some more coffee?"

Tahmila held up her cup, and he took it, trotting away to the coffee machine. She watched him go, smiling. "I'm glad he figured things out."

"Mm?" Rhys was working through his porridge.

Tahmila glanced at him. "It always takes him a while to work things out, relationship-wise. I'm glad he did this time."

"A compliment?" He scooped up another spoonful of porridge. "Or is this the carrot before the stick?"

She laughed, picking a grape off her plate. "No carrot. No stick. He's my friend, and he's more relaxed and happier than I've seen him in a long time." She met Rhys's eyes. "You watch out for him. It's good enough for me."

Rhys gazed at her. She'd known Qasim a long time. He wasn't sure how long, but at least five years. "He's a good person. He's worth watching out for."

She smiled. "Yeah, he is." She turned as Qasim returned, carrying two fresh cups of coffee. "And here he is, the sexy beast himself."

Qasim made a face at her. "Do you want to drink this coffee or wear it?"

She took one of the cups from him. "Love you too." She unfolded from the chair. "I'm going to do some reading. Meet me in the briefing room?"

Qasim nodded, wrapping his hands around his cup. "Sorry about Mila," he said to Rhys, once she was out of earshot. "She likes to tease me."

Rhys chuckled. "Do you think I mind?" He brushed his calf against Qasim's. "You know I like seeing you blush." He slid his leg a little higher. "When do you fancy going to the cinema?"

Qasim closed his calves on Rhys's. "Tonight? After the briefings and things are out of the way."

Rhys sucked thoughtfully on his spoon. "Gives me plenty of time to make sure no one else tries to join us and interrupt us."

"Rhys—" Qasim began, flushing.

Rhys laughed. "Like clockwork. I was talking about holding hands, you kinky beast." He leaned over the table and touched Qasim's hand. "You know what I said, *cariad*."

Qasim uncurled his fingers to take Rhys's hand. "Yeah." He tongued his lower lip as their fingers twined. "You're being so patient."

"Good things to those who wait," Rhys replied. He squeezed Qasim's fingers. "What kind of arse would I be if I pushed you just to get myself off?"

On the far side of the dining room, the doors opened again, and Qasim pulled his hand away. Rhys couldn't blame him. Even if they were involved, it didn't mean their lives needed to be a soap opera for the confinement crew.

"Tonight?" Qasim said as he got up, cup in hand.

Rhys smiled and nodded. "I'll arrange things."

Members of his own team were drifting in as Qasim hurried away. His agents came over to join him at the table with their breakfast.

"Do you think they'll tell us anything new today?" Dominique asked. She was a tiny brunette woman, smaller than Rhys, and one of their French and Spanish specialists.

"We can live in hope," Rhys replied. "At least we have a destination and a loose time frame now."

"Mm." Alexander grumbled around a mouthful of bacon roll. He was fourteen years older than Dominique and often ended up in the role of her father. There was a resemblance between them, making it a believable cover. "Paris. 1600s. Really narrows it down."

Dominique made a face. "It must be royals. I know it."

"You guess," Alexander countered.

Rhys munched on his porridge as they bickered. He had his own theories, but it was entertaining enough listening to them. They were like chalk and cheese but had been paired together for years. He'd only worked with them once before, but from all he'd heard, they were a good pair to run lead with. The only team he could have preferred for thoroughness and skill were Qasim and Tahmila.

"Have either of you had royalty before?" he inquired once he finished his porridge.

They exchanged looks, and then Dominique nodded with a grin. "Marie Antoinette. They wanted footage of her, up close. It was…challenging. Yes. Challenging is a very good word."

Rhys stared at her. "I didn't hear about anyone going to that era."

"One of the little secrets of lockdown." She shrugged, picking a pastry off her plate. "It was six years ago, so the public will have it soon. Everything was the same as it is now. The envelopes. The secrets." She smiled knowingly. "It is something special."

Alexander rolled his eyes. "They did it with loads of cases in those days."

Dominique nibbled on her pastry. "You will make a bet with me?"

Her partner eyed her suspiciously and shook his head. "Nah. You're all right."

Less than an hour later, the three of them were confined to the briefing room, and the seal was broken on the envelope.

As supervisor, Rhys was the one to read out the details: a three-day monitoring mission in the court of Louis XIV of France. Dominique beamed and spread her arms like a footballer who had just scored the last-minute winner at the World Cup.

"Say it! Who's the smartest person in the room? Who is it?"

Rhys shook his head, laughing. "And you're meant to be mingling with royalty…"

Dominique grinned. "Ah, but I am an actress."

"No flirting with the targets this time," Alexander put in.

She laughed. "I did not flirt with her. She flirted with me." She leaned towards Rhys. "If she had demanded her *droit de seigneur*, I would not have refused."

Rhys opened out the rest of the brief. Compared to Istanbul, it was child's play. The client didn't want any politics but were paying a fortune for two agents to wander about the court and take in as much as they could from clothing to etiquette.

"Sounds like the Marie business again," Alexander said with a sigh. "I'd kill for a chance to sit in on Marat instead of all this frilly royal nonsense."

Dominique snickered. "Don't listen to him. You give him some tights and a wig with powder, and he will prance and wave and enjoy every minute of it."

He sniffed. "Not the point." He turned to Rhys. "Do we have covers sorted out?"

"Analogue ones," Rhys confirmed, breaking off the two separate files attached to the brief. Each of them was sealed individually with 'For Your Eyes Only' stamped in red ink. Rhys shook his head in disbelief. "What is this? His Majesty's Secret Service?"

"We're history spies, Mr. Griffiths." Dominique took her file and struck a dramatic pose. "We move in secret, and no one ever knows we are there." She examined her file. "When is our first session?"

Rhys flicked open the folio he'd been given. The schedule for the next month was logged there. While the TRI still handled confidential work, it was a simple enough thing to gather references: lectures given by historians specialising in the period or contemporary records.

"This afternoon," he replied. "This morning, you need to familiarise yourself with your covers. We have a lecture feed coming in, and they'll sync the relevant texts to your folios."

"And your cover checks?" Alexander inquired.

Rhys shook his head with a frown. Normally a supervisor would have access to the covers as well and test the agents on them, but it was out of his hands. "There are half-hour blocks assigned each night, but someone will be chiming in to do them."

Dominique whistled. "It must be for someone who will pay very well. Fashion, maybe."

"Yeah?" Rhys frowned. "What makes you think so?"

She tapped the side of her nose. "If you wish to create something unique, you don't let anyone know. Fashion...it is a business of secrets. You don't want another designer to learn your secret and steal your idea."

"You've got to be joking," Rhys said in disbelief. "This much effort and expense for a fashion line?"

Dominique nodded. "They will do anything to move ahead of their rivals. It does not hurt our...managers when these people will pay well for this business. A little bonus for them this Christmas, I think." She glanced at Alexander. "Will you stay here or go to your room?"

The other man had already broken the seal on his file. "I think I'll stay here. If I get comfortable, I might not get the work done."

She laughed. "I'll be in my room if you need me." She saluted at Rhys. "Until later, Rhys."

The rest of the day went by briskly enough before the first tutorial.

It was surprisingly interesting, a study of manners and etiquette in the Sun King's court with images and paintings to help. Rhys made notes as the lecturer spoke and scribbled a reminder to check floor plans. Dominique was taking screen-snatches of the clothing in the paintings and examining the hairstyles, while Alexander was making careful notes about the accoutrements the men were carrying.

By the time they were finished, they had flung their notes all over the walls of the room, divided by attire, politics, diet, and etiquette. It was only the first pass. There would be a lot more in the coming days. The agents left to eat, talking animatedly. Rhys remained, examining the notes and removing any duplications. They needed the information to be as clear as possible.

Someone rapped at the side of the door frame several minutes later.

"Yeah?" Rhys didn't turn.

"Favour to ask. If you have time."

Rhys glanced over his shoulder. Qasim was standing in the doorway, one hand clenched by his side. The tightly reined energy, so familiar from previous briefings, was back. Qasim was in mission mode.

"Anything," Rhys said at once.

Qasim exhaled noisily. "Can we cancel the cinema and do some cover work? Mila—she's gone to the pool to clear her head, but I—" He rubbed his knuckles against his brow. "I want to work on it and I work better with someone to bounce ideas off and I don't know how long she's going to be and I hit the references about the guards and—"

Rhys crossed the floor in four steps and reached up to catch Qasim's hands. "Breathe."

Qasim smiled crookedly. "Sorry. I know you're busy."

Rhys shook his head. "It's all right. We'll do your prep. I don't have cover work to do with my pair."

Qasim nodded, squeezing Rhys's hand. "Thank you." He shook his head. "It's not—I just want to prep as much as I can this time. Just in case."

Rhys nodded. Now more than ever, especially after what happened last time. "Whatever you need."

Chapter Twenty-Five

QASIM WAS EATING, sleeping, and breathing fourteenth-century central Asia.

The briefing room walls were scattered with notes. Their research into clothing had been passed on to the prop team for costumes. Maps and plans were constantly rotating on the tables—some of the citadel, some of the surrounding oasis. Occasionally, the tabletop showed fragments of plates or tiles or a sword.

More than once, Qasim had woken in the night from a dream that was far too real. The swords weren't quite the same, but they were close enough for the nightmares.

One night, when sleep was gone and wasn't coming back, he went to the canteen and made himself a mug of cocoa. He then padded along the halls to the quiet room. It was more welcoming and cosier than lying in the dark.

There was plenty to do, and he opened up his folio, projecting as many notes as he could onto a table in front of the couch. There were maps and plans he wanted to study. There were even some images of fragile ancient documents from the period, which had somehow miraculously survived the centuries as well as the casual destructiveness of the Soviet Union.

Most of them related to Timur, which was useful.

The mission was technically recon only, but there was a request for footage of Timur if possible. All historical records confirmed he died of a cold in Otrar. It was the only reason they were being sent to a snow-blasted citadel in the middle of winter: they could guarantee where he'd be, instead of chasing his invasion forces across central Asia.

Qasim was privately relieved it wasn't a fixed directive to get up close and personal. Even if Timur was old and died of a sniffle, he was still a bit of a scary bastard. He wanted to be the Muslim equivalent of Genghis Khan, and by all accounts, he did a good job of it as well as killing a lot of people. Anyone who got an empire named after them wasn't the kind of man you wanted to cross.

He studied another summary as he sipped his cocoa, trying to fight the weariness dragging his eyelids down. His eyes might be tired, but he'd been in this position before, and sleeping wasn't an option.

Behind him, the door opened, and he twisted on the couch.

"Qasim?" Rhys was standing in the doorway, wrapped in a dressing gown.

Qasim gave him a sheepish wave. "You're up late."

"I'm not the only one." Rhys closed the door behind him. "You all right?"

Qasim hesitated. "Trouble sleeping. Thought I'd get some work done since I'm awake." He set his mug down. "What about you?"

Rhys nodded towards the bookshelves. "Fancied reading something old-school. Couldn't get to sleep, so I came to get one."

Qasim had to smile. "Nerves getting to you too?"

Rhys scratched his fingers through his hair. "It feels different, being on this side of things. Is it always like this?"

"Pretty much." Qasim glanced over at Rhys. In three days, he'd be in quarantine, and they wouldn't see each other for a fortnight. "You can stay for a bit, if you want. I mean, it's not as if you'll run and leak my work to everyone."

Rhys met his eyes. There was something in his expression, but Qasim was too tired to put his finger on it. Then Rhys smiled and nodded. "All right. I'll get something to read, and then you can show me what's keeping you up."

Several minutes later, Rhys joined him on the couch.

"Arabic?" he inquired, peering at the projection Qasim was studying.

"Persian," Qasim replied. "Similar style, but not quite the same." He shook his head. "I don't even know why I'm trying to read it. It makes me feel like I'm dyslexic, getting all my letters mixed up."

Rhys reached out and flicked it away. "No more tonight."

"And what am I going to do instead?"

Rhys leaned sideways and rested his head on Qasim's shoulder. "Could play?"

Qasim gazed down at him, so sleepy and cuddly, and smiled. "With you this tired? You'd end up nose down on the board."

Rhys turned to him and stuck out his tongue. He lay his head against Qasim's shoulder again. "When we get out, we get your new set, and I kick your arse from here to kingdom come."

Qasim settled back against the couch with him. "You wish."

"Mm-hm." Rhys nuzzled at Qasim's neck. "I'll take your rook."

"Fortress." Qasim closed his eyes, smiling at the ceiling as Rhys snuggled against him. "That set, it's a fortress."

Rhys snorted against his throat. "Sounds dirty." A warm kiss was pressed just under Qasim's jaw. "Lo, the Welshman took El-Fahkri's fortress, hidden between the twin hills, and breached his defences with a mighty thrust."

Qasim burst out laughing and swatted Rhys on the thigh. "You're a dirty great pervert. What piece are you, then? An undiscovered battering ram?"

Rhys lifted his head and blinked solemnly at him. "In your new set? I'm an elephant."

Qasim couldn't help himself. He glanced down at the front of Rhys's pyjamas. "Yeah. I can see the trunk."

They both dissolved into drowsy laughter.

"I think," Rhys finally said, "that's a sign we both need to hit the sack."

"Mm." Qasim stifled a yawn.

"Y'sound tired," Rhys murmured. He didn't sound even close to awake either.

Qasim forced his eyes wider. "I'm good. Just—trouble sleeping."

"Y'said." Rhys leaned forward and flicked Qasim's folio off. "Nightmares?"

It was embarrassing to admit they'd driven him from his bed. Still, Rhys was watching him with a knowing expression in his eyes, and he couldn't lie.

"Yeah." He rubbed his knuckles against his brow. "I just—I remember what happened last time."

Rhys patted his knee through his pyjamas. "Want to sleep by me?"

Qasim started in surprise. "What?"

"Sleep by me. Sometimes it helps." Rhys smiled. "Call me your own personal teddy bear."

It was the same wave of relief he had when Rhys had distracted him in quarantine and told him he didn't need to rewatch the footage. "Please," he whispered.

"On the condition you tell your super in the morning," Rhys added, stifling a yawn. "I know I'd be cross if my agents didn't tell me."

Qasim nodded, taking Rhys's hand. Rhys led him through the halls towards his room. One of the lamps was on, and the sheets were a rumpled mess, but Qasim couldn't care less as they both slid into the bed.

Rhys curled around him, warm and soft, and nuzzled along the back of Qasim's shoulder. "Better?"

"Yeah." Qasim touched the arm looped around his waist and ran his fingers along the back of Rhys's hand. "Thanks."

Rhys kissed his shoulder. "S'all right."

It surprised him how soon he fell back into sleep. Maybe it was having someone else's warmth close by or knowing that if the nightmares came, he wouldn't wake alone in the darkness.

Mercifully, he slept through the rest of the night until the time for prayers. Rhys's arm was still around him, and he slipped out from beneath it as carefully as he could, then made his way to his own room to purify himself and pray.

It was amazing the difference a decent night's sleep made.

After salat, he headed straight down to the briefing room. He and Tahmila spent the day arguing and sifting through the details, working out a plan for their few days within the city walls. The citadel overlooked the sprawling oasis of villages and settlements, a famous crossing point for travellers on the Silk Road. There would be plenty of places for lodging and plenty to examine for their anonymous client.

He didn't see Rhys during the day, but when night fell, he made his way to Rhys's door, his heart thumping loudly in his ears. To his relief, Rhys didn't even ask why he was there. He just opened the door and let him in.

Unfortunately, it turned out one good night was all he was going to get.

He jolted awake after a couple of hours. It was enough to wake Rhys, who murmured sleepily. Qasim patted his arm, said it was nothing, to go back to sleep. Rhys did. Qasim didn't. His heart was pounding too fast, the flash of the blade still vivid. He stared into the dark, fingers splayed on Rhys's wrist, and tried to even out his breathing.

He must have drifted again, because he woke just as sharply, sitting upright.

"Qasim?" Rhys's voice was muzzy with sleep. "You all right?"

"Yes. Yes," he lied as he scrambled from the bed. "Toilet."

The bathroom was blindingly bright. Qasim sank onto the edge of the bath, and braced his hands on either side of him, trying to calm himself down. It wasn't fair to keep Rhys awake, not when they both had work to do the next day.

There was an alternative, one of those worst-comes-to-worst options. He had a bottle of the tablets Dr. Bailey had prescribed to help him sleep. They worked—knocked him out cold, more accurately—but he had trouble with the after-effects. Tahmila called it a medicinal hangover.

With only two nights left before the mission, the last thing he needed was to be groggy and nauseous. Lack of sleep he could manage. A muffled, doped brain was another story.

He caught a glimpse of his reflection in the mirror. Well, on the plus side, he would definitely look like a weary traveller. He crept out into the bedroom. Across the room, he could hear Rhys's soft snores. As tempting as it was to curl up beside him again and feel safe and warm, it was selfish too.

Qasim slipped into the halls and made his way down to the canteen for a mug of hot milk and honey. The rest of the night was spent on a couch in the quiet room, his folio notes scattered around him.

He was poked awake by Tahmila and winced as he sat up. He couldn't remember lying down, and from the crick in his neck, he must have fallen asleep against the arm of the couch.

"You should have come and woken me," she said reproachfully as he rubbed at the side of his neck.

Qasim shook his head gingerly. "You needed the rest."

"And you didn't?" She sighed, shaking her head. "You're such an idiot."

She wasn't the only one to think so, judging by the expression on Rhys's face when they entered the dining room. Rhys was already working through his breakfast.

"You found him then?"

Tahmila nodded. "Our little workaholic." She pushed Qasim into a vacant seat. "I'll get you something to eat. Try not to fall asleep."

Qasim sheepishly glanced at Rhys. "Sorry."

Rhys took his time buttering a slice of toast. "It was kind of you," he finally said. "Not to wake me, I mean. I wouldn't have minded."

Qasim fidgeted. "I know." It was half the trouble. If he even suggested he was having a hard time, he suspected Rhys would sit up the whole night with him, which wouldn't help anyone in the long run. "I didn't want to disturb you."

Rhys set his toast down. "If it helps you for this mission, it's only one more night."

"And it's going to be him or me," Tahmila said, returning with a plate piled with toast and scrambled eggs. "Choose wisely."

Qasim made a face. "I'm a grown man. I can sleep on my own."

Tahmila and Rhys exchanged glances.

"Maybe we should toss a coin," Rhys suggested.

Qasim rubbed at his forehead. "I don't get a say in this, do I?"

"Not this time," Tahmila replied, slouching into the chair beside him. "I've been getting plenty of rest. I don't mind one broken night before we go. Mr. Griffiths or my good self. Your choice."

It was an easy decision to make. He only had a little time left with Rhys, and Tahmila was the one going on a jump with him. She needed the rest more than the man who would be staying in the present. Qasim glanced at Rhys. "You wouldn't mind?"

"I'd feel better knowing you weren't on your own," Rhys admitted, picking up his mug. He smiled crookedly. "And I'm not going to be able to see you for two weeks after."

"Normally, I'd feel rejected," Tahmila said, "but seeing you two make puppy-eyes at each other makes up for it." Qasim rolled his eyes at Rhys, who was doing a bad job of hiding a smile. "What? You were." She clasped her hands in front of her chest. "Womance isn't dead."

"Shut up," Qasim said, grinning. "You're embarrassing yourself."

She snickered. "Scientifically impossible." She leaned over and snatched one of the pieces of toast from his plate. "Now eat up. We have work to do."

The day went by far too fast. It always happened in the last hours before a mission: there was so much to get done and not nearly enough time to do it all. At least their schedule was in place, and they knew the maps well enough. Out of habit, Qasim still had his folio open as they ate their final meal before heading their separate ways.

"It's not like you're going to take anything else in now," Tahmila pointed out, twisting spaghetti onto her fork.

"You never know," Qasim retorted between mouthfuls of chicken and chips. "Something might stick."

It was the same conversation they had every single time, and it always went the same way. She would tease him and ask him questions, poking at his knowledge. It helped, because when he faltered, she would give him the answers. Teamwork, she reminded him. They were a team.

On any other mission, it would have been enough.

This time was different, though.

After he left her, he retreated to his room. Tahmila's pre-mission treat was a bubble bath. His was a scalding hot shower. Routines were good, but his had been broken, and as he stood under the water, he touched his side. There was no returning to the way things were before.

His scar had healed cleanly, but it was still raised against his fingertips. He traced his shaking hand along the length of it. An inch farther, an inch deeper, and he wouldn't have come back. He wouldn't have seen his family again. He'd never have gotten to know Rhys.

He had to go into the past again, and all he could think of was what if he wasn't as lucky? He pressed his fingers against his scar until it ached. There was no way to reach his family now, not with the mission so close, but Rhys...

His mind was whirling, but one thought was loud and clear: What if he never had a chance to let Rhys know how much he meant to him? They had tonight, which was more than he had left with anyone else. Tonight was as good a time as any.

By the time he finished his evening prayers, pulled on his pyjamas, and headed in the direction of Rhys's room, he had come to a decision. There would be talking and it would all be fine and he would make his intentions clear...

The minute Rhys opened the door, all Qasim's sensible thoughts went out the window. He stepped into the room and leaned down to kiss Rhys, sinking his fingers into the other man's hair. Rhys caught his breath, and then he wrapped his arms around Qasim's waist, pulling him closer.

When they broke apart, Qasim was breathless.

"That—" Rhys darted his tongue along his lower lip. "You sure this is a good idea? You need to get your rest."

Qasim nodded, curling his fingers down Rhys's neck. "I want to." His heart was pounding too fast, and he glanced towards the bedroom. "We could—I wouldn't mind if we—" It was sitting on his tongue, and he couldn't just say it. He swallowed hard. "I want to be with you tonight."

Rhys stared at him. It could only have been a few seconds, but it felt like much longer. Rhys loosened his arms from Qasim's waist and retreated a step. "I don't think it's a good idea."

Qasim recoiled as if he had been slapped. "You want to."

Rhys had his hands bunched in fists by his sides. "That doesn't matter now." He met Qasim's eyes. "You don't have to."

"I know I don't have to." Qasim reached for him again, but Rhys stepped away again.

"Qasim—" Rhys shook his head. "Take a minute. Think. This—it's a big deal."

"Think? What's there to think about?" Qasim pushed one hand through his hair. "I—" His voice shook, but he blurted out, "I love you."

Rhys closed his eyes as if he was in pain. Qasim felt sick down to his stomach. Was it possible he'd misjudged the situation so much? "And that's why you want to do this tonight?"

Qasim nodded uncertainly. "I did—I do."

"No." Rhys shook his head again, his expression creased in distress. "Qasim, I can't. We can't. Not tonight. Jesus, we haven't even officially gone out with each other yet."

Qasim stared at him. It felt like the floor had dropped out from under him. Rhys wanted him. He'd made it clear. Every day of lockdown, they'd been getting to know each other better, and Qasim was more certain of his feelings. On top of everything else, they were going to officially try the couple thing after the mission. But now, Rhys backed off?

"I *want* to," he said. "I know I want to."

Rhys reached out carefully, taking his hands. "I understand, *cariad*."

"Understand?" Qasim shook his head. He pulled one hand free and lifted it to Rhys's face. "What's to understand? I—I want to be with you."

Rhys pressed Qasim's hand to his cheek. "You're scared. You think what happened last time—"

A flash of metal. Blood. Pain.

"Don't." His voice sounded brittle. "It's not about that."

"Isn't it?" Rhys shook his head. "I can't let you do something you'll regret."

Qasim shook his head. "Won't regret it." He leaned down to try to kiss Rhys again, but Rhys moved away again, holding his hands up. It was like a blow. "Don't I get a say in this?" he demanded, his voice cracking. "I want to have this night with you, and now you're telling me I can't?"

Rhys wanted to touch him. Qasim could tell it from the way Rhys turned away, ran his hands through his hair.

"You said—" Rhys's voice was as unsteady as his own. "You said this was something important to you, for your faith. I'm not about to let you throw it away because you're scared, and you think this'll be the last chance you get."

That wasn't what it was about. It wasn't.

Qasim opened his mouth to protest, to tell him he was wrong, to tell him he was being melodramatic and stupid and all he wanted was to have a chance to be with the man he loved before he...

Rhys broke the tense silence. "*I'm* not ready for this."

"Liar." Qasim regretted the word the moment he said it.

Rhys turned sharply, looking up at him. There was something unreadable in his expression, the lines of his face deeper. "I want to fuck you, but I'm not going to do it." He removed his glasses and rubbed at his eyes. "When—if—we sleep together, it's... You said you were waiting for the right person. You don't know if it's me. Not yet. We—I need time to work us out."

"You would've done it before."

Rhys turned his glasses over in his hand. "And you wouldn't have. So, I won't." He smiled unhappily. "One day, we'll meet in the middle."

"But not tonight."

"No. Not tonight."

Qasim tugged at the end of his pyjama top. He wanted to be angry. He'd made up his mind, and he wanted to be angry. But Rhys wasn't wrong. He wasn't wrong, and Qasim felt ashamed of himself. It was pathetic, coming here and throwing himself at Rhys, after everything he'd said before.

"I'm going to go and see Mila," Qasim said abruptly.

"You don't have to." Rhys put his glasses back on. "You—if you want to stay, you can."

Qasim shook his head. "Not tonight." He hurried out before he could do anything else to humiliate himself. In the hallway, once the door was closed, he knocked his forehead against the wall. "Idiot."

His forehead was still tender when he reached Tahmila's room. She opened the door, surprised, and then sighed. "What did you do?"

Qasim rubbed at his brow. "Made a tit out of myself." He tried to smile, but it didn't work so well. "Can I come in?"

She stepped aside to let him into the room. "Tomorrow, you give me details. Tonight, we sleep as much as possible."

He nodded gratefully, padding through to the bedroom. As always, she had her candles lit, and it felt safe and warm. "Mila?"

"Yeah?"

He glanced back at her. "Thanks."

She smiled. "What are friends for?"

Chapter Twenty-Six

QASIM AND TAHMILA were gone.

Rhys had missed them by seconds. It wasn't anyone's fault, Qasim and Tahmila had eaten early and then went for a meeting with their supervisor. And he had last minute checks for his team's departure at noon. By the time the incoming transport notification rang through the building, he didn't have time to get to them.

He had hoped to at least see Qasim at the pickup dock.

The night before hadn't ended well. It wasn't the way he'd wanted to see Qasim off.

At the time, he knew it had been the right thing to do. Qasim was nervous about the jump—frightened, even—and it wasn't any state in which to make big decisions. Especially not when Rhys knew he'd regret it in the morning.

It had been the right thing to do.

Yes, Qasim had been upset, but he had to understand why. Surely, he had to understand Rhys was doing it for his own good.

He made his way through the building. His agents were in their rooms, grubbying themselves up to a historical standard for their scheduled departure in just under four hours.

His technical team had already transferred over to the other building to do system checks. All other teams in residence were restricted to their floors. Rhys felt like the only person in the whole building, and until Dominique and Alexander were ready, he had nothing to do.

He sighed and flicked out the screen of his folio.

A message was bouncing in the corner, sent from someone in lockdown.

Rhys's heart skipped a beat, and he popped it open.

Pawn to D6.

Nothing else, but it was enough and he laughed. Qasim still wanted to play. He pressed his hand to his mouth, shaken by how relieved he was. They were going to be all right, and Qasim still wanted to play. Christ, he wanted to kiss the bastard silly for letting him know.

It was daft how happy it made him. Happier than he'd been in ages. Rhys closed the message and took a breath. Jesus, it really wasn't the best time to realise how attached he'd become.

He went through to the hall and to the window facing the main building. Qasim and Tahmila were scheduled to make their jump in around ninety minutes. Dominique and Alexander's jump was set for exactly two hours later.

Standard protocol was two jumps per day, one late in the morning and another early in the afternoon. The jump and pickup usually took less than half an hour in-house. It meant Qasim would be back in less than two hours, at least by TRI time. On the other side of the gate and centuries earlier, they would have a week before they came home.

Rhys drummed his fingertips on the glass.

Unless he got special permission, he wouldn't be able to contact Qasim in quarantine. Supervisor privilege only went as far as his own agents. If he asked Jacob, it might be all right, but if he had to ask for permission from Qasim's supervisor, he had a snowball's chance in hell. Rhys had worked with her before, and she loved her rules.

He forced himself away from the glass.

The mission had to be completed first. It was the priority. Once all the agents were home and he was out of lockdown, he could worry about talking to Qasim. He got himself a coffee and went to the briefing room to wait.

It was almost an hour before Dominique and Alexander joined him.

The minute the door opened, he could smell them before he saw them. A stale, unwashed odour made him so grateful for regular showers, shampoo, and deodorant.

Dominique saw his expression and grinned, showing faintly yellowed teeth. "We warned you." She did a twirl on the spot. "Am I disgusting enough?"

Her sterile white jumpsuit was a stark contrast to the faint film of oils and grease on her skin and hair.

"I expected worse," he admitted honestly. "I'm guessing higher class than the staff, if you're this clean."

She tapped the side of her nose knowingly. "You'll see in the debrief."

"We'd better hope the costumes fit all right," Alexander said, scratching at his greying hair.

Dominique nodded. "I like to practise in my clothes. We need to know how to move. But with only a little time? It is impossible."

"I thought you were a great actress," Rhys teased with a smile. "Isn't an hour or two in wardrobe enough?"

Alexander chuckled at the indignation on her face. "You asked for it."

They all turned as the speaker buzzed. "Agents Lampard and Rose and Mr. Griffiths to the pickup bay for transfer."

Rhys rose from his chair. "That's us."

They took the lift to the pickup bay. There were two pods waiting for them: one to take the agents down to their prep room in the bunkers and one to get him to the main building.

He shook the agents' hands. "I'll speak to you before you leave, but for now, good luck."

The main entrance of the building was empty when he arrived, which was unusual. Only Jacob was waiting for him.

"We have a five-minute transfer window where the halls are clear," he explained as he led Rhys into one of the lifts to take him to the control room. "I'm the only one you'll meet apart from your team until this is done."

"I feel like I'm in some kind of post-apocalyptic film," Rhys admitted ruefully. "Empty buildings, abandoned halls, no one around."

Jacob chuckled. "Enjoy the peace while you can."

By contrast, the control room was bustling and loud. There was a projection of the gate room on one of the walls. Rhys could see two of the technicians going over all the connections and circuits to make sure everything was functional. Every gate was checked over multiple times before a jump as a precaution.

No Ben this time, he noticed, but it didn't worry him. The mission was a simple surveillance one, which meant a jumping flash wasn't likely to happen. Jacob had assured him; in ten years with the TRI, he said, there'd been three recorded flashes. Two of them back-to-back for the same super was a one in a billion chance.

Another projection showed the layover room. It was the docking point for the internal pod, which transferred agents between the gates, the prep rooms, and quarantine on their return.

"How are we looking?" he asked Tamara. She was one of the longest-term techs, tiny and skinny and covered in tattoos.

"Everything's on schedule," she replied. "They're on the final checks on the gate, and Lampard and Rose are safely in the hands of wardrobe."

Jacob patted Rhys on the shoulder. "I'll leave you to it, Rhys." He paused by the door. "You and your team will stay on restricted access until the debrief is complete. The hall outside, the bathrooms, and the snack suite across the hall are available, but all other doors are sealed."

Rhys snorted. "They must be paying through the nose for this."

"You know I can't comment," Jacob said, then tilted his head in the slightest of nods and winked. "I'll see you in a few hours."

Once he was gone, Rhys sat with Tamara. "Any problems so far?"

She raised a sceptical eyebrow. "You know you don't have to pretend to understand the technical terms every time, don't you?"

"I'm showing willing," Rhys retorted with a laugh. They'd worked together before. The first time he'd asked for details, she'd explained everything, and he guessed his panicked expression suggested his head was about to explode from too much information. "Are the machiney-things making the workiness?"

She snorted loudly. Everyone else in the room turned to gape at them. "Yes," she said as soon as she'd gathered herself. "The machiney-things are making the workiness. No sparky-booms or anything."

Rhys settled to watch the rest of the technical prep going on around him.

This time around, at least, there was no political coup.

Dominique and Alexander were going to be within the grounds of Versailles itself, which meant even less chance of anything going bloodily wrong again unless they managed to annoy the wrong nobleman.

A bell tolled through the speaker system.

"Team one, departing."

Rhys hoped his expression wasn't giving him away.

Any second now, Qasim would be doing his jump, no doubt remembering how badly the last one had gone. Rhys wasn't a religious man, but he could still remember his nan taking him to church and Sunday school and prayers, and a solemn, grey-haired man talking about God's mercy.

"Please let him come home safe," he whispered under his breath.

The lights flickered for a split second, a sign a temporal gate was in use.

Everyone in the room had paused, waiting. Maybe it was superstition. Maybe it was the nervousness of a team about to send their agents on a mission. Whatever it was, no matter how many missions he'd sat in on, they always waited to hear...

"Team one in place."

Rhys exhaled, and the room surged with sound and activity again.

The gate had done its job.

Now, he tried to concentrate on what his techs were doing and ignore the glowing numbers of the clock on the wall. Every minute seemed to take forever.

Another bell tolled.

"Primary rendezvous."

The lights flickered again and another pause.

Rhys's heart was pounding against his ribs. It was stupid. He'd sat through so many missions. He'd seen people go and return so many times. But all he could think of was the blood on Qasim's clothes and the scar on warm, brown skin.

The bell tolled a third time, but no confirmation of collection.

"That's unusual," Tamara said. "Wasn't it Samuels and El-Fahkri?"

A rush of trepidation made Rhys's stomach twist. "Unusual?"

She was frowning. "Those two are always primaries. Even with the flash, I've never seen them hit a secondary."

"Surely, they have at least once," Rhys said, trying to laugh.

Tamara's frowned deepened. "No."

Rhys pressed his knuckles to his lips, sick with dread. If they'd never missed the primary rendezvous point before, something must have gone wrong. Maybe Timur wasn't as sick and weak as everyone believed.

"Jesus," Rhys whispered. He wasn't sure if it was profanity or prayer.

Another five minutes. Another toll of the bell.

No one was even pretending to work anymore.

"Secondary rendezvous."

Another flare of the lights. Another bell. Another silence.

"Fuck," one of the technicians breathed.

It was as if Rhys was sitting a hundred miles away from his own body. He chewed his thumbnail. He stared at the monitor in front of him. There were people talking around him, but he didn't hear or feel or see any of it.

Another bell.

"Tertiary rendezvous."

Lights.

"Please," Rhys whispered against his nail. He tasted blood. "Please, please, please…"

The whole room was silent as a tomb.

Tamara reached out for Rhys's hand, clinging onto him. He held her hand as tightly.

A different bell. A bell Rhys had never heard before.

Others in the room must have recognised it.

One of the techs slumped forward at his station, head in his hands. Tamara released an explosive gasp. She had tears in her eyes.

Rhys didn't want to know. He could guess, but he didn't want to know.

There were others like him, confused, looking at the ones who knew.

"We lost someone," Tamara whispered. "We lost someone."

Chapter Twenty-Seven

QASIM WAS TOO hot.

It was strange when the moat was icy and winds from the north smelled like snow. Tahmila had all the luck, bundled up in her veils and more layers than he had.

He didn't know what he'd expected when they arrived. There were few references about the height and scale of the fortress. The ruins of the city only gave a hint of what lay ahead of them.

It was huge, a citadel on a high plateau.

All things considered, the architecture was modern. When Genghis Khan took issue with a place, he didn't leave much behind. It had been two centuries since he'd razed the city, and the signs of hasty rebuilding and where new walls overlapped the old were clear.

Qasim had been stunned as he walked through the massive clay-brick gates, so much taller than the estimates. *Look around.* That was what they were meant to be doing. *Take everything in: the locals, the different ethnicities visible in the streets, the architecture, the layout.*

The cold was down to the bone.

Furs and fires and clay mugs of warmed goat's milk were meant to stave it off.

Qasim rubbed at his brow. So cold, and yet, he felt dizzy with heat.

"They say the Amir is coming into the city tomorrow," Tahmila said by the light of an oil lamp in the inn where they were sheltering. It was warm and crowded and reeking of horses and dirt and the sweat of dozens of weary travellers.

"Which one?" he asked.

"Timur," she said. His army had set up camp below the city. The man himself was coming in.

A warlord. The ultimate kind of armed soldier. Qasim wanted to say no, but they had a job to do, so they would go.

There were hands on him again. He could swear someone was calling his name.

He had to ignore them. The mission was the thing.

They went out into the city the next morning, half-blinded at first by bright winter sunlight. It had snowed in the night, crunching underfoot, already frozen between the flat flagstones. The bells rang out on the walls, and they joined the crowd milling in the streets to see the Amir.

They were pushed so close—close enough to touch him as Timur rode by. Tall as Qasim, skin leathered by the wind and sun, he was old and grim. His beard, moustache, and thick braids of hair were reddish-grey against his furs. There was metal at his belt, weapons, and his expression was hard. He was exactly what Qasim expected in a man who had criss-crossed the continent and taken it by force.

It should have been terrifying when he turned his gaze to them, in the swarming crowd, but when he coughed wetly and shuddered under his fur-lined cloak, he wasn't a warlord anymore. He was just a man with only a few days left.

Qasim watched him ride on. Only a man, as vulnerable as anyone else.

His guards followed him, pushing the crowd back. Qasim recoiled then, from swords and shouting. Tahmila noticed. She touched his arm, suggested they move away. They wandered, explored, despite the bitter, biting chill.

They weren't the only ones to huddle by the fire at night.

The cold was the trouble.

Some people spoke with them, other travellers with broken Persian and stronger Arabic. A finely dressed trader from the Levant coughed and shivered as Timur had. It was the season for it, the locals said, but spring was coming soon.

On the third day, a snowstorm raged, rattling at the shutters, clattering the bells high in the guard towers. No one dared risk the streets. Qasim and Tahmila huddled together in their alcove in the inn. He was still cold, then, but she was hot. She didn't say anything, but he could feel it when they curled together under the blankets.

"My own hot water bottle," he teased as she squeezed his icy hands.

The fourth night, he started to feel warmer too.

"Qasim? Qasim, can you hear me?"

His head...

It was aching, and he rubbed at his temples.

"We should head out," he said, touching Tahmila's shoulder. "We need to get to the rendezvous today."

She was still curled under the covers. He couldn't really blame her. They'd slept badly. She'd started coughing on the fifth day, and by the nightfall, it had kept them both awake.

"Mila." He pulled the covers off and swore under his breath.

She was pale as ash and even opening her eyes seemed to be a challenge for her.

"Problem," she breathed, and he felt as if his heart had stopped. Her teeth were pink. There was blood on her lips. She stifled another cough, and there was more blood.

"Mila..." He caught her hands, squeezing them. Panic rose. This wasn't meant to happen, but he needed to do something. He had to find help, stop it, make her better. "A doctor. I'll find a doctor."

She didn't even argue. She didn't do anything except sink back down, and he pulled on his hat and ran into the streets. Ran, ran, ran, the cold air sharp, making him cough too. No. No. Couldn't start coughing. He had to find help and get them home and everything would be fine.

Someone shouted his name and he spun around, but there was no one and he ran.

The air cut like blades, and then it felt like it had gone. Everything was warm, and he was warm. So warm. Too warm. He grabbed at his tunic, his robes, his furs. Too warm, stifling him, making him dizzier with the heat.

He found a doctor. Physician. Alchemist with herbs and potions. One of them. All of them? He couldn't remember which now. This was common, the man (men?) said. A local ailment. There were remedies, potions to drink if the cough cleared. They would help, they said. If the cough cleared, and if she drank, she should see Ramadan.

It was the night he'd started coughing too. He wondered if she'd felt the knives in her lungs, the taste of metal in her mouth, and invisible bands around her ribs. She'd never complain. Now, she didn't. Too quiet. Not even teasing him and laughing.

Night fell again, a rendezvous missed, and he knew they had to leave in the morning.

Even though his head was a drum, hollowly beating, and his chest was full of broken glass, they had to. He was warm at least. He was staying warm, and as long as he was warm, he was alive and able to move, even if the ground was rising and falling under his feet.

Tahmila was worse come daybreak. Her lips were cracked and bloody, and she could barely open her eyes, but they had to go. Had to get to the gate. The second rendezvous. Home. Home to medicine and warmth and safety.

Bought a donkey.

Stole.

Borrowed.

Got a donkey.

The pain in his head was unbearable, and he was so damned hot. He wanted to lie on the icy cobbles. He tugged at his robe, his tunic. So thirsty, so hot, coughing and breathless. The city seemed darker than it should have by daylight, looming walls casting deep, sharp shadows.

The donkey's hooves sounded like thunder. *Bam. Bam. Bam.*

Home.

He had to get them home.

Tahmila was swaying on the donkey's back. He walked beside...beside her? In front? Why didn't it seem so clear now? There was him, there was her, there was the donkey, and the city gates gaping like a dark mouth.

Someone screamed as the shadows lengthened.

It sounded like him, and in his throat, sharp and metal.

The world turned bright. Noise and voices, and his blood was boiling in his veins. He wanted to scream, but darkness was suffocating him, and it was a long time until there was quiet.

The stars were out.

Tahmila was cold, but he was still warm. They were wrapped together in a blanket, huddled by a feeble fire. He could see the flickering torches of Otrar, a mile—two—three away. Far from the army on the plain below the city. Alone and quiet. They'd missed the secondary rendezvous. She was cross with him. She was trying to be cross with him. *Leave me.* Over and over, every word frothing with blood. *Leave me. Leave me. Leave me.*

He didn't have the words to tell her no. He couldn't leave her, not alone and cold and scared and-and-and...

It was a beautiful night. No clouds. Stars. A crescent moon.

He told her so, rocking her, trying to stir some heat back into her veins, holding her as tightly as he dared. He told her how bright the stars were. She should look. She really should look. So beautiful.

It was getting colder by the moment, even though he was hot and tight and hurting all over, and the fire crackled and snapped and stretched out long shadows all around. He prayed in broken fragments that tasted like blood, for her, for them, for home.

"We'll be home tomorrow," he whispered, red-lipped and hoarse. "We will."

He lied.

He lied he lied he lied he lied.

Qasim keened as the shadows reached for him again, and the memories were sharp and cut at him and he sobbed and screamed and thrashed.

She was still and pale and cold and dead. Dead dead dead. He woke and she was gone and he hadn't even been awake for her. She'd been alone and he had been sleeping and she was gone and he...

He left her.

He couldn't take her. Couldn't even bury her. No strength. No breath. Nothing left.

He crawled, fingers in dirt, crawling to the rendezvous, the last one. Protocol. To tell them what had happened, where to find her, to bring her home. Pain in his head, lungs burning, blood on his tongue and the light.

Light of the gate. Blinding.

No. No gate.

His eyes flew open.

Hands were on him, holding him. Decon-suits. Faces behind glass. Saying his name. Saying he was safe. Lying. Lying lying lying. He could hear the shrill beeping. His heart. Too loud, too fast and she was gone and she was dead and he had to tell them. He tried to sit up, tried to rise, tried to speak.

His world swam, and he fell back into the dark.

Chapter Twenty-Eight

RHYS WAS ANGRY.

He was worried too, but he was holding onto the anger.

The Board wanted everything to continue as if what had happened with Qasim and Tahmila was a minor problem. There would be no jumps made, but prep would continue, and as soon as the all-clear was given, work would resume.

Despite the fact one of their agents had been lost in time, and the other was currently...

They didn't know what he was.

Sick, according to the official announcement disseminated by O'Donohue. Some infection from the fifteenth century. Alive, but sick was all they'd been told. They didn't say 'stable' or 'under control,' which rang every alarm bell in Rhys. He'd spent enough time in hospitals to know what wasn't being said. His team had returned to H-block, but he'd refused to leave until someone told him what the fuck was going on.

It had been more than twelve hours since Qasim made it back. Since then, Rhys's team had been called into a conference room. A harried Mariam told them their mission was delayed, and they were to go back to H-block. The rest of the team had gone right away. *Shock*, Rhys thought grimly. *Not angry. Not yet.*

The conference room was empty, but still he sat. Stoking the fires of resentment, he kept reminding himself that upstairs didn't care about losing Tahmila, and Qasim's condition was just an inconvenience. Anything to keep from thinking about what was going on in the medical bay.

It was pitch-dark outside.

Another hour ticked by before the door opened.

Rhys wasn't surprised to see Jacob. The man was grey-faced and drawn, bracing his hand against the door frame.

"You should be back in H-block."

Rhys shook his head. "Not until I know what's happening. Is—" The question stuck in his throat. He had to take a breath, swallow hard. "Is he going to be okay?"

Jacob didn't move at once. He stared at a point on the floor, then walked forward and leaned heavily on the back of a chair. "We don't know."

Rhys closed his hands around the arms of his chair, squeezing until it hurt. "But we have modern medicine…"

"And this is something we've never dealt with before." Jacob stared down at his hands and then back at Rhys. "Tahmila didn't miss the gate. She…this illness killed her."

It felt like the world had dropped out from under Rhys. "No."

Jacob nodded without looking at him. "When Qasim was unconscious, the medical team managed to extract his digi-lens. Got us the footage. Tahmila took ill in the middle of the mission. They tried to reach the rendezvous. She—" There was a tremor in Jacob's voice. "He was holding her when she died."

It was as if he was hearing Jacob's words through a tunnel from a long way away. Tahmila dead. If the same thing was affecting Qasim, if she hadn't been able to fight it off when she was so sturdy and strong…

Jacob was still talking in an unsteady monotone. "…through the rest of the footage to see if they can identify a source and maybe point to a cure, but—"

"We use the gates. We get them before they get sick. Before Tahmila…" Rhys took a shaking breath. "If we can't save our own people, what's the fucking point?"

Jacob shook his head as if it weighed him down. "Can't. We don't know—it could be airborne. More contagious. We can't risk any more people."

"So, open a gate right in front of them! Fuck! You know where they were staying! Open it under then when they were asleep! Get them back!"

Jacob lifted a hand—shaking—to run over his face. "Can't. Qas is here. Can't cross your own timeline. It'd kill him faster, and Mila was— We can't find any way. She was too far gone." He shook his head again. "We *can't*."

Can't. Can't save them. Can't help them. Can't care for them.

"His parents." Rhys stared blankly at him. "Qasim's parents. They need to know."

Jacob took a slow breath, his voice strained. "You know the protocol."

Rhys stared at him in disbelief. "*Fuck* the protocol! Fuck them upstairs. If Qasim's…if…" He tightened his grip on the arms of the chair. "If he's dying, they have the right to see him."

Jacob rubbed at his brow. "I know." He pulled the chair out and sank into it. "I asked, given the circumstances. They said they would...consider it overnight, depending on whether his condition improves."

"Given the—" Rhys slammed his hand down on the arm of the chair. Pain shot through his arm, but he didn't care. "Those fucking shits! Qasim's parents have every right! He's their only son—and they might not even get a chance to say goodbye to him?"

Jacob held up a hand. "Rhys. I know."

Rhys shoved the chair out. "I'll go and talk to them."

"Talk to who? Them upstairs? Most of them have gone home for the night." There was a bitter, dark edge to Jacob's voice. "Nothing they can do. Can't just sit around and wait."

"There has to be someone up there!"

"O'Donohue. You really want to go head-to-head with him right now?"

Rhys almost said yes. He almost stormed to the door. Almost. He remembered the last time he'd crossed paths with O'Donohue, how his words got turned on him, how he ended up making things worse.

He turned in a tight circle on the floor, pacing back and forward. Christ, he was so angry, and he wanted to hold on to it. Yelling at O'Donohue would be something, but it wouldn't help, so he had to stay angry. He needed to hold on to it, because if he let go, and the fire and rage snuffed out, he wouldn't be able to keep it together.

"You've got high-security clearance," he said. "You could bring them in."

Jacob rubbed at his eyes. "Not into the med bay. Even if I got them as far as a screen link, Qasim's not in any state to know they're there. I don't know if it wouldn't be crueller to make them watch, knowing they can't do anything."

"Better than nothing. You know how important his family is to him."

Jacob scrutinised him. The lines around his dark eyes were sharper, the shadows beneath them deeper. "Not as well as you."

Rhys paused midpace, his back to Jacob. "No."

"What you said in my office..."

Rhys flinched. He didn't need to be reminded. He needed to be anything but caring and worried and fretful. It wouldn't help. "What about it?"

"Qasim. You care about him."

Rhys stared blankly at his reflection in the night-darkened glass. His hand ached where he'd hit the arm of the chair. He rubbed at his palm. "This isn't about me. This is about his mam and dad." He turned to face Jacob. "They're his world and he's theirs. You can't keep them away from him."

Jacob was pressing his hand to the edge of the table. "You know I'll do what I can. Hell, I'll go and twist O'Donohue's arm if it'll help." He rose. "You need to go back to H-block. Eat something. Rest. You know he'd want you to take care of yourself."

"Rest," Rhys echoed.

"Try, at least." Jacob touched the panel by the door. "They're doing everything they can for him, Rhys. I don't know what else I can tell you."

Rhys nodded, but he could think of a hundred, a thousand things. He silently followed Jacob out into the hall and towards the lift.

"There's a pod waiting to pick you up," Jacob said. "You'll be back in lockdown."

Rhys stared ahead at the door. "No, I won't."

"Rhys—"

"No." Rhys slowly turned to the other man. "I'm not doing any work until I know what's going to happen." He knew—hated—that he had to at least explain something. "If this was Kit, you know you'd be the same."

Jacob gazed at him, concerned, his eyebrows knitting together. "You didn't tell me anything had happened between you."

Rhys shook his head tightly. "No, I didn't." He clasped his hands together in front of him, tightening his grip until it hurt. "My team is ready, but they need someone in charge who can focus on the job. Right now, it isn't me."

For a moment, Jacob said nothing, and then he squeezed Rhys's shoulder. "You know you should have told me. I would've come down sooner if I'd known."

Rhys took a sharp breath. "It's private." His hands were aching. "No one else can know. Qasim was—is still working things out."

As the lift slid to a halt and they both stepped out, Jacob asked quietly, "Do you want some company? They can spare me for a bit."

Rhys shook his head. It wouldn't help to have someone make a fuss of him. If anything, it would make people ask questions. "I'll be all right. I'll..." He glanced towards the doors and the open courtyard beyond. "I want to get to my room." He turned back to Jacob. "Just let me know what's going on. I—don't like not knowing."

Jacob patted his shoulder. "If there's any change, I'll make sure you hear as soon as I do."

Rhys hesitated. "My team? They need to know why I'm not there."

Jacob grimaced. "I'll figure out something to tell them." He nodded to the pod. "Go. Eat. Rest if you can."

The journey to H-block felt like it took ages. For weeks, Rhys had been looking forward to getting out of lockdown, but right now, he would have given anything to be there indefinitely if it meant Qasim and Tahmila would both still be there.

It was late enough that no one was about in the halls. Even the canteen was deserted, but there were always ready meals and plenty of snacks and bread stowed for the night owls. He took one of the meals, some bread, a packet of biscuits, and retreated up to his room.

It took a few minutes for the meal to heat. He set the table. Place for one. Knife and fork all lined up. A glass of water. He ignored how much his hands were shaking as he sat down. He sent a message while he waited. It had to be sent. The words had to be said, even if the top brass didn't listen.

His appetite was in bits, but he made himself eat anyway. It helped. It always had in the past. It warmed him up from the inside, even if he barely tasted anything. He got through half of the food without even looking at his plate. It was enough. For now, anyway.

The next thing was to keep himself busy and his thoughts on the task at hand. There was a time and a place for getting weepy, but not yet. He washed the dishes. The water was so hot it turned his hands pink. He didn't even feel it. He wiped the table, put away the empty boxes for rubbish, and stood in the little kitchenette with nothing else to do.

Habit got him into the bathroom.

He remembered the first time he'd hidden in the bathroom at home. He'd been fourteen then, and his dad was in a bad way. Rhys hadn't done anything wrong, but he hadn't done enough right either. It was enough to set his dad off. His mam had to fetch the oxygen mask, and Rhys still remembered how much her hands were trembling when she tried to calm his dad down enough to put it on. Rhys'd tried to help her as well, but his dad was having none of it.

He'd spent the next hour sitting on the loo. Even from two rooms away, he could hear his dad coughing and wheezing. When it was quieter, his mam tapped on the door and hugged him when he let her in. She'd made all the excuses again—his dad was sick, he didn't mean what he was saying, he was having a bad day, maybe Rhys could try a bit harder not to wind him up. She'd been so tired, so he'd nodded and smiled. He'd kept on nodding and smiling, day in, day out. Anything to make it easier for her.

Two decades gone and another shitty bathroom.

He caught his reflection in the mirror. No surprise that he looked like cack. The lockdown uniform didn't help. He pulled it off, dropping it, and turned on the shower. It wasn't like anyone would interrupt him, not this late, but he turned up the pressure as high as it would go so the rush would drown out any other sound and stepped under the water.

It was almost too hot. He turned his face up into it, letting the water beat down against his eyelids. He pressed his hands against the smooth walls to hold him steady. He wasn't going to let it get to him. Not until he knew how bad it was. He couldn't—wouldn't—give them another person to worry about.

A stifled sound caught in his throat. It wasn't a sob. He couldn't let it be a sob.

The water was drenching him, and he couldn't hold himself up anymore. He sagged down to his knees, his hands sliding down the wall. Little by little, he sank forward, until his forehead was pressing to the tiles too.

And still, the water pounded down.

Chapter Twenty-Nine

SOMETHING WAS BEEPING.

Folio. Salat.

Qasim felt so tired. Head was hurting. Eyes were heavy, like they were glued shut. It took three tries to open them. White ceiling above. Bright lights. A smell, too. Familiar. The lights were blurry.

Medical bay?

A hand on his, covered. Someone saying his name. Echoing.

He tried to turn his head. It made the world swim, and he groaned. More pain in his head. Another hand at his brow.

That was familiar.

Tahmila, by his bed. She always took care of him.

But that—

Wrong.

That was wrong.

He fought to keep his eyes open.

"Don't move, *habibi*." An unexpected voice. Ummi's voice. Shaking. Worried. "Shh, *habibi*. Just rest."

He tried to focus on her. Not right. A spacesuit. Ummi wouldn't wear a spacesuit. He tried to tell her. His mouth was so dry, and words stuck in his throat. She was stroking his hair, over and over.

"Ummi?"

She smiled. Her eyes were shiny. "Yes, *habibi*. I'm here. So is Abi."

Another spaceman behind her. Abi's face. He was paler and thin. A hand squeezed Qasim's. Abi's? He tried to squeeze it back.

It didn't make sense. Ummi and Abi in the med bay? Why would...?

Sick.

He remembered.

Mila was sick.

He—

They—

He remembered.

He remembered her. Cold and still and dead.

He couldn't breathe. He couldn't breathe. Wanted to scream. Cry. His chest hurt, and he was gasping, choking.

Ummi moved. Ummi's arms around him, cradling him. She climbed on the bed, held him as his tears boiled over, burning down his cheeks.

Someone was shouting in English, shouting at Ummi. Not allowed, don't touch. Ummi held him tighter, humming to him. Humming old songs, songs from when he was sick and small, and she was shaking so much.

Abi was shouting in English too. She didn't speak English, she didn't understand. *Lies.* Qasim stared at the light. Lies, lies, lies. Like he told Mila. To make her feel better. White lies. Little. Small. To help.

The world faded around him again, less frightening this time with Ummi holding him.

She was still there when the light came back. He didn't realise at first. He was too warm again, dizzy with it. The pain in his chest made him gasp. Doctors were there too, and there were tubes and a mask on his face and cold rushing through his blood.

They were talking, loud and fast and urgent. His heart rate was tacky. His breathing was erratic. There was bleeding, but they couldn't be sure where from.

He must have cried out for his mother, somewhere in the faceless crowd of spacemen, because a hand grasped his, squeezing it.

"I'm here," she said, her voice breaking. "Can you breathe with me, *habibi*? Listen."

He tried to focus on her, but the light was too bright, and it hurt.

She realised and squeezed his hand again. "Breathe in when I squeeze." Her fingers tightened, and he tried to do what she said. It hurt and tasted like metal and plastic and filtered air. "Good," she whispered, releasing her grip. "Out, now."

He kept all his fraying attention on her. Ignored the doctors. Ignored the machines. Tried, tried, tried, to ignore the painful pressure as something was pushed into his chest.

Suddenly, his lungs were filling with air, and he gasped again.

"It's draining now," one of the doctors said.

Qasim gulped in air. It still hurt, but it was easier now, not the ground glass and bands around his ribs. The mask on his face was drowning him in air, and his mother's hand was squeezing his again.

"Good," she whispered again. She was crying.

His voice sounded like a stranger's when he whispered hoarsely, "I'm all right, Ummi."

Her hands were both around his, but he couldn't find her face behind the mask. Everything was hazy. It was enough to know she was there. He closed his eyes again, and later, when someone stroked his sweat-sodden hair later, he knew it was her.

At first, he didn't recognise Abi's voice through the mask. He was speaking softly in Arabic, as if he was afraid of waking Qasim. "I know, but we can't stay. They'll take us from here by force, if we don't leave."

Ummi sounded tired but determined. "They can't make me leave my child."

"Rasha, they can and they will." Abi sounded as tired as her. "You saw the papers we had to sign. If we don't leave, they'll do what they have to. You know you weren't meant to get so close to him. They're worried you might get infected yourself."

"I know," Ummi replied quietly. "But do you think I'll let some man who doesn't even know how to say our son's name tell me what is best for him?" Her gloved palm spread on Qasim's forehead. "They must see he's better now than he was."

"He is," Abi agreed softly.

Qasim managed to open his eyes. The heavy glue was back on them. He tried to smile, even though his mouth was bone dry.

His mother's face was distorted behind the mask, but she smiled at him. It was as if she was the one who was sick, all pale and sunken-eyed. "You're awake again, *habibi*?"

"Mm." He parted his lips. Wet metal on his tongue.

Footsteps came closer, and then his father was on the other side of the bed. "Here." He squeezed water from a bottle onto Qasim's lips. It was the sweetest thing Qasim had ever tasted, but swallowing was impossible. He managed a little and touched his tongue to his cracked lips.

"I'm sorry," he whispered, fresh blood on his tongue.

His father took his other hand. "No, Qasim. No. You don't have any reason to apologise."

Qasim's eyes were burning. "Ummi cried," he whispered.

Ummi laughed shakily. "*Habibi*, chopping onions makes me cry. It is an easy thing to do." She leaned down over him, as close as she could bring her face to his with the mask between them. The plastic was cool against his skin. "I only worry for you."

He had to ask. Didn't want to but had to.

"Better?"

His mother's face was close enough for him to see her expression and to see her eyes fill again.

Oh.

"They don't know," his father said softly. "They've never seen anything like this." He clasped Qasim's hand between his strong hands. "You've surprised everyone, fighting as hard as you have."

He should be dead already.

His eyes slid closed, too heavy to keep open.

"We can only stay a little longer." Ummi sounded unhappy as she stroked his hair again. "We only have today. This place of yours, they like their rules and contracts to keep quiet." She sniffed. "No manners, either."

Qasim's lips twitched. The world was caving in, and Ummi still found something so simple to grumble about. "Mm." He forced his eyes open to see them as they left. "Love you."

He shouldn't have said it. He saw Ummi's eyes grow bright and wet again. Abi's too. That was even worse. Abi didn't cry. Abi never cried. Both of them leaned down over him, despite the tubes and the wires and the needles, hugged him as much as they could.

His heart was aching, sharp and tight, as they told him in breaking whispers how much they loved him, how proud they were, how brave and good a son he was. His dry eyes burned again, and his cheeks were wet as they drew back.

His mother cradled his cheek, her hand shaking. "When you come home"—her voice trembling with emotion—"we will have such a feast. We will get a whole lamb."

"And some macaroni cheese," his father added unsteadily. "I'll even caramelise some onions in it."

Qasim wanted to laugh—and cry—but could only manage a faint, choked sound.

Ummi glanced at Abi, who nodded unhappily. She was weeping as she leaned down over him and pressed the top of her mask to his brow. "Rest now, *habibi.*"

She retreated from the bed. Qasim could hear her sobbing as his father took his hand. "We'll be waiting for you." He lifted Qasim's hand, pressing it to the brow of his mask, then close to his lips, then to his heart.

"Abi..."

His father nodded. "I know," he said quietly. "I know."

Chapter Thirty

RHYS WAS CLIMBING the walls with frustration.

Whatever was happening in the medical wing, he was only getting hints because the Supervisory Board were keeping the details quiet. All Rhys knew was Qasim was still sick, and they were struggling to stabilise him.

He also knew Qasim's parents had been given access because he'd demanded and begged and pleaded in dozens of folio messages to for them to be allowed in. He couldn't have done it face-to-face. Spamming the Board with written messages meant he could sit down, make his point, and not grab them by their shirt fronts and shake them until their teeth rattled.

They'd finally responded and told him—in more diplomatic terms—to stop being an irritating shit because we've brought the parents in, okay?

It was a small victory. Still, that had been days ago, and he was still out of the loop. Jacob was trying to keep him informed, but the TRI had locked down completely, takings its usual secrecy and notching it up to another level.

So, Rhys distracted himself. He read. He took walks in the grounds. He continued his flat-hunting. He visited Pisi, and if the cat used his face as a salt lick, no one needed to know about it.

He wasn't the only one who was on edge. On one of the rare times when he actually went to the canteen, Ben Sanders came and sat opposite him at the table. The boy was ashen, and his tray was shaking in his hands.

"Have you heard anything?" he asked.

Rhys shook his head, poking a piece of overcooked potato around his plate. "Sick. Not getting better." He glanced at Ben. The kid was the walking incarnation of Rhys's current mood. "I didn't know you knew him well."

A flush of colour spread across Ben's cheeks. "He was kind to me," he said defensively.

Rhys averted his gaze, taking a quick breath. "Yeah. He's like that."

Ben glanced around and leaned across the table. "Do you know if there are folio links in the med bay? I mean, I know there normally are, but this time…"

Rhys frowned. "I don't know. Why?"

Ben opened his mouth as if to speak, then shook his head. "Never mind. It's not like they'll let us have access." He prodded at the food on his tray, but it seemed like his appetite was shot too. "What's going to happen?" He sounded so young, barely more than a frightened child.

Rhys could only shake his head.

Ben stared at him, then rose and walked away, leaving his tray behind.

After forcing himself to eat, Rhys cleared up their trays before retreating to his room. He should have tried to be comforting, but he was so exhausted. He lay on the couch and only stirred when someone buzzed at the door.

He snatched up his glasses and put them on as he opened the door.

"Mr. Griffiths."

Rhys stared up at O'Donohue. Despite everything going to hell, the man still could've stepped out a catalogue. His long black hair was drawn back in an ornate braid, and he didn't have a tie on for once. *Casual summer collection.*

"What do you want?"

O'Donohue raised his eyebrows. "To the point, aren't we?" He motioned with one hand. "Please, I'd like to have a word."

Rhys didn't move. "About?"

"Something I can't legally discuss in the hallways of the building," O'Donohue replied. "Now, Mr. Griffiths, if you don't mind."

Rhys stepped aside to let him in. O'Donohue barely made a sound when he walked to the table. He folded gracefully into one of the chairs and gestured for Rhys to join him.

"I've been sent by Mr. Elwin."

Rhys sat opposite him, folding his arms over his chest. He'd been wondering when they'd get around to chastising him about his hundreds of messages. Of course, the boss would never do the dirty work himself. He'd always send his pretty lapdog to do it. "Yeah?"

"You know Mr. and Mrs. El-Fahkri were given special permission to visit their son."

Rhys nodded. "I know I had to send a load of messages to get you to even think about it. If you've come to tear me a new one and take my access away, get on with it and leave me be."

O'Donohue was sitting upright, but he was much more relaxed than Rhys felt, one hand resting casually on the table. He gazed at Rhys for a moment and then inclined his head. "And you think that's why I am here?"

Rhys hesitated, confused. "Isn't it?"

"There has been a...request." O'Donohue traced a circle on the table with his fingertip. "The El-Fahkris are in quarantine now as precaution, in case of infection. We're making them as comfortable as possible, and they've asked for you."

Rhys blinked stupidly. "Me?"

"Yes." O'Donohue's expression gave nothing away. "While the Supervisory Board would prefer to keep this situation on a need-to-know basis, they and Jacob Ofori have vouched you are a close friend of the family. Mr. Elwin has been persuaded you would be discreet, if you were given access." Those dark eyes fixed him with a steely look. "Yes or no?"

Rhys nodded at once. If it would help the El-Fahkris, if he could be useful in any way, he would say and do anything. "I—yes, I'd be discreet."

O'Donohue smiled slightly. "Good. Contact will be arranged for this afternoon." He rose from the chair. "Don't disappoint me, Mr. Griffiths. This took a lot of persuasion."

Rhys nodded, getting up. "Yes, sir. Thank you, sir."

Less than three hours later, he was linked in to the quarantine room.

Qasim's parents were waiting for him. They looked like hell. Qasim's father's hair had gone even greyer. No wonder. Still, Qasim's mother smiled unsteadily when she saw him, raising her hand in greeting.

"Hello." Jesus, he felt like an idiot saying it, but what else could he say. "Are you all right?"

"As well as we can be," Mr. El-Fahkri said. "Thank you for agreeing to speak with us."

"It's not a problem, honestly," Rhys said at once. "I'm—if there's anything I can do to help, you know you can ask."

Mr. El-Fahkri glanced at his wife, then back at Rhys. "You know what's happening?"

Rhys hesitated and shook his head. "The information was restricted."

Mrs. El-Fahkri murmured something to her husband, who nodded. "We can tell you, then. Qasim is—they can find no cure." Rhys tried not to flinch. "The doctors say he has a fever, but it won't break. They're using all the medicines they know of, but nothing has worked so far."

"But surely our medicines are more advanced than the sickness?"

Mr. El-Fahkri shook his head. "Medicines for modern illnesses. This is something different." He rubbed his face, the stubble rasping on his fingers. "We've been told we can't go back in."

"What?" Rhys exclaimed. "That's ridiculous! You have every right to—"

Mr. El-Fahkri raised a hand. "We were given orders when we saw him. We were meant to limit contact, in case of infection. We...didn't. They will permit video links, but nothing more now."

No wonder. If he were a parent to a scared, sick child, he'd want to comfort them as well. "But they can't leave him in there on his own. Not with medics who don't know him."

When Qasim's mother reached across the table, her husband took her hand in his and said something quietly in Arabic. Comforting.

Rhys wondered what it might have been like if the situations were reversed. If he was sick and his parents were in the quarantine room, would they have pulled together like that? Probably not. His mam would be there alone, like as not. Too much for dad, even if he gave enough of a shit to come.

"You can take our place." Mr. El-Fahkri said suddenly. "You have access, don't you?"

Rhys blinked in surprise. "What?"

"Qasim." They were staring at him hopefully. "We're not allowed to go back to see him. They won't allow it, but you...you're one of their staff. You've worked with him before. Can—will you go to see him?"

"Me?" Rhys wondered if they were reading his mind. He'd wanted to ask for days. He hadn't, though, not when Qasim's family was there and had to take priority. He couldn't go in and take what little energy Qasim had when his parents were there. He didn't have the right. But if they were being kept out, maybe he could. "I don't know if it would be allowed."

"He is alone," Qasim's mother said. Her voice was shaking, breaking. "Please. He needs— he needs not to be alone."

Rhys nodded. How could he not? They were right. Qasim deserved better, even though it was probably impossible. "I'll try. I'll do whatever I can."

They thanked him again and begged him to tell Qasim they would see him soon. It was like a punch in the chest. When he cut the connection, he sagged back in his seat.

"Shit," he breathed. "Shit, shit, shit."

He'd promised to do the impossible.

Right.

Right.

He needed to get permission to get into the medical bay. There were so many levels of authority he was going to have to get through. Direct supervisor first. That was the best bet. Test the waters and see if it might even be possible.

He headed out across the grounds to the main building and the offices.

Jacob was in his. He looked exhausted, and if he was anything like Rhys, he probably hadn't left the building or slept much in the five days since Qasim returned. "Did you get your connection to the El-Fahkris okay?"

Rhys nodded. "They're worried about him."

"No wonder."

Rhys swallowed hard. "They want me to go in and sit with him."

"Jesus Christ." Jacob eyed Rhys suspiciously. "And you said yes, didn't you?"

"What else could I say?" he demanded defensively as Jacob buried his face in his hands. "They're terrified of him being left alone in there." He waved a hand. "I know the medical team are in and out all the time, but—"

"But it's not the same as having someone he cares about there." Jacob propped his elbow on the arm of his chair and rubbed at his eyes. "Upstairs won't be happy about letting anyone else in, especially not with the Department of Health breathing down their necks."

"I'd be in full decon. No touching beyond hand-holding. Come on, Jacob. You can't leave him on his own in there."

Jacob lowered his hand. "If this is your attempt to guilt me into working for you, don't even try it." He pushed his chair back. "I'll go up. See what the options are." He touched the illuminated keyboard on his desk, and his projected screen lit up. "You stay put." He got up. "And whatever you do, don't type in ZR6193K, all in caps."

Rhys stared at him, and Jacob nodded curtly as he circled the desk then headed out of the room.

As soon as the door closed, Rhys ran around the desk and typed in the key.

A video link opened to the medical wing. Rhys pressed his hand to his mouth. He hadn't seen any footage since Qasim's return, and for a moment, it was like the Istanbul mission all over again—the same medical bay and everything.

Only it wasn't completely different.

Qasim was laid out in one of the beds, half-concealed by the mess of tubes and wires attached to him. The other bed was empty. There was no one else in there with him but a nurse in a decon suit. Rhys's hands shook as he tried to tighten the focus, drawing into a close-up.

Qasim was asleep. Or maybe unconscious. It was hard to tell. So much paler. His hair was matted to his brow, and his eyes were sunk into their sockets. He might have been a different man. Lights were blinking on the monitors. His breathing, his heart. Something at least. Even. Maybe he was resting now. Maybe a fever had broken.

Something must have happened, because machines started beeping. Doctors coming in, togged out in decon, checking everything. The sound, the chaos...

It—

Jesus Christ, it was—

Suddenly, he was twelve again, standing at the window, looking into the ward, watching his mam sobbing at his dad's bedside. Doctors checking numbers. The beeping. The rasp of breathing. Different. So different, but the same. The army had sent his dad off, and one chemical attack later, he was fucked for life. Qasim had gone away on a job and come back and now—

Now...

Rhys crushed his hand to his mouth to keep from crying out.

Jesus, if he went in there, how the hell was he meant to hold it together?

He fumbled to shut the screen down. It winked out, leaving the room darker, and he buried his face in his hands and tried to remember how to breathe.

He'd been there before. He'd seen it before. He'd lived it before. He'd managed it then. He could do it again. He'd smiled and done whatever his mam needed him to do. Got through it all, even if his dad had made it so much harder than it had to be.

It was different this time.

It was *Qasim.*

He forced his hands down from his face and took an unsteady breath. It was for Qasim. If he could smile and pretend everything was fine for his mam for twenty-odd years while his dad ranted at him for being a hopeless, useless lump, he could sit by Qasim's bedside and pretend he didn't want to scream at how helpless he felt. He reached out to open the link back up.

By the time Jacob came back, Rhys was back on the other side of the desk. He'd kept the feed on for several minutes after Qasim's stats stabilised and the doctors cleared out. It wasn't so bad when everything was calm, but that was always the way. Every minute he watched, he knew he had to get in there. No matter how hard it would be, Qasim needed someone in there.

"Well?" He turned expectantly to Jacob as he sat down.

"They're going to discuss the option. They'd prefer not to let anyone else in, but they can see how it might be considered...unnecessarily cruel to leave Qasim alone." He drummed his fingers on the edge of the desk. "They suggested a video link might be enough."

"No."

Jacob nodded. "I said as much." He scratched at his beard. "Go back to your room for now. Get some rest if you can."

Rhys nodded, rising. He paused. "If they let me in, is there somewhere on the med level I can stay? If I'm in the containment area, it'll be easier if I stay there until—" The words stuck in his throat. "I'd like to be close, in case Qasim asks for me."

Jacob was watching him too closely. "You're sure you want to do this?"

Rhys tried not to avert his gaze, but Jacob had the policeman's stare down pat. "If it was Kit in there, what would you do?"

Jacob sighed. "Hate every damned minute, but I'd be in there as long as they would let me be."

"Not really a choice, eh?" Rhys pushed his fingers through his hair. "You'll let me know as soon as they let you know?" Jacob nodded. "Good." Rhys headed for the door and paused again. "Thanks. For asking for me."

"We're a team," Jacob replied with a tired smile.

Rhys had to turn away, his throat tight with grief. Only days ago, he'd been joking with Qasim and Tahmila. They'd been sitting in the canteen in lockdown, laughing and speculating about whether they would ever be assigned the same mission again.

That question had been answered.

The walk back to H-block felt like it took much longer than usual. As soon as he closed the door behind him, he walked stiff-legged to the couch and sat down. Christ, he needed a drink. A big one. There was whisky somewhere in the suite. He couldn't remember where. It was there. He knew it was there. It...Jesus, he couldn't remember where it was.

He pressed his lips together and forced himself to take deep breaths. He was shaking again, and it wasn't good. Going to pieces wouldn't help anyone. Jacob might call him in at any second. If he called and Rhys was a blubbering wreck, they wouldn't let him in, and he couldn't let that happen.

Distractions. He needed to concentrate on something. Anything.

On reflection, his brain always did the stupidest things at the worst times.

It was why he ended up on a video link to Blato.

His mam answered. She was looking tanned and smiled when she saw him. They were so alike, him and his mam. His dad was taller and skinnier, but Rhys was her double.

"Rhys! You didn't say you'd be calling."

Yeah. Normally, he never got in touch without notice, but now wasn't normal. "All right, mam?"

"Well enough." She tilted the camera to let him see the sunlight pouring through the windows. "Your dad's out in the garden."

"Good." Rhys rubbed his left palm with his right thumb. It was good. It was the reason he'd gotten them over there in the first place. "Mam, can I ask you something?"

His mother sat at the table, adjusting the receiver. *She looks well. In summer clothes already. And happier too.* It was a relief, that. When the cold and the damp made his dad's chest worse, his mam had always been the first to suffer. "What is it, love?"

He dug his thumbnail into the middle of his palm. *Focus on the pain. Try not to think about the medical bay and Qasim and the fact you can't just ship him off somewhere warm to help him.*

"A friend of mine is sick," he managed to say. "It's—they have him in the hospital."

His mam looked stricken. "Oh, love, I'm sorry."

He shook his head. "It—it's all right. I just…" He trailed off, trying to find words. "Mam, when they brought Dad home…you went into the ward every day."

"I did." She leaned closer. "Are you visiting your friend, then?"

He nodded. "I'm going to, but it—" He swallowed hard. "Mam, how did you do it? When it was as bad as he got? And the doctors…"

She smiled, and for a second, it was the same awful, heartbreaking smile they'd shared when his dad was having a bad day. "Because I loved the grumpy bugger. You're not going in there for you, love. You're going in for them. I went in because your dad needed me there, even if he didn't know it."

Which was exactly what Rhys knew he was doing.

"Yeah," he whispered and drew his thumb away from his palm. There was a tiny crescent of blood where his nail had broken the skin.

"Rhys, are you all right, love?" For her to notice, it said how bad things were.

He pulled on his smile, the one she knew too well. "Yeah. I'm worrying over nothing, I am."

Maybe it was because she didn't have to worry so much herself now or because his dad wasn't about, but she was frowning and for the first time, he had a feeling she could see through him. "It doesn't sound like nothing. Are you sleeping? You're white as a sheet."

"Work's been rough," he lied. It was easy. Years of practise. "Just now, it's all a bit much."

"Well, if you need me to come over, you know you can ask."

He did, and even if some part of him wanted to, she'd spent nearly a third of her life taking care of his dad. He couldn't ask her to give up more of it, not now when she was looking happier and healthier than she had in years. "I'll be all right. Some sleep and a proper dinner'll be enough."

She gazed at him and shook her head. "Always so independent, aren't you?" She glanced over her shoulder and back at him. "Want me to call your dad in to say hello?"

Any other day, he'd have smiled through it and nodded, but not today. "I'm a bit tired, actually, mam. Tell him I said all right, yeah?"

She nodded with a brighter smile. "I will." She touched her fingers to her lips and blew him a kiss. "Talk to you soon."

He couldn't manage the lie. He could only nod and terminate the call without saying goodbye.

The next couple of hours crawled by. The only real distraction was dealing with paperwork from his solicitor. The flat had been snapped up. Last details were being checked. It should have been a relief, but Rhys couldn't care less. There were more important things, and he'd read the paperwork before. Nothing had changed.

He was staring blankly at the contract when his folio chimed.

Rhys's heart slammed painfully against his ribs. He flicked the contract out of the way and opened up the video connection.

"You've been cleared," Jacob said. "You've got four hours to do what you need to do on the outside, then you can go in. Standard quarantine protocols will apply until—well, as long as you're there."

Rhys nodded mutely. It felt like he was watching some strange film, everything not quite real. He thought he'd have been relieved, pleased for the chance, but he wasn't. He was tired and scared and numb, and no one could tell him it was going to be all right.

"You don't have to go in," Jacob said gently. He could sound so kind sometimes, and it only made things worse.

"No." Rhys fixed his gaze on a scratch on the tabletop. It was easier. Eye contact was the thing. If he acknowledged Jacob giving a shit, it would bring everything crashing down. "No, I need to go in. He—he's already lost Mila. I don't want him to be on his own."

"Rhys—"

"I want to." It wasn't a lie, but it wasn't completely the truth as well. It was less want and more need. He made himself raise his eyes back to the screen. "Do I need to do anything before I go in?"

Jacob shook his head. "The med team'll help you prep. You just need to have something to eat and get some rest. It..." He rubbed his forehead with his fingertips. "It's not going to be easy. I know you know, but I need you to understand it."

"Rest. Eat," Rhys echoed and nodded. "Yeah." He remembered it like a mantra from years ago: take care of yourself as well as the patient. "How—when I go, how do I go in?"

"I'll be playing escort," Jacob said. "I can come over now, if you want."

It was a generous offer and came from a place of good intentions, but when Rhys's guard was down, Jacob could read him like a book. The last thing he needed was to give Jacob the chance to work out just how shit he was feeling about everything.

"I'll see you in the lobby in four hours," he said. He tried to smile, but it felt false. "Thanks, Jacob."

Jacob inclined his head, watching him. "Remember what I said—food and rest."

Rhys nodded and terminated the link. He braced his hands on the edge of the table. Right. Food and rest. He could do both, and then, he would go and see Qasim.

Chapter Thirty-One

SOMEONE WAS HUMMING nearby.

Qasim stirred. Everything was...fuzzy. Fuzzy and quiet. There were beeps too, but they were normal now. He moved his hand—no, his finger. Awake. Let the hummer know he was awake. Eyes might catch up.

Something curled around his finger. Finger too? Felt like it.

"Morning, sunshine."

Familiar voice. Rhys.

It took time, but the awakeness finally spread. He opened his eyes, squinting. A new spaceman. Pink face behind the glass. Big blue eyes. The warm smile.

"You—" His mouth was too dry to speak.

Rhys leaned closer and squeezed some water onto Qasim's lips. This time, swallowing wasn't so hard. Better. Still sore, but better. "Slowly," Rhys warned. "Don't get overexcited. It's only water."

Qasim's lips hurt when he smiled. "Mm." He ran his tongue along his lip. His head felt odd. Kind of swishy. Medicine, he guessed. "Sorry. Tired."

Rhys covered Qasim's hand with his own. "It happens when you're sick, you silly bugger." He glanced up at something and back at him. "How are you feeling? The doctors would like to know."

Qasim managed to curl his fingers around Rhys's. Bits of him felt like they were reattaching, like they'd been off on their own and had decided to come back. Most of them were aching. Nice that they'd had a good time. Not nice to share the hangover.

"Swishy," he murmured. "Sore. All...weird."

Rhys stroked the back of Qasim's hand. Qasim could feel it like pins and needles. "They sedated you for a bit. They wanted to try to break your fever."

"S'why I'm swishy?"

Rhys nodded. The light was shiny on his mask. "It should fade." He squeezed Qasim's fingers. "I spoke to your mam and dad."

"Mm?"

Rhys nodded again. He was quiet for a minute.

Not using his words. Only happened when his head was busy.

"They're thinking of you," Rhys finally said. "They said they'll see you soon."

Qasim stared at him. They'd said...they'd said...what had they said? "Here?"

Another careful silence.

"Not in here," Rhys murmured. "They—" Paused. Frowned. Studied Qasim's hand in his. "They weren't meant to touch you as much as they did. There—it—" He exhaled, and his mask went misty. "They weren't meant to touch you."

Qasim knew there was something Rhys wasn't saying. They weren't meant to touch, but they had, and it was...bad? Bad because... because...because he was sick. He was sick, and the sick was bad, and the sick passed on like it did to Mila to him and-and-and...

He couldn't breathe. There were big hands around his chest, squeezing tight, and he gasped, choking.

Rhys was on his feet. Mask on Qasim's face. Mask and air and one hand under his head. "They're all right. They're all right. Breathe, *cariad*. In...and out...in...and out..."

He kept saying it, over and over, his eyes holding Qasim's. Qasim stared at him. In...and out. In...and out. In. His parents were all right. And out. His eyes were stinging, wet. In. They—like Mila—they might have...and out. In. Chest still burning, breathing too hard. And out.

"Do you remember Murad, the thief of Baghdad?" Rhys said.

Qasim nodded, gasping.

"In." Rhys held the mask in place. "I think he should have a bunch of flowers on a stick. And out."

"S-stick?"

Rhys nodded. "In. With ribbons. And out."

"Wha—?"

"Secret weapon," Rhys said. "In. Going to bugger someone up—and out—if they've got hay fever and you stick a bunch of flowers up their nose."

"Why?"

Rhys smiled at him, bright and warm. "In. Because why not?"

Why not? Qasim laughed breathlessly. "Yeah." He took another breath in. Easier now. And out. Rhys kept repeating it, squeezing his hand with every inhale. *He didn't panic. Saw someone who couldn't breathe and didn't panic.*

"I swear," Rhys said, when Qasim's breathing was even again, "you do it for the attention."

Qasim laughed hoarsely. He winced as Rhys laid his head on the pillow. His skin felt too tight, stretched thin. "Rhys..."

"Yeah?" Rhys smoothed his hair back.

"Ummi. Abi." Qasim's lips trembled. "Not sick?"

Rhys smiled and squeezed his hand again. "Not sick, I promise." He nodded towards the far wall. "They're in quarantine for a few days, to be sure, but definitely not sick now."

Quarantine.

Better than sick, but still not good.

Qasim curled his fingers against Rhys's. "You too?"

"Me?"

"Quarantine?"

Rhys was quiet. He adjusted the oxygen mask over Qasim's face. "Not yet." He smiled. Not his usual smile. Warm and bright, yes, but not to his eyes. "They've got me a room nearby so I can keep visiting you when you want to see me, until—" He bit the words off.

Until. Qasim stared at him. Until until until...

Until he didn't have to visit anymore.

Qasim closed his eyes, thinking of Murad and flowers on a stick. Ribbons. There would be blue ribbons. And gold, like Rhys's hair. He would make up a story, and Murad would fight off Death himself with the massive bunch of flowers. He would poke him until he fell, all rattling bones, then steal all the bones and tie them up with the ribbons and Death wouldn't catch him.

He swallowed hard. "Rhys?"

Rhys had sat back on the stool beside the bed. "Yes?"

Qasim tilted his head to look at his almost-lover. "The truth?"

He was watching closely enough to see Rhys's expression change. It flickered, like someone wiggling loose wires. "What about?"

Qasim tightened his grip as much as he could. "Am I dying?"

Rhys's expression froze. *Trying too hard. Trying not to show anything.* "I don't know."

"Rhys," Qasim breathed. "Please."

Rhys turned his hand under Qasim's and moved the other to close Qasim's palm between his. He was quiet for a long time. Maybe the mask was shiny or maybe it was his eyes.

"They can't stop the fevers" His voice was flat. "They drained the fluid off your lungs and thought it would help, but no matter what they try, the fevers keep coming back." He stroked his hand along the back of Qasim's. "If they can't stop them soon…" He frowned at their hands. "A body can only take so much strain before…" He shook his head. "I—we don't know what's going to happen."

Qasim's eyes were stinging but too dry for tears. "Right…" He pressed his fingers against Rhys's hand. "Thank you."

Rhys struggled to smile, but it didn't last. "They sent samples off to infectious disease specialists. Might even get you sent to them. They're trying everything they can to find something to help. A cure or something."

He didn't believe they would find one. His expression said it all. He didn't believe, and he'd still come into the room, to sit by Qasim's bedside, knowing he was probably going to watch him die. A whimper caught in Qasim's throat.

"Is there pain?" Rhys leaned forward, worry in his voice. "Do you need anything?"

"You—" It hurt to say the words. "You shouldn't come back."

Rhys flinched as if Qasim had slapped him. "Don't be daft."

Qasim shook his head, wincing as pain lanced through his temples. "No. Don't need to be here." He wanted to sound strong, brave, but…but he was scared. His voice was giving him away, shaking even as he forced the words out. "Don't need to see it."

Rhys lifted up their linked hands. "You know what this is? This is the fever talking."

Qasim tried to glare at him, but Rhys was holding their hands against his chest, and he seemed much calmer than Qasim felt. He took a rasping breath. "You deserve better."

Rhys wrinkled his nose, as if they were talking about anything but one of them dying. "I've seen worse." He propped his elbows on the bed and rested his chin on their linked hands. He was silent for a moment before meeting Qasim's eyes. "I never told you about my dad, did I?"

Qasim wanted to weep. Rhys was so private, but now, he was willing to tell stories when they were running out of time. "Don't need to."

Rhys's expression softened, and he offered a small, tentative smile. "I want to." He leaned his head forward as if he wanted to kiss Qasim's knuckles and made a face when the mask got in the way. "You know he was in the army, yeah?" Qasim nodded. "I was twelve when he was off in a combat zone somewhere out near Saudi. They never told us where.

Redacted or some cack." He gazed at their hands. "They said it was some kind of chemical attack. Came back coughing blood and bits of lung." He smiled wryly. "So, yeah. Seen worse. The day you cough lung bits on my best footie shirt, I'll leave."

Qasim stared at him. All the little pieces, the fragments he'd been gathering were fitting together. He squeezed Rhys's hand. Rhys was so drawn. No wonder. Showing all the little parts of himself. Qasim wet his lips. "You're not wearing a footie shirt."

Rhys grinned, bright and playful and almost convincing. "Catch twenty-two, innit? Can't cough lung bits on my footie top, so you can't make me leave." The grin faded. "Anyway, they managed to fix him enough to get home. If they can fix *him*, they better bloody be able to fix you."

"Not how it works."

Rhys snorted, and for once, didn't hide the bitterness in his voice. "No justice if you go and he gets to stay."

"He's your dad," Qasim murmured, wondering how bad things must have been to make Rhys hate the man so much.

"Yeah." Rhys sighed and shook his head. "Sorry. He—it—" He went quiet again. "You know when you get déjà vu?" Qasim nodded as much as he could. Rhys glanced around the room, at the machines and everything. "It...brought back some stuff. No big deal."

Qasim squeezed his hand again. He didn't know what he could say. They sat in silence for a while, just holding on to each other's hands. Coolness tingled into his skin, a fresh dose of painkillers, and he wondered how much he'd been getting for the pain to be reduced to a throbbing, all-body ache. Not for the first time, he wondered what would have happened if he'd managed to get Mila back too. Would they both have been lying here, dying minute by minute? It would have been a messed-up version of quarantine, and after...

"Rhys," he murmured, a thought creeping on him.

"Yeah?"

"Mitchell. Does he know?"

Rhys nodded. "Upstairs contacted him. Jacob went to visit."

Qasim let his eyes fall shut again, trying not to imagine Mila's husband alone in their flat with their ugly, funny little dog. They'd gotten the dog so he would have company when she was on missions. Now, that was all he'd have. He deserved more. Deserved Mila. He and Mila deserved each other, not this...mess.

The painkillers were working. The world faded out again.

Chapter Thirty-Two

RHYS SHIFTED QASIM up against the pillows. "Better?"

For the past couple of days, he'd divided his time between his quarantine room and the medical bay. As long as Qasim was conscious, he was there and doing everything he could.

"Mm." Qasim leaned back against the pillow. "Thank you."

Rhys patted Qasim's chest, trying to ignore the feeling of his ribs through the tunic. "Least I could do." He gently sponged the sweat from Qasim's face, which seemed even gaunter without Qasim's familiar beard. For once, it wasn't from a fever, but from the exertion of praying in his hospital bed. "I'm pretty sure you could have done it lying down."

Qasim made a face at him, his eyes half-closed. "Mm, but if you can sit up, you sit up."

"And if you swoon like a Victorian lady afterwards?"

Qasim cracked one eye open. It was bloodshot, but he was more alert than the first time Rhys visited him. "Fusspot."

Rhys smiled, sitting on the edge of the bed. "Did it help?" He didn't really need to ask. Even with Qasim swaying with effort, there had been an unmistakeable expression of peace on his face.

"Yeah." Qasim managed to open his other eye. "Missed it."

"Must be nice." He dabbed at Qasim's neck and shoulders. "Having something like that, I mean."

"Faith?"

Rhys nodded. A long while ago, his nan used to take him along to church, but it kind of fell by the wayside. They'd still gone on Christmas until his dad got sick, but it was more habit than believing any of it.

Qasim groped for his hand. "If I get better, maybe come to the mosque with me? See what it's like."

Rhys squeezed his fingers. If Qasim got better, if something—someone—out there decided to intercede when nothing else seemed to be working, Rhys would happily get down on his knees and give thanks for it. "Yeah, when you get better."

Qasim didn't bother to correct him, and Rhys knew why: if he wanted to delude himself to make things easier, then Qasim wasn't about to stop him. Denial was a safe, warm place compared to thinking about the inevitable.

"Can we play?"

Rhys smiled. "You're determined to kick my arse again, aren't you?"

Qasim's eyes were drifting closed again. "Take my fun where I can, Dumbo."

"Dumbo? Charming."

One dark eye opened a slit. "My little elephant."

Rhys couldn't help laughing at the mischievous smile twitching Qasim's cracked lips. "Well, I'm not tooting my trunk at you when we're on camera." He touched the folio console on the end of the bed and opened a chessboard.

Qasim laughed, but it trailed into a wheeze. Even so, it was enough to see him smiling.

Rhys set the board up, turning the white pieces in Qasim's direction. "Shock me."

It was a slow game, but Rhys didn't mind. Qasim was dosed to the gills on pain medication, which meant he wasn't as fast as usual, but he still knew what he was doing. Every move was calculated.

"I was playing Aisha," he murmured after he took Rhys's knight. "When you came on Eid."

"I remember." Rhys moved a pawn. "Do you play with her a lot?"

"Mm." Qasim took a slow breath. "All the time. Every year, three or four times. Thirty-eight to thirty-something. She's in the lead." He closed his eyes for a moment, and when he spoke again, his voice broke. "I don't want to go, Rhys. Not without saying goodbye."

"Qas—"

"I don't want to go." Tears were breaking from the corners of his eyes, and Rhys wished he was allowed to take him in his arms and comfort him.

"I know," he said, trying to keep his voice even. He slid one hand behind Qasim's head, the other stroking his cheek. "I know, *cariad*. I know. We're doing everything we can, I promise."

Qasim's face crumpled, and he clutched at Rhys's arm. He didn't have the strength to sob, Rhys realised. Every breath was a tiny gasp, and the tears were streaking silently down his cheeks. Rhys had to fight back his own tears.

It didn't last long. It couldn't, not when even sitting upright exhausted Qasim. Qasim sagged back against the pillows, eyes still wet and shiny, his hand still tight on Rhys's arm.

"I'm sorry," he whispered.

"Don't be," Rhys said gently, hoping his voice sounded steadier than he felt. "It's all right to get upset, *cariad*. No one would blame you."

"Thought I could pretend." He laughed tremulously. "I'm scared. I—I saw Mila. I—I don't—" He shook his head slowly from side to side. "I'm so scared."

"I'm here." Rhys smoothed his hair back from his brow. "Don't worry. I'm here." He glanced back across the room. "How about we see if we can get your parents to chime in again today, eh? I think they'd like to see you up and about. Maybe it'll help a bit?"

"Please," Qasim whispered.

It didn't happen often. Usually, Qasim insisted he didn't want them to see him in such an awful state. They had already seen him in agony, and he'd seen how much it upset them. Not the way he wanted to be remembered.

But when he asked to see them, Rhys made sure it happened.

He sat quietly by Qasim's bedside as he talked. Eventually, Qasim's exhaustion got the better of him. Sentences were reduced to single words and those finally turned into quiet sounds of acknowledgement.

Rhys got up. "I think he's ready to turn in." Qasim didn't even protest, which made it clear Rhys had probably let it go on too long.

"Thank you," Mrs. El-Fahkri said, her voice thick with emotion.

The link disconnected, and the only sounds left were the beeps of the machines and the quiet rasp of Qasim's breathing.

"Think you can sleep?" Rhys murmured as he lowered the incline on the bed.

Qasim managed to nod. His fingers twitched, and Rhys took his hand at once. The pressure of Qasim's fingers on his was barely even there anymore.

"Thanks," he breathed.

God, Rhys wished he could just lean down and kiss Qasim's forehead. "It's all right, *cariad*." He squeezed Qasim's fingers, then released them and adjusted the blankets over Qasim's body, avoiding the tubes and wires and everything else so horribly familiar.

By the time he was done, Qasim was already asleep.

One of the medical team was waiting to take over as Rhys made his way into the pod. He was swept along to the decon unit, where he was divested of his suit and sent back to the quarantine room.

It always felt eerily quiet after hours surrounded by the mechanical chirps of the medical equipment. The usual routine followed: a quick debrief with the doctors about Qasim's state; food from the delivery hatch, eat, drink; and, finally, stand in the shower until his eyes weren't burning.

Every day, it was getting harder to step into the medical bay.

Qasim had always been so calm. Today...

Rhys stared blankly at the wall, the water beating against his back. Qasim was scared, and there was nothing he could do. He couldn't even hold him or lie to him or do anything even a little bit useful.

His vision blurred, and Rhys closed his eyes, turning around to face the torrent from the shower.

He couldn't be scared. He couldn't, not when Qasim needed him to be there and at least try to make things feel safer. He reached out blindly to brace his hand against the wall. He'd managed for years, smiling when he was miserable and angry and scared. He could do it for a little while longer.

A little while...

That's all it would be, according to the doctors.

Christ, even thinking it hurt.

The shower took longer than usual. His eyes were still red when he finally made his way through to the main room. His folio was flashing on the coffee table. *A missed call.* He crossed the floor and picked it up. Doctor or Jacob or someone from on high.

Rhys sank onto the couch and opened the folio. He'd barely opened the message when it chimed. It wasn't likely to be a manager at that hour, but Rhys hesitated before opening the video link.

To his shock, it wasn't anyone he expected.

"Mr. El-Fahkri! Is—are you all right?" His stomach dropped. "Qasim?"

Mr. El-Fahkri held up a hand. "There's no change. I wanted to thank you for calling us to speak to him today. It meant a lot."

Rhys managed a weak smile. "I only suggested it. He was the one who wanted to." He stared down at his hands, not sure what to say. "I—" He raised his eyes again. "If he's well enough, I'll let you know again as soon as we can."

Mr. El-Fahkri nodded. He'd aged so much in the past few weeks. There were more lines around his eyes, his hair nearly all grey now. It made Rhys wonder if he was looking worse himself. Probably. None of them was getting much rest.

"What about you?" Mr. El-Fahkri asked.

Rhys sat back in confusion. "What?"

Mr. El-Fahkri was watching him too carefully. "When they let us in to see him..." He frowned and turned away for a moment, then back. "It was one of the hardest moments of my life, seeing my son in so much pain."

"It—it must have been awful," Rhys said quietly.

"Yes." Mr. El-Fahkri's voice trembled. "Yes, it was, but you—" He shook his head. "You go in day after day. You sit with him. It—you can't understand how grateful I am to you. You calm him, you comfort him, where no one else can."

Rhys clasped his hands one around the other. "He's my friend," he said, fighting to keep his voice steady.

"Mr. Griffiths..." There could be no mistaking the emotion in Mr. El-Fahkri's voice now. "Rhys, you're a good man. What you're doing for my son, my family..."

He broke off, and Rhys was stricken by the tears on the older man's face. "H-He's my friend. I-It's—I'm doing what any friend would do."

"Far more," Mr. El-Fahkri said quietly. "We owe you so much."

Rhys bowed his head, his throat tight. "Please, don't."

"It's the truth." There was the whisper of his hand running over his face. "I wanted to tell you now, because I— When it's over, I— It'll be difficult. I wanted to thank you now."

Rhys looked back up at the screen. "You didn't need to."

Mr. El-Fahkri smiled sadly at him. "You really don't understand how much you're doing for us, do you? For him?"

Rhys picked at his thumbnail, lowering his eyes. "I just wanted to help."

"Then you've done it, a hundred times over." Mr. El-Fahkri was quiet for a moment. "Rhys."

Rhys forced himself to meet the man's eyes again. "Yes?"

"Thank you."

Rhys wanted to protest he hadn't done anything. It wasn't as if he was doing anything to make Qasim better. Just sitting and watching and holding his hand—something any idiot could do. But Mr. El-Fahkri sounded so sincere and so grateful that he didn't have the heart to argue. He only nodded and lowered his eyes.

Chapter Thirty-Three

RHYS WASN'T THERE.

It was the first time Qasim had woken and Rhys wasn't already at his bedside.

The latest medical spaceman sat by the bed. "Good morning." It was the young Indian doctor. She helped him drink, enough so he could manage to speak. "How are you feeling?"

He managed a feeble shrug. "Where's Rhys?"

"Probably still asleep. The sun isn't up yet. Do you want me to chime through?"

Qasim shook his head at once. Every day, Rhys was more drawn and tired. He'd stopped shaving. He'd lost weight. He had shadows under his eyes. If he was resting, then it was a good thing. "Tell him—" He hesitated. "Afternoon."

The doctor nodded. "Give him a break?"

Qasim nodded gratefully, then frowned. Rhys probably wouldn't accept that. "Tell him I'm sleeping."

She patted his shoulder. "I'll leave a message for him. I'll put something in about us doing tests, in case he tries to come through."

Qasim managed a smile. "Thank you."

"No problem." She started checking the monitors, and the usual chorus of beeps and chirps sounded.

Qasim half closed his eyes, watching her through his lashes. It was something he'd always hated about quarantine: always being monitored. It was even worse now since there was actually something wrong and there was always someone there. It was constant.

At home, he could go off to his own room. Even in lockdown, he had some privacy, but not anymore. Every one of the medical team had seen every inch of him. Once, it would have mortified him. Now, he had worse things to worry about.

When she was done with her checks, she came back to the bed.

"You're holding steady today," she informed him, smiling. "Blood pressure and temperature are stable."

It wouldn't last.

Still, while it did, he wanted to take advantage of it.

"Please." His voice sounded like a stranger's, rough and raspy. "Can I have half an hour?"

"Half an hour?"

"Alone. Prayers."

Her expression softened. "I'd need to check with someone senior, but I'll see what I can do."

Less than fifteen minutes later, she returned to his bedside. "The cameras and monitors will still be on, but since your stats have been stable for a couple of hours, it should be all right. I'll be one bay over in case there's an emergency."

She helped him with the ablutions as best they could, and then she headed for the door, leaving him alone for the first time since his return.

With effort, he managed to turn onto his side to face the right direction.

Even though his mouth was dry and his head was light, he prayed. There was comfort in it. It let him be somewhere else for a moment, focussed on something more calming than blood and pain and death.

When he was done, he gazed at the window.

It was unfair to think he would never see a mosque again. He would never kneel among his brothers. The knowledge he would never share Friday prayers with his family was like a fist clenching around his heart.

The folio link at the side of his bed chimed.

Qasim opened his eyes to squint down at it. It was probably Rhys wanting to check in on him. With effort, he moved his hand and nudged the connection open.

A small video projection opened, barely a hand's breadth wide. A flushed face appeared.

Qasim stared at it. "Ben?" It wasn't possible. Access was restricted. Everyone had told him so. It was why he hadn't been able to speak to anyone except Rhys and his parents. Yeah, Ben had a lot of access, but he wasn't meant to be able to tap in here.

"Hi," Ben whispered. "Don't let anyone know you're talking to me. They shouldn't be able to see this projection on their screens."

Stranger and stranger.

"Okay," he agreed, leaning his head against the pillow.

Ben looked relieved but worried. "They weren't telling us how you were. They're only saying you're sick. I wanted—I didn't think—" He ran his fingers through his hair, which was already standing in all directions. "Are you—is it bad?"

What to say? The boy already had so much to deal with. It felt unfair to tell him the truth, but then, lying wouldn't help. "It's not great."

"Shit."

One side of Qasim's mouth turned up. "Yeah." He shifted his head up against the pillow, wincing. "S'good to see you."

"You too." Ben's voice was shaking. "Can I help?"

Qasim gazed at him and his video link, which technically shouldn't exist. "Yes." He managed a weak smile at the thought of outwitting the Board. "Can you take data out of here?"

Ben snorted. "That's easy."

Some part of Qasim knew he should chastise the boy, but now, there were worse things to think about than a small breach in security. "Got a favour."

"Anything."

"A message for my family." It was true the Board had agreed to let him make a video or two—Rhys had asked on his behalf—but they would censor it, censor him, and he wanted his family to see *him*, not some overedited robotic version. "A short one."

Ben nodded. "Easy. Now?"

Qasim lowered his chin in a nod. It might be the only chance he had, and he couldn't risk losing it. They didn't have much time, and Ben let him talk as long as he could manage. When the call abruptly disconnected, it took Qasim a moment to figure out why.

The door slid open, and the doctor walked back into the room. "Good prayer?"

Qasim nodded, rolling against the pillows. It was only talking, but it had taken all the energy he had. He closed his eyes, and when he opened them again, he wasn't surprised to find Rhys sitting by his bed, reading something on the folio.

"Afternoon already?" he murmured.

Rhys smiled. "Some of us can't be lazy beasts all day." He fetched the bottle of water and helped Qasim drink. "The doctors told me your stats have been holding steady today. That's good news."

Qasim managed a nod. "Still tired."

Rhys smoothed his hair. "I'm not surprised. You can sleep some more. I'll stay until they kick me out."

Qasim's eyes were so heavy, as if they were being dragged shut, and he let his head fall against the pillow. *So tired, again.* Rhys stroked his sweat-damp hair, over and over. The beeps and chirps of the machines faded into quiet dark.

For once, he wasn't woken by pain.

Apart from the machines, the medical bay was quiet. Qasim tilted his head, looking around as much as he could. One of the medical team was sitting in a chair at the far end of the room, apparently absorbed with a folio.

Rhys was gone.

The lights were low. Outside, it was dark. He'd slept all day?

He gazed at the windows, watching the reflections of the lights flickering on the glass, tiny red dots against the black.

There was still the ache, but it was bearable. The pain in his head was all muffled up in a cloud of medicine. He pressed a finger and thumb together, could barely feel them. It was odd, like squeezing a piece of *raha*.

It wouldn't last. Soon, the pain in his head would come back, and then his skin would pull tight again. It had been the same for hours, days, maybe weeks—quiet and calm for a bit, then it was if his blood was boiling and nothing could cool it down.

A body can only take so much strain...

Qasim gazed up at the ceiling. Rhys had said it the first time he'd come. Qasim knew he was going to die. His parents had tried to be positive. Rhys...Rhys had been honest, because he'd asked.

Qasim gazed at the light above his bed. He wasn't scared anymore.

It was strange.

He wondered if he should be panicking or hysterical or...or something. He'd been waiting for it to hit, the anxiety, which would have brought his end much faster. A panic attack or two and he would be done.

But he felt calm. Not happy about it, but calm. *Insha'Allah.*

He was the only one, though.

Ummi and Abi had wept over him. Rhys smiled and comforted and didn't even seem to realise how much his hands were shaking, giving his real feelings away. They'd all looked as bad as he felt, pale and hollow-eyed. They would waste away along with him, waiting for the last fever, and the...

He frowned at the ceiling.

The cough. He couldn't remember the last time he'd coughed.

A local ailment, potions to drink if the cough cleared. Was it a real memory? Wishful thinking? He didn't know, but maybe it was a chance. He moved his hand, touching the button to call the medical team's attention.

The woman at the other end of the room glanced up, startled. No wonder. He smiled weakly behind the oxygen mask. It was the first time he'd managed to use it.

"Mr. El-Fahkri?"

"My clothes," he breathed hoarsely. "From the mission?"

She shook her head, frowning. "Destroyed."

Qasim subsided against the pillow, disappointed. Of course. All the little sealed bottles in his bag would be gone too. Incinerated to protect everyone else.

The attendant checked his vitals. She asked if he wanted anything else, and he only shook his head, closing his eyes.

The doctors had talked about moving him when they thought he couldn't hear them. *Somewhere with specialists. Disease control unit. Somewhere not in the compound.*

Destroy clothes to keep a disease contained, but move the carrier? No. Bad idea. He pressed his finger against his thumb again. The ache spread this time. The medicine was wearing off. Think. He had to think while he had the mind to do it.

Yes, he was dying, but it didn't mean he had to lie down and wait for it.

Chapter Thirty-Four

"YOU CAN'T BE serious!"

Qasim was propped up among the pillows. He looked cack. It had been a bad couple of days when the fever spiked. For nearly twenty-four hours, the doctors struggled and finally stabilised him. It was the first time Rhys had seen him in two days, and while he was conscious, he was talking nonsense.

It has to be too many drugs. It's the only thing making any sense.

Qasim moved his head slightly, negative. "Serious." His voice was rasping, his lips cracked behind his oxygen mask.

Rhys walked in a circle. He didn't know what he was expected to say. He braced his hands on the end of the bed. "Have you gone crackers?"

For a few seconds there was silence, except for Qasim's breathing and the soft, repetitive *click-click-click* of the string of prayer beads slipping through his fingers.

"I'm dying."

Rhys straightened up. Wasn't a flinch. No one could say it was a flinch. "That doesn't mean—"

"Does." Qasim took a laboured breath. "Might be a cure."

"A cure." Rhys wished he could sink his nails into his palm, hold the terror—anger—God only knew what— in check. The decon suit was too thick. "Seven hundred years ago and they might have a cure we haven't found yet? Bullshit!"

The pale tip of Qasim's tongue moved along his dry lips. "Local illness. Local cure."

"And you expect them upstairs to send someone back to get it?" Rhys shook his head, not wanting to shatter Qasim's hopes, but knowing there was no other choice. "It's—we've already lost Tahmila. Do you think they're going to risk anyone else's life with this sickness on the off-chance?" There was something in Qasim's expression, in the tightening of his lips. "What?"

Qasim uncurled one hand and tapped his chest.

"No."

"Rhys—"

"No!" Rhys exclaimed. "That's suicide! You go back there and you'll die!"

Qasim raised his eyebrows. "Same here."

Rhys turned on the spot. His hands were shaking. "You can't even stand! How the fuck do you think you're going to go back and find some miracle cure? Even if they let you, you wouldn't get two steps beyond the gate! And don't say they'd send someone in decon and break every rule in the book! You know what they're like!"

Several more rasping breaths.

"Mila."

Rhys braced one hand on the end of the bed. Her name was like a damper on the frustration, the reminder of what was coming. The terror was back, suffocating. "What about her?"

"Her bag. Bottles."

Rhys's legs were shaking under him. He sank onto the stool beside the bed. Calm. He had to stay calm. Explain without breaking Qasim's fragile hope. "It'd be suicide." His voice sounded like a stranger's. "You'd be— you'd die alone. We—I can't let you do it."

Qasim uncurled one hand, and Rhys took it at once. "Might make it."

"Might not." Rhys turned Qasim's thin hand over in his. He could count the bones now. God, he wanted to scream at the unfairness of it all. "What am I meant to tell your parents if you died there? When they don't even get a body to bury?"

Qasim pressed his fingertips to the side of Rhys's hand. "Here either." He smiled sadly. "Contagious."

Rhys felt sick. Logically, he knew, but somehow, he hadn't even thought about it. If Qasim was so contagious their whole facility had locked down, then how could they justify passing on a contagious body to the family for burial?

"It's impossible," he said softly. "Qasim, you know they won't allow it." He squeezed Qasim's fingers. "Anyway, they've got permission to transfer you to the infectious disease medical unit. They might—"

"No." The word was as sharp as a whipcrack.

"What do you mean no?"

Qasim set his jaw, the muscles twitching in his hollow cheeks. "No transfer. Too risky."

Rhys could hear the catch in his breathing. It was too familiar. It wouldn't help. It might make things worse. Calm was what he needed now. "Qasim, they're experts." He kept his tone as passive as he could. "They know what they're doing."

Qasim jerked his head. "No. One mistake and people die." He swallowed hard. "Mila was—no more."

Rhys stared at him. "You can't be serious. If anyone's going to find a cure for this, it'll be them. They have more resources than we do. They'll help you."

"Might." Qasim stared back at him. "They might. I might."

"Qas—"

"Safer," Qasim whispered. "For everyone."

"They wouldn't let you." Rhys covered Qasim's thin hand with his. He'd seen enough of the senior management in the last few days to be sure of it. They were already in the shit for losing an agent in the past. Even if Qasim was in any fit state, there was no way in hell they would allow it.

Qasim gazed at their linked hands. "No," he agreed. His eyes rose. Bloodshot but determined. "We don't ask."

Rhys couldn't have been more surprised if Qasim had brained him with his heart monitor. "What?!"

"Ben."

Rhys shook his head in confusion. "Ben? What do you mean Ben?" It hit him. "Ben Sanders?"

"He has access." Qasim's voice was growing fainter by the moment. "Knows the system." His eyes sank closed. He was even worse today than before, his skin yellowed and tight over his bones. "He'll help."

Rhys could only hold Qasim's hand as Qasim slipped back between sleep and unconsciousness. It was a crazy idea. How could Qasim possibly think he'd be able to get through to a gate, let alone make a jump in his state? And all for some potion made by some mad quack centuries earlier? All the advances of modern medicine hadn't been able to push the infection back. How could he believe some potion thrown together by medieval chemists could do one better? The delirium was talking there. Or fear. Facing death had to do strange things to a man, even make him think of wild, desperate, impossible plans to save himself.

He rose from the stool and smoothed Qasim's sweat-damp hair back from his brow. If it distracted him, though, maybe it was a good thing. If he could think about other options, instead of what lay ahead, it might make things easier.

"Sleep well, *cariad*," Rhys murmured softly.

By the time he got back to his quarantine room, Qasim had been asleep for almost an hour. There wasn't much more he could do apart from watch him sleep and try not to think about Qasim's fantasy that he could still save himself.

It took time to go through the safety chamber and get out of the claustrophobic decon suit. A shower afterwards was a necessity, nearly two hours of sweat trickling down his back.

The folio link on the wall was blinking when he emerged from his bathroom into the quarantine chamber. It was a nice room, bright and spacious, but no matter how nice it was, it couldn't make him forget the reason he was there.

Rhys sat, towelling his hair, and reached out to touch the link.

Several seconds later, the video connection opened, linking to two other rooms in the facility. Jacob was visible on one of the screens, and Dr. Sullivan, Qasim's primary physician, was on the other. It sounded as if they'd been talking to each other before they linked Rhys into the conversation.

"Rhys," Jacob greeted him. "Anything to report?"

Rhys nodded in greeting, setting aside his towel. One of the conditions of his access was to keep them up to date with how Qasim was feeling. He hated breaking Qasim's confidence, but they needed all the help they could get to try to save him.

"I told him about the possibility of a transfer to the infectious diseases place. He said no."

Both Jacob and Sullivan frowned.

"What do you mean 'no'?" she inquired. "Surely, he knows they're the best people to help him now?"

Rhys rubbed at one eye. "Logically, he knows, but he—" He paused, frowning. "He's afraid if something goes wrong—the infection'll get out, and he'll be patient zero in an epidemic."

"Of course, he does," Jacob said with a sigh. "He's too good at looking for all possible outcomes."

"But it's incredibly unlikely," Sullivan said, shaking her head.

Rhys propped his arms on the table in front of him, looking at his folded hands. "You won't change his mind."

Sullivan raised her eyebrows. "Even if it could save his life?"

"Might." Rhys remembered how brutal the warning had been. "No guarantee." He shook his head, picking at his thumbnail. "He saw what happened to Tahmila. He doesn't want to risk it happening to anyone else, not because of him."

"All possible precautions would be taken."

"It won't change his mind," Jacob murmured. "Not if he's got the idea in his head now."

"Given the condition he's in," Dr. Sullivan pointed out, "we could transfer him, and he wouldn't have any idea about it."

Rhys had to admit he'd considered suggesting it. Anything to give Qasim a chance, but if Qasim realised and knew they'd risked the infection spreading, no matter how slim the danger...

"We can't do much for him," he said quietly, "but we can at least respect his wishes."

"He'll die." She wasn't one to mince her words. "We've done everything possible for him in this facility. We've taken the IDU recommendations and done everything they suggested based on the samples they had. There are no other options. We can only make him comfortable and wait for the inevitable."

Rhys gritted his teeth, trying not to let the emotion show on his face. "There was something he did say."

"About the IDU?" Jacob asked.

Rhys shook his head. "He said something about this being a regional infection. He said a doctor in Otrar gave him a remedy that would supposedly help once they passed the coughing stage. Do you think it could be possible?"

"Hold on." Jacob turned away, the light of another screen on his face. He was silent for a moment and then nodded. "There's a very brief exchange in the transcript of his digi-footage."

Dr. Sullivan sat back in her chair, frowning. "I don't mean to be dismissive of medieval medicine, but given the mortality rate of the period, I suspect it was little more than a placebo."

"I don't know," Jacob said thoughtfully. "Islamic medicine was known for being incredibly advanced for its time." He scratched at his chin. "We know what the man said, but we didn't see how it was made. Does he remember what was in it?"

Rhys shook his head. It would be so much easier if they'd known and could scratch a possibility off the list. "Qasim said they were both carrying bottles of the stuff."

"Which had to be destroyed," Sullivan said with a grimace. "I imagine they might have had some interesting herbal remedies. Even if it wasn't a cure, it might have been something lost to history."

Rhys hesitated. He didn't want to sound like he was clutching at the same straw as Qasim, but he had to know. "What if it was a cure?"

"I don't think it's—"

"I know it's not likely," Rhys interrupted, "but Qasim said the doctor was very specific about it. Once they stopped coughing, this potion would clear the rest. What if there was something in it to break the fever? I mean, it could be a basic penicillin or something, couldn't it?"

"Or some variation of quinine," Sullivan said thoughtfully. "It...might have been possible."

"With all the countries the Silk Road went through?" Jacob nodded. "Do you know of anything like that?"

Sullivan shook her head. "You'll know yourself how spotty the historical information is from those days, but I'll check in the medical archives and see if there's something we've overlooked."

Rhys's heart was pounding painfully fast. "So...they might actually have had a cure?"

"I'm not making any promises," Sullivan cautioned. "I don't think even their historical doctor was saying that. Whatever he gave them, he said it only worked after a certain point, which suggests it was only related to the fever, not the rest of the sy—" There was a chirp on her side of the connection, and she frowned, looking at something off-camera, then, "Shit!"

The doctor lunged out of shot, and they heard her scuffling around.

"Doc?" Jacob called.

"Spiking again!" she yelled from off-screen. The link to her screen disconnected.

Rhys sank in his chair. Again? Already? Until now, there'd been several hours of respite, even a whole day, once, when they were very lucky. But it had been less than three hours since his fever had been brought down and he'd woken.

"She'll report back as soon as she knows what's what," Jacob said.

Rhys nodded, but it could take any amount of time. "Buzz me in when she does." He terminated the connection and retreated to his bed where he sat, pressing his hands against his knees to keep them from shaking. It was bad. But now it was definitely getting worse, and even if they did hunt for Qasim's mystery cure, time was running out.

He gazed down at the band on his wrist, the braided ribbon of threads. He should have left it outside of the contamination zone, just in case, but with Qasim right there and still out of reach, he needed something to hold on to.

Rhys ran his finger along the band.

It—hurt knowing how little he and Qasim had been able to do for each other: a meal, a bracelet, some smiles, and badly played chess. It wasn't fair. Qasim deserved to have every chance. He deserved to grow old, surrounded by his family, still trying to outplay Aisha. He didn't deserve to die alone in a sterile, miserable medical bay.

It was another three hours before the connection chimed again.

Rhys hurried over to the table, tapping to open the link.

Sullivan looked exhausted. "He's not got long left."

"What are we talking?" Jacob asked. Rhys couldn't speak, all the air sucked out of his lungs.

"This morning, I'd have said a week or two, maybe more if he held steady." She shook her head, her hair clinging to her cheeks. "We're talking days."

"But he was—he sounded better this morning," Rhys choked out.

She rubbed her forehead. "He just crashed. Cardiac arrest. We managed to get him back, but we've sedated him again for at least twelve hours to reduce the stress on his body." She blew out a shaking breath. "I'll get our researchers into historical remedies, but right now, I don't think we're going to have the time to find them."

"Thanks, Miranda." Jacob nodded. "Go and get some rest. You need it."

When she disconnected, Jacob stayed on the line.

"Rhys."

Rhys was staring down at the band around his wrist, his fingers wrapped around it.

"Rhys," Jacob repeated. "Are you going to be all right?"

"He's going to die," Rhys whispered. "He—I mean, I knew—they said, but..." His eyes were burning, and Jacob was watching. He took a shaking breath, trying to gather himself. It wasn't working. Christ, it wasn't working and he couldn't breathe and he buried his face in his hands, trying to crush down the sobs.

"Rhys, if you want someone—anyone—in there with you, we can arrange something."

Rhys shook his head, breathing hard. No words. It made him whimper. Qasim always said he forgot his words when his head was busy.

Qasim, who would be gone soon, sooner than he wanted to believe, and there was nothing he could do about it.

No.

Not nothing.

He lowered his hands, looking at the feed. Jacob was watching him with concern. Rhys wiped his face with the back of one hand and cleared his throat. His voice still shook, but there was no helping it. "I need to speak to Ben Sanders."

"Ben?" Jacob frowned. "Why?"

It was amazing how quickly he came up with the lie, because it wasn't completely a lie. "Qasim asked me to pass a message on to him." He sniffed hard and exhaled noisily. "I—it's—I think it's better to pass it on before...when Qasim's still here."

He must have hit the right note. Everyone knew about Ben and how badly the loss of his dad had hit him. Most people knew he liked Qasim as well.

"All right," Jacob agreed. "I'll get him to call in." He studied Rhys's face. "I don't like leaving you in there on your own."

"I'll be all right. You—you just let Qasim's mam and dad know. They'll need the help more than I do. Tell them I'm watching out for their boy now. I'll be with him until... I'm staying until he doesn't need me to."

"Are you sure there's no one we can call for you?"

Even if they'd been able to bring someone in, who could he call? His mam was a continent away. He wasn't the type to keep friends close because of his work. The only other person he really had was Marc, and there was no way he was hauling him into it, even if Marc answered the call.

"You know we have people you can talk to if you need it. The counselling team would be more than willing to help." Jacob sounded too worried, and it was the last thing Rhys wanted. "Anything you need."

"I'll be all right. Just—Ben. I need to talk to him."

Jacob didn't look happy, but he nodded. "You know you can call me if you change your mind."

"Yeah. Thanks." Rhys terminated the link and headed for the bathroom. He was a state, his face red and his eyes puffy. He splashed cold water on his face, then filled a glass and drained the lot. No point getting hysterical when there was still something he could do.

It was half an hour before Ben chimed in to his folio. Unsurprisingly, he was as pale and worried as the rest of them. "Jacob said you wanted to speak to me about Qasim."

Rhys nodded. "Is this your private connection?"

Ben leaned towards the screen, and the video link flickered. "Is now. Why?"

Rhys took a steadying breath. He was about to break every rule in the book. "I need your help."

Chapter Thirty-Five

SOUND CAME BACK first. Beeping, again.

Habit made him move his hand, as if he could switch the alarm off.

"Afternoon, sleepyhead."

Rhys.

Qasim managed a smile as he forced his eyes open. Mask was in place again. Mouth felt dry and stale. Oxygen. "Hey," he whispered.

Rhys was right there. Chubby little spaceman. Close to the bed this time. Closer than before. He took Qasim's hand in one of his. "How are you feeling, *cariad*?" He sounded different, his breathing strange.

"Eh." Qasim shrugged as much as he could, though it made him ache all over. "Not dead." Rhys's laugh was a bit too sharp. Qasim eyed him. "Worse?"

Rhys nodded. The mask of his suit clouded around the edges as he breathed out. "Cardiac arrest."

Qasim stared at him. He remembered tight skin and pain and heat then nothing. "Oh."

Rhys cradled Qasim's hand between both of his. *His hands are shaking.* More than before. Something was different. "Do you remember what you asked me last time you saw me?" Rhys whispered.

It took a moment to piece together the memories. Tahmila's bottles. The past. A possible cure. He nodded slightly.

"Just as well," Rhys said more loudly. He turned and stared at the wall. Qasim followed his line of sight, confused, until one of the pin-lights on the wall turned green. Rhys whipped back around. "Right. We're getting you to a gate." He scrambled up and ran over to the pod access door, which shouldn't have opened, but it did.

"How?" he struggled to lean up on one arm.

Rhys was back beside the bed in a thundering heartbeat, a bundle in his arms. "Ben." He smiled shakily behind the mask. "If this is all I can do you for, then I'm doing it." He pulled back the blankets. "Come on. We need to get you disconnected, into clothes and a decon suit before they notice everything's been looped."

It took more effort than Qasim hoped. The monitors chirped noisily as wires and tubes were removed. Rhys ended up dressing him like Aisha dressed her kids—hoisting him up and dressing one limb at a time. He didn't seem to have any trouble, and all Qasim could think was he must have done it for his dad, back in the day. The dad he hated.

"Rhys."

"Yeah?" Rhys was pushing his arm into the sleeve of a heavily furred coat.

"I'm sorry."

Rhys paused, looking at him. "What for?"

"Your dad." He tried to smile, but it was so much effort. "Bringing it back."

Rhys didn't say anything, just finished getting Qasim into the coat.

"Not the same thing," he finally said. "He never wanted a chubby, short-sighted lump for a son to start with. Being sick just made him worse." He hesitated, as if he'd said too much, and stepped back. "Right."

The decon suit was trickier to get on over the flowing historical clothes, but it was at least three sizes too large, so Rhys managed to tuck everything in before sealing it up. Qasim wanted to argue about taking it into the past. Rhys must have seen his expression.

"You can destroy it when you get there," he said, showing Qasim a thick packet wedged into the belt. "Here." He turned it over, and there was a single flat button linked into an array of wires. "Get out of the suit, hold it for ten seconds, and it'll destroy it."

Neither of them brought up the question of how Qasim was meant to get out of the suit.

Before Rhys sealed the helmet in place, he pressed his hand to Qasim's cheek, and Qasim wished it could have been skin-to-skin contact, just for a second.

"Ben's got a pod off the grid," Rhys said. "He'll have the gate ready to get you as close as possible to Mila, but there's one more thing we'll need to do, and I don't think you're going to enjoy it."

"Oh?" Qasim leaned sideways against the pillows. The world was spinning unpleasantly.

Rhys headed for the medical cabinet by the wall. Qasim had no idea what was inside there. Most of it had probably ended up in his bloodstream at one point. Rhys poked through the contents and returned with a long, narrow packet.

"What...?"

"Adrenaline. If it works like Ben says it should, it'll give you enough of a boost to reach Mila."

Qasim gaped at him. "He knows medicine?"

Rhys smiled crookedly. "What the 'net told him, but it's not like we have a choice." He slid one arm under Qasim's shoulder. "Gate first."

The moment Qasim's feet touched the floor, his legs gave way under him. He wanted to scream. If he couldn't even get to the pod, he'd never reach the gate, Mila, and the medicine that might be his only hope.

Rhys didn't hesitate. He bent at the knees and scooped Qasim up as if he was as light as a child. If it wasn't for the strain in his face, Qasim might have believed it was easy. Rhys marched across the floor and plunged them into the darkness of the pod. The door slammed shut behind them, and the world was reduced to Rhys's arms holding him and their breathing.

Qasim leaned into him, wishing he had the energy to say something, to thank him. But he couldn't spare anything, not until they were at the gate, not until the adrenaline was in his blood. Then—only then—could he spare what little he had left.

"Not long now," Rhys said in the darkness as the pod shuttled them away. His arms tightened around Qasim's waist and under his legs. "You go. You get your medicine, and when you come back, we finish our chess game."

Qasim dipped his head in a nod. "Your move," he breathed.

Rhys was silent for several seconds. "Queen. F6."

"Queen. F6." Qasim murmured it, praying he would remember.

The pod whirred to a halt, and the door hissed open. The room on the other side was dark, but as they emerged, the narrow panels of light along the wall illuminated: a passage to a gate room.

Rhys's steps were laboured, but he pushed on, Qasim held tightly in his arms. Rhys wasn't speaking now. His face was red. Qasim could only watch him. All he could do now, when he couldn't stand or breathe or help. The doors ahead of them opened into the layover suite. Normally, there would be a crew there with makeup, costume, props. Now, it was dark. Only light from the hall on the other side, leading to the gate room.

"Ben says they're onto us," Rhys gasped, as he stumbled into the gate room. He dropped to his knees in front of the gate and set Qasim down. "Has to be now."

Qasim braced one shaking hand on the floor and pressed the other to his chest. "Here."

Rhys nodded, breaking the seal on the adrenaline shot. He grabbed Qasim by the shoulder and thrust the syringe into his chest.

Qasim gasped in shock as the adrenaline flooded his system, then flinched when the gate flared to life.

"Quick." Rhys grabbed him by the arm and hauled him up. Qasim drank in gulping breaths. It was as if he was watching his body from a long way away, but his legs were holding him, and even if he was stumbling, he was upright. "Protein tabs and water in your pocket. Got twenty-four hours. Pickup tomorrow. Same place. Means you get a stable gate."

"Rhys—" he began as they neared the gate.

"Go!" Rhys shoved him forward. Qasim hit the wall of light and fell.

The sand crunched beneath him as he landed on his knees on the ground. From the angle of the sun, it was early morning, the sky clear and cloudless and the wind gusting, tossing up sprays of sand. He groped for the helmet, twisting as much as he could. It took three attempts to break the seal. When he opened the mask and drank in the fresh air, the chill was sharp as a knife.

He stared around, trying to get his bearings, as he tugged at the collar of the suit.

There. That tree. He knew that tree. Close to the road leading to the city. Gnarled, with one branch low to the ground. He'd tried to tie the donkey to the tree, but it had escaped, and he and Mila had-had-had…

His heart was pounding in his ears. The cave, a crack in the cliff less than ten metres away. They'd sheltered there. Cliff. Cliff and crack and…and there. There. Mila was there. The cure was there too. He started to rise, but his legs were shaking too much under him.

The sand was cold between his fingers, cold and crisp as snow. Or maybe it was snow too. It was cold, and that was good. Staying cooler was good. The suit needed off, but not yet. *Keep it. Keep it till the cave and burn it.* Fire. It would help at night. Twenty-four hours.

He braced his weight on his hands and knees and started to crawl.

Chapter Thirty-Six

THE GATE CLOSED. The violet afterimage burned on Rhys's eyeballs. It reopened again, seconds later, blazing white and...

And...

And...

Nothing. No one.

Rhys stared at the frame as the light went out a second time.

No. Wrong. Qasim was meant to be back now. He was meant to fetch the medicine and come back. This was wrong. He wasn't meant to stay there.

The gate must have connected at the wrong time, because Qasim would have been there. He wouldn't have missed it. He'd never missed an important pickup before. He—he'd even done the flash, because he was so stubborn and stupid. He wouldn't miss a jump.

It was wrong.

He flinched when someone—two someones—grabbed him by the arms and pulled him to his feet. They dragged him, and he stumbled along, half carried, half frogmarched, back through the halls to the pod.

It was like watching through a thick pane of glass. Everything felt off. Muffled. Not right.

The two spacesuits were speaking at him, but all he could think of was the plain. Qasim said it was a plain on the other side. Some plants, but not many. Winter was cruel there. Everything was icy and dead.

He didn't fight them as they disinfected him and got him out of his suit. Another pod. Another two pairs of hands. The door of his quarantine room opening and closing behind him, and he stood there, staring blankly at the floor.

It wasn't right.

He made his way across the room and sat on the couch.

He'd done what Qasim had asked.

Qasim wanted to go back. Qasim wanted to try to save himself. Rhys had helped. It was a good thing. It was. He'd done what he could to help. It was the only thing he could do and he'd done it and it was good.

Even if it was cold, and Qasim was alone, and—

He gripped his knees, squeezing until it hurt.

He didn't know how long he'd been sitting there when the door opened. *Strange. Quarantine.*

Spaceman in the doorway, and behind the mask, he could see Jacob's face. Definitely wasn't good.

He got up.

The door closed behind Jacob.

"What the fuck did you think you were doing?"

Rhys pressed his fingernails into his palms. "He asked me to."

"He asked you to. He, the man who has been swinging between delirious and high on painkillers, asked you to." He shook his head. "Jesus Christ, Rhys, do you have any idea how much trouble you're in?"

Rhys's legs were shaking. He sank back onto the couch and whispered, "He asked me to."

"And you didn't stop to think, did you?" Jacob approached him. His voice wasn't so steady now. "Did you think I'd be able to pull some card out my sleeve and save your arse? Did you think what dragging Ben into this could mean?" He threw up his hands. "For fuck's sake, Rhys, I thought you had some common sense."

Rhys slid his hands together. Small and quiet and calm. Best way to stop people being angry. "I'm sorry."

"Sorry?" Jacob snapped. "Sorry?! You've abandoned Qasim to die God only knows where. His parents won't have the chance to say goodbye. You've shat all over Ben's future as an operative here." His voice was thick with disbelief. "And this is all because he 'asked'?"

Rhys made himself look up. He'd never seen Jacob angry before. He pressed his fist to his stomach, which was knotting up like someone had reached into it, grabbed and twisted. "I had to do something." It was a stupid, pathetic answer, but it was all he had.

Jacob stared at him. He grabbed one of the chairs from the table and pulled it over, sat, and propped his forearms on his thighs.

"They're going to fire you for this. I can't stop it now. You've gone way above my level. They'll fire you, and if you're lucky, they might not have you arrested."

The world swam around Rhys. "Arrested?"

"What the hell did you think was going to happen when you executed an illegal, unauthorised temporal jump?"

Rhys clenched his fingers around each other. He hadn't thought ahead. It was...a problem for another day. Right now, it didn't matter. He met Jacob's eyes. "He wanted to go."

Jacob sighed, folding his hands and tapping his thumbs together. "He was sick, Rhys. D'you think he was thinking straight?"

Rhys could remember the urgency in Qasim's voice, the plans within plans, the way he'd clung to Rhys's hand. "Yes, I do."

"Jesus Christ..." Jacob leaned back in the seat. He tried to rub at his brow, but the mask got in the way. He sighed again. "I get it. You wanted to do something for him. But this? How is leaving him to die out there alone a good thing?"

Rhys could feel his lips trembling. He pressed them together and took a breath, another. Calm. He had to stay calm. Falling apart wouldn't help anyone. "He was meant to come back."

"In the state he was in?" Jacob was quieter now. Even worse, the anger was winding down to grief and disappointment. He sounded older and tired. "Did you really believe he was in any state to do anything?"

Rhys pushed his thumb into his palm. Did he? He wanted to believe it, yeah, but did he? He'd hoped, like he had with his dad, that anything could help. Anything—as long as it was something. If his dad could get well again with one lung and a home in the Mediterranean, then why wouldn't Qasim, when he took his medicine and broke the fever?

Christ, he had been so desperate for it to work, and now, Qasim was dead and cold and alone...

His eyes stung and he blinked hard.

"Rhys..." Jacob said, gentle now.

No. No gentleness. No kindness. Jacob was right. Rhys had been reckless and stupid and selfish. He'd tried to make himself feel better, make himself less useless, and had left Qasim for dead because of it.

"His parents," he said without looking up. "I want to speak to them. This—I did this. I should explain."

"I don't think it's a good idea."

Rhys nodded unhappily. "I know." He raised his eyes. "Please. It's my fault. You don't need to be the one to tell them."

Jacob leaned forward, pressing his hand to Rhys's shoulder. His expression was too much, and Rhys had to duck his head. "You always watch out for everyone else, don't you? No matter what it costs you."

Rhys pressed his eyes shut, swallowing hard.

Jacob squeezed his shoulder. "I'm sorry."

"For what?" Rhys's throat was painfully tight around the words.

"For your loss."

It was too much, kindness on the back of the anger and frustration. He squeezed his hands together until the pain distracted him from the tears in his eyes and the sob fighting to get out of him. He didn't look up, not even when Jacob leaned closer. Jacob would have hugged him, Rhys knew, and he didn't deserve it. He pulled away from Jacob's hand, from the reassuring contact.

"His parents," he said again, hoarsely. "Please."

Jacob straightened up, watching him carefully. "If I can arrange it."

Rhys nodded. The skin of his hands was going whiter with pressure. He flinched when Jacob took them between his own.

"Don't speak to anyone else, not without me there, okay?" Jacob's hands were warm around his, even through the thick rubber of the decon suit. "I'm going to do what I can, but I need you to keep quiet until I'm there with you. Understand?"

"You'll get in trouble too," Rhys said, his voice shaking.

"You're my staff. My responsibility." Jacob released his hands and got up. "If you think I'm going to let you go down for this, you've got another thing coming. I'll get a solicitor in, see what we can do."

Rhys kept his eyes on his hands. Easier. Better. Safer. If he just focussed on his hands and counted the creases and folds and tried not to think, he could keep the grief closed down. He didn't need sympathy. He didn't need to be cosseted. Qasim's parents needed the attention. He didn't.

A bubble closed around him once Jacob left. There were no messages coming in, just walls all around him and the pounding, suffocating awareness that Qasim had died cold and alone.

He tried to think about something else. He took refuge in the shower. He tried to make himself eat, but all he could think of was Qasim's silhouette as Rhys threw him through the gate. Maybe he'd changed his mind. Maybe when he'd said Rhys's name, he was telling him to stop.

He was standing at the sink, glass in hand, when the door chimed and slid open.

He turned. Two figures in decon suits. It took him a second to recognise the pale, tearful faces behind the masks.

The glass slipped from his hand, clattering into the sink.

The couple stepped across the threshold, clutching each other's hands. Mrs. El-Fahkri swayed like she was about to collapse. Rhys moved towards her and hesitated. His breathing was too rapid. Calm. For them, he had to be calm, but it was so hard when his throat felt like it was closing up and his eyes were burning.

"It's true, then?" Mr. El-Fahkri said, sounding so much older now. "It was you? You sent him back?"

Jacob's anger and disapproval was nothing compared to the quiet grief of the El-Fahkris.

Mr. El-Fahkri guided his wife closer, both of them staring at Rhys, searching his face. They had trusted him to take care of their son. They were the ones who had asked him to go where they couldn't, and now, Qasim was dead and alone in the cold.

"Why?" His father asked. "They won't tell us why you sent him."

Rhys couldn't breathe. He couldn't remember how to breathe, his throat tight, and he fought to gulp in some air. "He—" The words were difficult. "He asked me." He took another choked breath. "There was medicine there. He thought—" His eyes were burning, and he had to turn away from them. "I thought it could save him. I wanted to save him." His face was wet, and he couldn't breathe again. The tightness around his chest was suffocating. "I'm sorry," he whispered, his voice cracking in a sob. "I'm sorry."

They didn't say anything, and he couldn't blame them. He groped out with one hand, leaning against the counter. He couldn't look them in the eye.

He flinched when a hand touched his arm. Mrs. El-Fahkri was right there beside him, looking at him. There were tears rolling down her face, and he was crying, even though he was trying not to.

"You try to save him," she said, smiling through her tears. She lifted her hands to brush the tears from his cheeks. "You try."

"But I didn't," Rhys choked out, shaking his head. "I didn't, and he died there."

"He ask," she said, "Yes?"

"Y-yeah."

She cupped his cheeks, forcing him to meet her eyes. "You do what he want. His wish. *Insha'Allah.*"

She was crying and she didn't blame him and Rhys couldn't stand up anymore. He folded to his knees in front of her, burying his face in his hands. The sobs were tearing through him, and when she knelt and she wrapped him up in her arms, they clung to each other. Another pair of arms joined them a moment later.

"*Insha'Allah*," Mr. El-Fahkri whispered, his voice thick with tears. "*Insha'Allah*."

Chapter Thirty-Seven

ADRENALINE WAS GONE.

It got him to the cave. Enough.

The cold was getting in now. Through his hands, into his blood. His teeth were clattering together, and he pushed at the suit. Burn it, Rhys had said. Fire was good. Fire was hot. Not cold to the bone.

Qasim keened softly, his hands shaking as he tried to tug the suit off his feet. Even sitting up made his head spin, but he had to. Had to. Stay warm. Stay alive.

It took a long time, a long time. He had to hit the burning part with a rock, his hands numb with cold. It snapped and hissed and burst into flames. Warm. Warm was good. He held his hands over it until they ached with heat instead of cold.

Warm. Good.

What else?

He was at the cave. He—the medicine.

He made himself turn, made himself look, afraid of what he would see.

Tahmila was where he'd left her, pale like stone. Wind had blown into the cave. She was like a princess in a fairy tale, dusted with sand and frost. Not sick. Not dead. There was no time to cry, no time.

He crawled across the ground to her, breathing hard. Used his arms, not his hands. Thick sleeves. Kept his hands up, warm. Meant he could pull at the bag, tug the clay bottles out. They were cold too. He broke the seal, shook one. Frozen.

No.

No no no.

Not all this way, not to freeze.

He managed to make it back to the fire at the mouth of the cave. He used his hands to dig a hole as near the flames as he could, shoved the bottles in. Burned his fingers, but there was cool sand and ice to stop them hurting.

Watched, watched, watched.

The sun moved, stretching across the ground. It might have been warm if it wasn't for the wind. He pulled his thick robes tightly around him, shivering. *At least not burning up now.* That was something.

Qasim touched the bottle now and then until something splashed inside. He wanted to cry with relief. A little longer, enough to melt the rest. Even if his head was swimming and he wanted to lie down.

The fire was burning lower when he started to list sideways.

With what strength he had left, he picked up one of the bottles with both hands. The contents were still cold enough to make him catch his breath. A sharp taste, bitter and unpleasant, but he knew he had to force it down.

The other bottle was there too, but he couldn't find the energy to lift it.

The wind whirled around him. He shivered.

Fire and medicine. Had both. All he could do now.

The sunlight was fading. Getting darker. Too early. He tried to lift his head, but his world swam and he fell into black.

Chapter Thirty-Eight

IT WAS ALL starting to sink in.

Rhys was exhausted after Qasim's parents left. He ended up sitting in the shower for an hour, his chin propped on his knees. There was something comforting about the hot water streaming down on him, but it couldn't keep reality at bay forever.

Going to bed and turning off the lights was a stupid idea. Without something to distract him, he was left with the dark and the memories of everything going so horribly wrong.

Qasim was dead.

Qasim's family had lost their boy.

Ben's career might be down the toilet.

Rhys was going to lose his job.

He might end up in jail.

His parents would lose their home, if he wasn't able to work and pay for it.

His dad would be proved right after all.

He stared blankly at the ceiling.

He didn't know how he still had tears left. They trickled down his temples into his hair. All he'd wanted was to help Qasim, and instead, he'd fucked everything up for everyone.

He lay there, wishing for sleep, but it didn't come. By three o'clock, he'd given up and taken refuge in a cup of tea at the table. He opened up his folio and stared at the screen. He had messes to tidy up before things got worse.

Right.

Right.

He tried to gather his scattered thoughts. First priority had to be his parents. They needed to stay where they were, which meant they would need the money for the house. Okay. His flat was selling. It was a start. It would make enough to pay off most of their—his—second mortgage.

He rubbed at his eyes with the heels of his hands.

Right. Pay off their house. Get them secure. Fine. He'd just have to resort to temporary accommodation for a while instead of buying somewhere new. Anyway, if he went to jail, it wasn't as if he'd need a new place.

Without his paperwork and files, he had to make guesses on the costs. Maths was never his strong point anyway, and it didn't help when his mind was all over the place. Lack of sleep. Grief. Fear. Guilt. God only knew what else.

The exhaustion must have gotten the better of him because the chirp of his folio woke him. He lifted his head from the table, squinting around. It was daylight, and one side of his face was all pins and needles. He groped for the folio, tapped to open the video connection, and immediately wished he hadn't.

It wasn't Jacob.

It was O'Donohue, and despite the early hour, Elwin's private assistant still appeared as if he had his own squad of personal groomers to keep him impeccable. There wasn't a hair out of place.

Rhys self-consciously pushed his fingers through his hair. "Um. Good morning, sir."

"Mr. Griffiths." O'Donohue inclined his head. *Surname*, Rhys thought bleakly. *Never a good sign.* "I expect you know why I'm contacting you."

Rhys's mouth was dry as a bone. He nodded.

O'Donohue folded his hands in front of him. He was as placid as ever. "There are laws in place for a reason, Mr. Griffiths, but you chose to take matters into your own hands. You not only breached company protocol, but the international statutes governing this organisation."

Rhys nodded, hooking his fingers around each other.

"You know you're not the only one whose future is at risk here."

Ben. He'd used his unrestricted access and got Qasim out. He could be in even more trouble than Rhys, genius or not. Better to be the villain and watch his back. "Ben had a crush on Qasim. I thought— He's lost so many people. I knew he wouldn't want to lose Qasim as well."

O'Donohue made a doubtful sound "You're saying you manipulated him?"

Rhys couldn't lie. Ben hadn't even needed much persuasion. He shrugged. "Why else would he do something so stupid?"

"Which makes me wonder." O'Donohue gazed at him with those expressionless dark eyes. "Why would *you*?"

Rhys blinked, confused. Surely, Jacob or the El-Fahkris or even the footage would have shown his superiors? "What?"

"I'm asking you why you did 'something so stupid,'" O'Donohue said quietly. "I want to understand why you felt you were above the law. Not what other people have told me. I want to hear it from you."

"He asked."

O'Donohue raised an eyebrow. "He asked? It's so simple? You defied the law, the company, your superiors, all because he asked?"

Rhys's nails cut into his fingers. He was tired and he was miserable, and he was...angry. "Because I had to do something. Because he asked. Because he was scared, and he was dying, and he asked me to help him. Because he thought—we thought there might be a chance we could save him."

O'Donohue leaned back in his seat, his head to one side. "Save him? Really?"

"It was all we had," Rhys burst out angrily. "Nothing was working. He was terrified of being taken out of the TRI—in case something went wrong and he caused an epidemic. D'you think I was going to let that happen to him? He said—" His voice broke. "He didn't want anyone else to die."

O'Donohue rubbed the hollow of his cheek with a knuckle. "And you didn't think to explain all of this and ask for permission?"

Rhys stared at him in disbelief. "To you lot? You go on about doing things for the good of the agents, but we all know it's bullshit! Why the hell would you open a gate when it would cost you money and not turn a profit?"

As soon as he said it, he shrank back in his seat, shocked at himself. *Shit, shit, shit.* Yelling never helped anyway, but yelling at the boss's right-hand man was so much worse.

O'Donohue didn't speak. He glanced out of shot, his blank expression giving way to a pensive frown. When he looked back up, his mask was in place.

"You make a compelling argument." He straightened in his chair. "Unfortunately, we can't overlook the breaches in protocol and law, Mr. Griffiths. Your contract with the TRI will be terminated with immediate effect."

Rhys had been expecting it, but it still drove the breath from him. "Yes, sir."

"A decision will be made in the near future regarding criminal proceedings," O'Donohue continued, but he was no longer looking at Rhys.

"The circumstances will be taken into consideration, and the El-Fahkri family will be consulted regarding their wishes."

Another burden to lay at the El-Fahkris' feet.

"Please," he blurted out, "don't make this harder for them."

Dark eyes flicked back to Rhys's face, and he felt like something on a scientist's slab. "We have no intention of tormenting a grieving family, Mr. Griffiths. They must be consulted, but it will be done as sensitively as possible."

Rhys nodded, clasping his hands tightly together. "Good."

"I'll be in touch, once decisions have been made." O'Donohue was still watching him. "Until then, you'll remain in quarantine for the standard period to be sure there was no cross-contamination."

Rhys nodded again. Two weeks, depending on regular medical checks, then maybe freedom. Best he could hope for, given the circumstances.

"And Rhys," O'Donohue murmured.

Rhys raised his eyes, startled.

The other man's expression softened, barely a flicker. "I'm sorry you lost your friend."

The video link disconnected, leaving Rhys staring at the spot where the screen had been.

It was over, then. He was formally done with the TRI. He just needed to do the cleanup.

He got up from the chair, his back aching, and retreated to the bedroom. He lay on his side, pulling a pillow under his head. Outside, the sun was bright in a cloudy blue sky. Maybe he would be allowed out there again soon. He closed his eyes. At least he'd made a start on trying to tidy up his mess.

Chapter Thirty-Nine

THERE WERE VOICES nearby.

Qasim could hear murmurs. Beyond them, the wind was wailing and heavy canvases were shaking at the force of it. Smoke. There was smoke too. Woodsmoke. A fire, somewhere nearby, meat cooking over it. The air was stuffy, but it was the warm rankness of a lot of people in an enclosed space.

He—

He couldn't remember what had happened.

The cave. He remembered the cave. Mila, still and pale as a statue, frost on her lashes. Laid out, hands on the furs covering her chest. Best he could do for her when he had to crawl. No time to weep. He remembered the bottles. The bottles and the fire and then darkness spreading over the sun.

Now, though...

Now, he was lying on his back on something softer than the ground. He was covered in more than just his clothing. Heavy and warm. He moved his fingertips. Fur or sheepskin under him. Thick. He moved his knuckles up. More furs.

Some part of him wanted to be afraid.

But for the first time in days—maybe even weeks?—his skin didn't feel like it was drawn tight. He was...warm. Not hot. Not feverish. Just warm. He was still alive and warm and wrapped up. Someone taking care of him. A stranger. Unlikely to be a thief or a killer, to tuck him in so nicely.

He was lost. Either he'd died or he'd made it home. This wasn't the plan, but now, there was no way around it.

It took effort to open his eyes, which were dry as if gritted with sand. There was light, dancing and flickering, and the sloping dip of a tent above him. He blinked slowly, trying to focus.

Someone called out in a language he didn't recognise somewhere over to his left, a few paces away. There was movement and a shadow stretched over him.

"Persian?" The silhouette said in the same language. Male, older, jovial. He rattled off a list of other words. Names of different languages, Qasim guessed and jerked his chin when he heard Arabic mentioned. It would make things easier. "Good." The man squatted beside him. "It is easier to speak to someone when you know their words."

Qasim turned enough to squint at the man. He'd come over from the fire, which cast a dancing glow on his face. Qasim could make out a long, crooked nose, glinting dark eyes, and a thick beard all framed by a thickly furred hat. "Thank you," he rasped.

The man chuckled and patted his shoulder through the furs. "Who am I, if I do not help a brother in distress?" He slid one hand under Qasim's head, gently tilting it, and lifted a brass cup to Qasim's lips. The water inside it was cool and sweet.

When his host laid him back down, he arranged Qasim's head so he could see his surroundings. It was a well-padded tent, the walls hung with layers to keep out the wind. By the light of the fire pit, he could make out maybe a dozen men seated or reclining on rugs and cushions.

"You must be hungry," his host declared, and immediately, painfully, Qasim remembered Rhys's first visit to his parents' home and the hospitality poured on him. "Do you think you could eat?"

Qasim didn't know. He couldn't remember the last time he had eaten. It— Before Mila passed. It must have been. Before the coughing and the blood and the pain.

His host gave his arm a squeeze. "We can try. It would do me no good to keep you alive only to starve you." He shook his head gravely. "My wife would be outraged."

There was a snort of laughter from one of the group, and his host turned towards them, calling out an instruction in another language—one Qasim didn't recognise. When he turned back to Qasim, he was smiling.

"I forgot to give you my name." He pressed his hand to his chest and bowed his head. "I am Abu Nasser."

It didn't feel right to give his real name, and the identity forged with Mila felt wrong too. He groped for a name, another name. He had a whole family to choose from, but even using one of them felt wrong. Wrong because he wouldn't ever see them again. Or Rhys. Rhys, who had risked everything to get him back here and would never know it had worked.

He spoke before he even thought about what it meant. "Riza."

Abu Nasser's smiled widened, and he nodded. "And now, we are friends." He rose from his crouch. "I will fetch food, then you must rest."

Somehow, Qasim managed to eat. Abu Nasser patiently fed him a porridge-like mess of ground grains, milk, and honey one small spoonful at a time. It was only a little, but it felt like a huge victory after days of tube feeding. He must have slipped back into sleep because when he was shaken awake, the tent was being dismantled around him, and sunlight was creeping across the landscape.

By daylight, he could see his host better.

Abu Nasser had to be at least fifty. His beard was peppered with silver, and his face was creased with age and too much sun. He was crouching by the makeshift bed Qasim was lying on. "Today will be hard, but we must move."

Qasim nodded, wincing as the other man helped him sit upright. His body ached, but it wasn't bone-deep pain anymore. The chill of the air hit him, and he caught his breath, then blinked and breathed in again. It stung, but it didn't hurt, not like before.

"You have colour in your face now," Abu Nasser said cheerfully. "*Alhamdulillah*! I think you will live!"

Qasim stared at him, then pressed his hand to his chest. "It worked," he whispered.

"Worked?"

"A medicine." Qasim couldn't help laughing. He could *laugh*, and it didn't hurt. "It worked."

Abu Nasser clasped his arms, as if checking how steady he was, and nodded, satisfied. "Then you may be well enough to ride."

Ride?

Qasim blinked stupidly at him, then stared around at the camp breaking around them. His world swam for a moment. There was no Otrar anywhere in sight. There was no familiar tree. There was no crack in the cliff face. There was no cliff face. He—he didn't know where he was. He was surrounded by strangers, and he didn't know where he was.

His sudden panic must have shown on his face.

"We are some miles south of Otrar. Not so far as the first *serai*, but far enough," Abu Nasser said. His warm smile shifted into something more serious. "It is better not to be in the city now." He glanced to the north, then back at Qasim. "They say the Amir is dying."

Of a cold-borne fever, Qasim remembered, or perhaps something more contagious. "*Insha'Allah*," he murmured.

They met each other's eyes, neither of them voicing any doubts about why leaving the city was the wisest course of action. A vast army without its leader was an unpredictable thing especially when the man was considered a hero to some and a bloodthirsty, murderous tyrant to others. Abu Nasser didn't so much nod but inclined his head. He was silent for a moment and then said, "We found your woman after we found you."

For a split second, it was as if the world had frozen. Qasim's throat tightened. "Tahmila."

Abu Nasser squeezed his shoulder again. "She—there was nothing that could be done for her. We gave her a proper burial."

It hit Qasim like a sledgehammer then, driving the breath from his body and folding him up over his knees. Not just Tahmila's death, but all of it: the illness, his parents weeping over him, Rhys giving up everything for him. The kindness of a stranger so far from home was too much. He covered his face with a shaking hand, swaying where he sat. Too weak to sob, too weak to do anything but let the tears stream down his face as he fought for every gasping breath.

Abu Nasser held him as he wept. The older man rubbed his back, comforting, speaking words from the *Qaf surah*. It was like a tide Qasim couldn't fight anymore, and when he was spent, his brow was resting on Abu Nasser's shoulder.

The other man squeezed the back of Qasim's neck gently with his leathery hand. "There will be time for grief." He sounded apologetic. "But now, you must rise and eat so we can be on our way."

Qasim nodded unsteadily, lifting his head. Going from somewhere he didn't know to somewhere else he didn't know with people he didn't know. If he'd had any strength left to care, he'd be terrified.

"Where are we going?" he asked as Abu Nasser pushed the furs covering Qasim's legs into the hands of one of the other men.

"Chachkand," Abu Nasser replied as he swept a thicker robe around Qasim's shoulders and wrapped him up like Qasim's mother used to on chilly winter days. "If we are lucky, we will reach the first *serai* before dusk."

Serai, Qasim thought, trying to remember all he'd read. It had to be a caravanserai—a walled complex serving as part travel inn and part taxation spot for traders on the road. "Is it far from here?"

Abu Nasser swayed his hand expressively. "Not so far, but the winds can make the journey hard, and if the snows come...." He shrugged, then tilted his head and studied Qasim. "Where do you belong? If you need to go in a different direction, we will pass Sayram if it is on your way."

Qasim stared blankly at him. Any direction, it didn't matter. Not when he had missed the gate and there was no way back.

No. Logically. He had to think.

Sayram had appeared in his notes. One of the cities where Timur's army was camped, wasn't it? Not enough information to be useful, but Chachkand was...it was familiar. Tashkent? It sounded right. One of the big crossroad cities. A good place for someone to get lost—or found—in.

"Chachkand is on my way."

Abu Nasser seemed relieved as he slipped an arm under Qasim's shoulder and practically carried him over to the larger fire, which must have burned outside the tent through the night. It was low now, little more than embers and ash, but still warm enough to huddle beside.

He was propped on cushions by the fire, left to pick at a bowl of porridge while the camp continued to break around him. When Abu Nasser returned, Qasim was swaying with the effort of staying upright.

The older man patted his shoulder. "You will ride with me today" He called out to one of the other men in a guttural language. The man led over a swaying camel. Its breath was misting in the air, and it had a broad, decorated saddle on its back.

It took the last of Qasim's energy to get up onto the animal. He clung to the saddle horn with both hands, his legs crossed over the camel's neck, as Abu Nasser mounted behind him. Abu Nasser put one arm around Qasim's waist, holding him steady.

When the caravan moved out, Qasim glanced back towards the north. Somewhere back there, Mila was buried, and a gate had closed, and his life was caught in an uncontrollable current. He pressed his eyes closed, trying to hold it together. At his back, Abu Nasser must have felt him shaking.

"It will be well," Abu Nasser said quietly. "*Insha'Allah.*"

"*Insha'Allah,*" Qasim whispered, groping under his robe for his prayer beads. "*Insha'Allah.*"

Chapter Forty

NO CHARGES WERE being laid.

It was a small mercy in a world rapidly swirling down the toilet.

Rhys had spoken to his lawyer. Two days later, a completely different solicitor showed up. She strode in like an empress and introduced herself as Victoria Cheung. Everything about her screamed authority, and she must have been good at her job because every piece of clothing was tailor-made. She asked a lot more questions, pushing him for answers when he hesitated, then left without ceremony.

Four days of fretting later, Jacob chimed in to tell him the news.

"It's as simple as that?"

Jacob nodded. "Qasim's parents made it clear they don't want charges brought for... for their son's loss, no matter how much the Board might want it. Whatever Cheung said, it was enough to get the Board to back down. Took them a while, but yeah. It's over."

Rhys knew he should feel relieved, but he was so tired. Part of him felt raw, like a chunk of him had been hacked away, and all he could do was stare at it. "That's good."

Jacob hesitated, then said, "The company feels there should be some punishment, though, even if criminal charges aren't proceeding."

Ah. The hammer, waiting to fall.

"Tell me."

"A substantial fine." Jacob didn't look happy about it. "You signed the nondisclosures and your severance paperwork, didn't you?"

Rhys could see the shape of what was going unsaid. The severance package had been surprisingly generous. It had lulled him into a false sense of security, convinced he'd be able to manage. "How much are they taking?"

Jacob grimaced. "We managed to argue them down to seventy-five percent. They wanted to cut it off completely."

Rhys braced his hand against the edge of the table. "Right," he said, his voice unsteady. "Fair enough."

"Bullshit," Jacob snapped. He pressed his knuckle to his lips and then asked, "Are you going to be okay?"

"Of course," Rhys said automatically. Christ, he would have to redo all his sums and see how much he could afford until he found a new job. If he spread it all a bit thinner, it could stretch. The last thing he needed was Jacob paying too much attention. "What about Ben? Is he still in trouble?"

Jacob shook his head. "He's going to be under supervision for the foreseeable future when he's using the TRI mainframe, but he's far too gifted with the system to be fired." He tapped his fingers on the tabletop. "I think they took his mental state for the past few months into account. He hasn't been— Things have been hard for him. Qasim's illness pushed him over the line."

Rhys nodded. He knew how it felt. "I'm glad he'll be okay. And he'll be here. The TRI is too important to him."

"Yeah." Jacob agreed. "But I'm not here to talk about Ben. This is about you, Rhys. I need to know how you're doing."

Rhys met Jacob's eyes defiantly. No one needed to make a fuss. He'd made the mess. He could work his way out of it. "I'll be fine."

"You should take up poker." Jacob sighed. "Look, if you need help, you have friends here. There's not one of us who doesn't understand why you did it."

Rhys had to take a steadying breath. Obligation. He understood, but if he let them help him, if the Supervisory Board knew, then his colleagues would be condemned with him. "Honestly, I'll be fine. New job. New flat. Nothing to worry about."

Jacob leaned closer to the camera. "I like you, Rhys, but you are the most pig-headed bugger I've ever had the misfortune of meeting." He gave Rhys a pointed look. "If I hear you've ended up living in a box, I'm going to drag you back to stay in my spare room, understood?"

Rhys nodded. "I'll be fine. I've been in a worse state than this before."

It was nothing more than the depressing truth.

There had been some tight times at university when he couldn't work as much as he and his mam both needed to. There were even those days when art students were willing to pay more by the hour for a model than his part-time job did.

Jacob raised his eyebrows. "Rhys, I swear to God..."

"I've sold my flat," he said firmly. "Got enough to get by on. Don't worry."

"You know I will anyway." Jacob sighed. He glanced off-camera again. "I've got to go. I'll try and chime in again before you're released, but things are hectic out here. We're trying to get through the backlog."

"I don't need babysitting, Jacob." Rhys managed to force a smile. "Just swing by when they let me out."

Jacob nodded. "Definitely. If I don't manage to chime before, I'll see you then."

As soon as the link disconnected, Rhys dropped his glasses onto the tabletop and buried his face in his hands. It felt like he'd been watching an incoming tidal wave after the earthquake of Qasim's death. Two more days and it would hit. He would be out in the world without a home or a job or any income. Without the man who had become his closest friend, who had trusted him and who had, perhaps, loved—

He took deep, shivering breaths, trying to focus himself.

Going down those roads wouldn't get him anywhere.

Okay. *Okay.*

Money. He had to work out the money side of things first.

He lowered his hands and retrieved his glasses, then popped out his folio screen. They'd given him access to his external data, and he opened the spreadsheets for his budgets. The money from the flat was gone already. Direct transfer, paying off most of a house he was never going to see.

He searched out and amended the severance figure.

Immediately, a rash of numbers dipped into the negatives.

"Shit," he whispered into his hand. Stubble rasped against his fingers. Shaving had seemed like such an effort.

He spent the afternoon moving numbers around. It didn't help much, not with the cost of accommodation in the city and how difficult it could be to get a job with NDAs slapped all over him. How could he explain why he'd left his last job when the job was secret, and he'd been fired?

He ended up retreating to the shower and sitting, eyes closed, as the water drummed down. He didn't know how long he sat there. It was meant to be until he felt better, but it felt like a pipe dream.

The next day was a struggle.

He tried to hold on to the few positive things he had left—no jail time, at least some of his severance package, the support of his colleagues, and for his first night of freedom, a discounted room at a small guest house in a decent part of town.

It was something, and it was safer than thinking of everything that had led him there.

And yet...

And yet, he couldn't stop thinking of Qasim's face, lit by the gate, the hope and fear and gratitude in his eyes. Every time he did, the regret hit him— the fact he hadn't at least tried to go with him, to carry him if he had to.

More than once, he ended up with his face pressed into his hands, smothering his sobs.

It was the isolation. There weren't enough distractions. Not his precarious situation. Not the media on the machines. Not even people chiming in. None of it was enough when he had screwed up so badly.

By the next morning, he had the numbers in some kind of order. He hadn't slept much, but he had a plan. He could take a day or two for mourning everything he'd lost, find somewhere quiet to get rat-arsed and forget for a bit, then get down to work. Things needed to be kept simple. If not...

Well, it didn't bear thinking about.

He showered, shaved, and dressed in his own clothes, which had been delivered for him. He needed to act as if he was good to go or Jacob wouldn't let him out on his own.

It was ten to ten when the door finally opened. A pod was waiting on the other side, and he stepped into it. A couple of minutes later, it emerged at the pod bay. He wasn't surprised to see Jacob waiting for him on the narrow strip of the platform. He was thankfully alone, and there was no one else in sight.

Rhys stepped out of the pod, taking his first breath of fresh air in weeks. It shouldn't have been a surprise when Jacob stepped closer and bent to hug him. He had to press his eyes shut against the emotion, and he could only pat Jacob on the back in acknowledgement.

Jacob straightened up. "I guessed you wouldn't want a big send-off."

"No," Rhys agreed hoarsely. He hesitated uncertainly. "I—my stuff. It's in H-block. Can I—" He remembered the paperwork and the clauses and the NDAs. No access to TRI properties once he left quarantine. "Oh."

"All sorted and packed up," Jacob said, his hand on Rhys's shoulder. "We'll send it all on for you."

Rhys nodded numbly. Just like that, turned out. "Right."

Jacob led him over to the lift, and they ascended into the lobby. "Do you want to get something to eat with me before you go? They won't stop you."

It was tempting to go, to sit and eat in the canteen as if nothing had changed, as if he'd be back the next day for his next mission. It would make things worse, though, knowing it was the last time.

He shook his head. "I need to go. Better to get it over with." He stepped back and held out his hand to Jacob, wishing he could stop it from shaking so much. "Thank you. You— I'm glad you were my boss."

Jacob brushed aside his hand, then stepped forward and caught him in another bear hug, nearly lifting him off his feet. "I'm going to miss you, Rhys. Who else is going to bitch with me when no one is looking?"

Rhys laughed unsteadily. "I'm sure you'll find someone." He had to clear his throat and blinked hard as he pulled away.

Jacob held out a folded leather wallet, Rhys's own wallet from his room in H-block. "You know where you can find me, if you need a hand."

Rhys nodded, taking the wallet.

"And one more thing..." Jacob stepped behind the reception desk and emerged with a carrier. Rhys caught his breath when he realised what— who—was inside it. Pisi. Qasim's cat. His cat now. "I think he'd want you to take care of her."

Rhys nodded, holding out his hand for the case. Pisi was complaining, and Christ, he wanted to take her out and bury his face in her fur and just forget for a minute. But he couldn't. Not now.

"Thanks," he managed to say.

He turned and walked away as fast as he could, out into the courtyard, before Jacob could see him crying. The wind was cool, but the sun was out, hints of a pleasant summer to come. He put his head down, hurrying towards the transport hub.

Once he got to the other side, his pod would be waiting. From there, he just had to get to the guest house and then find somewhere with the cheapest and most effective booze he could get his hands on and spend the rest of the night drowning his sorrows.

There shouldn't have been anyone in the hub, which was why he nearly shat himself when a shadow peeled away from the wall.

"Mr. Griffiths."

O'Donohue?

Rhys stared at him. Of course, they'd want someone from upstairs to make sure he left. "I'm going, okay?" He sounded miserable, but he couldn't help it. "You don't need to watch."

O'Donohue approached him. "I'm not here to gloat, Mr. Griffiths." He was only a few inches taller than Rhys, but he seemed so much more imposing. He extended a hand, holding a business card between two fingers. "You have an appointment on Wednesday. It's your choice whether you go or not, but I..." He shrugged elegantly. "It would give me peace of mind."

Rhys took the card warily and turned it over. It was the name and address of a therapist's clinic. He flushed with shame. "I don't—this—it's not necessary."

O'Donohue gazed down at him, his expression unreadable. "Perhaps not, but consider it this way—Dr. Richards is a neutral third party bound by doctor-patient confidentiality. If you need someone to talk to about all this...bullshit." He waved vaguely in the direction of the main building. "He's as good a person as any to vent to. Believe me."

Rhys read the card again. "Why do you give a damn? I'm out of your hair now. You don't need to give a shit."

For once, O'Donohue smiled. His sharp features seemed to soften, making him less intimidating. "Because you're a good man who did a brave thing, Rhys." He patted Rhys's shoulder with one of those long, slender hands. "I can't do much, but I can do this." He leaned closer, and his eyes were so dark they appeared black. "Like I said. Peace of mind."

Before Rhys could say anything, O'Donohue stepped around him and walked away, vanishing into the bright June sunlight.

Rhys looked at the card again. He'd been to a therapist once before, a long time back. His dad had told him it was a waste of time and money. You couldn't fix being a fat pussy by crying about it. He slipped the card into his pocket.

The shuttle was already waiting for him, and once it started moving, he took the card out again, studying it.

Of all the people to offer help, he hadn't expected it from O'Donohue. The last time they'd seen each other, he'd ended up shouting at the man, venting all his frustration and misery. Maybe that was why. O'Donohue could tell he needed someone to talk to and had given him an option which meant he wouldn't be breaking any NDAs.

There was a time and date written on the card in blue ink.

Rhys stared at it.

There was time to decide. Not today, though. Today was...today was for taking some time and then, after, he could start picking up the pieces. He tucked it into his pocket beside his wallet and gave in to the temptation to take Pisi out of her cage, wrapping his hand in the leash hooked onto her harness. Thankfully, she didn't try to run off, even when he hugged her closer and buried his face in the thick ruff of her fur.

Several minutes later, the shuttle drew into the hub, and Pisi wailed in indignation as he bundled her back into the carrier.

Rhys hesitated before getting up. This was it: his final moment in the TRI. It wasn't how he'd wanted to leave. Nothing about it was how he'd planned it. He took a deep breath and stepped out onto the platform. It didn't feel like anything had changed. It was all the difference in the world, but it was nothing more than stepping through a door.

"Rhys!"

He spun around, startled at a woman's voice.

Once upon a time, months ago, Qasim's family had swept in to collect their son. Now...

His eyes were burning, and he stared in shock as a tiny, plump woman in a hijab rushed towards him. She wasn't alone either. Familiar faces. All familiar faces. All much sadder than they had been, but all coming towards him, smiling.

Mrs. El-Fahkri reached him first and caught him in a tight hug. He staggered, dazed, and his free arm moved of its own accord, hugging her.

She was crying and he was as well. Other hands were touching him, and he was at the centre of a multi-armed embrace by more of Qasim's family than he could count.

"We take care of each other," Mrs. El-Fahkri whispered. "For him."

Rhys's vision was blurred with tears, and he nodded, burying his face in her shoulder. "For him."

Chapter Forty-One

SOMETIMES, ROAD TRIPS could be fun.

To Blackpool, or maybe down to Caernarfon. Those were nice trips.

Trekking through pre-Kazakhstan in winter on the back of a grumpy camel while recovering from a life-threatening illness was not. Especially when you were also trying not to get in the way of the sprawling restless army of a dying warlord.

Mercifully, Abu Nasser seemed to share his apprehension. Their passage through Sayram, where thousands of soldiers were impatiently awaiting news and orders from the north, was made swiftly. If anyone in the caravan questioned it, Abu Nasser told them they were free to take rest in the city, but he and his would continue on their way.

As warm and welcoming as the city walls were, Qasim was glad when they—and the ranks of soldiers and tents—were far behind them. It made the day longer and the journey harder, but it felt much safer.

In the courtyard of the latest *serai*, Qasim tried to slide off the saddle as smoothly as Abu Nasser, but his legs went out from under him again. Six conscious days on the road and he still wasn't even able to walk to their latest shelter. It was exhausting and frustrating, but Abu Nasser and his companions never complained.

They also paid his way into the caravanserais as they travelled south. Qasim wasn't sure what he'd been expecting, but it wasn't the miniature fortresses popping up along the road. Most of them were high-walled around an open courtyard, hemmed in on all sides by chambers. One even had a tiny mosque, Abu Nasser informed him. They had made sure of it, only a few years ago.

It was a strange kind of luxury, sitting by a fire in a neatly decorated room, a rich but well-worn Persian carpet beneath him and a cup of Chinese tea cradled in his hands. Sometimes, it made the hardship of the day feel like a dream.

A few of the men would join him and Abu Nasser, who was always honoured with the largest of the rooms. They, he came to realise, were the leaders of the whole caravan. They were the ones who had made the decision to bring him with them and nurse him back to health.

It surprised him how easily they'd accepted him, since he brought nothing to trade and was only a burden to them. He said as much one night as the wind wailed outside and the night muffled the sounds of the caravanserai.

Kaskil snorted. He was one of the northern men in the group. Siberian, Qasim guessed, or whatever Siberia was called in this era. He came from beyond the Aral Sea, much farther north than Otrar, and under his furs, his clothes were decorated with embroidery and beading.

"Is simple," he said in accented Arabic as he chewed on his long-stemmed pipe. "If you see fallen man, you help fallen man. If you fall, you hope other man help you."

There were nods around the fire.

"I could have been a thief," Qasim pointed out.

Kaskil grinned at him. His teeth were stained brown. "No. A thief is a dead man."

"He's right," Arzani, one of the younger men, said. He was sitting cross-legged opposite Qasim, working at a piece of wood with a knife. He shot a dark smile across the fire. "We know these roads. We know thieves. Thieves die."

Qasim's uneasiness must have shown on his face because Abu Nasser chuckled and nudged him. "Why do you think we travel with so many? It takes a brave thief—brave thieves—to try to rob us."

"And if they do?"

Abu Nasser shrugged prosaically. "Thieves have no honour. They will be punished."

Kaskil sniggered and slashed the tip of his pipe across his throat in demonstration.

It was comforting to know he wasn't seen as a threat, but it still made Qasim nervous to be around so many heavily armed men. A few of them carried swords. Abu Nasser had daggers at his belt. And yet, they managed to make him feel safe at the same time.

The nightmares had come back two days into the journey.

He had woken half the rooms in the *serai*, screaming. Abu Nasser was the one to wake him, and he would almost swear he could feel the eyes of the others in the doorway. He wished he could explain, but he could only lie there, clutching at his chest and trying to breathe. New nightmares now.

Mila, bleeding from the mouth. Rhys, reaching through the gate and being torn apart when it closed. His parents sobbing as they were ripped away. Swords of enemies and friends cutting him to pieces.

He was a sick man. A fevered, delirious, sick man.

The next night, in the next *serai*, he wasn't left to sleep alone. By the fourth night, half a dozen of them were piled together under thick blankets in the largest room available. *Better against the cold, Kaskil said gruffly. To be sure they all slept, Abu Nasser agreed.*

They drew blankets close around Qasim. It helped. Warmth and someone on either side seemed to convince his stupid, stupid brain he was safe.

As he lay in the darkness, surrounded by snoring men, he thought it was strange. He'd expected the nightmares, but he'd also expected the fear to set in about what he was meant to do next. It hadn't materialised. Exhaustion, he guessed. Still too weak and tired to be scared.

The journey was a distraction from everything as well. He had to concentrate so much on staying upright he didn't have time to worry about anything else. Now, in the quiet dark of the night, with the wind outside and the men around him asleep, he could think.

There were so many little things running through his head: Ummi's little smile when he hugged her unexpectedly; Abi slipping him extra candied petals from Ummi's special box; Aisha throwing a pillow at him and laughing in her wedding dress; Malika and Nasreen on the rollercoaster at Blackpool, their hijabs blown up in their faces; the kids. All the kids he'd never see again.

He pressed his lips together and blinked hard. No more stories. No more Murad the thief of Baghdad. No more laughing with them or fighting over the sugared almonds and dates or wrestling his game consoles back or...or...any of it.

And Rhys...

Oh, Rhys.

"Queen," he remembered in a whisper. "F6."

A chess game they would never finish.

An order, too: *You go. You get your medicine, and when you come back, we finish our chess game.*

An order from a supervisor, technically. It kind of made it a mission, didn't it?

The trouble was he didn't have a rendezvous point.

Even if he could remember somewhere—somewhen—the TRI had already visited in the past, approaching an old mission would have serious ramifications. Yes, it might have been enough to get him home, but he was already in their timeline. He'd heard horror stories of people who had crossed their own timeline: unexplained collapses and deaths, as the laws of physics tried to correct themselves.

Anyway, if anyone had been sent on a mission to this area, it would have been him and Mila.

So, the first problem was a pickup.

Outside, the wind was rising, and he curled onto his side. There had to be some way, something he could do. He lay in the stale darkness, turning over idea after idea.

There had to be some way to make use of getting caught in the fallout of the biggest political incident of the period—the death of Timur and the collapse of his empire. The trouble was Qasim hadn't done much research about what came after. He hadn't needed the information for the mission.

He must have fallen asleep because, next he knew, Kaskil was prodding him away.

"Today, we see Chachkand," he said, hauling Qasim to his feet.

"Soon?"

Kaskil shrugged. "Maybe soon. Maybe not soon. Snow comes."

He wasn't wrong.

By the time the camels were loaded up and Qasim emerged, unsteady, into the bustling courtyard, the air was thick with swirling flakes. The warmth of so many bodies and so many animals melted it on impact, leaving the ground thick with filthy slush as the procession of camels, donkeys, and people set out through the arched gateway.

It was a long day, and hard, but Qasim didn't mind. He had a mission. He had fragments of ideas. He held onto Abu Nasser as they rode, buffeted by the wind, his face buried in the older man's furred coat, and tried to come up with a plan.

Timur was important. After all, Abu Nasser and the traders had left Otrar based on rumours Timur may be dying, which meant they were carrying the message on to other cities. Other cities and other parts of the empire would soon hear about it. And that was before the man was even dead.

It was...significant.

Qasim knew it was, but his brain was still slowed by the illness. Timur. He had to use Timur somehow. The warlord was famous—notorious—in the history books. He was like Genghis Khan. People from all over feared him. There was...something there. Something he could use.

When Abu Nasser tapped on the back of his hand, he lifted his head to peer over his shoulder.

"Chachkand!" Abu Nasser called over the howling wind, pointing ahead with his stick.

Qasim squinted against the flurries of snow, spotting a darker shape on the horizon. For it to be visible, it had to be big.

As they got closer, he could make out the vast city walls riding up to meet them, huge with gates studded into them. There were at least three, and if the city was so big, there had to be more.

Mercifully, they reached one of the gates before sundown. There were processions of travellers making their way through, and Abu Nasser led their convoy to the northernmost gate, raising his stick in salutation to the guards with their swords and their matching armour. Qasim shuddered instinctively, remembering the last guards he had crossed. Four months ago already and more than two centuries into the future.

"*Assalamu alaikum!*" one of them called up. "You have braved the snows, Abu Nasser?"

"*Wa'alaikum al-salaam!*" Abu Nasser laughed. "For my own good," he called down as they plodded past. "You know my sons would never forgive me if I was trapped in the north again during Ramadan."

The other guard chuckled. "Nor your wife."

"*Subhan'Allah!* It did not come to pass!" He was twisting in the saddle. He raised his stick and waved again as they continued.

Qasim could feel the threads of something coming together. "Ramadan? So soon?"

Abu Nasser tapped the camel's shoulder with the stick, guiding it onwards. Despite the winter chill in the air, the narrow streets were thronged with people. "The next moon rise from now. It comes so soon every year." He tilted his head to squint back at Qasim. "Where will you go from here?"

Qasim shook his head, looking around at the city. He didn't know nearly enough. Timur. Ramadan. Chachkand. A time and a place, nothing more. Everything he knew about Tashkent could be scribbled on the back of a bus ticket. An essay written about medieval Islamic architecture when he was seventeen was useless in a time before the architecture was even built.

The scent of jewel-toned spices on a nearby stall reached him, even over the reek of the gutters and the scent of the people. There would be a mosque too. Several maybe. Missions were simple. This wasn't. There was so much he didn't know and couldn't be sure of. He needed information to build on the idea that could possibly maybe be a plan.

"I don't know," he admitted. "I'm a long way from home. I need to plan my journey."

Abu Nasser reached back and patted his knee through his thick robes. "Until you know your plans, my home is your home."

A weight dropped from Qasim's shoulders. Somewhere safe. It was the best chance he had now, but he still had to say, "You have done so much for me, Abu Nasser. I could not ask you for more."

It was a bluff, praying the rules of hospitality were the same here as they were at home. All the same, he held his breath.

To his relief, Abu Nasser snorted. "You must think little of me, if you think I will leave you friendless and alone in my city." He knocked Qasim on the knee again. "'Let whosoever believes in Allah and in the Last Day honour his guest.'"

"Then I will be happy to stay." Qasim smiled. Three days taken care of, at the very least.

Abu Nasser nodded cheerfully. "You will rest, and you will grow strong, and when you are well, we shall send you on your way to your people."

Qasim nodded, his thoughts four thousand miles and six hundred and fifty years away, as the camel plodded on through the winding streets. "*Insha'Allah.*"

Chapter Forty-Two

STAYING WITH QASIM'S family was like living in a different world.

Rhys had been given one of the spare rooms in the El-Fahkris' house. Mrs. El-Fahkri had refused to take no for an answer. She rattled off her reasons in Arabic and glowered sternly at him as her husband explained how Qasim had told them about the flat hunt. Until he had somewhere to live, the least they could do was make sure he had somewhere to call home.

Part of him wanted to say no. It was force of habit, not to want to get in the way or cause a fuss, but he remembered what Qasim had told him about the importance of hospitality to his family.

So, he said yes, and Mrs. El-Fahkri hugged him. He didn't want to let her down. It was what he told himself. It was for her. She was taking him and Pisi in, a pair of strays, because her son would have wanted it, and if it made her happy, so be it.

In a matter of hours, he was already settling. In less than three days, he realised he felt at home. He couldn't remember the last time he'd felt so comfortable. Even with Marc, there had been the undercurrents of things he wasn't happy about, but here...

Here, there were no threats, and no one was pushing him in ways he didn't want to go. There was comfort.

At first, the guilt was still hanging on him, but after a few days of sitting down for dinner with Rasha and Youssef—they insisted he call them by name—and helping around the house and even just sitting and watching films or streams with Pisi curled up in his lap, it started to sink in. It was...nice. It was safe, and he wasn't unwanted. He was even welcome, despite everything.

It was like a punch to the chest.

Rasha sat beside him and took his hand. He jumped and then blinked hard, startled to realise he was crying.

"You are sad here?" she asked, searching his face.

He shook his head, trying to find the words to explain. "Happy. You—you've been so kind to me. It—I haven't—it's different for me."

She brushed away his tears with her thumb. "You are kind for my son and lose all things for him." She smiled sadly at him. "He love you very much."

Rhys gazed down at their joined hands. "I loved him too," he confessed in a whisper.

She squeezed his fingers. "I know. We all know. You make him smile." She leaned her shoulder against his, and they sat in silence for a moment. She sighed quietly. "We will make memory-day for him. For all people to remember, not only family. For them to say goodbye too."

Rhys nodded, squeezing her fingers again, unable to speak. Qasim deserved so much more. His family too. He didn't know how she could be so calm about it all. He knew she must have cried, because more often than not, her eyes were red-rimmed, but she still managed to smile.

He wished he could do the same.

Despite his misgivings, he went to the appointment on O'Donohue's card, and he spoke with—at—Dr. Richards. It was meant to be about Qasim and the TRI. At first, it was...about all the anger and frustration and how useless he had been. But somehow, it turned into more: his childhood, his parents, the emotional abuse—yes, it was abuse, Dr. Richards said—and the scars he hadn't even noticed.

It left him wrung out like a damp cloth, but after the doctor had shone a light on it, he could see how he was still turned around by it all. It didn't take away any of the grief. It was like uncovering old wounds. Painful and awful, but like any wound, it needed to be cleaned out, instead of left to fester.

He made another appointment, even if part of him believed he was making a fuss about nothing. The fact he wanted to run told him how much he needed to be there. He didn't—there was no way it was something he could do on his own. The cost made him hesitate, but the doctor said not to worry about it, the first three were free. Rhys couldn't help wondering why—or maybe who had arranged it—but he nodded and marked the next appointment in his folio.

He took refuge in a bar for a little while on the way back to the El-Fahkri house. One drink, maybe two, until his chest stopped feeling so tight and his hands stopped shaking. It had been...a lot. So much. Even sending Qasim back had been a pushback against his father's tirades. Jesus, so many stupid things done, all because he needed to believe he could do better.

Even though he felt like cack, he did feel a little better too. Like he'd been tied up in cords and the doctor had cut some loose. It was as if he had room to breathe for the first time in...God only knew how long.

By the time he reached the house, he was feeling calmer. It was a good thing too. Qasim's memorial was the next day, and he wanted to get through it without falling apart again. He touched the console at the front door and had to dive down and capture Pisi, who tried to make a dash for freedom.

"No," he said sternly, carrying the cat back into the house. "You stay inside now, until we make sure you don't give us a legion of mutant historical cat-babies."

She squalled and wriggled indignantly, and as soon as he put her down, she raced off up the stairs.

"Rasha?" Rhys called. "Are you home?"

She was usually at the house, either surrounded by grandchildren or with some of her friends. Youssef was out most days until late. He worked in law, Rhys recalled, and even with his son's passing, he said he couldn't let his clients down.

From the smell of it, Rasha was working in the kitchen. She'd insisted on making food for the memorial, even though all her daughters said she didn't have to. Even her mother had been unceremoniously sent off to Aisha's until things were organised. Rhys had left her already working on pastries, and it definitely smelled like she'd moved onto the savouries.

Distraction. Everyone was trying to distract themselves.

He toed off his shoes and padded to the kitchen. As soon as the door opened, the smell went from being savoury to acrid, and there was smoke coiling up to the ceiling. Rasha was sitting on her small footstool, her face buried in her hands, and over the hiss from the pans, he could hear her sobbing.

Rhys rushed forward to turn off all the rings of the vast range and then knelt in front of her, gathering her up in his arms. She didn't resist, clutching at the front of his shirt and shaking in his embrace.

No wonder. She'd sent everyone else off, told them to go, and been left on her own with her grief. She didn't want to upset anyone any more than he did.

"I burn it all," she whispered minutes later, when the shaking had subsided. "All bad now."

He sat back on his heels. "We can fix it," he said, using the end of his sleeve to dry her cheeks. He glanced up at the hob. "I'm ready to help, I am." He tried to smile. "I'm not very good, but you can show me what to do."

She searched his face and nodded, letting him help her back to her feet. "Sorry for..." She motioned to her tear-stained face.

His throat felt tight and he hugged her again. "We take care of each other," he reminded her, his voice more choked than he'd hoped. She squeezed him tightly and nodded. When he stepped back, she winced at the mess on the stove. Several pans had boiled dry. "Where do we start?"

In the end, they didn't make half as much food as Rasha had planned. Too many of the ingredients were used up, and they didn't have enough time to get more. But with a little persuasion, Rhys managed to convince her to call around to her daughters and see if they could either put something together or arrange deliveries from restaurants.

She was frowning as she finished the calls, and he reached over to squeeze her hand and said, "It's all right not to do everything yourself." She gave him a doubtful frown which told him Qasim had told her far too much about him, and he smiled weakly. "I saw a therapist today. He gave me some advice. I'm trying to listen."

"You ask for help too?" She sounded surprised.

He hesitated and then shook his head. "I was offered this time, but I asked for next time." He settled back on the couch beside her. "See? We're both trying new things."

She gave his fingers a squeeze. "Better now?"

"Maybe. You?"

She glanced towards the kitchen. "We see for morning, when food come."

When morning came and Qasim's family started arriving with boxes, Rasha was clearly relieved—and surprised—though it didn't stop her checking all of the contents, just to make sure. He managed to weave his way between the flocking grandchildren to reach her.

"See? It's not so bad."

She smiled at him, and her eyes were bright. "And not all burned."

The official memorial was being held in the afternoon, so the morning was spent arranging tables in the garden and as many spare chairs and gazebos as could fit. The house was big, but with the number of people coming, there was no chance of everyone fitting indoors.

Rhys made himself scarce when the time for salat came, but as soon as it was over, he was called back down. Pisi was closed up in his room with a litter box, enough food, and a very securely locked door.

He wasn't sure what to expect of the memorial. He had only been to a couple of funerals in his life, and this was something different. He didn't expect the stories, the laughter, and the kids all squabbling over Murad the Thief's greatest adventure. Folios projected pictures of Qasim at various ages all around the garden and the house. Rhys wandered through the rooms and the garden looking at them all, his heart aching. It was ridiculous how happy one man could make so many people, but Rhys could feel it. There was sadness, but there was also so much joy.

It felt right, like they weren't mourning a death, but celebrating the life of a good man.

"Rhys?"

He turned from a picture of Qasim dressed up as a pirate and found himself face-to-face with Jacob. "Jacob. Hi." He shook Jacob's hand. "I didn't know if you'd come."

Jacob smiled sadly. He was dressed sombrely, which was out of place next to the colourful clothes of Qasim's family, who had decided unanimously to dress as Qasim would have liked. "A bunch of us came from the TRI. More would've, but the job still needs to be done."

Rhys nodded. "They'll be glad you're here." He glanced around the vast living room. "I think Youssef is in the garden, and it's a fifty-fifty chance Rasha's in the kitchen again."

Jacob studied him. "And things are okay for you?"

"I've got a roof over my head," Rhys replied. "Taking things as they come."

Jacob studied him a moment longer. "What I said still stands."

Rhys knew the man would only keep worrying, so at least he could ease some of his concern. "I'm seeing a therapist about everything." A bit embarrassing to admit it, but it was helping and knowing about it would comfort Jacob. "He—it's making a difference."

Jacob looked relieved. "That's good. Talking to someone always helps." He glanced around. "Speaking of, if you can find him, Ben was looking for you. He wanted a word."

Rhys could guess what it was about. The two of them had committed a crime. Only one of them had been fired. "I'll find him."

In the end, he didn't need to bother. As soon as Jacob headed to the garden, Ben was at his side, grabbing him by the arm.

"We need to talk," he whispered urgently. "Privately."

Rhys blinked at him in surprise. "Um. We could use my room?"

Ben nodded, looking around warily. "Quick. Before Jacob comes back."

Rhys led him out into the hall and up the stairs. "What's this about?"

"Privacy first," Ben said.

Rhys unlocked the door to his room and caught Pisi around the middle as she tried to bolt again. "In." he said, nodding through the door, and Ben hurried in. Rhys closed the door behind them and set the grumbling Pisi down on the end of his bed. "Why all the cloak and dagger?"

Ben spun to face him, a manic gleam in his eye. "Qasim's still alive."

If the floor had dropped out from under him, Rhys couldn't have been more shocked. "Ben..." He sat next to Pisi on the bed and stroked her fur, hoping he didn't appear as shaken as he felt. "I know we would like it if he was, but it's im—"

"No, it's not." Ben flicked open a folio screen from his watch and spread it in front of Rhys. "Qasim told me if he ever got lost in the past, he'd send me a letter." He pointed at a scrawl of Arabic letters. "It's his name. There."

Rhys stared through the projection. "You're joking."

Ben shook his head frantically. "I swear, Rhys! I have letters. I think they were from my dad. I told Qasim about them, and he said it was impossible, but if it was possible, if he ever got lost, he'd get a letter to me and this..." He was breathing too fast. "As soon as they gave me my computer access back, I went hunting in every historical archive, just in case. I found this."

"There have to be thousands of people with the same name," Rhys said, shaking his head.

"From the right time and the right area?" Ben sat on the edge of the bed beside him. "Look. Here. It mentions Timur, the guy who they were meant to be looking for. It's all about his death. That's why it was in the archives. Qasim is *insanely* smart, and he'd know people would keep something like this."

Rhys stared at the letter. It was a high-quality scan, but the original had been damaged. Not surprising if it was more than six hundred years old. There were tears along the edges, a few holes and stains. If it was true, it would have been a miracle, but it was impossible.

"It's just a coincidence."

"No!" Ben exclaimed angrily. "No, it's not!" He shifted the folio projection and brought up a document in English. "Look, I translated as much as I could. If you were a time traveller in the past and you needed someone to know where you are, what would you need to tell them?"

Rhys sighed. "Ben, this isn't—"

"Humour me!"

He studied the boy and then held up his hands. "Fine. You'd need a location."

Ben highlighted several points in the translation. "Chachkand. It's the old name for Tashkent."

"And you'd need an exact date."

Ben highlighted another paragraph.

Rhys leaned forward to read it: *With Ramadan close upon us, we mourn the death of the noble Amir Timur. He will be remembered with honour by his brothers at the Jumu'ah Masjid.*

"Ramadan," he murmured, looking at Ben.

"Ramadan 1405," Ben said excitedly. "Timur died in the middle of February. And look! He even gave us a day—at the Jumu'ah mosque. *Jumu'ah* is the word for the Friday noon prayers." He beamed. "Guess what day they'll be on."

Rhys felt a sudden rush of terror and hope. "Do you know the date? I mean, there has to be a record of—"

"March 15th, 1405," Ben interrupted, nodding. "That should be the first Friday of the Ramadan after Timur's death."

It couldn't be true. It wasn't possible. Qasim was so sick when he went through the gate. Even if he'd gotten to the medicine, how the hell could he have travelled so far? Rhys remembered Qasim's maps. It was at least a hundred and fifty miles between Otrar and Tashkent. It wasn't a journey a sick man could make in a fortnight.

"No." Rhys stood and rubbed his hands on his trousers, trying to stop them shaking. "No, I can't believe it. It's just a coincidence."

"Read it!" Ben expanded it out. "Please! If Qasim sent it, he would make sure we could tell. He'd put something in, some special clue for someone who knows him well. You...you were his." His eyes were bright with emotion. "*Please.*"

Rhys ran a hand over his face. "I—if there's nothing, you can't tell anyone else about this. It would upset too many people." He met Ben's eyes. "Do you promise to drop it if I don't see anything?"

Ben stuck out his chin stubbornly. "As long as you promise to tell me if there is something."

Rhys nodded, returning to sit on the bed. "Okay." His heart was fluttering as he pulled the projection towards him. "How good's your Arabic?"

Ben made a face at him. "I lived with Mariam since I was seven. I can read it as well as her sons."

Which meant it would be a decent translation.

Rhys took a shaky breath. "Right."

The first paragraph was a salutation and the news of Timur's death. The writer had heard the news in Tashkent and dispatched messages to those who would wish to hear it. He skimmed over the parts about the mosque and Ramadan.

It looked like any letter from the era. He glanced at Ben, startled by the desperate expression on his face. Whatever happened with this letter, it clearly meant a lot more to the boy than he was telling.

Rhys turned his attention back to the final paragraph. A couple of words caught his eye. "Ben..." he said carefully. "This part here. You've got 'mountain castle' with a question mark."

Ben nodded. He flicked open a copy of the original image. "Here." He pointed out a section. "I'm not good with landscape terms, so I found a translation by historians." He shook his head. "This bit's been confusing people for years. It's about an elephant getting into a castle between two mountains." He wrinkled his nose. "They can't agree which castle or what mountains or whose elephants or..." He frowned. "Rhys? Are you okay?"

Rhys was staring blindly at the message. His heart was pounding hard. "Not castle. Fortress. The fortress between two hills..." Their last nights in lockdown. The ridiculous joke he'd made. The elephant. Qasim's elephant. He pressed his hand to his mouth. "Jesus." He stared at Ben, trying to remember how to breathe. "He's alive."

Ben's mouth dropped open. "Really?"

Rhys started laughing, throwing an arm around the boy's shoulder. "Yes! He's alive!"

Chapter Forty-Three

THE CALLS TO prayer were ringing out across the city.

Qasim opened his eyes, listening.

It was still dark outside.

He'd been in Chachkand for a fortnight already, and every morning, he woke just before the *muezzin*'s call to listen, even if it was all he had the strength to do. It was something comforting and familiar in a strange place.

It helped, having a touchstone of reality.

He could barely remember the first week in Abu Nasser's home. He'd been fed, bathed, and then slept for hours, maybe days at a time. It was like some strange dream, but, little by little, he was growing stronger, and the world was becoming more tangible again.

Although he hadn't been able to venture out yet, Abu Nasser's house was high up in the city and let him take in the scale of the place. It reminded him a lot of Otrar with winding labyrinthine alleys and closely packed houses. From dawn until dusk, voices floated up from the street, no matter the weather.

From what he could tell, Abu Nasser's home was in a prestigious area close to one of the biggest markets and one of the biggest mosques. If he were somewhere like London, it'd be the equivalent of living on Oxford Street.

It told him more about Abu Nasser than days on the road had. He was a very successful businessman with the position to show for it. His continuing generosity and hospitality were also the signs of a pious man who took his charitable duties seriously.

The wind made the wooden shutters rattle in their frame.

Qasim sat up in his narrow bed.

The furs beneath him were warm, and the thick covers on top of him were keeping the worst of the winter chills at bay. He almost felt like himself again as he pulled the blankets around his shoulders and sat back against the wall. Still weak, but so much better. There'd been no more fevers or coughing or blood.

The soft tap of slippers sounded on the wooden floor, and a light appeared in the doorway of his room.

"Will you join us, Riza?" Abu Nasser was holding a small oil lamp, casting a warm glow around the room.

Qasim nodded gratefully. He managed to get up by himself, but it frustrated him how much effort it took to walk through the house. His host casually slipped his hand under Qasim's elbow, close enough to support him if he stumbled.

It was a fine house by Chachkand standards, with several large rooms and enough space to house a family as big as Qasim's. Once, Abu Nasser had told him, the house had been filled with his daughters. Now, only his wife, his two sons, and their wives and children remained.

Those same sons greeted Qasim as Abu Nasser helped him into the chamber where they were making their ablutions. For once, Qasim was able to do his without help. It felt like such a victory, and he couldn't help noticing Abu Nasser smiling like a proud father as he got up from the stool.

"Soon, you will be able to walk the length of the city walls," he said as he helped Qasim through to the other room where the prayer mats were laid out.

"*Insha'Allah*," Qasim agreed.

It took a lot of effort, but he managed to begin his prayers on his feet, even if his legs shook under him. Those were the small triumphs he thanked Allah for. They were small steps, it was true, but they were steps, and he was moving forward instead of standing still.

When they were done, Abu Nasser's sons quietly left the room. Qasim remained where he was, kneeling on the prayer mat. It had taken a lot out of him, but happily so.

"I think you will be strong enough for Friday prayers at the mosque," Abu Nasser murmured. He smiled. "It does me good to see you recovering so well."

Qasim looked at the older man. "I can't thank you enough, Abu Nasser."

Abu Nasser chuckled, waving his hand in a dismissive gesture. "I have given you little enough. Allah may reward me as he sees fit, but you need not thank me." He reached out and squeezed Qasim's shoulder. "Will you join us at the *masjid* on Friday?"

Qasim smiled. Another familiar touchstone in a different century. "I would be honoured." He hesitated, remembering how long it had taken him to walk from his room to the room they were now in. "Is it far from here?

Abu Nasser shook his head. "By then, it will be close enough for you." He nodded towards the window, which faced the city's main market square. "We are at close to the south edge of Chorsu Square. The mosque is there. Two hundred paces at most."

The name was familiar, and Qasim's heart leapt.

Once upon a time, he'd written about the mosques of central Asia. It didn't seem relevant when he rolled into Tashkent, since the earliest building he'd studied wasn't due to be built for another fifty-odd years: the Jumu'ah Masjid. The Friday mosque, which lay to the south of Chorsu Square.

It had been built on the foundations of an even older mosque, one whose name was now forgotten, at the heart of ancient Tashkent. His heart was racing. If he was right, then Abu Nasser's mosque had grown into the Jumu'ah mosque, and four centuries down the line, the Jumu'ah mosque would still be standing.

The threads of an idea were weaving together. It was an impossible chance, but if it worked...if it worked...

Ben had made him promise, after all.

"Abu Nasser," he said as calmly as he could as Abu Nasser helped him towards his room. "I must start to plan my journey home. Are there messengers who could carry letters for me?"

"More than there are birds in the sky," Abu Nasser replied. "Have some sleep now. I will fetch you ink and papers to write after you eat."

Qasim nodded gratefully. "If you have anything you would like me to write for you, I can do it," he offered. "Repayment for your kindness."

Abu Nasser chuckled. "Charity is worth nothing if it is paid for." He helped Qasim to sit again. "You write for yourself. Keep your strength."

Qasim nodded, subsiding on the bed. He retreated back under the covers and drifted back to sleep. He was woken well after sunrise by one of the servants setting out platters of food for him. It was far more than he could manage, but he wasn't surprised. There were fruits, bread, sticky pottage thick with honey, and tea.

He'd barely finished when another servant hurried in with writing implements and a sheaf of coarse paper. He cleared the table and left Qasim to his work. *Thank you, China,* Qasim thought. He ran his fingers over the paper. It was cheaper than the alternatives. At least he wasn't depriving Abu Nasser of valuable vellum.

The only concern was how fragile paper was compared to parchment, but it was all he had.

He laid out the paper and tools and stared at the wall, lost in thought.

Getting one letter out was good, but the more letters he could send, the higher the chance at least one of them would survive.

First priority had to be the recipient. It had to be someone with the means and tendency to keep written documents. Someone with an archive, which usually meant heads of state or royalty.

Timur's death was a useful means to an end. There were dozens of countries across the Middle East and Europe where news about the death of a tyrant would be gratefully received. He remembered the notes he'd made about the man and about the countries that had kept a careful eye on him. It was a start.

Next question was which ones archives had survived the intervening six centuries. So many places would fall to different imperial forces, which meant all the knowledge and records of the locals would be purged. So many archives would be lost through wars and conflicts. It narrowed his list down dramatically.

Qasim drummed his fingertips on the table.

The trouble was the content of the letter. Even if Ben managed to find it and was convinced, other people would need to be convinced too. If they didn't believe Ben's letters were from his father, why would they believe a fifteenth-century letter was from Qasim?

If Ben was smart—and Ben was very smart—he would know to show it to someone who knew Qasim well. It would probably be someone in the TRI as well, which meant...

Qasim grinned.

Well, he was an easy person to target.

He split each sheet of paper in half, picked up one of the narrow reed pens, and uncorked the ink bottle. It wasn't as easy as he would have liked. The first letter came out with a mess of blots and smudges, but it was a template to work from.

By the time the call came for *zuhr*, Qasim's fingers were black-tipped with ink, and there were a dozen identical letters all carefully rolled and sealed. There would be more later, as many as he could manage, but for now, it was time to pray for a miracle: for one of those pieces of paper to survive until the twenty-first century.

Chapter Forty-Four

RHYS DIDN'T RUN to tell Youssef and Rasha or the family.

He hated himself for it, but if there was one thing worse than losing a loved one, it was the false hope they might get him back. The last thing he wanted was to cause them more pain by telling them their son had survived but couldn't be brought home.

He considered telling Jacob, but it was so much bigger than him. They needed someone with access. Ben agreed, especially since—he said—Jacob didn't believe it was possible. He would call it a coincidence, and no one was going to open a gate for a coincidence.

Rhys and Ben discussed the possibilities.

There was no chance of Ben getting near any gate controls. They were monitoring him far too carefully. According to the boy, unless there was an official gate, there was no chance of getting to Qasim, and the chances of getting an official gate opened were between slim and none.

"I'll see if there's any way around it," Ben said, getting up. He paused at Rhys's door and held out a tiny memory chip. "Wait till Jacob's gone, then give them this. If I can't find some way around the gates, at least they'll have something."

Rhys took the chip from him. "What is it?"

Ben smiled crookedly. "Qasim. He asked me to make it for him. He wanted to say goodbye, his way."

Half an hour after Jacob left, Ben trailing in his wake, Rhys took the chip down to Youssef. "From Qasim," was all he could say.

Youssef stared at him, then hurried over to one of the folios, connecting the chip to it. Immediately, every image of Qasim was replaced with a video. Qasim, propped on his side among his pillows. Rhys could tell it was in the last days.

Around the room, there were cries and gasps.

Rhys heard the patter of feet a moment before Rasha appeared at his side, her eyes wide. "Qasim?"

"Bet you thought you'd seen the last of me," Qasim said, his voice rasping and little above a whisper. "Surprise!" He took a shaking breath. "I thought I would leave you the last adventure of Murad, the thief of Baghdad."

Despite every breath being a labour, he started to tell a story—a ridiculous, fantastic story about Murad, the stubborn camel, a box of candied rose petals, and so many personal jokes for every member of his family.

Rhys's eyes were burning. Even if Qasim was still out there, he'd taken the time and what little energy he had to do this for his family, to remind them of exactly who he was even as he faded away.

Rasha had her hands pressed to her mouth, and she wasn't the only one weeping.

Aisha approached Rhys and touched his elbow lightly. "You did this?"

Rhys shook his head. "All him," he said softly. "I had no idea."

She laughed sadly. "My baby brother always liked to surprise people."

Rhys could only nod and pray this wasn't the last time.

It certainly wasn't the only surprise of the night.

Rhys was helping Rasha wrap and pack up the leftovers for her daughters to take with them when the doorbell rang.

Rhys frowned. "I thought everyone was leaving now."

Rasha nodded. "Sef!" she called out, adding something in Arabic.

Her husband emerged from the living room. "More people?"

Rasha shrugged expressively, motioning to the door with one sticky hand.

Rhys couldn't see into the hall when the door opened, but he heard Rasha's sharp gasp. He remembered the sound. He remembered Eid and the sudden flick of the switch, and he was damned if anyone was going to come in and upset the family today. He set aside the box he was packing, wiped his hands, and stepped around her.

Youssef was standing in the hall with the old man from Eid. Qasim's grandfather. The homophobic bastard who had turned on his own flesh and blood.

But now, the man would play nice or he would get out. If he'd come to cast judgement on Youssef and Rasha's son, well, Rhys wasn't family. He could be rude and drive the man out, if it made things easier for Rasha.

The old man was speaking to Youssef in Arabic and then turned to Rhys, thick silver brows pulling down.

"Abi," Youssef said, his voice placid and neutral. "This is Qasim's partner. He is living with us now."

Rhys's defensive anger evaporated in shock. He gaped at Youssef, but Youssef's eyes were fixed on the old man, as if daring him to offend their guest, to treat Rhys as he had treated his own grandson.

They seemed balanced on a knife-edge, then the old man nodded grudgingly.

"I am sorry for your loss," he said, and he managed to sound sincere.

Rhys clenched his hands together. "Yours too. He was a good man."

The old man nodded again and turned to Youssef. "I would like to see my family."

Youssef glanced towards the kitchen, and Rasha must have nodded because Qasim's grandfather slipped his shoes off and padded through to the living room.

Rhys remained in the hall. "You knew?"

Youssef smiled sadly at him and patted his shoulder. "My son was good at keeping secrets about his work, but when he was in love?" He shook his head. "It was written all over his face."

Rhys felt his cheeks burning. "And so you asked me to stay?"

Youssef's smile softened. "You're family now."

It was all too much. The whole day had been so much, and now, he had people who wanted him as part of their family, who would choose to have him there despite the loss of the person who connected them. And if they knew he was keeping a secret about Qasim...

Youssef gestured towards the stairs. "If you need a break."

Rhys nodded gratefully as he stumbled up to his room. He sank onto his bed, scooping Pisi up into his lap. Christ, they wanted him around; they knew exactly what he was to their son, and they welcomed him.

They had given him a home. They had offered him a place in their family.

The least he could do was find their son, bring him home. But if Ben couldn't find a way, then he'd have to. He sank his fingers into Pisi's fur, stroking the cat and thinking desperately. There had to be something he could do, someone he could ask for...

Rhys's eyes widened.

Ask for permission.

And you didn't think to just explain all of this and ask for permission?

Could it be that simple?

He groped in his pocket for his folio, tapping it open. Pisi grumbled, butting her head demandingly against his hand. He nudged her head out of the way and opened up a message. He was out of the TRI, but Ben was as good a contact as any.

Once it was sent, he curled up on the bed with Pisi beside him. The cat lapped the salt from his cheeks in the dark.

Too much of a day.

By morning, he could at least pretend things were back to his new standard of normal. He was late for breakfast, and Rasha was already on her way out, but the previous night must have gone all right, because she smiled and rose on her toes to kiss him on both cheeks before she left.

He wasn't surprised to find she'd left his breakfast waiting for him, and he was halfway through it when his folio chirped. Rhys flicked it open. There was no sender name, but there was an address and a time later in the afternoon.

All right. Either a black-market organ harvester, or Ben had done good.

Half a day of fruitless job-hunting later, Rhys headed to the address in question. It was an elegant coffee shop, the kind of place well-off ladies would go after a day of beauty treatments and shopping. He wasn't surprised O'Donohue was already waiting when he arrived.

The man was sitting on one of the armchairs—a teapot and cup set out on a table before him—and was reading something on his folio. He didn't immediately raise his eyes when Rhys approached, but Rhys had the feeling O'Donohue had been aware of him from the moment he walked in.

When O'Donohue closed his folio down, he offered a slight smile that somehow felt more genuine than the one he usually wore. "Rhys," he said, rising and holding out a hand. Rhys shook it out of habit. O'Donohue motioned to the chair opposite his. "Please. Do you want something to eat? Tea? Coffee?"

Rhys shook his head. "I'm all right, thanks."

O'Donohue sat, crossed one leg over the other, and folded his hands in his lap. "Ben Sanders said you wanted to see me. He wouldn't elaborate on why. I guess either he doesn't know, or he wanted to make me curious enough to come."

Rhys rubbed the back of his neck. "A bit of both, to be honest." He hesitated, praying he didn't sound like a loony, and said, "We think Qasim might still be alive."

O'Donohue's expression smoothed out into the familiar and unreadable mask. "After six and a half centuries?"

Rhys winced. Right. No. It was coming out wrong. He pulled out his folio. "It's like this." He explained everything Ben had told him—about the promise of a letter, the documents he'd found, the translation, and the fact they had all the information to set a rendezvous point.

As he spoke, O'Donohue's brow creased in a thoughtful frown. He reached over the table and drew the projection of the letter towards him—the original, Rhys noticed, not the translation.

"It could be a coincidence," he finally said, examining the letter. "A strange one, it's true, but how can you be sure this is from our Qasim El-Fahkri?"

Rhys felt the back of his neck grow warm. It wasn't exactly as if he could admit Qasim had suggested he was definitely up for a shag in the letter. "There's a private joke in there. Something he must have known I would recognise."

"Relating to the elephant in the room, I presume?"

Rhys gaped at him. "You can read it?"

O'Donohue smiled, a glimmer of humour in his eyes. "I can do many things. For example, I can tell you for a fact this letter definitely wasn't written by someone from fifteenth-century Tashkent."

Rhys's heart stuttered. It was one thing to convince himself and Ben, but O'Donohue was something else, and if he believed it—

"Oh?" he managed weakly.

"Mm." O'Donohue tilted the projection and spread it on the table. "Whoever wrote it was trying to copy the formal style of historic documents, but some modern turns of phrase have slipped in, especially when he talks about the elephant and the fortress."

Rhys's mouth went dry. "You think it's him too?"

O'Donohue gazed across the table at him. "Do you know where this document was found?"

Rhys hastily riffled through Ben's mess of notes and then blinked in confusion. "Er."

"Er?" O'Donohue prompted.

"It looks like it's not the only one," Rhys replied, bringing up the notes to show O'Donohue. "It could be from a collection in Turkey, a copy of a copy from Egypt or... How would they end up in the English archives?"

"You'd be surprised what white people would steal if it wasn't nailed down." To his surprise, O'Donohue seemed amused. "Credit where credit is due—El-Fahkri's a smart one."

"Eh?"

"Let's say this letter is from our guy." O'Donohue tilted it back up. "He had useful political information—Timur's death. He must have sent a lot of these letters to people who would want to know about it, counting on some of them to keep a hold of anything so significant."

"The more copies, the more chances of us getting the message..." Rhys stared at him. "You mean it's really him?"

"I'm not saying it isn't." O'Donohue tapped his knuckle against his chin thoughtfully. "You said there's a private joke in there?" Rhys nodded. "How do you know it's a message for you and not a coincidence? There were a lot of armies using elephants to bust into castles back then."

Rhys must have gone scarlet, because O'Donohue's lips twitched.

"Ah. That kind of private joke, huh?"

Rhys knew he had a choice—get embarrassed or own it. He managed a quick smile. "It happens." He shifted on the seat, leaning back, hoping he looked more casual than he felt. "If you believe it's him, and we know where he'll be and when..."

"You want me to authorise a jump."

Rhys nodded. "I know it's a big ask after everything I did, but if there's any chance we can—"

"No."

Rhys flinched. "What?"

O'Donohue was looking at the letter again. "I don't have the authority. The only person who could authorise it is Mr. Elwin, and I don't think he's in the mood to play nice right now."

"That's it, then, is it?" Rhys stared at him. The fragile hope was shattering. O'Donohue didn't even seem to care he was condemning Qasim to a lifetime away from his family and his home. "You don't even fucking try?" He shook his head with a snort of disbelief. "I shouldn't have— I thought you were different. I thought—"

O'Donohue raised his eyes, and his expression made Rhys snap his mouth shut. "I said *I* don't have the authority. That doesn't mean I don't know how to make it happen."

Rhys rubbed his forehead. *Hold on to the anger. Better than giving way to the dread.* "Right. Fine. What do we do?"

O'Donohue leaned back in his seat and tapped the knuckle of his forefinger against his chin. "First, you're going to contact Ben. Tell him I said I couldn't help."

"That's your master plan?"

O'Donohue smiled benignly. "You're also going to make sure he tells everyone what he knows."

Rhys frowned. "Everyone? But they'll think he's cracked."

"Ben Sanders? The person who reliably knows more about the system than anyone?" O'Donohue shook his head. "They might think he's eccentric, but they listen to what he says. There's a reason he wasn't fired when you were. The boy's a genius with the tech. We couldn't afford to lose him."

"They didn't listen when it was about his dad," Rhys argued. "Why would they listen now?"

O'Donohue spread his hands. "This isn't someone blown to pieces when the gate malfunctioned, Rhys. This is an agent—one of them—who may be there and needs to be picked up. All it would take is one little jump. Nothing more."

Rhys was lost. "How's this going to help anyone? All you'll get is a bunch of pissed-off agents."

O'Donohue glanced away, looking up to the counter. He caught the server's eye, gesturing for the bill. The folio linked to the table chirped. He returned his attention to Rhys as he stood and pulled on his knee-length coat, drawing his braid out from the collar.

"Trust me," he said, "within three days, you'll have your gate open. Do exactly as I say, and I'll see to it."

"How can I believe you?" Rhys demanded. "You can't promise anything."

O'Donohue smiled as he fastened his coat. "Believe me when I say I want to get El-Fahkri back, and I'll do whatever is necessary to ensure it happens." He inclined his head as he picked up his folio from the table. "Good afternoon, Mr. Griffiths."

"Why?" Rhys rose from the chair. "Why do you want to get him back so badly?"

For a split second, O'Donohue's calm mask flickered. "Because I was the one who sent him to Otrar in the first place."

Before Rhys had a chance to say anything, O'Donohue turned on his heel and walked away.

Chapter Forty-Five

THE WEATHER HAD turned from winter to spring virtually overnight.

The bitter, biting gusts from the north were gone. As the temperature rose day by day, the rivers running through the city had swollen as the snows melted in the mountains. Everything smelled fresher and renewed.

The first time Qasim ventured out of the house with Abu Nasser, he didn't need his furs. The weight had dropped from his body, and the robes he had worn hung on him, soiled and travel-stained. Abu Nasser tutted and brought him some fresh clothes, borrowed from his sons.

Together, they had visited the *masjid* for the Friday prayers, even if Qasim nearly fainted from the effort. He'd wanted to attend the prayers, but he also needed to get the lay of the land for the Ramadan prayers. If he was going to use the place as a rendezvous point, he needed to know what to expect, even if he went over like a skittle afterwards.

Even after almost three weeks of Abu Nasser's care and hospitality, Qasim knew it would be a long time before he'd be back to full health. Now, at least, he could stand on his own, walk short distances without effort, and was able to eat more with each private meal.

He was pressing the bounds of hospitality, three days being the standard number for any guest. Any more would be bordering on rude. Mercifully, Abu Nasser had seen him preparing and making plans.

In a greater show of kindness, to ensure Qasim had enough funds to see him on his way, Abu Nasser had introduced him to several acquaintances who needed a scribe to write up some trade agreements for them. It was a simple enough task, and it pleased Abu Nasser to know he would be solvent, even if Qasim wouldn't need the money if his plan worked.

If.

That was the question.

The letters he'd sent had been as specific as possible. Every time he performed salat, he prayed one of them would fall into the right hands and, by the end of the week, someone he knew would come and take him home.

When the first Friday of Ramadan came, Qasim was on tenterhooks. It was out of his hands now. All he could do was wait, and it was terrifying. If it didn't work, was he going to spend the rest of his life chasing down major historical events in the hope he might get picked up? Or should he surrender and accept this was his life now? And if so, what would he do? How could he live?

The thoughts kept him awake, and even after the morning prayers, his mind was whirling in a thousand directions. He fled up to the roof, trying to calm himself as the sun came up. Nature always helped—watching it, reminding himself he was small in the grand scheme of things.

He was still sitting there, hours later, when Abu Nasser joined him.

The older man sat beside him, looking out over the city.

"You have not slept."

Qasim gazed at his hands in his lap. His nails were picked and cracked. "Too much to think about."

"Your plans?"

Qasim nodded, raising his eyes. He could see the mosque, their destination this afternoon, and he felt sick with dread at the thought. He was far too good at imagining the worst. It could go well, but it could also be the moment when he'd be stranded all over again.

"My friends should be passing through the city soon." He tried to smile at Abu Nasser. "Your hospitality will earn you great rewards from Allah. You have been far kinder than you had reason to be."

Abu Nasser chuckled, slapping him on the back. "At this time of year? No, no, no. This is the time when a man should be as kind as he can." He leaned closer. "It is easy to be a generous host to a generous guest."

Qasim grinned crookedly. "My mother said a man's worth can be measured by how he treats his guests. I think she would like you."

Abu Nasser smiled. "My mother once said the same thing. A wise lesson, worth remembering." He squeezed Qasim's shoulder. "I will leave you to your ruminations." He got back to his feet. "The bath will be made ready for you. Do not forget to have your breakfast."

Qasim nodded with a smile. "Thank you."

It felt strange staying in a Muslim household at Ramadan and being the only one who wasn't fasting apart from the children, but Abu Nasser was stubborn. Riza was too weak and still ill, the older man insisted. Allah would forgive him for it. It would do him no good if he made himself worse again.

Qasim had reluctantly agreed, though he wondered if he'd feel guiltier about it if it wasn't his second Ramadan in three months.

Once Abu Nasser was out of earshot, Qasim pulled out his prayer beads again. They *click-click-click*ed together between his fingers. It didn't help as much as he hoped, but at least he wasn't hyperventilating in a cupboard.

He had to think positively. He had to believe he'd soon be home and eat his mother's food and listen to his father's cheerful complaints about the economy. Aisha would set out the board, and they would play and...and everyone. Everyone would be there. Even his grandfather might be there and be nice. He stifled a bitter laugh. *That* would be the true miracle.

And Rhys...

Heat burned in his cheeks.

He'd told Rhys exactly what he wanted if he got home.

Click-click-click.

It was another part of the reason he was so terrified. There was the fear he wouldn't get home, but there was also the nervous anticipation he would, and he'd see Rhys and...

He rocked back on his heels, turning his face up towards the cloud-scudded sky.

There was no point worrying about it when it might never happen. Of course, logically, he knew, but his brain wasn't about to listen. He sighed, getting to his feet, and made his way down into the house. Better to focus on *Jumu'ah* and make sure he'd completed *ghusl*, the full ablution, in preparation.

Fresh clothing had been laid out for him, once he'd cleansed himself, and he smiled ruefully. Six hundred years apart and some things never changed—a casual reminder to be in his Friday best, even if his Friday best was borrowed from Abu Nasser's son.

He was combing his fingers through his damp hair when a voice rang out across the city. A pleasant shiver ran down his spine as the *muezzin* issued the call to prayer.

It was time.

Abu Nasser and his sons were waiting for him at the front doors, and as they emerged into the street, they were caught up in the wave of men heading towards the mosque. Qasim fell into step alongside them. Abu Nasser was talking animatedly, but Qasim couldn't hear a word he was saying, his blood throbbing deafeningly in his ears.

The world was a blur around him, too many faces and voices, as he trailed into the mosque with the three other men.

"Riza?" He jumped when Abu Nasser nudged him. "You are pale."

He shook his head and tried to smile. "I'm well." He glanced around, looking for any faces he might know, but there were too many, and he was breathing too fast. He had to focus on the prayers. He needed to be calm, and the prayers would help.

The mosque was small but beautiful inside with rows of carved wooden pillars supporting the roof. He smiled when Abu Nasser and his sons headed to exactly the same part of the floor they had occupied the previous week. He remembered how he used to herd his nephews to the place they considered 'their' spot in the *masjid* at home.

Abu Nasser beckoned Qasim to the spot beside him. "They will not mind if I have a guest."

Qasim translated it as "they can take it up with me if they have a problem" and nodded gratefully. The *mihrab* was in his line of sight as well as the familiar swell of bodies filling the hall. It was so far from home, but so similar in so many ways.

As more people filed in, he kept searching their faces, until the *khatib* stepped up onto the *minbar* and started to speak. Qasim didn't know who he was looking for or if there even was anyone.

He tried to listen to the *khatib*'s message, and when the prayer came, he had to concentrate hard to make sure he didn't make a mess of things. Different countries and cultures had their own ways of praying. He needed to be able to blend in. If he wasn't going home, he had to be sure he wouldn't stand out.

"I think it has been too much so soon," Abu Nasser said, once all the prayers and sermons were done. They were still kneeling on the floor, and Abu Nasser was watching him with concern. "You are pale as ash."

"Tired," Qasim demurred. "That's all." He glanced around the hall again, but there were fewer faces now and not a single person he recognised. It hadn't worked. They hadn't come. He swayed where he was kneeling, feeling dizzy.

So it was over, then.

He would have to find another way.

"More than tired, I think." Abu Nasser helped him to his feet. "Come. I'll take you home."

The walk back to Abu Nasser's house was like a dream. Qasim felt like he was watching his feet move from far away. Every step was like pushing through quicksand. A new plan. He needed a new plan. Something for now and something else to try to get him home.

Abu Nasser settled him in the main room of the house and pressed a cup of hot, sweet tea between Qasim's trembling hands. Delayed shock, he supposed. He'd been so caught up in the letters he hadn't planned anything else. Now the letters had failed, burned up across the continents.

Abu Nasser tried speaking to him, but Qasim had no words left. His tea was nearly cold when he remembered to take a sip and then jumped when someone pounded on the main doors. Tea slopped over his fingers.

"Wait here." Abu Nasser strode from the room. He had servants to open the door, but someone knocking so hard had to be about something important. Out of habit, Qasim listened.

"Forgive me, sir." A man, panting. "I have to seek for you." *Arabic. Not local, and not first language.* "Men say you are to care for my friend."

"Your friend?"

"Yes, sir. He was from Otrar. He was sick..."

Otrar.

Sick.

Qasim rose on shaking legs and walked through to the hall. The sun was bright outside, silhouetting two figures standing in the doorway. He couldn't see their faces. The speaker cried out Qasim's name. He was in the hall and in front of Qasim and hugged him. Qasim staggered from the force of it.

The visitor stepped back, grinning at him, warm and familiar. "Sorry we're late," Ibrahim said in English. "We only went to the wrong bloody mosque!"

Chapter Forty-Six

THREE DAYS HAD come and gone.

Rhys was trying to act like nothing was going on. He hadn't heard from O'Donohue, but he'd received daily rants from Ben: they're still not listening; everyone's getting pissed off about it; I think people believe me, but the Board is ignoring us; Jacob believes me, but he says we're up shit creek unless upstairs listens.

The last he'd heard, there were aggressive protests going on within the TRI. Ben had mentioned a rumoured walkout. All of the staff were up in arms with agents refusing to go for their assigned jumps. Only three jumps had been cancelled so far, but if they kept it up, it would be chaos.

If O'Donohue wanted to trigger anarchy, he'd done a bloody good job of it.

It had to be part of the plan, but Rhys couldn't see how it would help. Mr. Elwin was known for being unyielding. If he didn't want to do something, he wouldn't, no matter how much his employees were pushing him.

"Is something wrong?"

Rhys blinked, looking up from the book on his folio. "What?"

Youssef smiled. "You've been staring at the same page for twenty minutes."

"Oh. Right." Rhys shut down the book. "Just thinking."

Youssef nodded. "I know how it goes." He was sitting on another couch, a pile of analogue papers topped by digital projections on the table beside him. "I have a deadline, and can I concentrate on it?" He shook his head. "They say mourning—it takes time. Helpful, isn't it?"

Rhys nodded. He managed a smile for Rasha as she came into the room, carrying three mugs of tea. "You should have said. I would have made it."

She gave him a look. "You make bad tea."

Youssef burst out laughing at the indignation on Rhys's face. "I think she means you make *English* tea. She's not a fan."

"You drank it the other day," he pointed out, accepting one of the mugs.

"You ate her baby chicken without complaining," Youssef said with a chuckle. "Doesn't mean you like it."

It was Rasha's turn to be indignant. "You did not like?"

Rhys immediately hid behind the steam, which immediately misted up his glasses.

Youssef cleared the couch, smiling up at his wife as she sat beside him. "Just in time for your stream?" Rasha said something to him in Arabic, earning a fond smile and a pat on her knee. "If it makes you happy, I'll stay, even if it is soapy nonsense."

Rhys couldn't help smiling quietly as Rasha curled comfortably beside her husband.

In the days since he'd started living there, he'd seen subtle changes in the way both of them acted around him.

At first, there'd been formal politeness, but now, he was treated with the same teasing informality as their children. Rasha had even stopped wearing her hijab around the house. Rhys had a feeling it was significant, but he didn't want to make a big deal about it.

The programme—some melodramatic soap opera—was halfway through an episode when the house hub chimed, indicating there was a video link incoming.

Rasha grumbled under her breath but paused her show to pick up the call.

The air rushed out of Rhys's body as if he'd been hit in the chest with a two-by-four.

Qasim.

Qasim was on the video link, and he was beaming and waving frantically. "I'm back! I'm back!"

Rhys's vision was blurring. Youssef and Rasha were crying out, but he couldn't see them, and he couldn't see Qasim, but his voice was ringing out, chattering eagerly in Arabic and English, switching back and forth and laughing and crying too.

Rhys blinked hard, swiping at his eyes, and tried to focus.

Qasim.

Paler and thinner than he used to be, but so much better than the bone-thin dying man he had been. He was smiling and there were tears streaking down his face. He was saying something about Rhys, something about Rhys being the one to figure it all out, finding him.

Rhys felt Rasha and Youssef's eyes turn to him. He must have been out of frame because Qasim's breath hitched.

"He's there? Is he there?"

Rhys's legs were shaking as he got up and walked unsteadily across to the other couch. He raised a trembling hand to wave—and, shit, his vision was blurring again—and he saw Qasim press both hands to his chest, and his smile was even bigger.

"There's my elephant!"

Rhys was laughing and crying and he couldn't stop himself. He felt fingers on his wrist, and Rasha pulled him down to practically sit on top of her and Youssef, both of them hugging him.

"You have to come," Qasim said eagerly. "They said they'll send a pod to get you. I wanted to tell you before it arrived."

"A whole lamb," Youssef said, and he was crying as hard as Rhys and Rasha combined. "I'll find a whole lamb and we'll have a feast and you'll come home and we'll celebrate."

Qasim nodded, beaming. "You promised me macaroni cheese with it too!" He waved. "I'll see you soon!"

As soon as the video link disconnected, Youssef caught Rhys in a bear hug.

"You found him?"

Rhys's hand shook as he tried to wipe his face. It didn't help, not when the tears were still coming. "I—we couldn't be sure. I didn't want to tell you in case I was wrong. I—he—" He started laughing helplessly through the tears. "I didn't know if it would work."

Youssef caught him by the shoulders and kissed him on both cheeks. "*Alhamdulillah!* You brought our son home!" Smiling, his face was wet with tears. "You brought him home!"

On his other side, Rasha threaded her fingers through his, pressing her cheek to his shoulder. "Thank you."

Youssef nodded. "We need to tell everyone." He groped for the control for the hub, flicked up the main screen, and put out a family link to as many households as he could.

Rhys could only watch and listen. He was smiling so much his face hurt, and Rasha's hand was tight on his. His heart was throbbing, fit to burst, and all he could do was sit there and cry as dozens of El-Fahkris shrieked and squealed and cheered in delight as Youssef told them the news.

They were still on the call when someone buzzed at the front door.

Rasha scrambled up and ran for the door, pulling on her hijab as she went.

"That'll be our ride," Youssef said to the family at large. A babble of voices washed over them in English and Arabic, and even with his limited grasp of the second language, Rhys could take the meaning: tell him we'll see him soon. Youssef nodded, laughing. "I will! I will!"

Rasha reappeared in the doorway. "We go now."

Rhys hesitated. He knew he wasn't allowed within TRI facilities.

Youssef noticed his expression. "You're coming with us. If they don't like it, then they can face me."

The relief was overwhelming, but contracts could lead to problems. "You could get in trouble," Rhys protested.

"I couldn't care less," Youssef replied, pulling Rhys to his feet. "My son's alive, and we're going to see him."

Rhys was more than happy not to argue.

Thankfully, it was late enough in the evening that the rush hour was over, and the roads were clearing. The pod—one of the TRI's secure ones reserved for management or emergencies—sped out towards the TRI compound.

Youssef and Rasha sat on one side of the pod, holding each other's hands tightly, but every so often, Rasha leaned over to Rhys and squeezed his hand. They weren't talking. None of them had any words left, too overwhelmed with relief and joy. It was amazing, the feeling of weeks of misery and grief being lifted away.

It wasn't until they walked into the transport hub that Rhys remembered where they were actually going—to the company that had stripped away his living and his security. It was one thing for Youssef to say he'd be angry if Rhys was denied entry, it was another to expect access to a government facility given his past.

He froze, his feet rooted to the floor as the transport shuttle entered the hub.

"I'll stay here," he said, his voice catching in his throat.

Youssef and Rasha both turned, puzzled. "It's not much further now."

It was instinct to lie, to make things easier for them. "He's your son. You should see him first. I'd be a distraction." He motioned towards the shuttle. "I can wait for you here."

Youssef and Rasha exchanged meaningful looks.

"We won't make you come," Youssef said, "but you know Qasim would want to see you."

And God, he wanted to see Qasim, but he wasn't going to be welcomed. He didn't want to stop them from seeing their son because he was too stubborn to obey the order in his contract.

The shuttle pulled in to the platform in front of them, but it wasn't empty.

O'Donohue stepped out.

Rhys stared at him. The man had promised three days for a gate to be opened and Qasim to be found. Rhys had called him a liar and a bastard, but O'Donohue had done exactly what he'd promised. Rhys couldn't stop himself. He walked forward and hugged O'Donohue and felt the man chuckle.

"You're welcome, Mr. Griffiths," he said, patting Rhys on the back. Over Rhys's head, he spoke in a fluent stream of Arabic to the El-Fahkris. Youssef replied curtly, and Rhys heard his name somewhere in the middle of all of it.

Rhys stepped back, looking between them. "I'm not going to get in the way. I can wait here if I'm not allowed in."

O'Donohue's lips twitched, and he stepped side, motioning for them to get into the shuttle. "Exceptional circumstances mean certain allowances can be made."

Rasha had Rhys by the arm and into the shuttle before he could protest. Youssef followed them in, smiling, and took the seat next to his wife.

As soon as the shuttle moved off, Rhys made his way across the swaying floor to O'Donohue. "You got the gate opened. How?"

O'Donohue was watching the landscape flick by and smiled. "You just need to know where to apply the right pressure." He glanced down at Rhys. "A single voice can be ignored, but a hundred, two hundred, more..." He shook his head. "You'll find it's harder to drown them out or silence them."

Rhys stared at him in awe. "You sneaky bugger. You caused a riot, and no one will ever know it was you."

O'Donohue was the picture of virtuous innocence. "I have no idea what you're talking about. Mr. Elwin can make his own decisions."

"As long as someone pushes him in the right direction?"

O'Donohue smiled serenely at the window. "As I said, I have no idea what you're talking about."

Rhys shook his head in disbelief and made his way back to Rasha and Youssef. "If you want to thank anyone for getting Qasim home," he said in an undertone, "he's the man. He was the one who got the gate open. He couldn't tell you himself, because no one else knows."

It was funny to see the confused surprise on O'Donohue's normally expressionless face when two overjoyed parents hugged him. He raised his eyebrows at Rhys, who shrugged with a crooked smile.

When they reached the other end of the line, the forecourt and buildings were as deserted as they'd been the last time Rhys walked through them. It was unsettling, but right now, there were more important things to think about.

O'Donohue led them to the pod station for transfer to the quarantine facilities. They didn't need to be told what it was. From Rasha's expression, she remembered it well. Rhys reached out and took her hand.

"Better this time," he murmured.

She nodded, her eyes bright again.

There were quarantine techs waiting for them, and Rhys's heart jumped when he saw three decon suits. He'd expected video links or seeing Qasim through the protective glass, but they were going to see him, face-to-face. He looked at O'Donohue, trying to find the words to thank him. O'Donohue just smiled his annoyingly enigmatic little smile.

"I'll be waiting to see you out when you're finished," he said to the El-Fahkris. He met Rhys's eyes. "Try not to cause any trouble."

"You first," Rhys retorted and was shocked when a broad, brilliant grin spread across O'Donohue's face. He sketched out a mock bow and vanished from the room as Rhys was bundled into the oversized decon suit.

When the helmet was locked in place, Rhys remembered the last time he'd been in one of the suits—the day he threw Qasim through the gate and lost everything. Now, the best part of what he'd lost was back, and he was about to see him again and...

Rasha slipped her hand through his arm. "You are scared?"

He couldn't help but nod.

"I am too." She squeezed his arm. "Come."

The transfer pod doors opened for them, and they stepped in.

"Breathe," Youssef murmured, patting him on the shoulder. "We're here. We're all here together."

It helped more than he realised was possible. Not just the fact they were there, but that they didn't question the nerves or mock them. They took him in as he was, and didn't question it. He was part of their family now.

When the doors opened, when they saw Qasim standing there, waiting for them, he couldn't say which of them moved first. All he knew was that when Qasim's parents caught their son in their arms, Rhys was pulled into the embrace as well, and all of them were laughing and crying together.

Chapter Forty-Seven

"THIS WAY, PLEASE."

Qasim fell into step behind the woman from Mr. Elwin's office.

Another fortnight in quarantine had been frustrating with his family kept at a distance by masks and decon suits and screens. Now, the Board were delaying his departure because they wanted to have a face-to-face conversation with him, since every medical test showed he was in the clear.

They could have chimed in to speak to him during the week. It wasn't as if he'd had much to do apart from eat too much, spend too long in the bath, and talk to his friends and family through video links. The Board hadn't called, and he suspected why. Any conversations in quarantine were recorded. Face-to-face conversations weren't.

Whatever they were going to say, they didn't want it on record, which suggested they didn't want the world to know what had happened.

It wasn't the first thing they'd done to annoy him since he got back.

Ibrahim and Cyra had given him an update of everything from the TRI side of things when they'd made their way with him to their rendezvous point. They'd been, Ibrahim cheerfully admitted, a stone's throw away from anarchy. The Board had broken under the pressure, making bleating excuses about not risking any other agents and their health. But someone—they didn't know who—pointed out that if Qasim was well enough to survive a month, travel 150 miles, *and* plan an intricate time-travelling rescue, then there was little chance of him still being deathly ill and contagious.

The Board eventually caved, but it was clear to all sides they never really expected to find him.

Qasim had also only seen Rhys once since his return. His parents visited daily. After the third visit when Rhys didn't come back in with them, Qasim was worried. He'd chimed Rhys in the evening and asked him why. Rhys went quiet and then said Qasim's family had to be the priority. He was hiding something. Now Qasim knew to watch for it, he could tell, and the next day when his parents visited, he demanded the truth. What they told him made him angrier than he'd ever been in his life.

The lift doors slid open, and he smiled at the woman and headed towards the office where the top brass of the Supervisory Board were waiting for him.

"Mr. El-Fahkri!" A rangy, grey-haired man approached him as he entered the room. "I'm William Elwin."

The director. Once, Qasim would have felt intimidated. It surprised him how calm he felt, over the simmering anger. He shook Mr. Elwin's hand and examined at the other two in the room. One of them was a plump red-haired woman with a stern expression, and the other was a ridiculously photogenic man in a razor-sharp suit.

"Please, sit down," Mr. Elwin said, joining his companions on the other side of a broad desk. Their chairs were slightly higher than Qasim's own, so he would have to look up at all of them.

Office psychology. Make the person on the other side feel vulnerable. Put them in a position where they think they're weaker because you outnumber them and are looking down on them.

A few weeks ago, it might have worked.

Now, he had survived a deadly disease. He had crossed the winter-blasted plains between Otrar and Chachkand. He had travelled with sword-wielding men who would cut the throats of their enemies as soon as blink. He had broken the laws of time and space, and they expected to scare him?

He sprawled in the seat, gazing at them, and propped his elbows on the arms. "Is this going to take long? I'd like to get home. My father's making me macaroni cheese."

"Not long at all, of course." Mr. Elwin sounded surprised. "We wanted to express our joy at your safe return."

Qasim laced his fingers together over his middle and tilted his head, watching the man. "Really?"

"I beg your pardon?"

Qasim tapped his thumbs together, keeping his eyes fixed on Elwin. He'd learned a killer stare from Ummi. When someone did something wrong, and they knew it—make them squirm. He'd never done it before, but now seemed like a perfect time. "The way I heard it, you knew where I was, but you had no intention of sending anyone to find me."

Mr. Elwin sat back as if Qasim had slapped him. "I don't know where you're hearing that—"

"Your staff." Qasim sat up in his chair. "Something about three days of strikes and protests before the gate was opened." He inclined his head. "Or am I mistaken?"

"We had to verify the—"

Qasim sighed. "Are we really going to do this? I know you didn't want to send anyone back. Everyone downstairs knows you didn't want to send anyone back." He gave Elwin a look. "Maybe, you don't patronise me when we know I'm a problematic thorn in your side, and you brought me here to make sure I keep my mouth shut, okay?"

The man on Elwin's left pressed the knuckle of his forefinger to his lips. If Qasim didn't know better, he'd have thought the man was stifling a laugh.

Mr. Elwin cleared his throat. "The fact is you performed an illegal temporal jump without the consent or authorisation of the TRI."

"True," Qasim agreed, "but the Supervisory Board dispatched myself and my partner to a city where there was a known fatal illness."

"That's not—"

"I'm not finished," Qasim cut across him. "My best friend *died* there because your board approved the Otrar mission, and you bring me in here to tell me the jump that saved my life was a crime? Or would you prefer I was dead as well? Would you find it more convenient?"

Mr. Elwin glanced at the woman on his right. "Miss Quinn—"

"You didn't answer my question, *sir*."

Mr. Elwin didn't look happy. "We are—of course—relieved you survived, but—"

"There are no 'buts' here," Qasim said coldly. "My best friend is *dead.* I didn't make it back here for you to give me a smack on the wrist for daring to be alive."

"Mr. El-Fahkri, if I can interrupt," the other man said. He was softly spoken with an American twang to his accent. "We can agree mistakes were made on both sides. Your jump was...technically illegal, and there were delays in the gate being approved—"

"And Rhys Griffiths?" Qasim interrupted, gazing at the man. This had to be the one Rhys mentioned—the mysterious, good-looking one who was playing both sides of the board. "What about him?"

"He arranged and put the illegal jump in motion," Miss Quinn said. "He was fortunate not to be charged under the temporal offences act."

Qasim didn't bother looking at her. The man—O'Donohue—was the real power in this room. "Without Rhys's help, I would have died here, and my family would be suing the seven levels of hell out of you for putting me in that situation in the first place." He fixed his glare on Elwin. "And don't think I've forgotten that you kept my parents away from me when I was dying." He shook his head. "I wasn't happy, Mr. Elwin. You made my mother cry."

Elwin's features were taut. "What do you *want*, Mr. El-Fahkri?"

"Ah." Qasim braced his hands on the arms of the chair and sat upright. "This is where I'm open to negotiation." He smiled without humour. "Compensation, don't you think? For putting me in a situation where I had to watch my partner die. For separating me from my family with unnecessary and cruel restrictions when I was dying. For your little...delay in coming for me, even when you were well aware every member of staff in the agency knew where I could be found." He inclined his head. "What's the threshold for a man's life?"

"I'm sure we can come to a suitable figure." Rhys's ally was watching him with interest.

"I'm sure we can." Qasim met his eyes. "And while I'm here, I want to talk about reinstating the full severance package for Rhys Griffiths." He smiled again. "After all, if he hadn't helped me, you would be issuing the mortality payment to my family. I'm sure you would prefer the lower figure of Mr. Griffiths's payment, wouldn't you?"

"Now wait a moment!" Elwin started to rise.

"I did," Qasim said mildly. "Or are you forgetting the month I spent in the past?" He leaned forward in the chair and propped his forearm on the desk. Elwin sank back in his chair. "Oh, and one more thing. Mila. I know where she was buried. You're going to send a team back to bring her home."

"But the risk of infection in a corpse is—"

The glare Qasim shot at the woman silenced her. "We have *time machines*." He tapped a finger on the desk. "Let's say 1410. Maybe 1415. It should be clear by then." He inclined his head. "This is the part where you tell me how you're going to make sure this never happens again."

"You can't just make demands like—"

Qasim was astonished how the rage kept on coming, so much pent-up anger and the memory of Mila's blood on his hands. "I think I can." He rose and leaned forward, bracing his hands on the desk, looming over them, using their own dirty trick against them. "You would have left me for dead, and everyone knows it." He stared Elwin in the eyes. "Tell me how you're going to make sure this never happens again."

Elwin stared blankly back at him. "There are protocols—"

"There have always been protocols," Qasim snapped. "Tell me something better than protocols."

"A restructuring of the prep and research system," Rhys's ally cut in smoothly. Too smoothly. He was holding a lot of cards, and from Elwin's expression, Elwin didn't know about them. "More research by the Board and the agents before a jump is confirmed, with a detailed checklist of potential hazards to ensure all possible risks are assessed, even ones the Board might overlook."

"Lysander," Elwin hissed.

Lysander—if that was his name—glanced at Elwin. "The man's right. We overlooked the possibility of sickness because only one man was listed as dying. We didn't take into account localised diseases. Historians and agents might have noticed." He met Qasim's eyes. "Would that be acceptable, Mr. El-Fahkri?"

Qasim knew whatever happened beyond the room depended on what he said right now. There was more going on here than he cared to understand. "It's a start, but I want specifics." He straightened up from the table. "I want to see a timetable for it as soon as possible."

"Of course," Lysander said, rising.

"It may not be possible," Elwin added. "The board—"

"I wasn't talking to you." Qasim turned to Lysander. "I'll give you a day or two to discuss everything with the Board, but now, I'm going to go home to see my family." He inclined his head. "My father will come by in two days time to sort out the details."

"Mr. El-Fahkri!" Mr. Elwin seemed to have a death wish. "We need to discuss the nondisclosure agreement."

Qasim gave him a pitying look. "My signing depends on how you deal with this mess. Like I said, my father will come by in two days. If he's satisfied with what you've pulled together, then I'll consider signing your nondisclosure agreement. If not..." He shrugged. "You would have left me to die in the past. I can think of a few people who would want to hear about it."

"You wouldn't—"

Lysander laid his hand on Elwin's arm. "I think we should discuss this matter before we say anything rash, Will." He nodded to Qasim. "Mr. El-Fahkri, thank you for your time." Out of Elwin's line of sight, he winked at Qasim.

Qasim turned and strode from the room.

The moment the door shut behind him, he sagged against the wall, clapping his hand over his mouth. His heart was racing, and his blood was rushing in his ears. Everyone knew he was the family pushover. He giggled, dazed. He'd told people off. He *never* told people off. He turned over his hands. They were shaking as much as his legs, and he had to lean against the wall all the way to the lift.

By the time he reached the ground level, his legs weren't shaking so much, but he couldn't get the stupid grin off his face. Part of it was because he hadn't let them walk all over him, but the rest—oh, so much more—was knowing he was going home and would see his family.

The lift doors opened onto the lobby, and he stopped short as he stepped out of the lift.

There was only one person there, looking rumpled and nervous, twisting his hands together.

"Hi," Ben said with an awkward smile.

Qasim knew words. He knew a lot of words in a lot of languages. Words were good, but they all vanished from his brain. The only thing he could do was cross the space between them and pull Ben into a hug. Ben clutched at him, his fingers digging into Qasim's back.

"Thank you," he finally managed, wondering why his face was wet again.

Ben laughed damply against his shoulder. "You promised." His voice was as unsteady as Qasim's.

Qasim nodded, drawing back enough to see Ben's face. "You were right." He laughed, blinking hard as his eyes overflowed again. "Look at this!" He scrubbed at his eyes with the heel of one hand. "I'm happy! I'm honestly happy, but I can't stop leaking!"

Ben started laughing too, stepping back and knuckling at his own eyes. "I know! How stupid is this?"

Qasim could guess why it was hitting Ben as hard. It was proof his theory might be right and his father might still be out there somewhere, waiting to be found. He reached up and ruffled Ben's hair. "You did good. You can do it again."

"You—you think so?"

Qasim nodded with conviction. "I don't doubt it." A squeal from a nearby doorway made him turn, and he yelped as a cascade of people poured out from the canteen hallway into the lobby: agents and supervisors and researchers and everyone.

"There he is!" Gulshan exclaimed, descending on him with a hug. "Our boy! Back from the dead!"

She wasn't the only one as he was hugged and patted and kissed by more people than he could count, and all he could think was that the shuttle would be leaving any moment.

"You lucky fuck!" Dieter slapped him firmly on the back. "Had to show everyone how it was done, didn't you?"

Qasim laughed, smacking him on the arm. "Shut up."

Ben retreated, grinning, as Qasim was passed around like a new baby on display.

Over the enthusiastic babble of voices, Qasim heard Jacob's voice. "Sorry about this! They wanted to see you for themselves!" He pushed his way through to Qasim's side and slung an arm around him. "Right, everyone! You've seen him! The boy's on his way home from the longest quarantine you've ever seen! Piss off, and let him go!" He shouldered his way through the throng, hauling Qasim with him. "Let's get you back to your family."

"Wait!" Qasim turned under his arm. "Thank you! You persuaded them to come and find me! Thank you all!" There was a bellow of cheers from the crowd.

Jacob gave him a squeeze. "No man left behind," he said gruffly, hauling Qasim onwards.

Qasim glanced sidelong at him and thought of Ben and the hope in his face. "What about Tom Sanders?"

Jacob's eyes were on the door. "What about him?"

"You've seen Ben's letters. Maybe they were like mine."

They reached the steps down to the platform. Jacob loosened his arm around Qasim's shoulder, letting him walk down at his own pace, and said quietly, "Yeah. Maybe so." He looked at Qasim. "How did you know yours would get to us?"

Qasim shrugged. "I didn't. I had to try. Maybe Ben's father did the same thing." He reached out and touched Jacob's arm. "Promise me you'll at least try to look? Ben needs it. Even if you don't find him, just try?"

Jacob gazed down at his hand and then back at Qasim's face. "You pulled this off. Maybe he did too. We'll get a team on it." He stepped closer and pulled Qasim into a bear hug. "Don't you ever scare us like this again, d'you hear me?"

Qasim laughed unsteadily. "I won't. I promise."

Jacob stepped back, looking bright around the eyes. "Bugger off. Go and pester your family."

Qasim spun towards the shuttle. "I plan to."

The ride felt much longer than it ever had before. Everything was different since the last time he'd been in it. The fields were lush with wild flowers, and the sun was high in a cloud-puffed summer sky. The sight of it made him giddy, and he was practically dancing in place when the shuttle pulled into the hub.

He heard the shout of his name as he stepped out onto the platform and turned to see his family waiting. And among all the dark and veiled heads, there was one golden mop. He saw Rhys, and they both started running. The platform wasn't long. It wasn't big and dramatic when they met in the middle.

Qasim grabbed him in a tight hug, breathing in the smell of him, Rhys's curls rubbing against his cheek. "Hello, you."

Rhys drew back to smile up at him. "You're late."

"Oh, shut up," Qasim said happily and leaned down to kiss him as his family flocked in around them.

Chapter Forty-Eight

IT WAS STRANGE the difference a few months made.

Rhys couldn't help pondering it as he helped Rasha and Nasreen carry bowls of food to the extended tables occupying most of the living room. Six months ago, the noise and the chaos would have been too much, but now it felt safe and welcoming and home.

Even without Qasim there, it would have felt the same.

It was like navigating an assault course of people to get to the tables, and somewhere in the middle of the throng, he knew Qasim was being hugged and kissed more than he had been the first night Rhys visited. Even Qasim's grandfather was in there somewhere.

When he arrived, Rhys felt the change in the room, the familiar tension, but to his—and everyone else's astonishment—Qasim was the one who shattered it. Instead of staying put, Qasim walked across the room to his grandfather and welcomed him with a smile. The old man stared at him and pulled him into a hug, and it was like all the air had returned to the room.

The atmosphere was incredible. The house was full of laughter and smiles. No one seemed tense or on edge, and Rhys couldn't be happier to be there and be part of it.

A small hand tugged his trouser leg.

Ranim beamed up at him. "Can I have some now, Khali?"

"Not yet!" Nasreen scolded, waving her away. "Not until Sitto says so."

Rhys smiled, watching the girl stamp off. "Everyone loves a trier." He glanced at Nasreen. "What was she calling me?"

Nasreen nudged him with a grin. "Uncle."

He blinked at her. "Eh?"

She laughed. "Well, you're Uncle Qasim's other half. She can hardly call you auntie, can she?" She took the bowl from him and nodded back towards the door. "Can you see if Ummi's got any more salad made? I don't think this'll be enough."

Rhys nodded, dazed.

Logically, he knew he'd pretty much been adopted into the family. Logically, they knew about his relationship with Qasim—the kiss at the hub wasn't exactly subtle. Logically, it made sense.

It hadn't sunk in that it wasn't just Youssef and Rasha who had laid claim to him.

He was grinning like an idiot when he got back to the kitchen.

Rasha raised her eyebrows at him. "Why so happy now?"

He caught her in a hug and swung her off her feet. "Because I'm home and he's home and everything's great."

"Yes, silly boy." She laughed, swatting him. She picked up a dish stacked deep with flatbread. "Here. Be useful."

By the time he finally managed to get back to Qasim, well after the meal was finished, he wasn't surprised to find him in a battle to the death with Aisha over a chessboard.

Rhys perched on the arm of the chair Qasim was sitting on. "Who's winning, then?"

"Mum's taken more of Uncle Qas's pieces, but I think Uncle Qasim is winning," Kamila said.

"He's playing faster than he used to," the younger Youssef added.

"You're sure she's not letting him win?" Rhys hazarded and promptly received matching glares from both players. "What? He came back from the dead. You might have softened up a bit."

"In his dreams," Aisha snorted and made a move.

"She knows I'd never forgive her if she didn't make it interesting," Qasim agreed, gazing at the board. He reached up and gave Rhys's thigh a lazy squeeze. "The only person around here who would let me win is you."

Rhys could feel his cheeks grow warm. He didn't know all the details of Qasim's weeks in the past, but something had changed. In the brief time they'd had together, Qasim seemed so much more confident and direct. It was different, and, oh, it was good. Still, he couldn't let Qasim think he'd been domesticated, not when it was his job to make Qasim blush.

He leaned down to Qasim's ear.

"Hey!" Aisha exclaimed. "No conferring."

Rhys didn't sit back. Instead, he propped his arm on Qasim's shoulder. "Your elephant is being neglected."

Qasim snorted so hard he almost dislodged Rhys.

Rhys met his eyes, trying hard to hide his grin.

"You're a twat," Qasim said, giving his thigh another quick squeeze.

"You love it," Rhys countered.

It was still a surprise—a good one—when Qasim reached up and wrapped his hand behind Rhys's head and pulled him closer to kiss him, especially with all the family right there. When they broke apart, Rhys became aware of the kids making kissy noises and several of the boys groaning.

Qasim was pink-cheeked but smiling. "Less neglected now?"

"It'll cope," Rhys agreed, shifting his weight on the arm of the chair. It kept his thigh snug against Qasim's arm for the rest of the game. Qasim only made it worse by stroking Rhys's calf through his trousers between moves.

In the end, Aisha barely scraped a win, but from the impressed expression on her face, it had been a tough battle.

"Not bad," she said. "Less hesitations. It's a good look."

Qasim tilted sideways in his chair to rest his head against Rhys's hip. "Next time, you're going down," he said happily as his sister packed up the pieces. She snorted, crossing her eyes and sticking out her tongue at him.

Rhys gazed down at Qasim fondly, stroking his fingers through Qasim's unruly hair. "You couldn't be a gracious loser, could you?"

Qasim shook his head. "Never." He smiled up at Rhys. "I'm glad you're here."

Rhys wondered how wide and silly his smile was. "Me too."

Qasim's fingertips slipped under the end of Rhys's trouser leg, skimming the skin, and his cheeks were getting pink again. He nibbled his bottom lip, and Christ, the combination of the blushing and those teasing fingers was enough to make Rhys breathless.

The only trouble was it was a welcome-home party and Qasim was the guest of honour.

In the name of decorum and not running out of the room to hide a potential hard-on, Rhys moved his leg. "You should go and see your other guests." He untangled his fingers from Qasim's hair. "I'll still be here when they're gone."

"Promise?"

"An elephant never forgets." Rhys was proud he managed to keep a straight face, but he couldn't help himself when he leaned close enough to murmur, "Especially when there's a fortress involved."

Qasim's cheeks flamed, and he grinned, scrambling up from the seat. Aisha chuckled as he walked away. "You two are awful."

Rhys watched Qasim plunge himself into another cluster of relatives and smiled. "I know."

He wanted to last out the whole party for Qasim's sake. There were so many people, though, and every hour, it felt like there was a revolving door of even more relatives. There was music, and Qasim was dancing, joined by half a dozen male cousins, all clapping and whooping encouragement.

Someone sat on the couch beside him, and he turned to find Qasim's father there.

"You're not used to this kind of celebration, are you?"

Rhys shook his head with a crooked smile. "I had one aunt. No cousins. This is—it's big."

"Mm." Youssef chuckled. "Bigger than usual. We've never had a family resurrection before." He patted Rhys's shoulder. "He'll understand if you need some quiet. It's been a big day."

Rhys nodded gratefully. There was so much of Rasha in Qasim, but so much of his kindness came from his father. "I'll be in my room if he asks." He got up from the couch. "Thank you, Youssef."

Youssef waved him away with a smile. "You brought him back. Nothing I can do can repay you." He rose too and nodded towards the door. "You should escape before the little ones notice and ask you to dance."

Rhys fled.

Even on the top level of the house, he could hear the music and laughter, muffled through the walls. He lay back on his bed and smiled. Even if he hadn't managed to stay till the end, he was glad Qasim could. He deserved every moment of the celebration.

It was a long while before the noise started to wind down and the voices moved from the living room to the hall. Doors were opening and closing. Pods were purring to life outside. Dishes were clattering in the kitchen. All the sounds of a party drawing to a close.

Someone tapped lightly on the door.

Rhys sat up on the bed, setting aside the book on his folio, then padded over to the door. He blinked in surprised. "Qasim? Is the party finished?"

Qasim didn't move for a moment, then he was across the threshold and his hands were in Rhys's hair and he was kissing Rhys demandingly. Together, they stumbled back into the room, and Qasim kicked the door shut behind them.

They were both breathing harder when Qasim broke the kiss. He searched Rhys's face by the light of the bedside lamp, his eyes as dark and liquid as pools of ink. "Are you ready now?" he asked, the hope and plea hanging on every word.

Rhys stared at him and remembered a night a lifetime ago when he had turned Qasim away, before everything fell apart. Everything had changed so much since then. They'd both been through so much. He smiled. "I am if you are, *cariad*."

Qasim's face lit up and his cheeks got redder. "Now?"

Rhys had imagined so many different ways for it to go, all the things he wanted to do for and with Qasim, and right this second, he couldn't remember any of them. Either way, he leaned up and kissed Qasim again, pulling him closer, because it was never a bad place to start.

Qasim made a soft, happy sound and God, Rhys wanted to hear it again.

He slipped his hands to Qasim's waist and pushed up the bottom of his shirt until his fingers skimmed along bare, warm skin. Qasim shivered and drew back from his lips.

"Anything you want, tell me," Rhys murmured, tracing his thumbs above the waistband of Qasim's trousers. "Anything you don't like, tell me." Christ, he was nervous. Of course, he was. It was *Qasim*. "All right, *cariad*?"

Qasim nodded, kneading at Rhys's shoulders through his shirt. "D'you—d'you remember Eid? What you said then?"

Rhys could remember all too well. "Yeah."

Qasim darted his tongue along his lips. "That. I want that."

Jesus Christ. Rhys's heart was pounding. Those months of restraint were about to come in really handy, especially when his pyjama bottoms were starting to feel too tight.

"All right," he murmured, leaning in to kiss the corner of Qasim's mouth. "I'll see what I can remember." He trailed his lips along Qasim's cheek, under the corner of his jaw, his throat, adding a soft, sharp bite there that made Qasim clutch at his hair.

Rhys withdrew one hand from under Qasim's shirt to start undoing the buttons. He started at the top, working down, and with each new inch of skin revealed, he moved his head down, kissing and teasing with his teeth and lips. When he caught one of Qasim's small dark nipples between his teeth, Qasim jolted as if he had been electrified, his fingers yanking in Rhys's hair.

Rhys soothed the bite with a flick of his tongue, then moved his mouth back up in a lazy, meandering path to the other side of Qasim's throat. "Like this?" he murmured against the stubble-prickled skin.

"Yeah..." Qasim sounded breathless already. He swallowed hard, throat bobbing against Rhys's lips. "More?"

"Shirt off," Rhys murmured, drawing away from Qasim's hand.

Qasim released him to shed it at once, and Rhys caught him by the front of his trousers, pulling him across the room. Christ, Qasim was so much thinner and breathing so hard and it wouldn't do any good if he managed to kill his lover on their first night together.

He paused by the bed, running the backs of his fingers up from Qasim's navel to the middle of his chest, barely touching, making Qasim shiver again. "Do you want me to get rid of your trousers?" he murmured, watching Qasim's face.

There was nervousness there, but anticipation as well. Qasim nodded, and Rhys trailed his hand back down, easing the button of Qasim's fly undone. The zip followed but Rhys kept his eyes on Qasim's face. When he curled his fingers over the waistband of Qasim's trousers, Qasim caught his breath as they were pushed down over hips, thighs, and dropped to puddle on the floor.

Rhys didn't look down at once, even with his hands on the warm flesh of Qasim's hips, not until Qasim leaned in, kissed him, smiled.

"I'm not made of glass," he whispered. "Don't need to be so careful."

Rhys laughed ruefully. "I'm a bit new at this," he admitted, trailing his fingers down to blatantly pinch Qasim's arse. "First times and all that." He leaned closer, until their bodies were a breath away from pressing against each other and murmured, "I'm a bit of a letch."

When Qasim burst out laughing, it felt like some kind of tension between them had broken. "No!" Qasim grinned at him. "I couldn't tell."

"I'm subtle, like."

Qasim considered him for a moment, then to Rhys's astonishment, grabbed him by the front of the pyjama bottoms and squeezed. He was scarlet in the face when he did it, but he *still did it*. Rhys's eyes flew wide, his hands tightening on Qasim's bum.

"Qas..." he said hoarsely. It was one thing to hold himself in check for his sick lover, but Jesus Christ, Qasim had a hold of him, and it was enough to make him forget about caution.

Qasim was staring at him, heat in his eyes. "Have you any idea how long I've been waiting?" He fumbled at Rhys's pyjamas, pushing them down enough to catch Rhys by the cock, just like he had the lazy morning so many weeks ago. "I've done subtle. I'm tired of subtle." His other hand curled into Rhys's hair, clenching, sending delicious heat charging through him. "I *want* this. Not softly-softly. I want *you*."

"I—" Rhys tried to remember how to breathe. The gleam in Qasim's eyes, the grip, the hunger in his voice. "You're not at full strength."

Qasim laughed breathlessly. "I crossed hundreds of miles. I crossed time. I think I can manage one elephant ride."

They stared at each other, before dissolving into helpless laughter. "Fine!" Rhys exclaimed, pulling Qasim flush against him. "You win."

This time when he leaned up and kissed Qasim, he didn't hold back, opening his mouth to Qasim's hungry, eager kisses. He rocked his hips against Qasim's palm and shifted his weight, insinuating a thigh between Qasim's, nudging his legs apart. Qasim groaned as his cock rubbed against Rhys's belly.

Rhys slid one hand up to the middle of Qasim's chest. All it took was a push and Qasim fell back onto the bed, sprawled there, panting and flushed. His legs were dangling over the edge of the bed, and he pushed himself up on his elbow, holding out his other hand.

"C'mere."

Rhys couldn't have refused, even if he'd been under orders. He pressed one knee to the edge of the mattress between Qasim's legs and leaned down over him, bracing his hands on either side of Qasim's head. "You're sure?"

Qasim caught his hair again and pulled his head down, kissing him hard enough to bruise their lips. "Yes."

Rhys wet his lips with the tip of his tongue, then rose back on his knee and leaned over to the bedside cabinet. He had been mortified when he'd open one of his boxes from storage—labelled bedroom stuff—and realised he'd brought all his sex gear into the El-Fahkris' home. It felt better to hide it in his bedside cabinet rather than risk offending anyone.

Now, though, it was there and Qasim was here. He caught Qasim watching him from the corner of his eye as he picked out one of the tubes.

"Lube," he explained, wondering if he'd ever blushed so hard during sex before. There was so much blood in his face he was amazed his cock was still up. But then there was a naked Qasim right in front of him, wide-eyed and breathing hard and just as flushed. He smiled cautiously. "So it doesn't hurt."

Qasim bit his lower lip but spread his legs a little wider.

All Rhys could think was *gently*. His hands were shaking as he slicked his cock then his fingers. He reached down to stroke his hand the length of Qasim's cock. Qasim's hips jumped, and he made another of those small, sharp sounds which shot straight from Rhys's ears to his knob.

"If you want me to stop..." He trailed off as he ran his fingers along the crease of Qasim's backside. Qasim's breath caught, and he trembled under Rhys's hand. But the heat was still in his eyes, and when Rhys eased a finger into him, he pressed his head back on the duvet. A stroke, another, deeper, then another finger, curling just...so. Again, then again.

Qasim's fingers were bunching in the covers under him, and his cock was seeping, dripping on his quivering belly. "Rhys..." He was keening breathlessly. "Please."

Rhys nodded mutely, withdrawing his hand. He slid both hands under Qasim's backside, lifting him just enough and pressed close against him. Qasim's eyes were bright and wet and he reached up to pull Rhys's mouth down on his. When Rhys pushed into him—slowly, Christ so slowly—he swallowed Qasim's low moan. Fingers were in his hair again, pulling tight, nails in his shoulders, and Qasim's thighs were hard around his hips.

He tried to hold back. Christ, he tried, but Qasim growled his name against his lips, pushed against him, and he couldn't stop himself from moving. And every time he did, Qasim made small, urgent sounds, and his nails pressed and his fingers pulled and his thighs squeezed tighter, and Rhys's brain just...stopped.

All that mattered was Qasim. All he cared about was kissing him and breathing him in and fucking the living daylights out of him, making him pull and cling and grab and leave Rhys's senses a smouldering ruin.

He only faltered when Qasim pushed at his shoulder, his breath coming too fast, and his cock throbbed hard and wet against Rhys's belly. Done. He was done, and he was staring wide-eyed at Rhys, a mortified expression on his face.

"Sorry!"

Rhys wondered how it was possible to love the adorable, silly little bugger even more. He leaned down and kissed him again, reassuringly. "It's all right, *cariad*," he promised, catching Qasim's hips again. "It's not the end of it." He started to rock his hips again, felt Qasim move under him, wrap his legs around him, and well...that just helped as he shifted his position just enough and caught Qasim's prostate. "There..."

Qasim pressed his head against the bed. "Oh!"

The gasped sound threw Rhys over the edge. Not even half a dozen strokes, watching Qasim's eyes press closed and lips fall open and the feel of fingers in his hair and those fucking beautiful little noises he was making…

They were both sheened with sweat as they lay side by side on the bed. Qasim's eyes were still half-closed, and he had a small, dazed smile on his lips. His cheeks were pink, and he was breathing hard, but Rhys had never seen him so peaceful.

"Rhys?" he murmured, groping out and finding Rhys's hand.

"Yeah?"

Qasim tilted his head to meet his eyes. "Can I stay here tonight?"

Rhys's heart was swelling with happiness. He rolled onto his side and pressed a soft kiss to Qasim's lips. "For as long as you want."

Qasim gazed at him, his eyes dark and shining. "Could be a long time."

Rhys kissed him again, barely a brush of their lips. "I think I can cope."

When Qasim smiled, it lit up the room.

Chapter Forty-Nine

SOMEONE WAS TAPPING on the door.

Qasim lifted his head and squinted around. It took him a second to get his bearings in the dim room, but the new aches in his body, the warm arm around him, and the bare chest against him brought everything back. He flushed and shifted in Rhys's embrace.

Rhys was still asleep. It softened the tense lines around his eyes and mouth, but it didn't hide the silver threading in his hair or how much weight he had lost since those weeks ago in lockdown.

There was another light tap at the door.

Qasim squinted at the clock by the bedside.

Salat!

He eased himself out from under Rhys's arm and grabbed his shorts, then headed for the door. Pisi bolted in when he opened it, and Qasim's father raised his eyebrows as Qasim closed the door behind him. Qasim could feel the blush accelerating towards his hairline.

"Your mother would like you to join us," his father said as if he hadn't found Qasim in bed with a man in his house. He nodded towards the bathroom. "You have some ablutions to make, I think."

"Yes, Abi," Qasim said sheepishly.

He couldn't help feeling a little ashamed of himself. He'd always insisted he wouldn't throw himself at someone—anyone—before they were married, but after the past few months, after everything that had happened...

It wasn't an excuse. Well, it was. Sort of.

He loved Rhys, and when they had come so close to losing each other permanently, even wild horses couldn't have kept him back. Maybe vows hadn't been exchanged, but to Qasim, it felt as near as made no difference. The fact his family had practically adopted Rhys was the icing on the cake.

He did his ablutions with even more care than usual—he definitely needed *ghusl* after the night before—then dressed and joined his parents in the living room. His prayer mat was laid out beside his father's, like it had been the first time he'd been old enough to pray.

"Like old times?" he said, failing to hide the emotion in his voice.

"Like old times," his mother agreed, taking and squeezing one of his hands.

Qasim always loved praying with his family. Their presence was calming at the best of times and combined with salat, it felt like every weight on his shoulders was lifted away.

When they were done, they sat together.

It was the first time they were alone together since his return, just the three of them, with no one watching and no decon suits and machines and distractions. He reached out and took each of their hands, wishing he had the words to say everything he wanted to say.

His mother laughed softly, releasing his hand and moving closer to embrace him. "We know, *habibi*. We know."

"Thank you," Qasim finally managed. "For Rhys. For taking care of him for me."

"You know we will always take care of our children and the ones they love," his father murmured, a mischievous glint in his eyes. "Even if they don't bother to tell us."

Qasim ducked his head. "I didn't think I was so obvious."

"Ha!" His mother ruffled his hair. "Everyone knew. It was written on your face at Eid." She cuffed his cheek gently. "He's a good man. We like him."

Qasim couldn't help the widening smile. "He is, and I do too."

His mother considered him thoughtfully. "You should make him breakfast. Since you were sick, he hasn't eaten enough. He might eat more now you're here with him, especially if you make it."

"You remember how well I cook, Ummi?"

She wrinkled her nose. "Toast then. We have bread for him and jam and English tea with milk."

"You let Tetley in the house?" Qasim feigned horror. "Ummi! I'm shocked."

She swatted his head fondly. "The things I do for my son's intended."

"Ummi!" Of all the things for his mother to say, he hadn't expected that.

"It's too early for him yet," his father said. He smiled at Qasim. "I think you should get some more sleep too. Yesterday was a long day, and you're still recovering."

Qasim nodded gratefully, glad to dodge the inevitable questions about his apparently forthcoming marriage neither he nor Rhys knew anything about. "We'll both be down for breakfast," he promised, kissing his mother's cheek before getting up.

If he were sensible, he'd have gone to his own room and slept in his own bed, but he'd spent his whole life being sensible. There was something to be said for a near-death experience shaking up his life choices. He crept back into Rhys's room and shed his clothes again, smiling when he spotted Pisi curled up in the warm space he had left in the bed.

"No stealing my spot," he murmured to her, scooping her up so he could sit back down. She grumbled, wriggling out of his arms, then indignantly stalked over to his pile of still-warm clothes and curled up on them instead.

Qasim laughed quietly, slipping back under the covers. Rhys was woken by the bed shifting under Qasim's weight and immediately nestled closer, burying his face in Qasim's throat, one arm wrapping across his middle.

"M'rnin'."

"Shh," Qasim murmured, stroking his fingers along the back of Rhys's arm. "Go back to sleep."

Rhys nodded, his yawn a warm gust on Qasim's throat.

Qasim wished it was as easy to drift back off, but he had no idea how he was going to explain to his parents that no, in fact, they weren't engaged, they hadn't even officially been on a date yet. His mother didn't know where he'd spent the night. If she did, he would get an earful about it as well.

He didn't know how long he'd been lying and staring at the ceiling, turning over explanations in his head, when Rhys's fingers brushed his ribs.

"S'wrong?"

Qasim traced his fingers on Rhys's arm. "Nothing. Just thinking."

Rhys pushed himself up on one elbow to peer short-sightedly at him. His hair was standing in all directions, and he looked even more adorable than usual. "Bullshit," he said with a yawn. "You're stiff as a board. S'not good."

Qasim lifted his hand to push a rogue curl back from the middle of Rhys's forehead. "You know me and my brain."

"Mm." Rhys tilted his head into Qasim's touch. "Is—was it last night?"

"No!" Qasim sank his fingers into Rhys's hair. "No, not at all." He smiled shyly. "I'm glad I came. I liked it."

"Mm?" Rhys's hand on Qasim's ribs moved down. "Really?"

Qasim laughed, but even he could hear the edge in it, as he reached down and caught Rhys's wrist. If he didn't say it now, Ummi would be the one to explain, and it would be all kinds of awkward. "There's something I need to tell you."

Rhys immediately moved his hand back up. "So something *is* wrong?"

"Not...wrong exactly..." Qasim reluctantly sat up in the tangle of bedding, pulling up his knees to prop his arms on them. "It's..." He shook his head self-consciously and laughed. "Ummi's got it into her head that we're engaged, and I didn't know how to tell her we're not."

"Ah." Rhys flopped onto his back.

Qasim shrugged helplessly. "I—it's—she'll probably start asking about plans. I mean, you saw how much she likes to throw a bit of a do. She hasn't had a wedding for more than ten years."

"She does like a party," Rhys agreed. He leaned over to the side of the bed, groping for his glasses on the bedside table. When he managed to find them, he rolled back. "I think I know how we can keep from disappointing her."

"Oh?" Qasim looked down at him and blinked.

Rhys had his hand open, and there was a ring lying in his palm. Qasim stared at it, then back at Rhys's face. Rhys shrugged with a small smile. "We'll give her an excuse."

Qasim's eyes slid back to the ring. "What?" His voice felt all choked up.

Rhys sat up, still smiling. "You're going to make me ask, aren't you?"

Qasim gaped at him. "Are—you're serious? Are you serious?"

In answer, Rhys scrambled off the bed and went down on one knee beside it. "Serious enough?"

Qasim's vision blurred with tears, and he pressed a hand to his mouth to keep from shouting out in shocked delight.

"I thought I'd lost you once," Rhys said, and his voice was shaking. "I don't want to do it again, not ever." He held up the ring. "I don't know how this is meant to go, but I—I love you, *cariad*. You invited me in. Gave me somewhere I can call home. If you'll have me, I promise I'll do the same for you."

Qasim could feel the tears streaking down his face, and his cheeks were hurting from the width of his smile. "Ask me," he urged.

"Qasim El-Fahkri." Rhys gazed up at him, all earnest and stark bollocking naked. "Will you marry me?"

Qasim threw himself off the bed, tackling Rhys onto the floor, and kissed him. "Yes! Of course!" He pushed himself up over Rhys, still half tangled in the sheets. "You never said anything!" He stared at Rhys, who was beaming from ear to ear. "Wait, did my parents know...?"

Rhys just started laughing and pulled him down again. "Come here and give us a *cwtch, cariad.*"

Qasim leaned back from Rhys's kisses, prodding him in the shoulder. "Did you ask my father's—" He dodged another kiss. "Did you actually ask my father's permission?"

"You're ruining the moment a bit." Rhys chuckled, giving Qasim's bum a squeeze through the sheets. "You know I'm a bit traditional."

Qasim had to kiss him. "I love you."

Rhys somehow managed to roll them over, sheets and blankets and all, and Qasim ended up on his back. "I thought you might," Rhys said, smiling down at him. He held up his hand with the ring. "You want to make it official?"

Qasim immediately held up his right hand and couldn't stop himself from giggling as Rhys slipped the ring onto his finger. It shone like silver, not gold. Rhys must have asked what was all right and what wasn't. No detail forgotten. He held up his hand, examining it. "Well, Ummi's going to be delighted."

"Her bachelor boy finally growing up," Rhys said, smiling. He pushed himself up onto his knees. "Shall we go and tell them?"

Qasim sat up. "One thing, first." He wrapped his arms around Rhys's middle and tilted his head up. "Can I get a cudge? I mean, whatever one of those is, it sounds nice."

Rhys burst out laughing. "*Cwtch.* It's a hug." He pulled Qasim into a hug to demonstrate and murmured close to his ear, "We'll need to work on your Welsh."

"And your Arabic," Qasim said happily. He leaned back enough to meet Rhys's eyes. "You do know the family comes as part and parcel with me, don't you? In case you want to run a mile..."

Rhys shook his head. "They sealed the deal. I want the whole package."

Qasim's cheeks were aching from smiling, and he pulled Rhys's head down to kiss him again.

They were delayed for breakfast, but he was too happy to care as they meandered into the living room, which was already wafting with the smell of coffee and toasted bread.

Before he even said anything, his mother threw her arms up with a delighted cry and leapt up from the table, rushing towards them. They were both caught in an enthusiastic hug that almost squeezed the breath out of them, and then she caught Qasim's hand to examine the ring.

His father lowered his folio and raised his eyebrows. "So you did it, then?"

Qasim beamed at Rhys, who was trying unsuccessfully to hide a smile. "Yeah, he did."

Chapter Fifty

THE WIND WAS up, but it was a beautiful day.

The park was dotted with flowers, and the scent of freshly cut grass filled the air. It was the right kind of day for the funeral.

Somehow, someone in the TRI had managed to get the gate open to retrieve Tahmila's body. Rhys didn't want to know who had twisted their arm to do it. What mattered was Tahmila finally got a ceremony, and her friends and family had the chance to mourn her.

Everyone had shown up in vivid colours on Mitchell's request. Mila would have wanted it, he'd said. Qasim donned a bright pink blouse with ruffles down the front and made Mitchell laugh so hard he cried.

Rhys had kept out of the way during the small gathering at a community hall although he moved a little closer as the funeral party headed for the park. Qasim and Mitchell were the ones who knew Mila best. Mitchell was the one who needed the support now, and Qasim was right there beside him. They were at the head of the rainbow-coloured group of dozens of people. So many people were there from the TRI. So many people had known Tahmila and liked her.

Mitchell led them through the park to a hilltop overlooking a pond and the sprawling green and flower-speckled grounds. There were benches, and in the summer light, it was beautiful.

"This was her favourite spot to come," Mitchell said, turning to face the mourners. "I think it'd give her a good laugh to know she ended up fertilising the place." His voice shook and broke, and Qasim stepped closer and squeezed his shoulder.

Mitchell gathered himself and then held out dog he had tucked under one arm. Qasim took it and stepped back as Mitchell opened the urn and scattered his wife's ashes into the wind. Rhys wasn't surprised when he dropped the empty urn and buried his face in his hands. No one ever expected to lose a loved one before they even hit thirty-five.

Qasim stepped closer and wrapped an arm around Mitchell. One by one, the other mourners approached and hugged him too, then gradually, the party started to break apart, until there was no one left but Qasim, Mitchell, Rhys, and the ugly little dog.

Qasim glanced at Rhys. "Can you give us a minute?" he asked quietly.

Rhys nodded. "Want me to take..." He paused, looking at the dog. "I want to say Boris?"

"Boris Yelpsin," Mitchell corrected with a damp laugh. "She thought it was funny."

Rhys took the dog and hooked on his leash, then retreated a little way down the path. The dog snuffled his way along the side of a bench as Rhys sat and gazed back up the hill.

Qasim was talking quietly to Mitchell, one hand on Mitchell's shoulder, the other holding one of his hands. Mitchell was openly weeping, but to Rhys's surprise, he smiled and stepped close, pulling Qasim into a tight hug. Rhys glanced away, not wanting to intrude on something private.

Several minutes later, Mitchell and Qasim joined him at the bench.

"I should get back to the hall," Mitchell said. "Everyone was heading back there. Mila insisted on putting a disco in her will." He shook her head. "S'pose we should count ourselves lucky she didn't go for the bouncy castle."

"I don't know," Qasim said with a laugh. "I could go for a bouncy castle. I'd look like a radish on a spring."

Mitchell's expression was brighter than it had been. "Maybe save it for your wedding?"

Qasim's eyes widened, and he swung around to face Rhys with delight. "Yeah!"

Rhys recognised the manic gleam in his eye. "Maybe," he said diplomatically. "We can talk about it later." He offered Boris's leash to Mitchell. "We'll come back down in a bit, if it's okay."

Mitchell nodded. "Don't take too long. We need Qas to get everyone dancing."

Qasim preened, fluffing the ruffles of his shirt. "You know it." He patted Mitchell's shoulder. "Don't start without us."

"Of course not."

As Mitchell walked away, Qasim sat on the bench beside Rhys and exhaled a long breath.

Rhys reached over and took his hand. "You've been amazing today."

Qasim gave him a brief sad smile. "Yeah, but I've had plenty of time to process it all, remember. No legal ramifications or enthusiastic parents to distract me back in the day." He threaded his fingers between Rhys's. "It's still rubbish, though."

"Yeah." Rhys slid a little closer, until they were pressed side by side. "Looked like you said something to help Mitchell, though."

Qasim leaned into him, rubbing his thumb along the back of Rhys's. "Yeah. Dad and me went over the formal paperwork. It was all signed two days ago." He smiled, looking down at their hands. "They're putting new safeguards in place, guarantees for the well-being of all other temporal agents. They're calling it the Samuels protocol. Named it after her and everything."

Rhys couldn't hide his surprise. The division between the Supervisory Board and the agents had been a long one. "Who swung that?"

A smug little smile crossed Qasim's face. "Didn't I tell you? I got Elwin fired."

Rhys's jaw dropped. "You did *what*?"

"Mm-hm." Qasim snuggled against him. "'Parently, the board saw the reports on everything, and Mr. O'Donohue explained my conditions for signing the nondisclosure and why I needed them validated, and they weren't too happy with Mr. Elwin."

Rhys stared at him in astonishment. "Your dad did all of it?"

To his ever-increasing surprise, Qasim giggled and hid his nose in Rhys's shoulder. "Nope." He leaned close and whispered conspiratorially, "I told them off before I got out. They wanted to shut me up. I didn't let them. Gave them a piece of my mind and used Ummi's best glare." He kissed Rhys on the ear. "You'll be getting a letter of apology and your full severance back in about a week."

Rhys had a feeling he was gawping. "You did it? *You*?"

Qasim stifled another giggle, his chin resting on Rhys's shoulder. "Mm-hm."

Just when Rhys thought it was impossible to find something else to like about the bugger, he pulled out even more amazing tricks. "Christ, I love you."

Qasim kissed his cheek fondly. "Well, yeah. That's why you're marrying me."

Suddenly, something dawned on Rhys. "Did you get Mila back too?"

Qasim nodded. "Least I could do for Mitchell." He sighed, covering their linked hands with his other hand. "They've asked me to keep working there. Well, Mr. O'Donohue has. Said something about me bringing 'valuable insight' to the TRI."

As much as Rhys wanted to tell him no, he couldn't stand the idea of Qasim going off on temporal jumps again, he knew it wasn't his decision to make. "Well," he finally said, "at least one of us'll have a job, eh?"

He could feel Qasim's eyes on him. "You'd be okay with it?"

He couldn't lie, not to Qasim. "I can't say I'd be happy if you went on jumps again, but if it's what you want to do, I wouldn't stop you."

Qasim lifted one hand to touch his cheek, drawing Rhys's face around to his. "Never said anything about jumps." He smiled at Rhys's confused expression. "I'm there to supervise and train newcomers. I lasted a month in the past and didn't die. They think I can teach the babies a thing or two."

The relief hit Rhys like a truck, and he wrapped Qasim in a hug. "Thank God!" He laughed shakily. "Don't scare me like that."

Qasim patted his shoulder "I'll try not to." He drew back and glanced down the hill. "We should get back." He unfolded from the bench and straightened up. "You heard what Mitchell said. I can't let down my audience."

Rhys hesitated. There was a question he'd been meaning to ask for days, but it wasn't something for a crowd or even in front of Qasim's family. "Qasim."

That made Qasim turn to him, frowning. He never said Qasim's full name so seriously.

"Yeah?"

Rhys fiddled with his fingers. "You remember when you were sick, you asked me if I'd come to the mosque with you?"

Qasim nodded. "I remember."

Rhys gazed up at him. "I'd like to go with you next time." He smiled cautiously. "I mean, not just because you asked, but it's important to you. I'd like to understand it all better."

Qasim's smile was as bright as sunshine. He swept down and kissed Rhys again. "I love you so much."

Rhys wrapped one hand around the back of Qasim's head and held him there for a moment, brow to brow, nose to nose, sharing each other's breath. "Same." Qasim curled his fingers into Rhys's hair and, for a moment, the world was just them, and Rhys couldn't remember ever feeling happier.

When Qasim pulled him to his feet, it felt natural for Rhys to slip his arm around his lover's waist as they started down the hill.

"Rhys."

"Yeah?"
"Just so you know, you're about to dance with me."
Rhys made a face. "I don't dance."
Qasim looked at him and smiled. "You do now."

Epilogue

REUNION: FIVE YEARS LATER...

Ben smoothed down his shirt and neatened up his jacket before pressing the doorbell.

He'd never been to this particular house. The El-Fahkris had moved since his last visit, and he had to admit he was a little curious. It was only a flying visit, he told himself. In, eat, and straight back out again. No need to get tangled up with anyone affiliated with the TRI again.

As soon as the front door opened into the bright, warm hall, Ben had a sinking feeling he wouldn't be leaving anytime soon. The smells wafting through from the kitchen made his stomach growl, and from the smug grin on Rhys—no, not Rhys anymore. Riza, after he converted four years back. Damn it, he always forgot—Riza's face, he knew it.

"You made it all right, then?" Riza hadn't changed. His beard was a bit thicker and there was silver starting to show in the blond, but he was still the same short, plump, pink-cheeked man he'd always been.

Ben made a face at him. "You weren't exactly subtle."

Riza laughed. "It was only six invites, since you ignored them last year."

Ben flushed. "I didn't ignore them!" he protested, following Rhys into the house. He braced a hand against the wall as he toed his shoes off. "I didn't get them until it was too late. We were—I was away on a trip."

"We, eh?" Riza frowned. "You should've said. There's always room for one more at the table."

Ben hesitated. Sometimes, it was tempting to pretend his life was nice and normal, and he could go on nights out like any normal couple. But this wasn't just any night, and it definitely wasn't a celebration a nice, normal couple would attend. "At a 'yay we got Qasim back from history despite all the odds' anniversary do?"

Riza nodded with a wince. "You could've said it was a normal anniversary?" he suggested, leading Ben into the house. "I mean, it is, technically."

"Technically," Ben echoed. It was true, but it also marked the anniversary of the month Ben defied the temporal laws and opened an illegal time gate and got himself into an awful lot of trouble with the TRI. Not that he regretted it. Doing what he had to, to save a friend's life, didn't feel like a crime, and he still stood by it. Yeah, he'd done some stupid shit in his life, but when it was for the right reasons, who could blame him? "Maybe another time, when it's not about time travel?"

Riza nodded, pushing open the door into a kitchen and dining room. It was a huge, bright room, the back wall all windows and the side walls pale cream and golden. The evening sunlight made it even warmer.

On the far side of the room, Qasim was at the stove, a small child sitting on the counter beside him carefully dropping handfuls of peas into a pot. She was tiny, her black hair braided with floral clips holding strands back from her round cheeks, and a white apron neatly tied over her frilly skirt.

"*Cariad*, we've got a miracle!" Riza called.

Qasim turned with a grin. "Ben! We didn't know if you'd make it."

Ben rolled his eyes, smiling. "I miss one time, and it's the end of the world?" He peered at the girl beside Qasim. He'd heard about their adoption going through but hadn't had a chance to meet the newest addition to their family. "And who's this?"

The girl gave him a curious stare.

"This," Riza said, swinging the girl off the counter and into his arms, "is Mirmah." He chuckled when the girl hid her face in his collar. "She likes to pretend she's shy." He leaned closer to Ben. "It's a trap."

Mirmah giggled, tugging at the front of Riza's shirt. "Not."

Ben had to smile. He offered his hand. "Hello. I'm Ben."

She reached out and tugged his finger, then ducked her face down again. "'Lo."

Riza gave her such a soft, doting smile and something twisted up in Ben's chest.

"So," he said, turning away, "this is the new place? Nice."

"Thought it was about time to get out of my parents' hair." Qasim set down a lid with a clatter. "They're only up the road, so they're happy."

"And you two?" Ben wandered across the room. "Everything okay?" He risked a glance over at them and saw the affectionate smiles they exchanged. "Stupid question?"

"Happy," Riza agreed. "Especially now we've got this one to keep us on our toes." He bent to set Mirmah on her feet and glanced at Qasim. "Ben's seeing someone."

"And you didn't bring th—"

Riza clapped a hand over Qasim's mouth. "Been there, done that, cancelling the guilt trip," he said, grinning. "Think about the top of the cake. D'you want to explain it to a civilian?"

Qasim's eyes widened and he shook his head, then brushed his husband's arm aside. "Good point." The oven beeped, and he glanced at it. "The food should be ready. Mirmah, can you show Ben where to sit?"

Mirmah nodded, holding out a small hand to him. "I show you."

She led him to the table, which gave Ben pause. There were five places laid.

"Who else is coming?" he inquired.

Mirmah beamed up at him. "Uncle Sander."

"Uncle Sander?" Ben's stomach dropped like a rock. "Lysander?" He glanced back at Riza. "You didn't mention O'Donohue'll be coming."

Riza was helping his husband dole out the food. "All the conspirators in one place. He's on his way, but he let us know he's stuck in traffic."

Conspirators. Right. Of course. He'd helped get Qasim five years ago, but things had changed since then.

Ben felt sick.

It was almost three years since he'd seen O'Donohue, when Ben stormed out of the TRI in a fit of useless rage. Not the best note to leave on, but then, they had just terminated the two-year search for his long-missing father. Mariam Ashraf—former head of the TRI and Ben's foster mum—had made the call, but Lysander O'Donohue had signed off on it and nearly got punched in the face for his efforts.

It was a dramatic exit, which Ben couldn't deny. The fact he'd wrecked his office, smashed a bunch of his machines, and told them exactly what he thought of them only made it worse. It was less burning a bridge and more firebombing the living shit out of it.

Since then, he'd screwed up even more, but at least they didn't know about it. He'd avoided them as much as he could, blocking their calls, deleting their messages, and trying like hell to pretend everything was fine and normal. Time away, he'd said. Experiencing life, he'd said. Anything that meant they didn't come to check on him to make sure he was okay.

And now, he was meant to sit and eat dinner with the man and smile like everything was fine?

A small hand tugging on his jerked him back to reality.

"You need to sit," Mirmah informed him.

"Oh. Right. Yes." He sank onto the appointed chair, his heart purring rapidly in his chest.

"You're sitting by Uncle Sander." The girl climbed onto one of the other chairs and beamed at him. "And we got cake."

"Cake," he echoed. "Yeah. Cake is good."

And it would be, he thought, if they could just get through dinner.

"I THOUGHT HE knew," Qasim whispered to Riza as he stacked *yalangi* in one of the bowls. "Last time he came, Lysander was here."

"Maybe he forgot." The front door buzzed, and Riza touched his arm. "I'll go and run interference with Ben. You let Lysander in."

Qasim nodded, handing the bowl to his husband. He wiped his hands, hurrying through to the hall, and opened the front door. Lysander O'Donohue greeted him with a smile. It was a rare expression for such a serious man, but the more Lysander visited, the more often he smiled.

"Hey."

"Right on time." Qasim motioned for him to come in. "We're just serving up."

Lysander laughed. "I could smell it from the yard." He held out an elegant paper bag with ribbons for handles. "I thought I'd add something to the feast."

"Ly..." Qasim sighed, shaking his head. "You know you don't need to."

Lysander gave him an amused look. "I'll let your mom explain to you why that's never going to happen." He shrugged off his jacket, hung it one of the pegs by the door, and slipped his shoes off as well. "I'm surprised I don't have someone climbing up my leg already."

"Yeah"—Qasim couldn't help himself—"Riza's trying to behave himself. I like to think I have him domesticated now."

Lysander's shoulders shook, but he made a game effort not to laugh out loud. "Sure."

Qasim stepped closer before Lysander could head towards the dining room. "There's something, though."

Lysander's dark eyebrows pulled down. "Oh?"

"Ben." Those eyebrows rose again. "He didn't realise you'd be coming."

Lysander stared blankly at him for several seconds, then groaned. "Ah."

"It'll be the first time he's seen you since—"

"Since he quit." Lysander nodded. "Yeah." He ran a hand over his beard. "Guess I'd better bite the bullet. He can't avoid the TRI forever, even if he wants to."

Qasim nodded. "Only...no furniture damage, okay? We just finished decorating."

"On my best behaviour," Lysander promised, hand to his heart. "Now, where's your troublemaker?"

"Senior?" Qasim asked, grinning as he led Lysander towards the kitchen, "or Junior?"

"Either."

Qasim pushed the door wide. "Mirmah!" He stepped to the side as footsteps pattered closer, out of the way in time for Mirmah to slam straight into Lysander's leg and hug him around the middle.

"Uncle Sander!"

Lysander swept her off the floor and spun her around. "Hey, trouble." He propped her on his hip. "Have you been making me dinner?"

Mirmah beamed at him, nodding. "I helped Abi."

Qasim chuckled. "She did this time. She cooked the peas."

"I like peas best." She hugged Lysander around the neck and then pointed towards the table. "We need to sit down for dinner."

Qasim glanced over. Ben was sitting stiffly in his seat, fidgeting with his knife and fork. Riza met Qasim's eyes with a helpless shrug. "Riza and I'll bring the food over. You go and make yourself comfortable."

Riza hurried back towards the kitchen. "It's not going to be much of a party," he said apologetically.

Qasim reached out to squeeze his hand. "It'll be fine. Give them a little time to thaw out."

They both spun around when Mirmah screeched.

"Not that chair! That chair is mine! I sit by Tad!"

Lysander hastily got up and shifted around to the seat next to Ben as ordered. Ben's lips twitched, and he offered Lysander a sympathetic glance. "Better?" Lysander inquired, folding his hands on the table.

Mirmah climbed onto her seat, kneeling up. She frowned and straightened her fork and spoon, then nodded imperiously. "Yes. My seat."

Qasim pressed his lips together to keep from laughing. "Or," he murmured to Riza, "we unleash Mirmah and spend the rest of the night hiding out back here."

"Tad!" Mirmah yelled over her shoulder. "I want peas!"

Riza snorted. "So much for our cunning plan." He patted Qasim's bum to nudge him out of the way to fetch the bowl of peas and one of the dishes of rice. "Our princess commands. We must obey."

Qasim grinned. "You're so soft."

"Coming from the person who makes me the softest?" Riza leaned up to drop a kiss on his cheek. "Bring the rest. I'm not being the referee on my own."

"Wimp."

"Always."

THE MEAL HAD gone okay.

As promised, no furniture had been broken. Lysander tried to stick to neutral topics, which Mirmah made easier by telling everyone about butterflies, a spoon, and the new duck she had for her bath. It almost made it possible to ignore the elephant in the room.

The elephant himself softened up around Mirmah. It was hard not to. She was such a happy, bubbly kid, and from the looks of things, Ben had forgotten how sweet small kids could be. He even smiled once or twice, which she rewarded with beaming grins.

Lysander couldn't help watching the younger man out of the corner of his eye.

By the time the search for his father had been shut down, Ben was thin and hollow-eyed. He'd worn himself to the bone, and the search was proving fruitless. Mariam Ashraf insisted it was time to end it all. She'd seen his father go through the same hopeless obsession hunting for his missing wife, she said, and didn't want it to consume Ben's life as it had his father's. Lysander had agreed.

It had been nearly three full years since Ben left the TRI in a rage, and no one was sure where he'd been or what he'd been doing.

His eyes were still shadowed, and he was still thin, but it wasn't the same now. He had some colour in his face, and he seemed like he'd at least been trying to take care of himself. Still anxious and always fidgeting, Lysander noticed, but then, Ben always had been highly strung.

"Tad!" Mirmah knelt on her seat. "I want to play outside!"

Riza and Qasim exchanged looks, and Lysander suspected there was a conspiracy underway.

"Uncle Lysander and Ben can take you outside for fifteen minutes," Riza said. "I'll clear up in here, and Abi'll go and get your bath ready."

"I can help," Ben said too quickly.

Lysander narrowed his eyes at Riza, who seemed to be fighting down a grin, as Mirmah wailed, "Don't you want to play with meeeeeeeeee?"

Ben—to his credit—only recoiled, panicked, for a few seconds. "Uh, yes! Yes, of course, I want to play with you!" He shoved back his chair, scrambled to his feet, and offered his hand. "Can you show me where to play?"

Mirmah's distraught expression vanished, and she ran around the table to grapple Ben's hand with both of her own. "Outside!" she declared happily, hauling him towards the door.

Lysander raised his eyebrows at Riza. "Really, Riza? Weaponising the kid? Doesn't it breach the Geneva Convention?"

Riza shrugged his shoulders, grinning. "I use the tools I—"

"Uncle Sander! Hurry up!"

Qasim propped his elbow on the table and cupped his chin in his hand. "You better go," he said, grinning as widely as his husband. "She gets antsy if she doesn't get her way."

Lysander snorted, pushing his chair back. "I blame the parents."

Riza chuckled, wrapping an arm around Qasim's waist. "We're great teachers."

"Uncle Sander!"

"I'm coming." Lysander followed Ben and Mirmah out into the garden, trying to ignore Riza and Qasim laughing behind him.

The sun was sinking, but it was still warm enough to be pleasant. Ben was sitting—no doubt instructed—on the edge of the stone terrace as Mirmah ran up the lawn. He was leaning forward, hunched over his knees, his forearms propped on his thighs. If a human could turn into a knot, Ben was definitely trying.

"She's getting her ball," Ben said, though he didn't turn. "She'll want you to sit down too. I was too big."

Lysander nodded, stepping down from the terrace onto the grass and sitting an arm's length from Ben. "I've been tricked like this before. She's got a mean right arm."

To his relief, Ben actually laughed, although it was strained. "Yeah?"

"Mm." Lysander waved when Mirmah turned around to make sure he was there. She beamed at him and then poked around in one of the flower beds. "She's just like her dads." He glanced sidelong at Ben. "Everyone thinks they're such pushovers."

Ben snorted. "Have they *met* them?"

"I know, right?" Lysander shook his head. "It's like they forgot everything that happened five years ago."

"Yeah." Ben was quiet for a minute. "They seem happy. Qasim and Rh—Riza."

"They are." Lysander watched Mirmah skipping back up the lawn, her sparkly, flashing ball clutched in her pudgy hands. "I'm glad we helped."

"Catch!" Mirmah lobbed the ball at Ben, who yelped and ducked.

Lysander tried to hide a laugh, curling a finger over his lips. "What did your tad say last time?"

Mirmah sighed. "Don't throw a ball at a head." She held out her hands for Ben to toss the ball back to her. "He should've put his hands up."

"Now, you know," Lysander said with a solemn nod to Ben.

"Now, I know," Ben agreed, throwing the ball back to her.

For several minutes, they tossed it back and forth between the three of them, until Mirmah demanded, "Throw it far!"

"Will you fetch it?" Lysander asked, hefting the ball in his hand.

Mirmah nodded. "It goes wheeeeeeeeee when you throw it far!"

Ben was laughing. "Wheeeeeee?"

"Wheeeeeeeee!" she confirmed, hopping from one foot to the other. "Throw it! Please!"

Lysander hurled the ball as far as he could and, as advertised, it screamed through the air. The girl shrieked just as loudly in delight and raced off after it. "She's doing well here," he murmured once she was out of earshot. "You wouldn't believe the change since she arrived."

Ben was watching her. "I s'pose I've been a bit out of the loop."

Lysander hesitated, considering his next words carefully. "You don't...have to be."

Ben stared at him, his expression twisted up and conflicted. "Lysander..."

Lysander held up a hand, nodding. "I know. No pressure. You've been missed is all. At the TRI. People have been worried about you."

Ben's face contorted even more, and he turned away, hunching over his knees. "They shouldn't."

"You know that's not how people work."

"Yeah." Ben propped his feet on the edge of the terrace, his chin on his knees. He wrapped his arms around his legs, his knuckles going white. "I made such a mess of things," he finally said, barely above a whisper.

Lysander hesitated again and then carefully touched the younger man's shoulder. "You can make up for it, if you want."

Ben laughed sharply. "Can I?"

"Why not?"

Ben turned to stare at him. No, it was more like he was staring through Lysander, weighing up his options. "You'd really let me come back? After everything I've done? The number of laws I broke? All the trouble I caused?"

Lysander nodded. "The TRI is your family's legacy. You know the tech better than anyone. If you want to come back, I wouldn't even have to press the board to let it happen."

Ben continued to stare at him and then ducked his head with a crooked grin. "Oh. I get it. You can't find anyone smart enough to handle the tech. That's what this is about."

Lysander leaned closer to him. "If I'm being honest..."

It earned him a small smile. "You're so full of shit."

"Only the best for you," Lysander replied with a grave nod.

"What's shit? Can I have some?"

They stared at each other in horror and turned to the small girl in her frilly skirt and pigtails standing three feet away from them.

"It's...um..." Ben stared imploringly at Lysander and frantically jerked his head towards her.

Lysander leaned forward. "It's a smelly thing silly old men have." He held out a hand for the ball. "I don't think you'd like it."

Mirmah considered him before dropping the ball in his hand again. "Okay. Throw it again."

Lysander lobbed the ball as hard as he could, and the girl skipped off again.

"Okay? She believed it?"

Lysander shook his head. "No, but at least you might be able to escape before she asks her parents what it is."

"Before they string me up by the balls, you mean?"

Lysander chuckled. "Yeah. *Les papas sans merci.*"

Ben unfolded, some of the tension leaving his body. "Don't I know it." He was quiet for a minute. "I'm sorry, y'know. About the way I left."

Lysander nodded. "We all knew."

Ben chewed his lower lip, staring at his hands in his lap. "I've... I started working on some new ideas. I mean, I can't do much with them, but

I was trying to develop timers for the gates. Automated ones so we—you don't need to worry about the manual count and things." He glanced nervously at Lysander. "I could bring them in. Show the engineers."

It felt like an unbearably heavy yoke had lifted from Lysander's shoulders. "That," he said sincerely, "would be amazing."

When Ben smiled, even if it was uncertain, it felt as though things were finally getting back to the way they always should have been.

Author's Note

After almost 3 years, welcome back to the Out of Time world! Thanks so much for your patience and I'm excited to be continuing this journey with you, with book four coming later this year and book five in early 2020.

This was definitely one of the most challenging books to write from a historical perspective. The dates and historical events around Timur's death in the 15th century have been checked, but because of differences in the Western (Julian and Gregorian) and Islamic calendars, some approximations have been made regarding exact dates.

I've attempted to stay as close to fact as possible, although some of the characters Qasim encounters along the way are, of course, fictional. As much as I hope to have avoided any discrepancies, information from that era is spread thin and often contradictory. When faced with five explanations for Timur's death, I chose the one that worked best for the story.

And lastly, my biggest hope is that I've done Qasim and his family justice. They are my love-letter to the amazing and sometimes gloriously overwhelming Syrian and Arab families I have known in my life. And yes, Rhys's initial reaction was entire influenced by personal experience. Once, I too was that stunned deer in the headlights.

Glossary

Note: The translations, transliteration, and spellings of these terms can vary from country to country. For the sake of consistency, I have used the spelling recommended by my cultural consultant, according to his lived experience. The author is also aware that 'Qas' is not a nickname in Arabic and that it makes no sense. Qasim is also aware of this. He just never had the heart to tell his non-Arabic-speaking colleagues.

Phrases:

ALHAMDULILLAH—Praise be to God

EID MUBARAK—Muslim greeting reserved for use during the Eid festivals

INSHA'ALLAH—As God wills it

MASHA'ALLAH—As God willed it

SALAAM ALAIKUM / ASSALAMU ALAIKUM—Peace be with you

SUBHAN'ALLAH—God is perfect (often used when extolling the greatness of God and his creations)

TISBAH ALAL-KHAIR—Good night

WA'ALAIKUM AL-SALAAM—And also with you (response to *Salaam alaikum*)

Terms:

ABI—Arabic; father. Varies depending on region.

BACH—Welsh; term of endearment; literally 'little'

CARIAD—Welsh; sweetheart

CWTCH—Welsh; a cuddle or hug

DROIT DE SEIGNEUR—French; the alleged right of a medieval feudal lord to have sexual intercourse with a vassal's bride on her wedding night

EID—a Muslim celebration that takes place to mark the end of Ramadan

FAJR—Arabic; literally, dawn prayer; one of the five daily prayers (*salat*) observed by practising Muslims

FITRA—Arabic; human nature

FUTOOR—Syrian dialect; the evening breaking of the fast during Ramadan. Also called *Iftar*.

GHUSL—an Arabic term referring to the full-body purification mandatory before prayers or religious ceremonies

HABIBI—Arabic; 'my darling'. Literally, 'my one who is loved.' A term of endearment.

HAMMAMS—public bathhouses. Also known as Turkish baths.

JEDU—Arabic; grandfather. Varies depending on region.

JUMU'AH—gathering/assembly. Also used in reference to the congregational worship of Muslims at the Friday midday prayers.

JUMU'AH MASJID—the Jumu'ah mosque

KA'AK—a savoury Syrian cookie with spices and sesame seeds which is popular at Eid

KHATIB—the person who delivers the sermon during the Friday worship and Eid

MASJID—mosque

MIHRAB—a niche in the wall of a mosque at the point nearest to Mecca, towards which the congregation faces to pray

MINBAR—a short flight of steps used as a platform by a preacher in a mosque

MISBAHA—Prayer beads

MUEZZIN—a man who calls Muslims to prayer from the minaret of a mosque

NASHEED—Arabic; chants and vocal music, usually making reference to Islamic beliefs, history, and religion

QAF SURAH—a chapter of the Qur'an

RAHA—a Syrian variation of lokum (Turkish delight)

SALAT—the ritual prayers of Muslims, performed five times a day in a set form. One of the five pillars of Islam.

SERAI—caravanserai. A stopping place for caravans on the Silk Road. Usually, a small, walled fortress with a courtyard in the middle and rooms around the sides.

SITTO / TETTE—Arabic; grandmother. Varies depending on region.

TAD—Welsh; father.

UMMI—Arabic; mother. Varies depending on region.

VALIDE—Ottoman Turkish, from Arabic; mother. Sultan Valide is both title and descriptor of the mother of the Sultan.

YALANGI—Syrian dialect; stuffed grape leaves

ZUHR—the second of the five daily prayers of *salat*

Acknowledgements

First, my usual suspects Beth and Ash, thank you for putting up with me as I flailed my way through this. Arshad, your help has been invaluable. Gus, your support and encouragement for these lads means the world. And lastly, to the lovely people at the masjids I visited, thank you so much for your hospitality and your patience with my endless lists of questions.

About the Author

C.B. Lewis is small, Scottish, and writes pretty much anywhere, any time. She loves to travel and tends to bring home at least four new plot bunnies from every trip she goes on. She's very excited to continue the adventures of the *Out of Time* series.

Facebook: www.facebook.com/cblewisauthor

Tumblr: www.tumblr.com/blog/cb-lewis

Website: www.cblewis.co.uk

Coming Soon from C.B. Lewis

Time Turns

Out of Time, Book Four

When he got back to Carrigan's office, the woman was still on a call. Audio only, but Danny wasn't surprised. The poor old bat already had a dozen screens projected over her desk, and from the sound of it, she'd sent them on to their client to spread the shit around.

"Right." Carrigan was frowning, her grey-salted brows pulling together. "That's...unorthodox."

"Given the circumstances, I consider it necessary." The speaker was male with a softly-spoken American-accented voice. "Discuss the matter with your colleague, and if he's amenable, I'll make the arrangements."

Carrigan terminated the call and looked across the desk at Danny. "Well, you're either going to love me or hate me for this."

"That's...ominous."

"The client wants you to go up there and work in-house for a few days. Weeks if necessary."

Danny gaped at her. "Eh?"

"That was my reaction." Carrigan pushed her fingers through her sandy hair. "If there's a security issue, they want to clear it up in-house. The CO believes that if you can access all their coding data, you may be able to pinpoint a source."

"But we don't go in-house," Danny said, and then a horrible sneaking suspicion crept up on him. "Have you got me working on Government stuff?"

Carrigan looked shifty. "Not exactly, but it's...complicated."

Danny scratched his cheek. "And this would be monitoring for as long as I'm there?"

"As far as I know," Carrigan said with a sigh. "Look, I know it's a terrible assignment, but you're the one who spotted the anomaly, and you're the one they want there."

Danny leaned back in the chair. "They really want me, eh?" He folded his arms over his chest. "So what do I get?"

Carrigan gave him a look. "If this is about that bloody chair again, do you want me to promise I won't touch it?"

Danny inclined his head. "It's a start. What about travel? Will I have a commute? Is it far? Do I get compensated for any extra travel? Do I get put up somewhere if it's not nearby?"

"Ah." Carrigan frowned. "I can't tell you exactly where but..."

Danny almost groaned. "So it's in the backside of nowhere then?"

"Just a minute." Carrigan's fingers flew across one of the screens, and she sent off a message. "Can't hurt to ask."

"Do I even get to know who I'd be working for?"

Carrigan shook her head. "Not until you get there."

"Sounds like I'm joining spies." He made his accent stronger as he said, "The name's Fergushon, Danny Fergushon. Shaken not shtirred."

"This isn't a laughing matter, Danny." The screen blinked with an incoming message. Carrigan flicked it open, and Danny read it—backwards—through the transparent projection.

"Manchester?" He leaned closer to be sure he was reading it right. "Not a chance in hell! If I wanted to stay up north, I would have stayed in Paisley!"

"Danny—"

"Look, tell him he can take anyone else. I'm not going all the way back up there."

"Danny—"

"No! He can't expect me to—"

"Danny!" Carrigan rotated the projection and scaled up the bottom half of the message and the lump sum he would receive if he was willing to temporarily relocate and identify the problem in-house.

Danny stared at it. There were a lot of zeroes. "Fuck me..."

"Does that change things?"

"Aye..." Danny counted the zeroes again and then met Carrigan's eyes through the projection. "What the hell have you got me into?"

Also Available from NineStar Press

Connect with NineStar Press

Website: NineStarPress.com

Facebook: NineStarPress

Facebook Reader Group: NineStarNiche

Twitter: @ninestarpress

Tumblr: NineStarPress